Shiké
Last of the Zinja

Available in Piatkus Editions
by the same author

Shiké: Time of the Dragons

The author gratefully acknowledges quotations from the following:
Reprinted by special arrangement with Shambhala Publications, Inc.,
1920-13th Street, Boulder, Colorado 80302. Excerpt from *The Diamond
Sutra and the Sutra of Hui Neng* translated by A. F. Price and
Wong Mou-Lam.

Excerpt from *China's Imperial Past* by Charles O. Hucker, with the
permission of the publishers, Stanford University Press. © 1975 by the
Board of Trustees of the Leland Stanford Junior University. This excerpt
includes six lines from a poem by Liu Yin.

Excerpt from *The Ten Foot Square Hut and Tales of The Heike*,
translated by A. L. Sadler. Reprinted with permission of the publishers,
Charles E. Tuttle Co., Inc., of Tokyo.

Excerpt from *The Samurai: A Military History* by S. R. Turnbull.
Copyright © 1977 by S. R. Turnbull, with permission of the publishers,
Macmillan Publishing Co., Inc., of New York, NY, and Osprey
Publishing, of London. The excerpt is two lines from a poem by
Yorimasa.

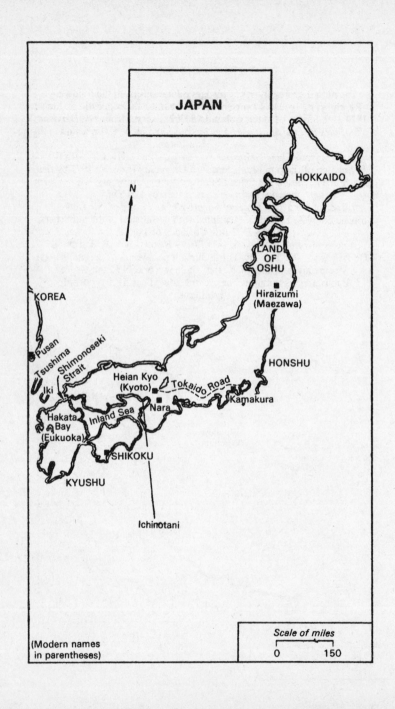

JAPAN

HOKKAIDO

N

LAND
OF
OSHU

KOREA

Hiraizumi
(Maezawa)

Pusan

HONSHU

Tsushima   Shimonoseki
            Strait

Heian Kyo
(Kyoto)   Tokaido Road

Iki   Kamakura

                Nara

Hakata   Inland Sea
Bay
(Fukuoka)

                            KYUSHU   SHIKOKU

Ichinotani

(Modern names   Scale of miles
in parentheses)   0   150

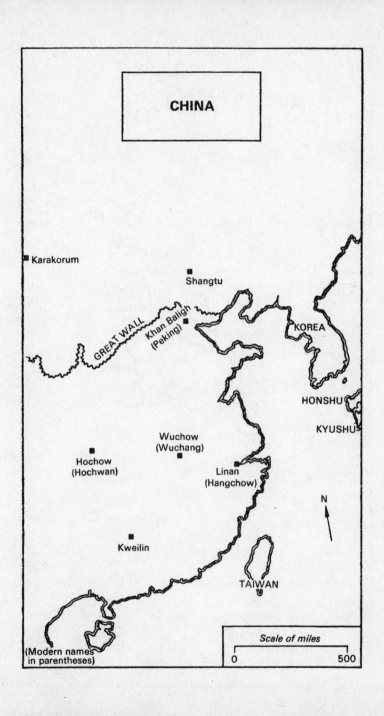

CHINA

Karakorum

Shangtu

GREAT WALL

Khan Baligh
(Peking)

KOREA

HONSHU

KYUSHU

Wuchow
(Wuchang)

Hochow
(Hochwan)

Linan
(Hangchow)

N

Kweilin

TAIWAN

(Modern names
in parentheses)

Scale of miles

0   500

A summary of SHIKÉ: TIME OF THE DRAGONS

The Shiké Jebu, a master of the martial arts taught by the Order of Zinja, stirred uneasily in meditation. He sat in the bow of a huge junk sailing eastward from China. Ahead, the night sky paled to blue violet, and his heart raced, for he was about to see the sun rise over his homeland, the Sacred Islands, for the first time in seven years. Yet he was not sure whether he could rightly call the Sunrise Land his home. He seemed condemned to be a wanderer and a native of no country.

Long ago Jebu's father, a rebellious Mongol chieftain known as Jamuga the Cunning, had fled to the Sunrise Land, pursued by a death sentence decreed for himself and his descendants by the Mongol conqueror, Genghis Khan. Marrying a woman of the Sunrise Land, Jamuga had fathered Jebu, then was tracked down and slain by an officer of the Khan, Arghun Baghadur. Jebu was saved by the Zinja, an order of formidable warrior monks. Taitaro, the local Zinja abbot, married Jebu's mother and adopted him. Raised and trained as a Zinja, Jebu grew up tall, red-haired and grey-eyed – traits common in certain Mongol families – forever marked, to his sorrow, as different from all the other people of the Sunrise Land.

The Zinja were an austere order with high ideals, who sought to increase their influence in the realm. But they were few in number and could only hire themselves out to one side or the other in the feudal wars that were increasingly dividing the Sacred Islands. After his initiation into the Order as a full-fledged shiké, Jebu had been sent to Kamakura on the north-eastern side of the island of Honshu to escort Taniko, a daughter of the wealthy Shima family, down the Tokaido Road to the great city of Heian Kyo, capital of the realm, where she was to marry Horigawa, a prince of ancient aristocratic lineage. On their long journey Jebu had killed a warrior who was trying to kidnap Taniko, and made a lifelong friend of a little carpenter named Moko, whose life he had spared. Jebu and Taniko fell deeply and irrevocably in love on the Tokaido, but

9

Taniko's duty to her family and Jebu's to his Order forced them to part.

For centuries the Sunrise Land had been peacefully governed by the Emperor and his Court. Lately, however, a new force had arisen – the samurai – ferocious and highly skilled warriors who served landowning warlords. Among the samurai, a fierce rivalry between the two most powerful clans, the Muratomo and the Takashi, was tearing the nation apart.

When the Muratomo raised a rebellion in Heian Kyo, the Zinja sent Jebu to serve Domei, the gallant Muratomo chieftain. Because Taniko's husband, Prince Horigawa, a treacherous, conniving courtier, was allied with the Takashi, he and Taniko fled the capital. Domei's rebellion was quickly put down by Sogamori, the power-hungry head of the Takashi clan, and his brilliant son, Kiyosi. Domei and almost all his sons were killed, except for the two youngest, Hideyori and Yukio. Jebu helped Hideyori escape to Kamakura, where he was taken in custody by Lord Bokuden, Taniko's father. Yukio, a child, fell into Sogamori's hands.

Wandering through the countryside, still serving the fading Muratomo cause, Jebu found himself at Horigawa's country estate. The prince had exiled Taniko there for crossing him by helping to save the lives of Hideyori and Yukio. With Taniko was Moko, who had promised to be the link between her and Jebu. The lovers spent a blissful night in Taniko's bedchamber, but in the morning Jebu barely escaped Horigawa and his guards.

Jebu went back to the temple of his foster father, Abbot Taitaro. There Taitaro initiated him into deeper Zinja mysteries, showing him a vision of the Tree of Life and giving him a carved crystal, the Jewel of Life and Death, as an object for meditation. But the Mongol warrior Arghun Baghadur was pursuing Jebu again. At the temple they met and fought, and Arghun nearly overcame Jebu, who escaped death only with Taitaro's help.

'Until you can go against Arghun stripped bare in mind, he will always be able to get the better of you,' Taitaro warned him.

In the course of time, Taniko gave birth to a daughter. Knowing she was Jebu's child, Horigawa drowned her in a waterfall, after which he abandoned the distraught Taniko to her family. She remained in seclusion until visited by Kiyosi,

Sogamori's son, who had long been attracted to her. Kiyosi's love brought Taniko back to sanity. Eventually, Taniko and Kiyosi had a son, Atsue.

At the command of the Zinja, Jebu rescued Yukio, the younger of the two surviving Muratomo brothers, from Sogamori. Awed by Yukio's almost supernatural skill in the martial arts, Jebu vowed to serve him for life. Together Jebu and Yukio, joined by Moko, travelled up and down the Sacred Islands eluding Sogamori's samurai. At last it came to Yukio that his skirmishes with the Takashi were futile, and he decided to seek a new fortune across the sea in China. He sent out a call to all samurai still loyal to the Muratomo to accompany him. They would offer their services to the Chinese Emperor in his war with the Mongol invaders.

Yukio and his little army prepared to sail from Hakata Bay on the southern island of Kyushu. But Sogamori was determined to destroy Yukio once and for all and sent a fleet against him under Kiyosi's command. In the battle of Hakata Bay, Kiyosi aimed his bow at Yukio, but Jebu killed the Takashi scion with an armour-piercing arrow in the chest. As the Muratomo fleet set sail for China, Moko told Jebu that Kiyosi had been Taniko's lover and the father of her son. Feeling that he himself had never been able to offer Taniko anything, Jebu bitterly regretted killing Kiyosi.

Taniko was crushed by the news of Kiyosi's death. The ageing Sogamori, also grief-stricken but having no respect or sympathy for Taniko, saw his grandson Atsue as a substitute for Kiyosi, who had been his favourite son, and took the boy from Taniko by force. Her life ruined, Taniko made no resistance when Horigawa, reasserting his position as her husband, forced her to accompany him on an embassy across the ocean to the Court of the Emperor of China.

Yukio and Jebu and their men were already in China, defending the city of Kweilin against a huge Mongol army. Commanding the Mongols was Arghun Baghadur, who saw the siege as another opportunity to kill Jebu. The Chinese Emperor's chief minister was plotting to betray his country to the Mongols and intended to sacrifice Kweilin and the samurai by not sending reinforcements to the beleaguered city.

The same minister commissioned Horigawa, as a neutral

party, to negotiate with the Mongol lord Kublai Khan, grandson of the great Genghis Khan. To avenge himself on Taniko for her many past offences, Horigawa handed her over to the dreaded Mongol barbarians to be used as a courtesan. But her fate, after Horigawa departed the Mongol camp, was not as unpleasant as he had wished. She attracted the attention of Kublai Khan himself, a man of intelligence and sensitivity, who made her part of his harem.

The current Great Khan of the Mongols, Kublai's elder brother, died unexpectedly on campaign in China. Following their rigid law, Mongol generals everywhere broke off their battles and headed back to their steppe homeland to elect a new Great Khan. Kweilin and the samurai were saved. The Chinese Emperor's treacherous minister sent an army to arrest Yukio and his men, but the samurai escaped with the help of the governor of Kweilin, who revealed himself as a member of the Chinese branch of the Order of Zinja.

Now a civil war broke out between the cosmopolitan Kublai Khan and his traditionalist younger brother, Arik Buka, each claiming the title of Great Khan. To Taniko, whose understanding of affairs of state impressed him, Kublai confided that he hoped to complete the work begun by his grandfather, Genghis Khan, and combine Chinese science and Mongol mastery of warfare to unite all nations under Mongol rule.

The Zinja abbot Taitaro, in China on a mission of his own, advised Yukio, Jebu and their men to offer to fight for Kublai Khan, since they had no further reason to be loyal to China. When Kublai Khan met his brother in a final battle at the edge of the Gobi Desert, the samurai found themselves facing an army led by Arghun Baghadur, one of Arik Buka's chief supporters. Arghun changed sides in the middle of the battle, helping Kublai Khan to win. Then Arghun's army fell upon the samurai in an attempt to kill Jebu. Mongol officers stopped the fighting and brought the quarrel to Kublai Khan for judgement. The new Great Khan decreed that, since Jebu had served him well, the command of Genghis Khan calling for his death was now rescinded. He reprimanded Arghun for treacherously attacking the samurai after the battle was over, and asked Jebu, who had nearly been killed, what would compensate him for his ordeal. Jebu's daring request was that Kublai release Taniko to him.

When Kublai reacted with jealous anger, Jebu assumed that he and Taniko were doomed. But, surprisingly, soon afterwards the Great Khan arranged their ecstatic reunion.

All these memories passed through Jebu's mind as he sat in the bow of the junk carrying him back to the Sacred Islands. Yukio had accepted Arghun's offer to join the expedition, bringing along with him ten thousand Mongol cavalrymen. Arghun said he had given up trying to kill Jebu, but he felt he had been dishonoured by the Great Khan and wanted to find new wars to fight elsewhere. Yukio could not bring himself to refuse such a massive addition to his fighting strength.

Today the first ships carrying Yukio's forces were about to make landfall at the mountainous northern end of the great island of Honshu, far from the regions controlled by the Takashi. And, watching the sun rise over the coastline of his homeland, Jebu tried to meditate but was deeply troubled by the prospects before them all: civil war . . . the likelihood that Arghun would betray them . . . the threat to their island nation from the vast Mongol empire that was engulfing the world. And between Jebu and Taniko, too, there was a shadow. Jebu had been unable to admit to Taniko that it was his hand that had let fly the arrow that killed Kiyosi, thus depriving her of her son and destroying the happiness she had found with the Takashi heir.

Now the sun's red disc floated above distant, snow-tipped peaks. The thunder of breakers carried faintly on the breeze. Jebu did not know what would happen. He only knew that there was no turning back. They were home again. Whatever good or evil might come of it, the choice was made.

PART ONE

THE BOOK OF YUKIO

Government is always for the benefit of the governors, at the expense of
the governed. Sages who observe
this are ever beset by the question:
why is it that he who is most able to
rule is never he who is most worthy
to rule?

—*The Zinja Manual*

CHAPTER ONE

The little house was perched on pilings over a pool at the
bottom of a waterfall. A winding pathway of great black rocks
led to it from the bank. The only sounds were the prattle of the
waterfall and the sighing of the wind in the pines. The site had
been chosen and the little house designed for seclusion and
meditation.

It had been built ages earlier by the ancestor of their host,
Fukiwara Hidehira. Hidehira said his ancestor, banished from
Heian Kyo, had almost died of longing for the capital until he
built this meditation hut and found peace. It was kept in repair
and used by every generation of these Northern Fujiwaras.

Jebu took off his clogs and set them on the mossy
embankment before trying to walk across to the house. The
stepping stones were wet and slippery. When he had reached the
house, he climbed steep wooden stairs and stood on the porch.
'Ho, Yukio.'

'Come in, Jebu-san.'

Yukio, seated cross-legged before a low table, was wearing a
violet robe with a yellow butterfly pattern. The robe looked
strange to Jebu: he had grown so used to seeing Yukio in
Chinese and Mongol garments. Yukio had brush, ink and paper

before him, and when Jebu entered and seated himself, Yukio handed him a scroll.

'You are the first to read this. I plan to have it sent immediately to every province.'

Jebu unrolled the scroll and read, while Yukio sat watching his face. It was a proclamation whose message was familiar to Jebu. Towards the end he read, 'Most sorely oppressed by Sogamori and his clan is the illustrious family of Muratomo. Sogamori despoiled and murdered my grandfather, my father Domei, and all my brothers, as well as many other members of my family. I alone, Muratomo no Yukio, survive to avenge them. I now claim the chieftainship of the Muratomo clan and call upon all relatives and allies of the Muratomo, from the farthest provinces to the capital itself, to rally to the White Dragon banner.'

Yukio urged all who read his words to rise at once and attack their Takashi overlords. He promised that all meritorious deeds would be noted and rewarded.

He concluded, 'We vow to rescue the sacred person of His Imperial Majesty from the clutches of the Takashi. The Muratomo clan, always loyal to His Imperial Majesty, will sweep away the clouds that obscure the glory of the Imperial house and burnish it till it once again shines as brightly as the sun.'

Yukio's round eyes were eager. 'Well?'

'It's beautifully written, Yukio-san. Especially that last sentence.'

Yukio bowed. 'Thank you. Is there anything I've neglected?'

Jebu hesitated. Lately, Yukio had been asking his advice and then doing just the opposite. These Muratomo were stubborn, wilful men. Yukio's father, Domei, had been like that, refusing to listen to advice, gallantly leading his family and his samurai straight to disaster. Probably Yukio's grandfather, beheaded after supporting the losing side in a struggle between rival Emperors, had been the same way. Now Yukio had brought the Mongols to the Sacred Islands against the advice of Jebu and his stepfather, Taitaro. He had insisted on landing in the far-northern land of Oshu against advice. Jebu and Taitaro and many other samurai were convinced that there were more warriors in the south ready to spring to Yukio's support. Now this proclamation. Jebu sighed inwardly. He could do nothing but try.

'By scattering copies of this declaration up and down the realm, you put Sogamori and the Takashi on notice that you're back and are going to fight them. Why throw away the advantage of surprise? They outnumber us twenty to one.'

Yukio smiled. At least he had not yet lost his temper, Jebu thought, as he often had when Jebu's advice contradicted his wishes.

'We have no advantage of surprise. It has taken us most of a month to collect all our men here. By now Sogamori's agents have reported our presence. I learned my lesson when we fought our way out of Hakata Bay. If we couldn't keep the departure of a thousand samurai a secret, how can we expect to hide the arrival of twelve thousand warriors? Since the Takashi know we're here, it's best that all who might rally to our side be alerted as well. Also, as you and Taitaro warned me, there will be people who will imagine I'm an invader, because I brought Mongols with me. This proclamation will allay their suspicions.'

'How?'

'It at once makes plain that I belong here and have a just cause. I want everyone to think of me as a loyal subject of the Emperor. Which I am.' He looked challengingly at Jebu, as if expecting disagreement.

'You talk of rescuing the Emperor from the Takashi. When we left here, the Emperor was Sogamori's son-in-law. What makes you suppose he'll want to be rescued? Remember how your father tried to rescue Emperor Nijo from the Takashi, and His Imperial Majesty fled to the Rokuhara the first chance he got?'

'It's worse than that,' said Yukio with a grin. 'Fujiwara Hidehira tells me there's a new Emperor on the throne, Sogamori's grandson. When I wrote about rescuing the Emperor from the Takashi, I meant rescuing the office, not the man – or in this case the boy.'

Jebu was surprised. 'Don't you believe that the person of the Emperor is sacred?'

'Do you?'

'It's not a point on which Zinja teaching dwells overmuch. I certainly thought you and all samurai believed in the Emperor's divinity.'

Yukio looked melancholy. 'I gained much by travelling to China, but I lost much, too. I've learned that every nation declares its ruler divine or divinely appointed. In every nation it is really the powerful men who decide who the divine ruler will be. If I'm to win this war for my family, I must be a maker of Emperors, just as Sogamori has been.'

Jebu stood up. 'At the moment I must be a maker of Zinja. Or near-Zinja.'

'Then Taitaro-sensei has given you permission to instruct some of our men in Zinja arts of fighting?'

'Yes. He says there are so few Zinja left these days that there can be no objection to sharing our knowledge with others.'

'Only our own people, though. No Mongols or other foreigners.'

'I'm glad you're at least somewhat wary of the Mongols.'

'Of course.' Yukio stretched himself and sighed. 'Ah, Jebu-san, it's good to be home again, isn't it? To see landscapes that excite the eye, instead of endless, dreary wastes. To eat our good food and get away from the infernal stink of meat. To hold the exquisite women of our islands in our arms again. No more clumsy, smelly foreign women.'

'I didn't have that much to do with foreign women,' Jebu said.

'You have always belonged, body and soul, to the Lady Taniko. Which reminds me.' Yukio grinned proudly. 'I'm getting married to the lady Mirusu. You and Taitaro-sensei and the Lady Taniko and Moko-san are invited to the feast.

Jebu climbed the hill between the samurai camp and Lord Hidehira's citadel. Yukio was right. It was a great happiness to be back in the Sacred Islands. Here, near the city of Hiraizumi, the land was hilly and wooded. To the south rose a chain of blue mountains. The hills and rocks, the trees and streams, were a delight to an eye exhausted by the bare brown plains of northern China and the steppes of Mongolia.

Yukio getting married. That was surprising news, but it shouldn't have been. Yukio always liked women around him, and he always pined for the women of home. Jebu was happy for him. Who was the woman, though, and how had Yukio found her so quickly?

If only he and Taniko could be married. It would give him much pleasure to have Taitaro-sensei bless their union. Long ago his mother had urged him to marry and raise children. It would please her, wherever she was, if Taniko and he did that.

But Horigawa lived. And Kiyosi remained dead by Jebu's own hand. Could that make a difference to her? Or did she no longer care how Kiyosi had died, now that she had Jebu?

He was afraid it did make a difference.

He reached the top of the hill and was looking down through the pines at a wide valley. The camp of Yukio's army filled the valley from end to end. The tents of the samurai, the Chinese and other foreign auxiliaries were scattered, seemingly without pattern, near at hand. Beyond them the Mongol *yurts* stretched in their regular grey rows. Jebu could make out a few horses grazing in the wooded hills. Fortunately there was enough uncultivated land here in the far north to provide their thousands of horses with room to forage. When they began to move towards the capital, peasants would suffer wherever they went.

He sat down on the hilltop with his back to the camp, facing the distant mountains. His students would wait a while. He was wearing only his simple grey robe. His fingers went without conscious direction to the pocket inside the robe, the secret place grown so familiar over the years. The Jewel sparkled in the mid-morning sun. He composed his mind and held the Jewel up just far enough away from his face to focus on it. His eyes followed the knots and twists of the Tree of Life pattern etched on the crystalline surface, his fingers slowly turning the stone. Soon he was looking through the Jewel at the pattern as it appeared on the other side. The lines swam up to his gaze through the depths of the Jewel, which magnified them and gave them solidity.

He heard the beat of wings descending from the sky above. It was the White Dragon of Muratomo, the beast he had ridden in his initiation vision. He looked up, raised a hand to reach for the dragon. It hovered above him. Its eyes were Yukio's huge brown eyes. Looking at him sadly, it rose again and at last disappeared into the blue sky. Jebu felt a sad sense of loss.

Slowly, the Jewel reappeared in his gaze. After a time he put it away and stood up, sighing. His foreboding about this expedition was confirmed.

He started down the hill. Today he would teach his students how to kill with any one of thirty-four common objects to be found in any household.

CHAPTER TWO

Taniko and Lord Hidehira's wife had worked together preparing the dinner, and together they served it to Yukio, Jebu and Hidehira. When not serving, Taniko knelt in a corner beside Hidehira's wife with her eyes downcast and pretended not to hear the conversation. At first, she told Jebu, she resented being expected to play the role of a woman of the Sacred Islands, submissive and hidden. But now it relaxed her. After the uncertainties of life in China and Mongolia, it was pleasant to know exactly what to do in every situation.

The hall they were in was built of roughhewn logs. The pillars that supported the roof were barbarously carved and painted. Hidehira liked to imagine that his palace rivalled anything in Heian Kyo, but to his visitors' eyes, it was so different there was really no comparison.

'I never forgot her,' Yukio was telling Lord Hidehira and Jebu. 'When I came back here after so many years I was amazed to discover that she was still unmarried. That was my fault, though. Her father had many daughters and it was difficult to find a husband for Mirusu after she had given birth to a wandering stranger's child.'

'Shame, shame,' said old Hidehira, chuckling and wagging a finger at Yukio. The top of his head was bald. The long white hair that grew from the sides of his head flowed together with his luxuriant white beard and moustache, all of which spread over his chest like a great river fed by its tributaries. He was a dainty eater and kept his beard scrupulously clean. He was eighty-nine years of age.

He was the tenth-generation chieftain of a clan known as the

Northern Fujiwara, who had settled here in the land of Oshu hundreds of years earlier, after losing out in a power struggle with the Fujiwara branch that dominated in the capital. Like the Muratomo and the Takashi, the Northern Fujiwara had become landowning samurai. They had been allies of the Muratomo for generations. They took part with them in joint expeditions against the barbarian hairy Ainu who had once held these northern reaches. Fujiwara Hidehira had sheltered Yukio once before, years ago, and it was while staying at Hidehira's stronghold that Yukio got the idea to go to China.

'Ah,' said Jebu. 'You are marrying the girl whose father owns Sun Tzu's *Art of Warfare*.'

'Exactly,' said Yukio. He recounted the story to Hidehira, of nights divided between reading the classic on warfare and enjoying the delights of the lovely Mirusu.

'Ah, the energy of the young,' Hidehira laughed as he levered a prawn to his mouth with chopsticks. 'Coupling half the night and studying till dawn.'

'You sought the girl out again as soon as you got back here?' said Jebu. 'I thought you were only interested in reading the books.'

'Hardly,' said Yukio. 'She was an exquisite creature, pale and delicate as moonlight. She has not changed that much since we parted.'

'Her father was a Takashi supporter,' said Jebu. 'Didn't he object?'

'It seems he lost a bit of land in Omi province to Takashi double-dealing. Now he hates them passionately. Also, he feels a son-in-law with twelve thousand troops behind him may have a promising future.'

'Did you learn much from the Chinese book on warfare?' Hidehira asked him.

Yukio smiled and nodded. Taniko thought, it's too bad his teeth stick out every time he grins, and he grins so often. If it weren't for those protruding teeth and bulging eyes he'd be a handsome man. Still, his new bride was getting a marvellous man. Almost as marvellous as Jebu.

'I learned that deception is the key to victory in war,' said Yukio. 'A principle that was confirmed for me while riding with the Mongols.'

Hidehira waved a hand in dismissal. 'That is not the samurai way of fighting.'

'I know,' Yukio said solemnly. 'I expect to beat any samurai army sent against me.'

'I do not like your Mongols,' said Hidehira, looking sourly down at the small table on which his food was arranged. It was a feeling, Taniko thought, which would be shared by many people of the Sunrise Land, of high and low station. Yet, Hidehira had so far allowed the Mongols to camp outside his provincial capital, Hiraizumi, had sold them provisions and was adding a detachment of his own considerable army to Yukio's.

'Our people don't like any foreigners,' Yukio said with a laugh. 'But we had better learn from them. Their way of making war has won them territories so vast, Lord Hidehira, that you might not believe so much land exists on the earth. To travel from one end of the territory ruled by Kublai Khan to the other takes most travellers a year. Of course, he has post riders who can do it in twenty days.'

'Kublai Khan,' said Hidehira. 'An absurd name. What are post riders?'

Yukio looked at Jebu, raised his eyebrows and shrugged. 'Couriers. They ride the fastest horses. All travellers must clear the road for them. They ride from one post to the next, where they change mounts. They continue day and night. Being able to send and receive messages so quickly enables the Great Khan to hold his empire together.'

'I'm glad we have no such thing here,' said Hidehira. 'The Northern Fujiwara would never have been able to enjoy as much independence as we do if messages could travel with such lightninglike speed.'

'Your isolation is good for you but a problem for me,' said Yukio. 'I need so much more information before my army can start to move.'

'All you need to know is that everyone hates Sogamori,' said Hidehira. 'He issues whatever orders he pleases. Neither laws nor officials can oppose him. Even my cousin, the proud Fujiwara of Heian Kyo, must kiss the soles of his sandals. For a year now, Sogamori's grandson, Antoku, has reigned as Emperor.'

Taniko remembered a conversation she'd had long ago with

Kiyosi, when Sogamori was just planning the marriage of his daughter to Takakura, one of the Imperial princes. Takakura had an older brother whose claim to the throne must have been overruled if Sogamori's son-in-law, and later his grandson, had become Emperor.

Full of eager curiosity, she blurted out, 'What did Prince Mochihito do when Antoku was made Emperor?'

Hidehira whirled, his hair and beard flying, and stared at Taniko. Out of the corner of her eye Taniko could also see Hidehira's wife staring at her in shock.

'Did the lady speak?' Hidehira said in a wondering voice.

'Lady Taniko intended no discourtesy, my lord,' Jebu answered. 'She has just returned from an embassy of many years at the court of the Mongol Great Khan. At the Great Khan's court women frequently participate in discussions with men.'

'Barbarous,' said Hidehira, shaking his head.

Pompous old fool, thought Taniko, giving a little snort.

'What about Prince Mochihito?' said Jebu quickly. 'First he was passed over in favour of his younger brother. Now he is passed over again for his nephew. Did he protest?'

'There are rumours that he is furious,' said Hidehira. 'But he has done nothing in public. It is that way with everyone in these times. Outwardly, all submit to Sogamori and his relatives. Inwardly they hate the Takashi rule.'

'That's what I'm counting on,' said Yukio. 'As my proclamation spreads, there will be a general rising throughout the country.'

'The realm is ripe for it,' said Hidehira. 'Every province has a governor appointed by Sogamori who extorts huge taxes and imprisons anyone who fails to pay. The landlords drain the fiefs of all they produce, leaving the farmers nothing to live on. Every Takashi-appointed official abuses his power. Sogamori is once supposed to have said that anyone who is not a Takashi is not a human being. It would be more true to say that anyone who is a Takashi is a tyrant, a murderer and a thief. People are harassed in everything they do. No one is left alone. The Northern Fujiwara have always hated the Takashi. Now everyone hates them. My son Yerubutsu will return shortly from a trading mission to Maizuru, which is not far from the capital. We will have more news from him.'

'Let's hope he doesn't come here with a Takashi army snapping at his heels,' said Jebu.

'The Takashi are incapable of moving that fast,' said Yukio. 'But I would welcome their coming. If they came here I'd show you the art of warfare, Lord Hidehira. The Takashi survivors would never stop running.'

'Hidehira fancies himself a great lord because he has this mountain stronghold where no one bothers him,' said Taniko. 'Actually, he's backward and ignorant.' They were alone and lying together in their little guesthouse in the Fujiwara citadel. Her hands pressed against the hard muscles of Jebu's chest. 'Not even willing to answer a simple question because it was a woman who asked it.'

'Would you prefer to be back among the Mongols?'

In the darkness Jebu was no different from the man she had held in her arms so many years ago on Mount Higashi. His body was as hard and lean, his voice still smooth and quiet, with a trace of hidden power. His Zinja training included so many amatory postures that she believed that since their reunion at Khan Baligh they had never coupled in the same position twice.

'I would prefer that my people make one or two sensible changes in their customs,' said Taniko. 'I have spent too much of my life hovering in the background at dinners where my thoughts were far more interesting than most of the male conversation I heard.'

Jebu laughed. 'That's why men won't lēt you talk. They're afraid you'll shame them. It may well be that I'll be the only man who is aware of the full power of your mind.' The laughter went out of his voice. 'Taniko, we'll be on the march soon. We'll have to find a safe place for you to wait it out. Perhaps you could stay here at Hiraizumi.'

'I wish I could rejoin my Uncle Ryuichi at Heian Kyo. Of all the older men in our family, he is the one I like best. I did blame him for letting Sogamori take Atsue from me and for not protecting me from Horigawa, but those things were out of his control. The moment that cruel arrow struck Kiyosi, my fate was decided.'

There was a note of uneasiness in the gentle voice that came to

24

her out of the darkness. 'If Kiyosi had not died, you and I would not be together today.'

'I know,' said Taniko. 'But the world in which Kiyosi lived and died, the world in which Atsue was born, seems to me a completely different one from the world you and I inhabit. By your thinking, I should be grateful to the man who killed Kiyosi. I could never feel anything but hatred for that man.'

Jebu was silent for a long time. At last she reached out and stroked his cheek. It felt cold, hard and smooth under her hand, like a jade mask. He is thinking that he owes his happiness to the death of a good man, and he is ashamed, she thought. It isn't his fault, though.

At last he said, 'You can't go to the capital. You'd be in the thick of the fighting. What do you want to do?'

'I really have no alternative,' Taniko said. 'If I can find a way to make the journey, I want to go back to the place where you met me, my family home in Kamakura.'

CHAPTER THREE

Fujiwara Yerubutsu, Hidehira's son and heir, arrived at Hiraizumi at the end of the Third Month, after the sun had dried up the mud of the spring thaw. There was even a summerlike dust cloud over the road along which Yerubutsu and thirty Fujiwara samurai had come, escorting a baggage train loaded with pottery and silk from the southern provinces.

A few hours after Yerubutsu's arrival, Hidehira sent for Yukio, asking him to come to the great hall of the fortress. Accompanied by Jebu, Yukio walked through the gardens between the guesthouse and the donjon. There was a different feeling in the air. Samurai who had been friendly only the day before, now greeted them gruffly or pretended not to see them at all. Many more men seemed to be in armour than on the previous day.

By the time they entered Hidehira's great hall, Jebu's senses were as alert as a hunted animal's. Hidehira sat on the dais wearing a stiff black robe of state with upswept shoulders. A row of councillors and generals, similarly dressed, sat on his right and left. All wore their two samurai swords, the long and the short, the hilts thrusting out from under the robes. All were stone-faced except for the aged Hidehira, who wore an uncomfortable grin, as if trying to dispel the unpleasant atmosphere.

Hidehira began by introducing his eldest son to Yukio and Jebu. Yerubutsu was nearly seventy years of age, his topknot grey. His head was as perfectly round as an iron ball fired from a Chinese *hua pao*. His mouth was wide and at first glance, lipless; his eyes were slits.

Servants brought sake, and a round of polite questions and answers concerning Yerubutsu's journey to the southern provinces and Yukio's sojourn in China seemed to Jebu to take all morning.

At last Yerubutsu said, 'It's a good thing I was only in Maizuru, not in the capital, Lord Yukio. Otherwise, your proclamation could have caused me grave embarrassment. As it was, I barely had time to get out of Tango province with the goods I had acquired before a detachment of Takashi samurai arrived in Maizuru with a warrant for my arrest.'

'I regret that my activities caused you distress, Lord Yerubutsu,' said Yukio with a low bow. 'My oversight was unpardonable.'

'Nonsense,' said Hidehira testily. 'I knew Yerubutsu was in some danger, being so close to the capital when you issued your proclamation. I said to myself, if he can't get himself out of trouble, he's no son of mine.'

'I appreciate your confidence in me, Father,' said Yerubutsu coldly. 'Still, you could have lost a son. Of course, now that Lord Yukio is here again, you may feel you can spare a son.'

'Lord Yukio's father, Domei, was a brother to me,' said the old man sternly. 'His son is my son. You have no right to resent that.'

Yukio quickly interrupted the bitterness between father and son. 'Lord Yerubutsu, I'm most anxious to learn what impact my proclamation had in the provinces to the south.'

Yerubutsu gave Yukio a long, hostile look. 'I had little time to learn its effect on others, since its effect on me was to force me to flee for my life. You can be sure, though, that now that the

26

Takashi know you are in Oshu, a huge army will be on its way here before long.'

'Let them come,' said Hidehira fiercely, his white beard quivering.

'My father's generosity and his loyalty to old friends are legendary in Oshu,' said Yerubutsu. 'Because so many of our forefathers were comrades-in-arms, he extended his hospitality to you. Please forgive me, Lord Yukio.' Yerubutsu's eyes glittered with hostility. 'I fear you may have abused my father's generosity. Unwittingly, I'm sure.'

A man with less self-control would have been provoked into drawing his sword. Yukio merely replied calmly, 'If I thought that were true, Lord Yerubutsu, I would have to kill myself.' Having lived as long with Yukio as he had, Jebu understood that this was a threat. If Yukio were to cut his belly open because of Yerubutsu's unjustified accusations, Yerubutsu would be disgraced.

'Certainly the matter does not warrant such extreme measures,' said Yerubutsu, shifting restlessly on his cushion. He'd love to hack Yukio's head off and be done with it, thought Jebu. 'I merely meant that by taking refuge with my father and issuing your proclamation of rebellion against Sogamori from here, you have placed us all in grave danger.'

'Sogamori has always been my enemy,' said Hidehira grumpily.

'I assure you, Lord Yerubutsu,' Yukio said, 'the forces I have are more than ample to protect your domain from the Takashi.'

'We do not need your protection,' Yerubutsu snapped. The polite mask was slipping away. Rage was turning the ball-shaped head a deep orange colour. What was troubling Yerubutsu, anyway? It must be that he had plans of his own, and Yukio's activities were interfering.

Yerubutsu said, 'I presume by your forces you mean the swarm of barbarians camped on our land. I'm sorry to say it, Lord Yukio, but I'm shocked that the bearer of so illustrious a name as yours would lead foreigners in an invasion of our soil. Even Sogamori would not bring foreign troops to fight against his people.'

It was just as he and Taitaro had warned Yukio, thought Jebu. The Mongols would never be trusted.

27

Yukio continued to smile, just as if he had not been accused of treason to the realm. 'The early Emperors invited Korean artisans and Buddhist missionaries to our shores. The honoured founder of your family, the Great Minister Fujiwara no Kamatari, brought Chinese law to the Sacred Islands, together with Chinese scholars to teach and administer the law. These were not invasions. We simply made use of the talents of foreigners for the greater glory of the Sunrise Land. The Mongols are not craftsmen, missionaries or scholars. But they understand one art better than almost any other people in the world – warfare.'

Jebu spoke. 'If the great lords will permit a comment from this humble monk, Sogamori did bring at least one Mongol into the realm to fight against his people. Many years ago the Mongol leader Arghun Baghadur acted as an officer in Sogamori's service.'

'Formerly he fought for Sogamori,' said Yerubutsu. 'Now he fights for you. See how little loyalty these barbarians have.'

Yukio shrugged and said, 'The past is the past and the present is the present.' It was the slogan samurai had always used to justify changing sides in the midst of a war.

Yerubutsu took another tack. 'I have heard that these Mongols have conquered half the earth. I am sorry if I seem to question you, Lord Yukio, but is it not foolhardy to bring ten thousand of them here?'

There was something to be said for the polite style of discourse cultivated in the Sunrise Land, Jebu thought. At least, Yukio and Yerubutsu were still talking. By now two Mongol chieftains would have exchanged coarse insults and been at each other's throats.

'I see that you are well informed on our troop strength, Lord Yerubutsu,' said Yukio with a chuckle. 'The fighting men of the Sunrise Land outnumber my Mongol contingent a hundred to one. The Mongols are masters of strategy and tactics, but I believe we can learn from them. We will have them under our control at all times.'

'I do not believe my father realized how many troops you would be quartering on our lands when he gave you his permission,' said Yerubutsu. 'These savages take whatever they want without paying for it. They turn their horses loose to graze anywhere they choose. Several of our peasants have been injured in quarrels with the barbarians.'

Yukio bowed. 'As I have already assured your noble father, we are prepared to pay for everything we requisition. We have gold, silver, copper and an abundance of trade goods.'

'Peasants who have lost all their rice cannot eat copper,' Yerubutsu growled.

'Enough, Yerubutsu,' Hidehira snapped. 'I'm far from dead yet. I am still chieftain of this clan.' He straightened his back, and his son and the family retainers on the dais bowed in unison.

'I was well aware that Lord Yukio was landing a huge army in our domain,' Hidehira went on. 'I am proud that the struggle to free the Sacred Islands from the Takashi has begun here at Hiraizumi in Oshu. Yerubutsu, you seem to have forgotten the long list of injuries done to us by the Takashi. As for the Mongols, who but a fool would reject an army of ten thousand well-armed, experienced warriors, no matter where they came from? I'd use hairy Ainu to fight the Takashi if they'd do any good. You know perfectly well our peasants won't starve. Lord Yukio has already reimbursed us generously for quartering his army. Your complaints are nonsense, Yerubutsu. If you don't have more wisdom that that, at your age, you'll never have it.' Breathing hard, Hidehira sat back and glared at his grey-haired son.

One time you don't have to be polite, thought Jebu, is when you are scolding a son. Hidehira's withered face was as red as Yerubutsu's.

'I'm sorry, honoured Father,' Yerubutsu muttered. 'I'm only trying to protect our clan.'

'By driving a wedge between us and our age-old allies?'

'I don't know whether Lord Yukio has a right to appeal to that alliance. His claim to the chieftainship of the Muratomo clan is false.'.

Yukio leaned forward, ready to spring. 'Who says my claim is false?'

'Your brother Hideyori is chieftain of the Muratomo, my lord,' said Yerubutsu with a triumphant smile. 'I doubt that he welcomes your attempt to usurp his office.'

Yukio stared at Jebu. 'I thought Hideyori was dead. We had

heard Sogamori had him executed.' He turned to Yerubutsu with a sudden grin. 'This is wonderful news.'

'Your brother may not find your call for an insurrection and your assumption of the chieftainship so wonderful,' Yerubutsu said sourly. 'After all, the Shima family still hold him hostage in Kamakura for the Takashi.'

Yukio turned to Jebu. 'We must send word to Hideyori at once.'

'There is something else you must do at once,' said Yerubutsu angrily. 'We want your army out of here, as far from Hiraizumi as you can march them, before the forces Sogamori sends against you can reach here. For two hundred years the land of Oshu has been virtually our kingdom. I will not allow it to be destroyed by a war not of our making.'

Yukio raised a hand in a placating gesture. 'The warriors I have brought with me, especially the Mongols, have little experience in mountain fighting. I would prefer to meet the Takashi somewhere south of here.' He stood up. 'If you will forgive me, Lord Hidehira, Lord Yerubutsu.' He bowed. Jebu stood and bowed with him.

Yerubutsu held up a finger. 'Before your army leaves here, I will go over the accounts my stewards have kept. You will repay us in full for all food and supplies taken from our people. I will determine the amount you owe. I have been to the Home Provinces, and I know better than any of you what current prices are.'

Yukio bowed again. 'I'm sure your assessment will be fair.'

Staring at the floor, the ancient Hidehira muttered, 'Clearly, the age of noble-spirited samurai is gone.'

CHAPTER FOUR

On the outskirts of Hiraizumi stood the proudest achievement of the Northern Fujiwara, the Chusonji Temple. A complex of forty buildings, the Chusonji was as richly decorated as any of the great temples of Heian Kyo. It boasted two famous statues of the Buddha as well as innumerable other works of art. Its most splendid building, the Konjikido, was coated with black lacquer and plated with gold.

Taniko and Jebu sat on a bed of pine needles on a wooded hill overlooking the Chusonji. Jebu was full of apprehension, far more frightened than he had ever felt going into battle. He had decided that today he must tell Taniko the one secret that lay between them.

'Yukio wants me to go to Kamakura to see his brother Hideyori,' Jebu said. 'If necessary, I'm to rescue Hideyori from your father. I'm to bring Hideyori the message that Yukio only claimed the clan chieftainship because he mistakenly thought Hideyori was dead.'

Taniko bowed her head. 'It was I who misled Yukio. If there is bad blood between the brothers because of this, it is my responsibility.'

Jebu shook his head. 'You gave us the only information you had. I warned him not to be so impulsive about sending out that proclamation.'

Taniko smiled at him. This morning her beauty was as radiant as the golden temple below. Since their return to the Sunrise Land, Taniko's beauty had acquired a new vividness. She was like a plant that had been kept in a room too long and was fading, but had now been put outdoors and was growing vigorously again.

'I'd hoped all along you would be coming with me,' she said.

'We'll have to travel quickly. A day's delay could mean Hideyori's death. You'll have to be ready this afternoon.' He wondered if she could hear the tension in his voice as clearly as he could. He had to tell her now. With each day that passed there was more chance that circumstances would intervene to prevent him from telling her that he was Kiyosi's killer.

Now that he had made up his mind to speak, he was almost paralysed with dread. He reminded himself that, as a Zinja, he should simply speak out and let the consequences be what they would. Whatever her reaction, it would be the reaction the Self wanted, and therefore the right reaction.

'I will be ready when you want me,' Taniko said with a small smile. 'The Mongols taught me how to travel quickly. They consider a breakneck speed a dignified pace for a lady. We don't have to cover the whole distance overland, either. We can go by horseback to Sendai and from there hire a boat to take us down the coast to Kamakura. That would save us half the time.'

'What do you think your father will do to Hideyori?'

She frowned. 'Whatever he does will be decided by the situation. I know that after Kiyosi was killed Sogamori ordered my father to send him Hideyori's head. For some reason my father did not obey. Hideyori is worth much more to my father alive than dead.'

At the mention of Kiyosi's name, Jebu felt as if he had been stabbed with an icicle. Taniko looked at him curiously, half smiling, half concerned.

'Jebu-san, you didn't bring me to this beautiful spot just to tell me you're coming with me to Kamakura.'

'No, there is something I must say. It's something I would much rather forget, much rather we could both forget, but it cannot stay hidden forever.' How to say it? He cast about frantically in his mind for words that would not hurt her. Finally, he gave up. Just say it as simply and plainly as possible, the Zinja way.

'Taniko, I killed Kiyosi.'

He felt a momentary relief at having at last said what, for so long, he could not say. But the look on her face turned the relief to anguish. It was a look of disbelief, one he had seen hundreds of times, usually on the faces of men he had just killed. He wanted to rush on, now that he had started, to tell her everything that had happened that day on the waters of Hakata. But he checked the impulse. First, he must find out what she wanted, and needed, to know.

When she spoke, it was no help. 'What did you say?'

'I killed Kiyosi,' he repeated. He would have to explain. 'At Hakata Bay. We were fighting from ships. He was about to shoot Yukio. I used an arrow with an armour-piercing head. He died instantly. Fell overboard. I didn't know who it was. Moko had to tell me. Yukio was angry with me at first. He had given strict orders – don't shoot at samurai. But I explained that the man I shot, Kiyosi, had been about to kill him. It was over so quickly. You know how these things happen in battle. One moment a man is alive. The next he's dead. No, you don't know what it's like. You've never been in a battle.' He checked himself. This was just what he hadn't wanted to do. He had

32

wanted to help her, not merely purge himself. He waited for her to speak. Her look was changing from astonishment to pain. Just like a wounded man, he thought.

She said softly, 'I've seen people killed, Jebu. I once killed a man.' He waited for her to say more. Her lustrous eyes held his. Her mouth was slightly open. After a moment she said, 'Oh, Jebu-san. Poor Jebu.'

Now he was surprised. 'You feel sorry for me?'

'You've been living with this ever since it happened. Especially since we came together again. You've been holding this in and suffering all alone.' She rested her hand on his. Her hand was cool and dry. She looked down at the large, brown hand under hers and slowly drew her hand away.

She whispered, 'Homage to Amida Buddha. Homage to Amida Buddha.' There was bewilderment on her face.

'I've learned to bear the death of Kiyosi,' she said. 'I can even bear the loss of my son. I don't know if I can bear this, that it was you who killed him. I looked at your hand just now and thought, this is the hand that released the arrow. I couldn't touch you any more. Help me, Amida Buddha.' She was not talking to him now, Jebu realized, but to herself. For a moment, when she spoke of feeling sorry for him, he thought she was going to understand. But now, watching the tears begin to form in her eyes, he knew it was not going to be that easy. He had often found that his worst fears were not realized, so that it sometimes seemed that to fear a thing would insure its not happening. Once in a while, though, exactly what he feared came to pass, and those were always the worst times of his life. Like this. His fingers strayed to his chest and felt the lump of the Jewel inside his robe. The Jewel gave no comfort, either. It was hard and cold.

She drew her index finger delicately over her eyelids. The tears that had brimmed her eyes were wiped away. She turned and looked at him, and her stare was dark, fathomless.

'Tell me exactly what happened. I didn't grasp all of it the first time.'

Slowly and carefully, Jebu told her, starting with the first appearance of the Takashi ships at the mouth of Hakata Bay and ending when his galley had fought free and was on its way to China.

'All these years,' she said wonderingly. 'I've hated the man who killed him, without ever once suspecting that it might be you. Unthinkable that my karma could bring me that much pain.'

'Taniko, there is no need for pain.' She was slipping away from him. He felt panic, as if he were holding her with one hand at the brink of a cliff and was losing his grip.

'No need to feel pain?' She looked at him in amazement. 'Jebu, I don't choose to feel pain. Pain happens to me. All my life, it seems, has been filled with pain. Except for two times. One was the year with Kiyosi. The other was the last few months with you. You brought each of those times to an end.'

He closed his eyes. Her words hurt past bearing. He wanted to get up and run from her, run down the hill to the golden temple. He would throw himself on the floor and lie there in the cool peace of the temple until he died. Now, at last, he yearned for death as the samurai did. Plunging a dagger into his belly and tearing his guts open could be no worse than this pain in his heart.

'The Buddha said that life is suffering,' Taniko whispered.

Again Jebu tried to tighten his fingers on the wrist that was slipping over into the abyss. 'The Buddha also said that suffering can end. That the poisoned arrow can be pulled from the wound and the wound can heal.'

Taniko's eyes were quite dry now. 'Yes. He said that the cure for suffering is to kill desire.'

'Desire for what is past, for what cannot be brought back.'

'All desire,' said Taniko quietly. 'As long as I desire you, I will feel pain, knowing that I desire the man who killed Kiyosi.'

'You might as well kill me,' Jebu said, 'if you are going to kill your desire for me.'

'Are not life and death all the same to a Zinja?'

Thinking still of the belly-cutting of the samurai, Jebu said, 'At this moment, for me, death is preferable to life. If it will give you any comfort, any peace, I'll give you my sword and you can run it through me.'

The look in her eyes was almost hatred. 'For the Zinja and the samurai it's the same. Life is nothing. Death is everything. So easy. Easy for everyone except those you leave behind.'

'Forgive me. It was a foolish suggestion.'

'No. Typical. Not foolish, typical of you Zinja, of all

warriors. Even of Kiyosi. He was no wiser than you, after all.'

'I know that Kiyosi was a man to be admired.'

She was still looking at him with near hatred. 'So you killed him.'

He began to feel angry. If she couldn't understand how men who respected each other might fight and kill each other, she understood nothing about this matter. She had no right to hate him.

'Taniko, in battle you can't pick and choose your targets. You try to kill everyone on the other side. They are all trying to kill you. I didn't want to kill Kiyosi. I didn't even know it was Kiyosi I was shooting at. All I knew was that I couldn't let Yukio be killed. I didn't even see it as a choice. I was guided by the Self.'

'Ah, I see. It was not you who killed Kiyosi. It was your god, the Self.'

'The Self is not a god. Taniko, nothing will bring back Kiyosi. Your son Atsue has been lost to you for eight years. Nothing can change that, either. Yes, my hand launched the arrow. But you must know, if you know me at all, that I felt no hatred for Kiyosi. If I had known what he was to you, perhaps I would have hesitated to shoot. I've always wanted you to be happy, and I've never been able to give you happiness.'

The dazzle of Konjikido blurred and swam in his sight. He heard blackbirds calling in the cryptomerias that towered above them. Their cries sounded like the battle shouts of samurai announcing their lineage.

'The last time I cried was when Taitaro-sensei told me how my mother was killed,' he said.

Taniko's face was a mask, the powdered, painted face of a noble lady of the Sunrise Land. It was unreadable. She did not answer.

'If I could restore him to life I would, knowing that it would mean losing your forever,' Jebu went on. 'All I've done is bring you suffering. When you found a new life with Kiyosi, I killed him. And now that we're together again, I'm destroying it by telling you this.'

'It would have been so much easier not to tell me,' she said, her voice a cold silver chime. 'It would have saved us both so much grief. Why did you have to?'

'Because you mean so much to me that I could not go on lying to you. If the shadow of falsehood had fallen between us throughout our lives, we would never truly have been united, body and soul. Our union would have been eternally blighted. That would have been as painful for me to live with as it would have been for us to part and never see each other again.'

'Then you told me this to spare yourself pain. I might have been perfectly happy with you if you had not told me.'

'Would you really wish to spend your life with me, not knowing this?'

She looked down at her small, pale hands folded in her lap. 'That is a question that can never be answered. How can I say whether I would prefer not to know?'

'The man who unknowingly drinks poisoned wine enjoys it but dies all the same.'

'He may die happy, perhaps not even aware that he is dying.'

She had pulled her hand away from him earlier, but he had to reach for her now, to hold her hands again. It might be the last time he would ever touch her. She did not resist when he took her hands, but they lay lifelessly in his grasp.

'Taniko, you can spend the rest of your life hating me for Kiyosi's death, but that will not bring him back. You and I might be happy together, if you were able to forgive. Otherwise, you will lose me as well as Kiyosi.'

She smiled faintly. 'I can forgive, Jebu. I have already forgiven you. I know what you say is true – that you meant no evil when you fired that arrow into Kiyosi's breast. Once, Kublai Khan told me about the Mongols killing all the children of a captured city. He explained that, since the men and women had been killed, the children would only have starved to death had they been left alive. The Mongols believed that killing the children was the right thing to do. You, of course, have never killed a child, but I can't help thinking how much harm men do when they mean no evil. Even so, these hands, holding mine, were the hands that sent Kiyosi to the bottom of the sea forever, that took away my son's father, destroyed my protector, left me defenceless when Sogamori took Atsue. None of it was your doing, Jebu. I realize that. I could never hate you. I can forgive you.'

Again, for a moment, Jebu felt hope and relief, but there was something in her tone that warned him against hope. Slowly, gently, she pulled her hands away from his.

'What I cannot do is forget.'

Jebu reached for her again, but she rose to her feet gracefully and drew away from him.

'You could not call back the arrow that killed Kiyosi,' she said. 'Nor can you call back what you have told me. I can never forget what I now know.'

'Did Kiyosi mean more to you than I do?'

She shook her head. 'That question is not worthy of you, Jebu. Kiyosi was with me almost daily for ten years. He fathered Atsue, who gave me more pleasure than any other human being ever has, including you. But in all those happy years with him I never forgot you. If what happened were reversed, if Kiyosi had killed you, I would feel towards him as I do towards you now.'

Jebu stood before her with his hands dangling helplessly at his sides. If only he could break down this wall between them by holding her, by crushing her in his arms.

'How do you feel towards me now, Taniko?'

A slight frown creased the white-powdered skin of her forehead. 'If I say it, I will hurt you, but since you consider the truth so important – I shrink from you.'

Jebu turned away from her so that she could no longer see the tears streaming down his face. Her voice followed him.

'Years ago you killed Kiyosi. Now you have killed Jebu. The Jebu I was happy with just a few moments ago no longer exists. A stranger is there. I recoil from that stranger.'

Jebu sank to the ground, his hands over his face, feeling as if a great rock pressed on his back, crushing him into the ground. The worst of it was the self-hatred mingled with despair. If this went on much longer he knew he would take out his sword and, as the samurai did, destroy himself.

Taniko's voice went on behind him, musingly, as if she were alone and talking to herself. 'I've often wondered why so many of our samurai men and women welcome death, and why I do not. Even at this moment, I cling to life. It's almost vulgar, peasantlike. Perhaps I simply lack the courage to kill myself. I am tempted to suggest that you and I, since we seem to have lost everything, should die together.'

'I am ready to die,' Jebu groaned through his hands.

37

Her hand settled on his shoulder, as light as a falling leaf. 'Stand and look at me, Jebu.'

He saw now that the tears she had dried away in her cold revulsion were now flowing freely, tiny rivulets cutting through the powder on her face.

'Death is what brought us to this agony,' she said. 'Kiyosi sought death and you gave it to him. I will not add my own death to it, and I forbid you to seek death. If you care for me, if you want to atone for Kiyosi, do as I tell you. Live, Jebu.'

Jebu stared at her, astonished. 'Those were the very words my mother spoke to me after my initiation into the Zinja.'

Taniko smiled, though her tears were still falling. 'The women who care for you think alike. Even if life seems unbearable, Jebu, I demand of you, as one to whom you owe an obligation – carry that burden. It may be that death will come to you as you serve your Order and Yukio, but do not go looking for death.'

'Why should you care whether I live or die?'

'Because everything you say is wise and true, Jebu. Only, I can't forget what you've done or continue to feel about you as I did. I told you that for years I've hated Kiyosi's killer. I always pictured him as a faceless samurai, a warrior in a steel mask. I never thought I would actually know who he was. The vision of you as the man who killed Kiyosi is too new, too shocking for me to bear. It's strange. I've never wanted to forget any great wrong done to me before this. I've never expected to be able to avenge myself on Horigawa or Sogamori, but I've never had to forgive such people, either, or forget what they did. I'm not very practised at forgetting. With time we may go back to what we were, or something like it. We might even have some of the happiness we had before today.'

The weight crushing him seemed a tiny bit lighter. 'You want to try to go on as before?'

'That is not entirely possible. I assume we will be leaving for Kamakura today?'

'We must leave at once.'

'We will travel together. We will sleep in the same tent. You must not touch me.' She paused and levelled her piercing gaze on him. 'Do you agree?'

His shoulders sagged. 'I understand. Yes.'

38

'When we get to Kamakura, I will stay with my family, if they will accept me. After you've delivered Yukio's message to Hideyori, you'll return to Yukio. You and he will wage war on the Takashi together. When it is over, you will come back to me. Then we will see.'

'I may not come back to you.'

'If you are killed, I will hate the man who kills you as I've always hated the man who killed Kiyosi. I will probably never forgive myself for having sent you to war this way. But I cannot do otherwise. I can control my actions and my words, but I cannot control what I know and feel. Will you go on with me, on those terms?'

'I will go on with you on any terms you name. Tell me, though, Taniko. Was I right, do you think, to tell you about Kiyosi?'

She stood silent for a moment, thinking. 'You always said the Zinja does not recognize right and wrong. Who can say which would injure us more – to have spent our lives with a lie between us, or to have our happiness smashed by the truth? It is a question I will ask myself many times as I sit alone at Kamakura.'

CHAPTER FIVE

Kamakura had been growing when Taniko left home to marry Prince Horigawa. It had now spread out into the surrounding hills until it covered almost twice the area she remembered. Most of the new buildings were the homes of wealthy families, surrounded by parks and walls. Even this larger Kamakura seemed a tiny hamlet to her, though, in comparison to the vast cities of China.

She saw at once that the Shima mansion had grown, too. It had swallowed up the estates on either side, so that its newly built earth and stone wall enclosed a park three times as great as the old wooden-palisade had. Beyond the high wall was a sight that made Taniko gasp. A three-storey donjon tower dominated the estate, topped by the gilded dolphins to protect it from fire and lightning.

39

'Clearly my father has prospered,' she said to Jebu.

The flag over the main gateway was no longer the Red Dragon that had defiantly proclaimed Shima loyalty to the Takashi in the Muratomo-dominated eastern provinces. Instead, the flag bore the Shima family crest, a small white triangle inverted within a larger orange triangle. My father's ties to the Takashi must be weakening, Taniko thought. He declares himself a power in his own right.

Another sign of her family's new position were the guards at the gate. No less than ten samurai stood there, looking relaxed, alert and very competent, all carrying two swords and dressed in handsome suits of full armour, the strips of steel lashed together with bright orange lacings. Their captain's helmet was decorated with a white horsehair plume.

The party with Taniko included Jebu, Moko and five samurai guards, men who came from the area around Kamakura and who volunteered to accompany Jebu and Taniko so they could visit their homes. All rode horses, and three more horses carried their baggage.

No one would suspect from looking at them, Taniko thought, that each was moderately wealthy with spoils brought back from China, or that they were the harbingers of a powerful army newly landed on the Sacred Islands. They were tired, and their travelling robes were dusty and stained. It had taken them twelve days to get here from Hiraizumi, coming down from the mountains of Oshu by horseback, then hiring a coasting galley to make the long voyage from Sendai. The stunning scenery of the far north helped Taniko, to some extent, to forget her sorrow. The soaring crags and rushing, foaming streams, the huge rocks laced with white ribbons of falling water were wilder than any landscape she had ever seen – even a bit frightening. When their party reached the sea there were countless islands scoured into strange shapes by wind and wave, and covered by precariously clinging pines leaning at odd angles. A Heian Kyo courtier would find such sights barbarous, but having lived among barbarians Taniko could see the beauty in it. As they rode along, she and Jebu were silent most of the time. There was nothing left for them to say to each other now. Time was their best hope. She expressed the thought in a poem she gave him on shipboard, a poem inspired by the scenes through which they had passed.

> To carve a hollow in the island rock,
> A shelter for the sea birds,
> Many winters, many summers.

She handed it to him silently just before their galley docked at Kamakura, and silently he read it, nodded and put it inside his robe.

Now the captain of the Shima estate's guards was swaggering towards them. Jebu climbed down from his horse and approached him.

'Another monk, by Hachiman,' the captain snarled before Jebu could open his mouth. 'Every ragged monk from here to Kyushu has heard that there are rich pickings to be had in Kamakura. Well, not at this house. Lord Shima Bokuden has given strict instructions that monks are to be sent away with their begging bowls empty. Go.' The captain laid a threatening hand on his silver-mounted sword hilt.

A typical samurai of the eastern provinces, Taniko thought, blustering and rude.

Taniko watched as Jebu turned his left side towards the samurai captain, bringing the sword dangling from his belt into view without making a threatening gesture. 'Excuse me, captain,' he said politely. 'I am escorting Lord Bokuden's daughter, the Lady Taniko, who has come a long way to visit her father. Would you be kind enough to allow us to enter and to notify Lord Bokuden that his daughter is here?' Jebu did not mention his own message for Hideyori. They must manage to find out Hideyori's situation without expressing any interest in him.

'Oho, one of those weapon-carrying monks, eh?' the captain growled. 'What sort are you, Buddhist, Shinto or Zinja? None of you armed monks is either holy or skilled in the martial arts, so there is no need to fear either your curses or your swords. That woman on horseback claims to be Lord Bokuden's daughter, does she? Lord Bokuden's daughter is a great lady who lives at the capital. She would not come riding up here on a horse, like some camp follower.'

41

'Pay no attention to him, my lady,' said Moko in a low voice. 'His mother was a yak.' Taniko wanted none of the men with her to quarrel with her father's guards. She decided to assert herself and spurred her horse forward. She addressed the captain in a small but sharp-edged voice, like the dagger all samurai women carried.

'The Lady Shima Taniko has not resided in Heian Kyo in seven years, captain, as you should know. As for my riding a horse, I am samurai by birth and upbringing and can perhaps ride as well as you. I advise you to change your tone and let us in at once, or you'll answer to my father when I report this to him. If, that is, you do work for my father and are not some filthy ronin who happened to be idling by the Shima gate when we rode up.' There were some mild chuckles from Taniko's party, and even some from the gate guards, at this last jab. The captain blushed.

'I have my duty to perform, lady. A party of assassins might try to enter here in disguise. If you'll dismount and the men will disarm themselves I'll admit you, and you can wait inside the gate to be properly identified.'

Her father had always suspected the worst of his neighbours, but he had never worried about assassins. Another change in the Shima family since she left.

Grooms took their horses through the double set of gates, leading them to the stables. Two of the guards collected swords from all the men except Moko, who did not carry one. Once inside the gate they walked single file through a maze made up of wooden walls and the sides of buildings, a maze designed to trap any attackers who might get through the gate during a siege. At last they found themselves in a courtyard full of boxes and barrels. It appeared that the Shima were still in trade, more so than ever.

'You have good horses and good swords,' the captain remarked. 'If you're a band of thieves, you chose victims of good quality.'

This was too much for Moko. He reddened, turned to the captain and said, 'Not being a man of much quality yourself, you couldn't be expected to recognize it in others.'

The captain stared at Moko. Taniko's heart started pounding. Moko had forgotten where he was. He had come up in the world, had travelled with Yukio's samurai and talked with them on equal terms. Everyone, of whatever rank, talked freely among the Mongols. A commoner did not speak sharply to a samurai in the Sacred Islands, however, and Moko might lose his life for it.

Without a word the captain moved towards him, sliding his long sword out of the scabbard that hung at his left side. Moko paled, but did not try to run. The captain drew his sword back, holding it with both hands, for a stroke that would cut Moko in half at the waist.

Jebu stepped between them.

'Out of the way, monk,' said the captain. 'No commoner can insult a samurai and live.'

'I beg you to reconsider, captain,' said Jebu quietly, 'or you'll end by looking even more foolish than you do now.'

'Out of my way, or you'll die before he does.'

'Please put your sword away, captain.'

Taniko was terrified. Jebu's own weapon had been carried away. He might be cut down before her eyes.

The captain lunged at Jebu, swinging his sword. Jebu hardly seemed to move, but the blade cut through empty air, and the captain rushed past him. Jebu quickly shifted position again, to keep himself between the captain and Moko. The captain swung at Jebu's legs, and Jebu leaped high into the air. Now the captain had forgotten Moko and was determined to kill Jebu. Jebu ran up the side of a pyramid of boxes and kicked them, sending them tumbling down on the captain, who tripped and fell under the avalanche. He picked himself up and came after Jebu again.

Easily ducking and dodging the sword, Jebu led the captain back across the courtyard towards a high wooden wall. The captain brought his blade down in a ferocious two-handed swipe. The sword thumped into the hard wood of the gate. The captain was furiously trying to pull the sword out of the wood when Jebu, robe flapping, swooped down on him like a falcon on a rabbit and picked him up, leaving the sword stuck in the gate. Jebu hefted the captain into the air and hung him by his belt from an iron hook used to suspend a lantern over the courtyard at night. He pulled the samurai's shorter sword out of its scabbard and laid it on the ground, then freed the long sword from the door and laid it across the short one. Bowing to the

43

captain, who wriggled frantically to free himself from the hook, Jebu turned and walked away. The courtyard shook with laughter. Elated by Jebu's unarmed triumph over the samurai, Taniko clapped her hands with glee.

'Taniko.'

Standing at the top of the steps entering the donjon was her Uncle Ryuichi. Her heart gave a surprising little leap of gladness. She wondered what he was doing here instead of Heian Kyo. Then she remembered with a sinking feeling how she had accused him of failing her and had walked coldly out of his house seven years ago. Yet she was happy to see him today.

Ryuichi had grown fatter in the interval. His eyes and mouth were tiny in his white moon of a face. Powdered and painted like a courtier, he wore gorgeous robes that glittered with gold thread.

Taniko bowed to him. 'Honoured Uncle. I have returned from China.'

Ryuichi looked at her, astonished, then his expression changed abruptly to a frown. 'What is happening here? Why is that man hanging there?'

The captain managed to unbuckle his belt, drop to the ground with a clatter of armour, and kneel. Taniko noted that the whole courtyard had fallen silent as soon as Ryuichi appeared. He had an air of command she had never seen in him before.

'Your captain of guards was about to kill one of my escort,' she said. 'This Zinja monk, who is also a member of my party, hung him up there to give him time to calm himself.'

Ryuichi took immediate charge. He sent the guards back out to the gate, and looked reprovingly at the captain who had allowed himself to be disgraced. He ordered Taniko's party fed and quartered in the estate's guesthouses.

'Niece, if you will forgive me, I think we ought to talk immediately. After that you can refresh yourself. Please come with me.'

Not looking back at Jebu, Taniko followed Ryuichi into the donjon. They climbed up winding flights of stairs in the dark interior. At last he drew her into a small chamber whose window overlooked the courtyard. They knelt facing each other across a low table.

'My esteemed elder brother will be astonished when he learns

44

his daughter has returned. I am happy to see you.' He looked at her uncertainly. 'I hope you are happy to see me.'

'I am, Uncle. Very.'

Unexpectedly, tears began to roll down his whitened cheeks. 'I never thought to see you again. I was sure you would die in China, and I blamed myself. You were a daughter to me, but I could not save you. I was tormented. I felt I had two choices: to die or to try to become the sort of man who does not let such things happen. I decided I was not worthy to die. So I have tried to become a better man.'

She smiled. 'I noticed a difference about you, Uncle.'

He nodded. 'I am no longer afraid. I have learned that there is worse suffering than death. Being unafraid, I can look samurai in the eye and order them about. I dress myself as a man of the Court to further impress the people here in Kamakura. Now, you must tell me everything about yourself. These are dangerous times, and I must know what your circumstances are, so I can advise you how to act. What happened to you in China? What connection is there between you and Horigawa now? That monk who was with you in the courtyard and made a fool of our captain of guards – is he not the same Zinja monk who escorted you to Heian Kyo years ago, when you were to be married to Prince Horigawa? Did you come back from China with Muratomo no Yukio? Do you know anything about this proclamation of his?'

Taniko took out her ivory fan and briskly waved it in front of her face. 'So many questions at once, Uncle. I'm tired from travelling. But I'll do the best I can.' As she had already agreed with Jebu, she said nothing about her relationship with him. It would only disturb her family, and just now there was no need to reveal it. She told Ryuichi that Horigawa had left her with the Mongols, but said she had simply been a lady-in-waiting to Kublai Khan's Empress. Yukio and Jebu had been fighting for the Great Khan, and they agreed to take her back to the Sacred Islands with them when their service with the Mongols was finished. Ryuichi's eyes widened as he heard her story. Even with certain intimate parts left out, it was a remarkable tale.

'Now, Uncle. What are you doing here instead of the capital?'

'The most terrible war these islands have ever seen is about to descend on us, Taniko-san. When the clash comes, my family and I will be among those whom Sogamori will either kill or hold as hostages. So we moved back here.'

'Did Father send for you?'

Ryuichi laughed. 'No. He was furious. He expected me to stay there, looking after Shima interests to the very end. Though I no longer fear death, I don't intend to sacrifice myself and my family to my brother's greed. I told him so.'

A servant brought a tray of food, along with sake and two cups. Glad of the opportunity to serve sake the way she had been taught as a girl, Taniko poured a cup for Ryuichi and held it out to him. She offered him a seaweed cake on chopsticks, but he shook his head.

'You eat. You have travelled far, and you need refreshment. Let me tell you our situation here. As you can see, our family is much wealthier than it was when you left. At first we prospered because of our connection with the Takashi. But now we grow on our own. We have extended our holdings in the Kanto. Wealth and power go hand in hand. Samurai flock to us. We have built up a network of alliances all through the eastern provinces. The Shima are the first family in the north-east because we are hosts to Hideyori.'

'Hosts? No longer guards?'

'Not guards for many years. Twice Sogamori has ordered your father to have Hideyori executed, but we are so far from the capital we could evade the order. Hideyori has grown stronger. He has built friendships and alliances throughout the Kanto. The husbands of your two older sisters, who have large holdings in the north, both wear the White Dragon now. My unworthy son, Munetoki, your cousin, wears our family crest still, since he is heir to the clan chieftainship, but he worships Hideyori as much as Hideyori worships the war god, Hachiman. Meanwhile, Sogamori's problems have multiplied.'

'What problems does Sogamori have?'

'Most of the nobles who are not Takashi hate him. He has forced hundreds of men out of office and replaced them with his relatives. He has quarrelled with the Retired Emperor, Go-Shirakawa. He is blamed for all the troubles of the realm, the plague, the starvation, the failure of crops, the bandits who roam the land. Many say he is pursued by the angry ghosts of all

46

those who have died at Takashi hands. He has ruled unwisely since Kiyosi's death. Kiyosi's younger brother, Notaro, serves Sogamori as a second-in-command. But he utterly lacks Kiyosi's ability.' Ryuichi paused and looked sadly at her. 'Forgive me for bringing up what must be a painful subject.'

Taniko sighed. 'I suffer Kiyosi's death every day anew. What has happened to Atsue?'

Ryuichi shook his head. 'I know little. Sogamori is said to dote on him. He lives at the Rokuhara and spends time at other Takashi estates. Those who know him say he is a most charming and accomplished young man. I've seen him several times on public occasions. He is quite handsome. He dresses beautifully, like a young prince, as all the Takashi do. He rides well and wears his sword with grace.'

'Perhaps it was best for him that Sogamori took him from me.'

'I will never think so. Tell me, Taniko-chan, now that you're back with us, what are your plans? Will you stay here?'

'For the time being, Uncle, I have no plans beyond the next few months. As you said, these are dangerous times. Now I would like you to see my father and Lord Hideyori and arrange an audience with them for the Zinja monk, Jebu.'

CHAPTER SIX

After her talk with Ryuichi, Taniko spent the afternoon in the palatial new women's house of the Shima estate, enjoying her reunion with her mother and her Aunt Chogao. She bathed and unpacked a set of robes for the night. When the time came for Jebu to deliver Yukio's message to Hideyori, she emerged from her chamber dressed in her finest silks. The older women objected. It was unthinkable for her to dine with men discussing important affairs. She brushed aside their disapproval and strode out of the women's house and over the covered bridge to the main hall.

At the doorway of Lord Bokuden's formal dining room two samurai tried to stop her from going in.

47

'I am Shima Taniko, Lord Bokuden's daughter, and my presence is required.' The guards let her pass.

For the first time in twenty-one years, she saw her father. The old rage he had always provoked in her stirred within, but she kept her face composed. He stood up when she came into the room, which had been set for a small dinner. Three low individual dining tables were arranged in a semi-circle. The walls of the room were adorned with landscapes painted in green and gold.

Jebu, wearing his plain monk's robe, knelt facing Bokuden's place. He looked up at her, expressionless. She felt a pang of longing for him. The central place was empty. Was Ryuichi to join them?

Bokuden's smile of greeting faded when he saw Taniko.

'Well, Father, since you seemed too busy to send for me, I thought I would visit you,' said Taniko calmly. 'I can help serve your guests.'

Where Ryuichi had put on weight, Bokuden had grown smaller and thinner. His beard and moustache were longer and streaked with white. His small eyes narrowed with annoyance.

'I cannot greet you properly tonight, Taniko. Please go. I will speak to you in the morning when I have time.'

'I haven't travelled all this way to hide in the women's house, Father. I was a party to many of the decisions that led to this moment. I know what is happening in Hiraizumi. You may find me useful.'

Bokuden glowered at her. 'Yes, you always did imagine that I stand in need of your advice. Look about you. You see we have done rather well in the years you were gone.'

'I understand Hideyori is the key to your prosperity. Who was it advised you to take him in, in the first place?'

Bokuden flushed. 'We are discussing matters of state. It would be unthinkable for a woman to be present. Please go, before Lord Hideyori arrives and you embarrass me in his eyes.' He turned to Jebu. 'You have been her escort. Can you not advise her to leave?'

'I have heard correctly, then,' said a strong voice from the doorway. 'The Lady Taniko has returned to Kamakura.'

This day has brought me a whole succession of faces from the past, thought Taniko. It was hard for her to remember what Hideyori had looked like the last time she saw him. Atsue today was older than Hideyori had been then.

The Muratomo chieftain was now a handsome, big man who carried himself with the assurance of a leader who knew no superior. Taniko found herself thinking of Kublai, even though Hideyori was neither as tall nor as old. Nor, indeed, anywhere near as powerful. Hideyori had the bulging Muratomo forehead, straight eyebrows, a hawklike nose and a prominent chin. His moustache was small and neatly trimmed. It was when she looked into his eyes that she remembered him. Those cold, black eyes had not changed.

Taniko dropped gracefully to her knees and bowed low. Her father followed suit, and Jebu gave a short bow, as was the Zinja custom.

Hideyori bowed in turn to Jebu. 'The warrior monk who brought me safely from Heian Kyo to Kamakura. I'm pleased to see you alive. A man with an occupation like yours shouldn't have lasted past his twenty-fifth year.'

'Your younger brother Yukio helped me to survive, my lord,' said Jebu with a smile.

'Yes,' said Hideyori shortly, turning away from Jebu. 'Lady Taniko. I have never had occasion to compliment you for your clever deception at Daidoji. Had you not been such a fine actress, Prince Sasaki no Horigawa would now be nineteen years dead.'

'I apologize for deceiving you, my lord. I have had cause to regret it,' Taniko said with a wry smile.

'I do not regret it,' said Hideyori, kneeling behind the table in the place of honour. 'The prince has been very useful to me.' In what way? Taniko wondered. Horigawa, the Takashi toady, helping the Muratomo chieftain?

'Well, now that you have paid your respects to Lord Hideyori, you may leave us, Daughter,' Bokuden said. He glared at her, his wispy grey beard trembling.

'Must you go, Lady Taniko?' Hideyori asked.

Laughing inwardly at her father, Taniko said, 'I am yours to command, my lord.'

'I understand that you, like the monk Jebu, have just returned from China with my brother and his army of barbarians. Perhaps

49

you can tell me things about Yukio's adventures that may have escaped his holy friend's attention.'

The implication was clear; he doesn't like Yukio, she thought, or trust him. He doesn't trust Jebu very much, either. Perhaps I could be the link between the brothers. They need someone to draw them together if they're to have a working alliance.

'I'll be happy to tell you anything you want to know, my lord,' said Taniko. After all, Yukio had no secrets from Hideyori.

Hideyori turned to Jebu. 'Yukio hopes to win me over by sending this charming lady and an old comrade-in-arms as emissaries. But I find it curious that he does not come to me himself.'

Jebu's clear grey eyes held Hideyori's. 'My lord, he has an army to command, and there is always the threat of a Takashi attack. Please, if you will, read this letter from him. He acknowledges you as chieftain of the Muratomo and is prepared to meet with you whenever it becomes possible.' Jebu drew a sealed bamboo tube from an inner pocket of his robe and offered it to Hideyori, who laid it unopened on the table beside him.

'Yukio feels safer with his army,' Hideyori said curtly. 'Let us dine now. You can both tell me about China and the Mongols.'

Hideyori gave Bokuden a slight nod, and Taniko's father clapped his hands. The shoji panel slid back and servants brought in a succession of dishes and deposited them on their tables. At another glance from Hideyori, Bokuden, barely concealing his exasperation, ordered a table set for Taniko.

Taniko told Hideyori the acceptable story she had devised to cover her years in China. Bokuden and Hideyori might know that Horigawa had other reasons for taking her to China than a diplomatic mission, but she doubted that either would be rude enough to contradict her.

Hideyori was intensely curious about the personality of Kublai Khan, the strategy and tactics of the Mongols and their ultimate ambitions. He questioned Jebu and Taniko in turn. For Taniko, the evening was reminiscent of her first meeting with Kublai, when he asked her so many questions about the Sunrise Land.

'Do you think the Mongols plan to invade our islands?' Hideyori asked.

Bokuden laughed. 'How could they transport a big enough army across the sea?'

'Yukio did it,' said Hideyori quietly.

'Yes, lord, but Lord Yukio's army landed in friendly territory where provisions could easily be obtained,' said Jebu. 'It landed piecemeal over the course of a month. Nor is it large enough to be an invasion force in its own right. It is only meant to be part of a general uprising against the Takashi.'

They had finished eating. Taniko waved away the maid and poured sake for the men herself.

'Very good,' said Hideyori. 'It's best our cups be filled by someone we know and can trust.' He took up Yukio's letter, drew the scroll out of the bamboo tube and read it slowly and carefully.

'He apologizes for his proclamation. Well he might. He was foolish to issue it so hastily, without even knowing whether I was alive or dead. He has no idea what he has stirred up. I will write to him, and you will carry my letter back to him. It is important that our efforts be planned in such a way that all blows fall upon the Takashi at the same time.'

A look of fear crossed Bokuden's face. 'You're not thinking of going to war, Lord Hideyori?'

'There'll never be a better time. Yukio's army moving down the west coast, an uprising in the capital, and our army marching from the east. Would you have me wait here until Sogamori decides he's strong enough to come after me?'

'An uprising in the capital?' Taniko echoed.

'Sogamori's grandson, Antoku, a boy of four, now wears the Imperial necklace,' said Hideyori. 'Prince Mochihito, the child's uncle, was bypassed, though his claim to the throne is much better.' Taniko nodded. All this she knew. 'A secret opposition to Sogamori has formed around Mochihito,' Hideyori went on. 'It includes Fujiwara no Motofusa, the former Regent, contingents of the palace guard, and the Retired Emperor Go-Shirakawa. And Prince Sasaki no Horigawa.' Hideyori looked at Taniko.

Jebu said, 'Forgive me for speaking bluntly, my lord. If I ever encounter Prince Horigawa, I will kill him.'

51

Hideyori frowned. 'Why? What grievance do you have against him?'

Jebu's grey store was level. 'I am not free to say. He has committed unspeakable and unforgivable acts against – those I love.'

'I always thought Zinja monks were utterly detached and impartial,' said Hideyori.

Jebu gave him a faint, bitter smile. 'I will spend the rest of my life repenting and trying to be detached, after I have killed Horigawa.'

Bokuden was livid. 'Prince Sasaki no Horigawa is an ally of this house and always has been. I will not have threats uttered against him in my presence.' He turned to Taniko. 'He is your husband.'

Taniko burned with envy of Jebu. It should have been her right, not Jebu's, to threaten to kill Horigawa. If Jebu did kill him, it would only be in her behalf. Why must women always have men do their killing for them? Her father's suggestion that she ought to defend Horigawa shocked her. She answered with understatement.

'The prince has treated me badly,' she said quietly.

'It is your duty to be loyal to him,' her father said. 'How he has treated you does not matter.'

'Prince Horigawa helped me, even though I once tried to kill him,' Hideyori said. 'Long ago, as the Lady Taniko knows, I led a party of Muratomo samurai to his country estate to kill him. He escaped me. Many years later, when Kiyosi was killed by Yukio's men, Sogamori was so enraged that he ordered Lord Bokuden's brother, Ryuichi, to have me executed.' Taniko could not help a glance at Jebu. He was gazing calmly at Hideyori, his face attentive, revealing nothing. 'Horigawa asked Ryuichi to let him handle my execution. Horigawa then wrote a letter to Lord Bokuden urging him not to kill me, but to protect me. He advised Bokuden on what excuses to make to Sogamori. He helped persuade Sogamori that I was harmless, loyal, and thoroughly disapproved of Yukio's crimes, and that it would be pointless to kill me. So you see, where my brother very nearly caused my death by killing Kiyosi' – Hideyori's face grew ugly with long-felt bitterness – 'my old enemy Horigawa saved my life.'

'You were the last Moratomo leader in the realm,' Jebu said. 'Why would Horigawa want to save you?'

'He sensed the turning of the tide. Whoever put that arrow in Kiyosi's chest at Hakata Bay doomed the house of Takashi. If Kiyosi had lived to advise Sogamori and eventually succeed him, Takashi rule might have been fastened on the realm forever. Kiyosi was the only one of them who combined a warrior's prowess with a sense of statecraft. Sogamori is nothing but a blustering tyrant. His other sons are stupid and arrogant. The Takashi are doomed. They have misgoverned too long. They have made too many enemies. Horigawa saw all that and sensed that I am the man who can bring down the Takashi.'

'But why would he want the Takashi brought down?' asked Taniko. 'He seems to have devoted his entire life to their advancement.'

'Oh, he has his own reasons,' Hideyori said with a laugh. 'He wants to see the samurai destroyed and the old courtier families like the Sasaki and the Fujiwara once again supreme. He hopes the great samurai clans will kill each other off.' Hideyori smiled. 'I will give him the war he wants, but not the outcome he desires.'

'Excuse me,' said Jebu. 'Lord Hideyori, I sense that you hold Lord Yukio to blame for endangering your life. I was at the battle in which Kiyosi was killed. Lord Yukio had nothing to do with his death. Now Lord Yukio submits himself to your leadership and offers twelve thousand veteran troops, men who have been fighting for the past seven years or more, while the Takashi have been growing soft. Surely you will accept his brotherly obedience?'

Hideyori pursed his lips. 'I was nearly beheaded because of him. He came back here thinking I had died and proclaimed himself chieftain of our clan. Now he does not come in person to resolve our differences but sends a henchman with a letter – I mean no disrespect to you, shiké. I will accept his submission, but there is much to be settled between Yukio and me.'

Jebu's remark about Yukio's troops having been in combat for years reminded Taniko that Hideyori had been leading an inactive life in Kamakura ever since the age of fifteen. In all that time he had had to suffer the perpetual fear that Sogamori might at last bring about his execution. Bokuden and Horigawa must

53

have seemed utterly untrustworthy protectors. Living with such fear for so long had undoubtedly scarred Hideyori, but in what way?

'I will send my brother a letter,' Hideyori said. 'I will tell him I am prepared to raise an army and go into battle immediately. I will command him to strike from the north-west down the Hokurikido Road, and I will come down the Takaido from the east. At the same moment, Mochihito and his supporters will rise in the capital.'

He raised his sake cup and stared deep into Taniko's eyes. She felt herself blushing. 'By the end of summer we will be in the capital and the Takashi will be as forgotten as last winter's snow.'

Why, Taniko wondered, did he say that especially to me?

CHAPTER SEVEN

Takashi no Atsue went to the treasure box in his chambers, unlocked it and took out his father's sword, Kogarasu. The sword was wrapped in heavy red silk. Atsue uncovered it, laid the two-edged blade on a blackwood stand in the tokonoma alcove, and burned incense to it on a small brazier. Kogarasu glistened like a lake under a full moon. Atsue had made it his personal duty to polish the sword every day. He prayed now to Kogarasu, asking that he be a worthy son of his father in the battles to come. In the sword, if anywhere, his father's spirit must reside.

Then he went to see his grandfather. In the main audience hall of the Rokuhara, Sogamori, fat and shaven-headed, wearing his orange monk's robe, was bawling orders at Atsue's uncles, cousins and other high-ranking officers.

Prince Mochihito, the Emperor's uncle, had proclaimed himself Emperor and immediately fled the city. A contingent of the Imperial Bodyguard had gone over to Mochihito and left the city with him. They were led by a Muratomo relative who had not been purged from the guards because he had avoided involvement in Domei's insurrection. With Mochihito, also, was the former Regent, Fujiwara no Motofusa, an old enemy of the Takashi; it was Motofusa's men who had caused the street brawl that had terrified Atsue as a boy.

Mochihito had echoed Muratomo no Yukio's proclamation, calling for a general uprising against the Takashi, declaring that those who made war on Sogamori would not be rebels but loyal supporters of the rightful Emperor – himself. The pretender and his little band were headed, Sogamori believed, towards Nara, two days' journey south-east of Heian Kyo. There they would probably seek refuge with Buddhist and Zinja warrior monks who supported their cause. They might try to hold out in Nara until Hideyori, who was raising an army in the east, could reach them.

Sogamori ordered thirty thousand samurai mobilized and sent after Mochihito and his followers. They were then to go on to Nara and attack the monasteries that favoured the Muratomo. From Nara, he commanded, they were to march north and meet Hideyori on the Tokaido. Hideyori defeated, they would return to Heian Kyo, gather reinforcements, and advance into the north-west provinces on the Hokurikudo Road to crush the other Muratomo brother, Yukio.

'They think to defeat us by attacking from three directions at once,' Sogamori growled. 'But we will meet each threat in turn and defeat them one at a time.' He held up a finger and repeated. 'One at a time, that is the secret of victory.' His sons and generals bowed.

'I have been too magnanimous,' Sogamori went on. 'Having taken holy orders, I have tried to live according to the Buddha's teaching. I let the Muratomo brothers live. I tolerated untrustworthy officers in the Imperial bodyguard. I left the Northern Fujiwara in peace.' He stood up suddenly and kicked over an ancient and beautiful four-panel screen. 'When this war is over, every close relative of Muratomo no Domei will be sent into the great beyond, even infants at the breast. The Muratomo imbibe treason with their mothers' milk. All officials and samurai who have come under suspicion of disloyalty, no matter how slight, will be executed. All orders of warrior monks will be suppressed. The Northern Fujiwara will be stripped of their lands. No longer will Takashi no Sogamori show compassion.' He stamped the screen to splinters.

Sogamori's officers hurried out, their silks and satins rustling, the gold scabbards of their ceremonial swords twinkling. Sogamori turned to Atsue, and his broad faced opened in a huge grin.

'Atsue-chan. What does my beautiful grandson want of me?'

Atsue prostrated himself and swallowed nervously. 'Honoured Grandfather, I want to fight the Muratomo.'

'Get up, child. Come sit with me.' Sogamori pointed to cushions beside him. There was a pained expression on his face. 'Fighting is butchery, foul work. My ancestors were samurai, I am samurai, my sons are samurai. Now, though, I have one grandson on the Imperial throne, and I have always hoped that other grandsons of mine would be above going to war, would serve as scholars and men of state.'

'Honoured Grandfather, you're afraid something will happen to me,' Atsue said, smiling at Sogamori. He knew that with that smile he could get his grandfather to agree to anything.

'Nonsense,' Sogamori chuckled. 'What could possibly happen to you? You are the favoured of the Kami.'

'The spirit of my father calls me to war, Grandfather,' Atsue said. 'Ever since I came to live with you, you've been telling me over and over again how my father drove the Muratomo out of the Imperial Palace. I want to have a great battle against the Muratomo, too, as you did and my father did. Then I can settle down to serve my Imperial cousin at his Court.'

'The Takashi have always fought,' Sogamori sighed. 'Have you arms and armour?'

'I have a beautiful suit of armour with blue lacings, Grandfather, which you gave me last year when we performed my manhood ceremony.' He touched his samurai topknot. 'As for arms, I was hoping you would let me take Kogarasu.'

Sogamori sighed. 'Take Kogarasu. Kill many Muratomo with it. I want to see all the Muratomo go into the next world before I do.'

'Yes, Grandfather.'

'One more thing, Atsue-chan. As you know, it is my wish that you marry the Imperial Princess Kazuko. You may go to the war tomorrow, but tonight you must pay your first-night visit to the princess's bedchamber at the palace. I trust you are as eager to acquit yourself well there as you are to display prowess in battle.'

Atsue bowed. The blood raced through his body. To lie with a beautiful princess tonight and to go to war tomorrow – it was too perfect. The world was heaven.

Atsue arrived at the scene of battle late and tired. Princess Kazuko had kept him awake all night. No, to be fair, he had wanted to stay awake all night with her. Even when she had complained of soreness – she had been a virgin when he crept into her room at the beginning of the night – he could not restrain himself from coupling with her one last time.

He had cheated a bit and written his next-morning letter and poem the previous afternoon. He could not have managed to stay all night long with the princess, then to arm himself and leave for Nara in the morning, and also find time to compose a decent letter and a suitable poem.

He had told her he was going to pursue the rebel prince who was fleeing to Nara. Her parting words echoed in his mind. 'You are as tall and beautiful as a heron. Fly back to me safely and quickly.'

He began to see the bodies before they reached the Uji, where, he had been told, the main battle had taken place. Most of the dead had been stripped of their armour, and they lay like heaps of stone or bundles of cloth on the side of the road. Atsue's horse shied, and he had trouble controlling it. This annoyed him, because Grandfather had sent an escort of twelve veteran samurai with him, and he didn't want to look like a poor horseman before these experienced warriors. The samurai didn't seem to notice the bodies. The worst sights, Atsue thought, were the parts of bodies, the men who had been cut in two, the severed limbs. Most of the corpses lacked heads. Each samurai received honours and pay according to the number of heads he could produce after a battle.

From wounded Takashi samurai passing on their way back to the capital, Atsue learned, to his disappointment, that there was no more fighting. The battle had been fought late the night before and finished in the morning. Vastly outnumbering Prince Mochihito's supporters, the Takashi fell upon them and overwhelmed them at sunset. During the night many of the rebels disappeared into the countryside. Most of their leaders had cut open their bellies early this morning, choosing a temple called Phoenix Hall on the southern bank of the Uji as the site of their self-immolation. The former Regent, Fukiwara no Motofusa, had been captured. As for Prince Mochihito, he had fled to a Shinto shrine further down the road to Nara, where the Takashi caught up with him and finished him off with a volley of arrows.

The Uji was a broad, fast-flowing grey-green river running through wooded hills. Simple Shinto shrines and elaborately painted Buddhist temples lined its banks on both sides. Atsue and his escort rode over the bridge with a clatter of hooves on planks. Atsue turned downstream in the direction of the Takashi camp.

The Takashi had set up camp before Phoenix Hall. Samurai sat on the ground beside their tethered horses, repairing their armour and polishing their swords. Many of them recognized Atsue and called respectful greetings to him. He had always been popular with the samurai.

The Phoenix Hall was an elaborate building in the Chinese manner with two wings and upcurling roof corners. It had once been the country villa of a nobleman, who had willed it to religion. Now Red Dragon banners fluttered over it. Atsue's uncles and the other Takashi officers sat at their ease in the shade on the front steps of the hall.

In the dusty courtyard before the temple stood a lone man, tied to a pole, his arms bound behind him with ropes. He was small and slender and wore a dark, dusty robe. His head was bowed, his shoulders bent.

Atsue walked around the man to get a better look at him. He recognized him at once, even though his face was unpowdered and he was shabbily dressed. It was the former Regent, Fujiwara no Motofusa. The small black eyes looked back calmly and incuriously at Atsue. Doubtless many men had gone up to Motofusa to stare at him today.

Atsue had seen Motofusa in public many times after the day of the carriage fight. Eventually, though, as the Takashi hold on the government grew stronger, Motofusa had been pushed out of the Regency and replaced by a younger relative more amenable to Sogamori's influence.

Now that he and Motofusa were staring at each other, it would be rude not to speak to him. Atsue bowed deeply.

'My respects to you, Lord Fujiwara no Motofusa. I am sorry to see you in this uncomfortable position.'

Motofusa smiled at him, showing blackened teeth. 'Your manners are exquisite, like those of all the younger Takashi.' The implication that fine manners were not enough was clear. It stung Atsue and made him want to remind Motofusa of their encounter years before.

'I'm sure you don't remember me, my lord. I am Takashi no Atsue, son of Takashi no Kiyosi, grandson of Takashi no Sogamori. In the Year of the Horse your carriage had an unfortunate meeting with one in which I and my mother were riding.' Atsue realized that he had not thought of his mother in years. The helpless hunger for her, when it did arise, was so painful that he quickly pushed the thought of her from his mind. Lately he had been telling himself that he really didn't miss her, but her face kept appearing in his dreams.

'Ah, yes,' said Motofusa. 'You must be the son of Kiyosi and that little woman from the provinces who was married to Prince Sasaki no Horigawa. I warned Horigawa that he was making a mistake, marrying beneath him. Well, forgive me for saying that. I have no wish to hurt your feelings, young man. The occasion you spoke of caused me considerable discomfort thereafter, as you may also recall.'

'After all, you humiliated our family, my lord,' said Atsue.

'That's the difference between us, young man. Your family can be humiliated. I, on the other hand, can suffer endless indignity, I can even be put to death, and remain a Fujiwara.'

Atsue swallowed hard. 'Are they going to kill you?'

'Don't look so shocked, young Lord Atsue. You are samurai. Samurai are expected to revel in the sight of blood. Your generation of Takashi has not had the opportunity to see much blood spilled before now. Instead you powder your faces and blacken your teeth, you paint, you write poetry in beautiful characters, you dance and you play musical instruments. The power of the Takashi is not based on these attainments, however, but on military prowess. You younger ones are somewhat lacking in experience of bloodshed. Don't worry, though.' His eyes hardened. 'You're going to see a great deal of blood spilled before this war is over. Oceans of it. I only regret that when it is done, the world I knew and loved will be even more distant than it is now.' He began to speak in Chinese.

> But when I look back and speak of things that were,
> With glowering brows I find I loathe my life.
> The streams and hills now shelter thieves and bandits;
> The fields are now abandoned to brambles and thorns.

He paused, looking sadly at Phoenix Hall. Atsue couldn't resist providing the final two lines of Liu Yin's poem:

> Our heritage is a burden of moral obligations,
> But we lack a ruler who grieves at committing murder.

Motofusa smiled with pleasure. 'Thank you. Your literary learning is extensive. I did not wish to finish the poem myself because you might think it an offensive reference to your grandfather.'

Atsue stiffened. 'I know what my grandfather's enemies say about him. I don't consider him a ruler who approves of murder. My grandfather loves religion, nobility and learning. He hates the necessity of killing. He fights to preserve peace.'

Motofusa's smile seemed to say that Atsue couldn't actually believe that. 'You must know something of the history of the realm, young man. For hundreds of years, from the founding of Heian Kyo until the disturbances of the last twenty-five years, there was peace in the realm. You samurai are not protectors of peace. You yourselves have destroyed it.'

Atsue felt a certain pleasure, knowing he could trap the former Regent. 'Excuse me, sir but wasn't it rival members of your family, the Fujiwara, who first enlisted bands of samurai to settle differences between them by fighting?'

Motofusa bowed his head. 'Humiliation is endless.'

Atsue felt sorry for him. He had no business winning arguments with a man of Motofusa's age and dignity, especially when he had only a short time to live.

'Forgive me for disagreeing with you, my lord. Is there anything I can do for your comfort or peace of mind?'

Motofusa sighed. 'Only I can pacify my mind, I'm afraid. But these ropes around my arms and hands are a dreadful nuisance.

I'm perspiring, and I can't even wipe my brow. On the honour of my ancestors, if you remove these ropes I won't try to escape. Not that a man of my age could get away from thousands of samurai.'

'Allow me to ask permission to free your arms, my lord.'

Atsue strode across the dusty open space to the entrace of Phoenix Hall, where the Takashi leaders sat. They had all changed out of armour and into handsome red, green and blue robes. They were drinking sake and one of them was playing a lute.

Atsue's Uncle Notaro, second son of Sogamori, sat in the centre of the group. He had inherited Sogamori's tendency to stoutness, but without the muscular solidity that lay underneath it. Even here in the field his round face was carefully powdered and painted and his robes as thoughtfully chosen as if he were about to appear at Court.

'We were wondering if you'd ever catch up to us, Nephew. Wasn't last night your first-night visit with the Princess Kazuko?' Notaro's younger brother, the handsome Tadanori, laughed. Atsue felt his face grow hot.

'Honoured Uncle, I just want to ask a favour for the Regent Motofusa. The ropes are hurting him. May I untie him? He has sworn not to attempt escape.'

'Why was I keeping him alive? I forget,' Notaro said. 'All the other prisoners were sent into the Void this morning. Well, no matter. If he's uncomfortable, let's kill him at once and end his suffering.'

One of Kiyosi's older sons, a half-brother of Atsue, spoke up. 'Honoured Uncle, perhaps he should be spared because he is a Fujiwara and a noncombatant?'

'That may have been in my mind earlier,' said Notaro, 'but we've executed Fujiwara before this. As for his being a noncombatant, the Fujiwara never soil their hands with blood. Oh, no. They get others to do their killing for them. He helped start this rebellion. He deserves to die. Let him feel the edge of the sword. Immediately.' With a wave of his hand Notaro sent two officers to see to Motofusa's execution.

Atsue pressed on. 'May I untie him first, honoured Uncle? Whatever he has done, it is a shame for him to die trussed like a common criminal.'

61

Notaro smiled indulgently. 'Go with those officers and unbind the prisoner, Atsue-san.'

The ropes on Motofusa's arms were so tightly tied that Atsue quickly gave up on the knots. He drew Kogarasu, hearing the officers with him draw breaths of admiration at the sight of the famous sword. Atsue had been handling swords since he was four years of age, and Motofusa's bonds fell away with a flicker of the two-edged blade.

'Thank you, young Lord Atsue,' said Motofusa with a black-toothed smile. 'That is the closest a sword stroke has ever come to me – yet.'

One of the officers bowed. 'I must ask you to prepare for death, my lord.'

Rubbing his arms and wrists, Motofusa frowned slightly. 'Is it to be at once? There are favours I would like to ask, if the Takashi lords will be good enough to allow me.'

'We were ordered to help you into the Void immediately, my lord.'

'May I have writing materials? I would like to write a poem before I die.'

'I'm afraid that won't be possible, my lord.'

Atsue's face grew hot with sudden anger. 'This is barbarous. This is the former Regent, a man who was spokesman for the sacred person of the Emperor. We are taking his life. Let us give him the chance to make something that will live after him. Let paper and ink be brought.'

Reddening, the officer snapped his fingers to a servant and sent for writing materials. They brought brush, ink, green-tinted paper and a writing table. By now word had got round the camp that Motofusa was to be executed and was writing a final poem. The samurai formed a ring at a respectful distance from the old nobleman, who knelt before the small table. Motofusa thought a moment, then sent his brush flying down the page. Finished, he contemplated his poem for a moment, then without rising held it out to Atsue.

Atsue's eyes blurred as he read.

> Like a fossil tree from which we gather no flowers
> Sad has been my life, fated no fruit to produce.

'Beautiful,' said Atsue, shaking his head.

Motofusa waved away the writing table. Now he knelt in the dust in the centre of the circle of warriors. Even the Takashi commanders, led by Notaro and Tadanori in their flowing robes, left their pavilion to witness Motofusa's death.

'At my age it is difficult for me to kneel and stand and kneel again, so if there is no objection I will remain kneeling – for the rest of my life.' Motofusa smiled. 'It is the custom, I know, among samurai for a man who performs self-immolation to be helped by a close friend. I wish, too, that I might die by a friend's hand. I have no such friends in this camp, but my last moments have been made more pleasant by the kindness and courtesy of the young Takashi no Atsue. If he is willing and if his commanders permit, I desire him to do me the final service.'

Atsue's body went cold. He had never killed a man. A picture suddenly appeared in his mind: his mother standing over a dead samurai, a dagger in her hand, her robe spattered with blood. He remembered the terror he had felt, as if his mother had turned into a murderous devil. He had forgotten that terror completely. Now it flooded back inside him, full force.

Notaro smiled and nodded. 'My nephew will be honoured to take so distinguished a head.'

Motofusa's dark eyes looked into Atsue's. 'It will further your education in bloodshed, young Lord Atsue.'

All eyes were on Atsue. If he refused now, he would bear the shame the rest of his life. After all, he had asked Sogamori to send him to this war so he could kill the enemies of the Takashi. He had expected to do his killing in the heat of combat, though, not to bring his sword down on the neck of a helpless man with whom he had just had a friendly conversation. He must do it, or he would disgrace not only himself but the name of his father.

He bowed his head and in as strong a voice as he could muster said, 'I will be honoured, Lord Motofusa.'

What if my hand trembles? Atsue thought. What if I miss? What if I have not the strength to do it in one stroke, and he suffers?

He remembered what his mother always said in time of trouble and for the first time in many years whispered, 'Homage to Amida Buddha.'

He must forget that he was killing a man. He must imagine

63

that he was back at the Rokuhara, taking a practice swing at a bundle of straw suspended from the ceiling. He knew how to aim the blow, and just how much force to use. He could do it perfectly, as long as he resolutely put out of his mind the thought that he was killing a man.

He tried to forget, too, that hundreds and hundreds of samurai, many of whom doubtless had followed his father, were watching him.

He drew his sword. 'This is Kogarasu, Lord Motofusa. It was given to my ancestor, Emperor Kammu, by a priestess at the Grand Isle shrine and has been in our family ever since.' He held it out for Motofusa to see.

'You handled it dexterously when cutting my ropes,' Mofotusa said. 'I am sure both the sword and you will serve me well. Please see that a copy of my poem is sent to my son at the capital. You may keep the original yourself.'

'Thank you. I do not deserve such an honour,' Atsue whispered. 'May you be reborn in the Pure Land, Lord Motofusa.'

'I'm hardly worthy of that. I shall have to suffer through quite a few more lives before I reach the Pure Land, I'm afraid.' Motofusa bowed his head, exposing his neck.

Atsue took a deep breath, planted his feet firmly and wide apart, clenched his fists around the hilt and drew the sword back over his right shoulder. He had practised this stroke ten thousand times. He did not need to think. He fixed his eyes on a spot in the centre of the slender, white neck. He said in a clear, strong voice, 'Homage to Amida Buddha.' He brought the sword down with all his might and severed head from body.

His ordeal was over. The life of Fujiwara no Motofusa was over.

He stood breathing heavily, still holding the sword in both hands, staring at the gilded roof of the Phoenix Hall. The cheering of the samurai around him came faintly to his ears. He was vaguely aware of the corpse at his feet being dragged away.

Notaro was standing beside him. 'Well done. You're a Takashi and a worthy son of your father.'

'Thank you, honoured Uncle.'

Atsue's orderly came up to him. 'Let me polish Kogarasu, sir. You know how quickly blood can pit the steel.'

Atsue handed him the sword without a word.

Atsue went through the travel box strapped to his baggage horse until he found his flute, Little Branch. He trudged up a pathway of flat stones on a slope shaded by towering cryptomeria. At last he came to a spot where he could overlook the rushing Uji, Phoenix Hall, the other nearby temples and the samurai camp.

All that afternoon, while his uncles and half-brothers caroused at the entrance to the Phoenix Hall and the other samurai repaired their equipment, Atsue sat on the hillside playing every song he knew.

Many men in the camp below stopped what they were doing to listen to him. His playing was beautiful to hear.

CHAPTER EIGHT

From the pillow book of Shima Taniko:
On receiving word of Prince Mochihito's uprising, Hideyori at once led a glittering procession of Muratomo and Shima samurai to a shrine to Hachiman, the god of war and patron of generations of Muratomo. Hideyori had the shrine built several years ago, at what my father feels was a ridiculous expenditure. But Hideyori believes in the power of the Kami and of prayer, whereas my father only believes in the power of wealth.

Returning from the Hachiman shrine, Hideyori assembled all the nearby warlords and called on them to march south with him. He told them that Hachiman had promised him victory. I was reminded of Kublai's telling me that the Great Khans of the Mongols always commune with the spirits before sending their armies on campaign. Hideyori told the samurai that their numbers would grow to a hundred thousand before they reached Heian Kyo. He reminded them that they are warriors of the eastern provinces, and eastern warriors are said to be the fiercest in all the islands.

I listened to all this from a window in the tower. Hideyori's speech was not impressive. He lacks fire. He is a man who has lived in fear more than half his life, and it shows, at least to me. Yet, he is very ambitious and very intelligent. He is determined to destroy the Takashi and restore the glory of the Muratomo, no matter what the cost.

After his speech to the samurai, Hideyori led them out of Kamakura to attack Takashi Kanetake, the most powerful Takashi lord in this area.

—Eighth Month, seventeenth day
YEAR OF THE OX

'I can't understand a lady of your station conversing with a carpenter,' said Chogao. 'Especially not that carpenter. Those enormous white teeth make him look like a shark. And those eyes. You can't tell where he's looking.'

'Moko is a very old friend, Aunt.'

'One does not have carpenters for friends.'

Taniko received Moko in her chambers behind a screen of state painted with peonies. In the dimly lit room the little man looked downcast. He stared at the floor.

'This is ridiculous,' said Taniko. 'I'm not going to talk to you through a screen.' She started to get up.

Moko raised a warning hand. 'No, my lady, stay where you are. Everything we do and say can be seen and overheard. If you talk to me without a screen it will only cause a scandal and make it more diffcult for me to see you in the future.'

'All right, Moko.' Taniko settled down on her cushions again. 'Have you found a home in Kamakura?'

'I have bought myself a fine piece of land on a hill overlooking the beach, my lady. I am building a house on it. I've sent to Hakata for my son and his mother, whom I plan to marry. I may even at last acquire the five children – or was it six? – I told you of when we met so many years ago. I have also been accepted into the joiners' guild of Kamakura. That wasn't easy. They're a tightly knit lot. I couldn't do any work here without being accepted into the guild. I promised to help pay for a new guild-hall for them, and I showed them a new system of construction proportions which I learned in China. In the long run I hope to become a shipbuilder.'

A silence fell between them. Suddenly Moko said, 'I'm sorry you and the shiké couldn't stay together.'

Taniko sighed. 'Jebu has a war to go to. I must fight a battle inside myself.'

'I was there,' said Moko softly. 'I saw him kill Kiyosi.'

'Jebu told me that.'

'I was the first person in all the world to weep for Kiyosi's death, my lady. Lord Kiyosi was a great and good man. But it is madness to let his death years ago inflict so much suffering on the living today.'

'I agree, Moko. Madness seizes us, though. It does not go away when we tell it to. I can only hope that this madness will leave me in time. I think that it will.'

Taniko felt a tapping on her shoulder. She woke instantly. It was one of her maids. The maid beckoned her. Taniko stood up, pulling her kimono closer around her. A driving summer rainstorm was hammering on the roof of the women's building. It must be past the middle of the night, Taniko thought. She followed the maid to a partly opened screen overlooking the Shima mansion's courtyard.

A small band of horsemen was just coming through the main gateway. Their heads were bent against the rain, their faces hidden under hooded cloaks and sedge hats. Something more than the rain had beaten these men down. Their movements were heavy, weary, hopeless. As they dismounted lightning flashed and Taniko recognized Hideyori.

'Does Lord Hideyori have a wife or woman to attend him?' Taniko asked the maid.

The maid shook her head. 'His one wife died in childbirth two years ago.'

'Go to him. Tell him Lady Shima Taniko offers to serve him and see to his comfort, if he wishes it.'

The maid looked shocked, but said nothing and hurried away. I'm not going to lie with him, you idiot, Taniko thought. But after what he's been through, a man needs dry clothes, food, warm sake and someone pleasant to talk to. Surely the head of the Muratomo clan deserves that much.

Hideyori was shivering. He drained four cups of sake in quick succession, each time holding the empty cup out to her without a word. He stared at the wooden floor, his face impenetrable.

67

This was the first time she had been in Hideyori's chambers. The room was utterly bare except for a writing table, a plain wooden pillow and a rolled-up futon. In a tokonoma alcove stood a small blackwood statue of the war god, Hachiman, grim of face, on horseback, armed with bow and arrows. Hachiman hasn't been much help to Hideyori so far, Taniko thought.

At last he looked up at her. 'I do not deserve to live,' he said in a voice faint with fatigue.

He's trying to find out what I think of him, Taniko thought. 'My lord, you have an obligation to live. The whole future of the Muratomo depends on you.'

He shook his head. 'I watched my father lead our clan to disaster. I vowed I would never make the same mistakes. Nineteen years later I have my first opportunity to lead a Muratomo army into battle, my first chance to strike back at the Takashi. Another disaster.' He waved his hand vaguely southwards. 'I had five thousand men under my command. I lost four thousand.'

Taniko wanted to console him, but she could find nothing to say that was both kind and honest. 'I am sure the eastern warriors displayed the courage for which they are famous,' she said at last.

'Courage.' He laughed bitterly. 'They ran away in the night. I ran with them. But women aren't usually interested in talk of war.'

'I do not like war, my lord. Still, I consider it too important to ignore.'

'I have always thought you an unusual woman. I marched out of Kamakura, then, as you saw, at the beginning of this month, with high hopes. Many landowners and their men joined us as we went. By the time we were ready to besiege Takashi Kanetake in his stronghold, we were three thousand. We took Kanetake's castle and put him and all his people to the sword.'

Taniko felt a hollowness in her stomach just as she had when Kublai talked to her about the Mongol massacres. 'You took no prisoners, I suppose.'

'Samurai never take prisoners. My aim, when this war is over, is that there be not one Takashi left alive. At least, that was my aim, until Ishibashiyama.'

'What happened there?'

'After our victory over the Takashi governor we felt invincible. More samurai flocked to us. We were five thousand. Then I received word that Mochihito, Motofusa and their followers had been wiped out by the Takashi. Now there was no reason to march south, I thought. Unless Yukio was continuing to push southwards. He and I might take the capital together. Otherwise it would be better to stay here, to consolidate our hold on the north-eastern provinces and the Kanto plains. Let them stretch their lines coming after us.

'Then new messages arrived. The Takashi were on their way north, coming up the Takaido. My officers were all of one mind. We must go to meet them. We must not allow the Takashi to invade our home provinces, murdering and pillaging. I would have preferred to retreat, drawing the enemy into our territory until we could ambush them somewhere. But my brave eastern warriors wouldn't hear of that. They were all for attacking at once. I couldn't put up much opposition. After all, I've never proven myself in war, and if samurai get the notion that their leader is a coward, they'll never fight for him again. So I let myself be led by my followers.

'We marched south through the Hakone mountains. We crossed the neck of the Izu Peninsula. I stopped to pray for victory at the Mishima Hachiman shrine. At last our scouts brought us word that the Takashi were at Shimizu. They estimated that there were thirty thousand of them. We were outnumbered six to one. Now I insisted that to attack was madness. There were those among the officers who were still convinced we could win. The Takashi aren't fighters, they said, but effeminate courtiers. Five thousand real samurai could easily beat ten or even twenty times that number of decadent fops.

'Finally, one officer who knew the countryside nearby came up with a proposal that satisfied everyone. Near the sea coast, north of Mount Fuji, there is a valley called Ishibashiyama that cuts through the Hakone mountains. It is so narrow that no more than a hundred men can stand abreast at its widest point. At this pass we could make our stand. The Takashi could not go around us, because then we could strike at their rear. They would try to come through the pass, but in that narrow area their numbers would be useless to them. They could come at us only a hundred men at a time. We could inflict such casualties on them that they might eventually give up and retreat. News of a setback to the Takashi like that would bring many more samurai to our side.

'It took nearly two days for us to take up our positions at Ishibashiyama. By then it was the twenty-third day of the month. A Takashi advance guard had pursued us. Before entering the pass we turned and slaughtered them. This gave us even more confidence.'

Atsue could have been riding with that advance guard whose slaughter Hideyori so casually described, thought Taniko. I must not think about that.

'Would the Takashi follow us or had we guessed wrong? Would they try to bypass us instead? It wasn't till almost nightfall that we heard taiko drums and flutes playing martial music and saw rank after rank of mounted samurai climbing over the foothills.

'Our two armies camped a short distance apart for the night. I thought it might be a good idea to retreat under cover of darkness, but my officers refused to listen.

'Then, in the middle of the night, there was a thunderous noise from behind us, the north end of the pass. Men jumped up in the darkness. Someone shouted, 'It is the army of the Takashi coming to attack us! There are hundreds of thousands of them.' They thought the Takashi had stolen around the mountains in the darkness and were attacking us from the rear. Our samurai, half-armed and half-dressed, ran forward, right into the Takashi camp. The Takashi slaughtered hundreds of them.

'By this time some of us realized that the noise that set off the panic was the whirring of the wings of a flock of water-fowl that had taken off in the middle of the night from a lake at the north end of the valley. We started to retreat up the pass, but the narrowness of the valley slowed us down. The supposedly effeminate Takashi fell upon us like a bear chewing up a deer. Less than half our men got out of the valley alive.

'I fled into the forest beyond the pass. It was every man for himself by now. I was alone. I lay with my face in the mud while enemy troops searched the bushes a few feet away.' He looked at Taniko. He could not say that he had been nearly mad with terror, but she could see it in his eyes.

'For five days the Takashi scoured those mountains and forests, killing every Muratomo samurai they found. Most of all, though, they were looking for me. Throwing off my armour, keeping only my sword, I fled them and hid from them.' His face brightened. 'The worst moment of those five days was also the best. I know the kami are protecting me. I hid in a hollow tree. I could hear a band of the Takashi crashing through the underbrush. Then they were all around me. One of them approached the tree. I recognized him. He was a samurai who had served in the palace guard under my father. He looked into the hollow where I was hiding and right into my eyes. I clenched my fist around my sword. I was determined that I would kill him before he killed me, even though I could never escape his comrades. Then he smiled at me. He stepped back from the tree and struck it twice with the flat of his sword. Three doves that had been perched in the upper branches took flight. 'No one over here,' he called and walked away. Do you see? The gods must be watching over me.'

Taniko remembered how, long ago, Kiyosi had seen Moko hiding in a tree and spared his life. On that same day Kiyosi had beheaded the father of this man sitting before her.

She said, 'Even in time of fiercest strife some men feel kindly impulses.'

'Kindly impulses?' Hideyori looked at her, surprised. 'No, it was not the warrior who saved me. It was Hachiman. The dove is the messenger of Hachiman, and there were three doves in that tree. Hachiman clouded that man's mind so he would not see me. It was Hachiman who smiled at me through the man's face.' Hideyori walked over to the alcove. He knelt and prostrated himself before the statue.

'Are the Takashi coming here?' Taniko asked when he had seated himself with her again and drank some more sake.

'No. After five days they regrouped and withdrew down the Tokaido. Yukio must be threatening the capital.' Hideyori glowered at the Hachiman statue. 'The thought of that upstart half-brother of mine in the capital before me makes me want to cut my belly open.'

He's never been able to trust anyone, Taniko thought. He's spent most of his life knowing that anyone around him might be willing to kill him and take his head to Sogamori. 'Your brother

Yukio has never spoken of you except in terms of the deepest respect, my lord,' said Taniko.

'How well do you know him?'

'I met him at the beginning of this year,' Taniko admitted. 'I knew his mother at Court long ago.'

'I think I know Yukio better than you do, then,' Hideyori said with a hard smile. 'I watched him grow up. He was a snivelling, ugly little snake whose mother turned my father's head. She enticed him to forget his true family and give all his attention to her and her child. When he grew up he sneaked away from the Rokuhara and drifted about the country, living like a bandit. He never cared how his crimes endangered my life. Twice Sogamori ordered me executed because of things Yukio did. Only my ability to build alliances saved me. Can you wonder why I wanted to be in the capital before him? I wanted it so much, I made the same mistake our family has made for generations, the mistake that has led us into defeat after defeat.

'We are impetuous. We act rashly, prematurely. That's what got my grandfather and my father killed. It caused the destruction of the Muratomo who followed Prince Mochihito. It nearly got me killed at Ishibashiyama, because I was in such a rush to get to the capital I didn't wait until I had gathered a large army here at Kamakura before setting out to attack the Takashi. For that matter, I should not have gone into battle at all. A leader can't plan intelligently in the heat of battle. You don't see Sogamori riding at the head of his troops. He sends his sons and his generals to do his fighting for him. He sits like a spider at the centre of his web, taking advantage of his victims' mistakes, growing fat on their bodies. Ishibashiyama is the last time I'll ride to war at the head of troops. From now on I'll stay here, making my plans, organizing my supporters, sending out my generals and troops, praying to Hachiman for victory. I believe I can fight this whole war from right here in Kamakura, better than I could if I were riding about the countryside like some ancient prince.'

'Perhaps you're right,' said Taniko. 'Especially since you have fine generals like Yukio to take the field for you.'

Hideyori eyed her coldly. 'You keep trying to tell me that Yukio is a help, rather than a danger to me. If you weren't so open about it, I'd suspect you of being a spy for him.'

72

Taniko smiled and shook her head. 'I'm not a spy for anyone.'

'Of course not. You are staying here, are you not, with your family? You and I will be together throughout this war, then, Lady Taniko.' He smiled at her. There was no warmth in the smile, but there was desire. Taniko suddenly felt uneasy. She had put herself in a compromising position, coming here to his chambers, because she hadn't expected him to be interested in her.

'I have never forgotten that day at Daidoji,' he said softly. 'To save your husband's life, you emerged from behind your screen of state, your pale face modestly turned aside, your ivory fan held up before you. I thought you the most beautiful woman I had ever seen. Now there is no screen, and you are still the most beautiful woman I know.'

'You're too kind, my lord.' She felt her heartbeat quicken. There was something frightening about this brooding man full of cold anger. He lived among memories. He hated Yukio, it seemed, because as a baby Yukio had supplanted him in his father's affection. He nurtured the recollection of that one glimpse he'd had of her nineteen years ago, and he saw her as she was then, not as she was now. She felt no desire to lie with him, certainly not after these past months with Jebu, but she had to be careful how she went about putting him off.

'Excuse me, my lord, but I know I can't be as beautiful as you say. I'm thirty-four years old now, practically middle-aged, and I look it. It would take a girl closer to fifteen, as I was then, to equal the picture of me you carry in your mind.'

Hideyori reached for her across the table. 'Some women do not age. Or they grow more desirable with age.'

Trying to move gracefully and wishing not to offend Hideyori by seeming alarmed, Taniko backed away from the table. 'I think I have done all I can for you tonight, my lord. You need rest. I'll bid you good night.'

She and Hideyori stood at the same moment. 'You have not done all you can for me,' he grated. 'I have never forgotten you. I have hungered for you for nineteen years. Even while you were giving yourself to Kiyosi, the son of my worst enemy, I longed for you. You came to me tonight of your own choice. You set up no screen between us. You said you wanted to comfort me.' He moved around the table and put his arm around

73

her waist. He pushed her towards the sleeping area of his room.

He was far stronger than she, and Taniko knew she would not be able to resist him if he tried to force himself upon her. He knew she had lain with men other than her husband; at least, he knew about Kiyosi. So she could not claim to be a chaste married woman. If she tried to fight him off, she would offend him, with possibly disastrous consequences. She did not want to go to bed with him, though. What a fool she had been to separate from Jebu.

She whispered, 'Homage to Amida Buddha.'

'What did you say?' said Hideyori in a low voice full of tension.

She remembered that this was a man who seemed convinced he could accomplish more for his cause by praying to Hachiman than by leading an army in the field. She thought quickly.

'I was calling upon the Buddha, my lord. I hope you will not force me to break my vow. It might bring bad karma to both of us.'

Hideyori's hand fell from her waist. 'What vow?'

'As you may have guessed, my marriage to Prince Sasaki no Horigawa was not a happy one. In my resentment of my lot and in the strength of my youthful passions I turned to Kiyosi when Prince Horigawa separated from me. When Kiyosi was killed, I felt with absolute certainty that my lying with him had displeased the gods and caused his death. I promised the Buddha then that I would never again go to bed with a man other than my husband.'

Hideyori stared at her. 'Thousands of women have lain with men who are not their husbands, and the men usually don't die.' He laughed. 'Unless the husband kills them. Why should your favours be so dangerous?'

Taniko cast her eyes down. 'You may joke if you like, my lord. I realize that Kiyosi was your enemy. But his death was one of the great sorrows of my life.' That is the simple truth, she thought, even if it is not the reason I don't want to lie with Hideyori. That reason is a living man, and his name is Jebu.

It was as she had hoped. She was beginning to accept Jebu as Kiyosi's killer. When she saw him again it would be as it had been between them in the best times.

Hideyori's eyes smouldered with frustrated yearning. 'At

74

least tell me that you would couple with me if this vow did not stand in the way. Do you find me desirable?'

'It has been so long since I went to bed with a man that I've almost forgotten what it is like,' Taniko said. Now that was not the truth. 'Even so, my lord, I do find you a very attractive man, and if I were to lie with any man in Kamakura it would be you.' That was true enough. She felt stirred by his desire. He was the sort of man who moved her, a man like Kiyosi or Kublai. He even reminded her of Jebu a bit. He had the same sort of haunted quality.

'Good. I want no one near you, then, but myself, while you are in Kamakura. Perhaps the day will come when we will find a way to release you from your vow.'

As she lay alone, her head resting on the worn wooden pillow that had been her companion throughout her life, Taniko could not sleep. Hideyori frightened her. She seemed to feel his desire surrounding her as solidly as the bars of a cage. She had stepped into that cage tonight, not knowing the danger she was in. She wondered whether it would be as easy to escape from it.

CHAPTER NINE

At the top of the hill called Tonamiyama, Atsue reined in his horse to admire the view. To the east rose row upon row of snow-streaked mountains, glowing gold in the setting sun. To the west was the sea that lay between the Sunrise Land and Korea. Somewhere beyond that sea was the strange country from which Muratomo no Yukio had brought the barbarians who made up most of the army.

Atsue felt a twinge of fear. No one knew what Yukio's barbarians were like, or even how many there were, but everyone had heard frightening stories about them. They were twice the height of a normal man. They lived on raw meat and smelled like tigers. Their skin was black. The Takashi leaders like Uncle Notaro had ridiculed the notion that ignorant savages could pose any threat to forty thousand superbly trained, well-armed samurai. The stories were nonsense, they said, but they did show that the barbarians were subhuman.

Not far away, Takashi no Notaro, commander of the army, astride a black horse and wearing the red brocade robe of a general under his armour, was conferring with a semi-circle of mounted officers. They were gesturing to a distant ridge where a line of white Muratomo banners rippled in the purpling sky. Between Tonamiyama hill and that distant peak was a pass called Kurikara. The valley and the mountains around it were thickly covered with pine trees. Behind Atsue, spread over the hills to the south, forty thousand samurai were labouring up the slopes. The pines made it hard to see the men. Once in a while Atsue caught a glimpse of a man or a group of men struggling through a clearing.

Isoroku, a young samurai from Hyogo, whom Atsue had befriended because they were the same age, rode up beside him. 'Looks like more of them than there were at Ishibashiyama,' Isoroku said, pointing to the banners.

'Well, we can't go into the pass while they occupy that hill,' said Atsue.

Little information had come to the Takashi from the country through which Yukio's army had passed. They knew it was a large army and that it threatened the capital. So, after their autumn victory at Ishibashiyama they crossed the narrow neck of Honshu to Heian Kyo, where they spent the winter and collected reinforcements. Apparently Yukio had gone into winter quarters as well. Then, in the Fifth Month of the Year of the Tiger, the huge Takashi army moved away from the capital and started marching northwards to find Yukio and destroy him.

They had paused for a day to admire Lake Biwa, the largest lake in the Sacred Islands. The entire army had waited while Notaro took a boat to a pine-covered island called Chikubushima, where he sang and played the lute at the shrine of the kami of the island. He even composed a poem in her honour. Later a rumour went around the army that the goddess had appeared to him in the shape of a Red Dragon and had promised him victory over the insurgents.

Yesterday they had started climbing the mountains that formed a rampart between the Home Provinces around the

76

capital and the wild country to the north. At midday Atsue had found himself on a peak from which he could look back and see Lake Biwa, a silvery sheet of water, and look ahead to the rolling sea on the long north-western coastline and rank upon jagged rank of mountains. He felt a pang of longing for Heian Kyo. Any day now Kazuko would be giving birth to their child, conceived after his return from the great victory at Ishibashiyama. As they descended the peak and Lake Biwa disappeared, he felt he was leaving home and safety behind and venturing into unknown and dangerous territory.

Atsue hated to admit it to himself, but he did not like war. The actual fighting was never what he expected. There might be hours of waiting or riding about. Then suddenly someone was at your throat, and just as suddenly it was over. Most of war seemed to consist of looting, raping and massacre. Atsue was particularly upset by the memory of the destruction of the temples around Nara. Even the women and children who lived in the temples had been burned to death or cut down with swords. The great Todaiji, five hundred years old, had been burned to the ground on Notaro's orders. A huge statue of the Buddha had been melted down to a heap of slag.

Atsue tried not to notice when a group of his men were abusing peasants or torturing captured enemy samurai to death. It was hard to ignore such things, though, when they shocked him so. Some incidents he had witnessed would burn in his mind forever. Only his flute playing took his mind off such horrors.

Now the order came to set up camp on the crest of Tonamiyama hill. 'Didn't we get enough rest the other day at Lake Biwa?' said Isoroku impatiently.

'Would you rather cross the valley and charge uphill at that enemy army?' Atsue asked. 'Look at all those Muratomo flags. There could be fifty or a hundred thousand of them over there. That's why we're stopping.'

Atsue's servant got his tent up, and Atsue lent the man to Isoroku to set up Isoroku's tent beside his.

As night fell, Atsue and Isoroku sat in a circle with the armed retainers who followed Atsue into battle. They enjoyed a dinner of coarse rice and broiled lake trout. Atsue's men were skilled at finding provisions, which was a blessing, since the army's food supply had run out shortly after they left the capital. They had been living on the land like locusts ever since, stripping bare every farm in their line of march. It was a shame, because the country through which they passed had always been loyal to the Takashi. Atsue wondered why these things couldn't be better organized. He liked to think that if his father, great Kiyosi, had been leading the army, enough food would have been provided to get at least as far as the unfriendly northern provinces. Now they were in the mountains, and farms were few and far between. The shortage of supplies was becoming a real hardship.

After they had eaten, Atsue took his flute out of his belt, where he now carried it all the time, and played the melody called 'Peach Blossoms'. Those nearby remained respectfully silent for a long time after he had finished.

'You play so well, I think you will bring us good fortune,' said Isoroku. 'The kami will notice us, and they will give us victory.'

'Then victory goes to the best musicians?' Atsue said with a smile.

'Are not the Takashi more cultured than the Muratomo?' Isoroku asked earnestly. 'And have we not always defeated them?'

'We've always outnumbered them,' said Atsue. 'In my father's day, we often outsmarted them as well. We do not know what is waiting for us beyond the ridge now.' He gestured to the hill where the Muratomo banners had flown, now invisible in the darkness.

'Would you like to die in battle, Atsue?' Isoroku asked.

Atsue his head. 'I would like to live. Of course, it would be better to die in battle than be taken prisoner and treated shamefully. But why else would anyone want to die?'

'I sometimes feel that I would rather die when I am young and handsome and strong, doing something brave, then grow old and ugly,' said Isoroku. 'One cuts a flower when it is most beautiful, not when it has withered. Your father died a hero's death, and all remember him that way. If he had lived he would be greatly respected, I'm sure, but he would not be worshipped almost as a kami by the Takashi.'

'I'm old enough to know that I'm very young, Isoroku-san. I

78

know very little of life. I want to know and do much more before I die. I don't care whether people think of me as a hero or not. As for my father, I would much prefer him to be alive and respected than dead and worshipped. I miss him terribly.'

The humming-bulb arrows, screaming like falcons, began to fall on the Takashi camp just after sunrise. They killed no one. Crouching, a bit nervous, Atsue looked across Kurikara pass to the hill bedecked with white banners. A row of about a hundred archers was standing there, bows aimed high so their whistling arrows would carry across the valley.

'How civilized of them to wake us up,' said Isoroku, laughing. 'They might have started with arrows that gave us no warning. This is a gesture worthy of the Takashi.'

'Not really like the Muratomo, is it?' Atsue said uneasily. The enemy was controlling the situation, he thought. First, by displaying their banners on the opposite hill, they had determined the place where the Takashi would stop for the night. Now they had chosen the time and manner of opening the battle. Where were those mysterious barbarian troops everyone talked about? The archers across the valley looked like ordinary samurai.

The Takashi were lining up, pulling their man-high bows, releasing their own whistling arrows. After a few moments they drew first blood. A Muratomo archer fell, to much cheering from Tonamiyama hill. Atsue and Isoroku joined the crowd gathered a short distance behind the bowmen. No one wanted to be too close to the archers – even a humming-bulb arrowhead could kill a man if it hit him in a vulnerable spot – but to stand very far away could look like cowardice.

Two Takashi archers were hit. There was a rumble of anger. Someone suggested switching over to willow-leaf arrows. Someone else said it was too soon for that. Two more men took the place of the fallen, who were only wounded and were dragged out of the line to be cared for by their friends. Atsue saw Notaro and several other officers standing a small distance away, watching. Notaro called out praise when another Muratomo archer fell.

I wonder what plans he has for the battle, Atsue thought. It was odd that they couldn't see any more of the Muratomo than those few archers. Maybe there weren't as many of them as the Takashi had thought. He squinted at the line of white banners. Clever of them to start a fight with arrows when the sun was in the east, blinding the Takashi.

Just when the incessant screaming of the humming-bulb arrows was becoming more tiresome than intimidating, the Muratomo switched to willow-leaf and armour-piercing arrows. The Takashi archers did the same, and more samurai joined in the contest.

Some of the bolder warriors mounted horses and charged partway down the eastern slope of Tonamiyama. Immediately the Muratomo made a dash down their hill to match them. Atsue glanced to the top of the Muratomo hill. Would they attack now? The white banners remained in place. Only about two hundred Muratomo archers faced twice that number of Takashi. Soon the two groups of archers had halved the distance between them, and men on both sides were falling in threes and sixes, instead of ones and twos. Now some of the Takashi fell back, and some Muratomo did likewise.

The archery battle continued most of the morning. Once in a while a Muratomo samurai would get off a particularly long, accurate shot and kill or wound a Takashi in the watching crowd. Most of the injuries were confined to the archers themselves.

Both Atsue and Isoroku were devotees of the sword and not particularly proud of their skill with bow and arrow. While many other samurai joined or dropped out of the archery combat as the spirit moved them, the two young men stayed out of it entirely.

Just when the sun was directly overhead, the Muratomo stopped firing. They began to withdraw up their hill. Three horsemen rode down towards the Takashi lines. One of them held aloft a white banner. They stopped in an open meadow at the bottom of the pass. Takashi samurai, some on foot, some on horseback, began to drift down the slope towards the Muratomo riders.

'I am Saito Kiji of Nakatsu,' the samurai carrying the white banner shouted. 'I have fought both in China and in the land of the Mongols, and I have won many victories.' Kiji went on to describe the martial careers of his father, grandfather and great-grandfather. He claimed descent from the Brave of Yamato, legendary son of an ancient Emperor, subduer of malignant kami and of barbarians. He called upon the Takashi to send a warrior of suitable pedigree out to meet him.

'Let's get closer,' Atsue called to Isoroku. 'I want to see this.'

A Takashi officer rode down the hillside and exchanged words with the Muratomo challenger. The two men rode a short distance apart, then charged each other with drawn swords. Atsue and Isoroku were part of the crowd cheering for the Takashi fighter. Atsue felt himself trembling with excitement.

It was difficult to strike a killing blow from horseback. The two samurai circled around each other, swords mostly missing or glancing off their armour. Then Kiji, the Muratomo samurai, stood up in the saddle on his short stirrups. With two hands he brought his sword down on the Takashi warrior's right shoulder. Stunned, the man fell from his horse with a crash.

He scrambled to his feet just as Kiji rode down upon him. Kiji brought his horse to a sudden stop, grabbed the Takashi's chin from behind, and pulled him against his saddle. With one quick downward swipe of his sword the Muratomo warrior cut the Takashi's head off.

The head was still strapped into its helmet. Holding it high by one of the helmet's decorative horns, Kiji rode in a circle around the meadow. Isoroku, Atsue and the other Takashi samurai groaned, while the Muratomo opposite them cheered.

Another Takashi rode out to challenge Kiji. More Takashi rode down the hillside shouting their own lineage to anyone on the Muratomo side who might be a worthy opponent. The scene in the valley was becoming quite confused, with more and more samurai riding about bellowing their ancestors' names and looking for someone to fight with. All the Muratomo wore something white, an armband, a streamer on the helmet, a robe. Each Takashi wore something red.

Excitement, fear and eagerness swept through Atsue. He had been too late at Uji bridge and in the rear ranks most of the time at Ishibashiyama. Now was the time for the youngest son of Kiyosi to ride forth and bring back his first Muratomo head. What terror the Muratomo would feel when he announced his father's name.

'Let's get our horses,' he called to Isoroku, scrambling up the hill. He looked back over his shoulder. Samurai were fighting all over the meadow.

Back in the camp, he was about to mount his warhorse, a grey with black spots, when he heard his name called. His Uncle Notaro, in full armour but bareheaded, was hurrying towards him.

'Where do you think you're going?'

'To issue a challenge, Uncle.' Notaro's manner gave Atsue a sinking feeling.

'Your grandfather made me swear to bring you through this campaign safely. I forbid you to go into battle now.'

Atsue was so frustrated he felt on the verge of tears. 'It will tarnish our family name if I hang back while these brave men fight.'

Notaro shook his head. 'Only the most experienced and skilled samurari get into these single-combat duels at the beginning of a battle. They're old veterans, who know all the tricks. Especially these men of Yukio, with all the devilish foreign ways they've picked up. Of course you may fight, Atsue-san. Eventually. Wait till the battle becomes more general. If I let you go now you wouldn't have a chance.'

Atsue walked back to Isoroku, his head hanging. 'Battles aren't the way I thought they would be at all.'

CHAPTER TEN

Atsue forgot his disappointment as he watched master swordsmen on both sides display their skills in duel after duel. It was no pleasure to see men killed outright or lose their heads after being badly wounded. He didn't care to notice the way blood spattered everywhere, gradually staining red the grass of the meadow. Still, he had seen enough blood in the past month to take it calmly. He could ignore the ugly parts of fighting and focus on the mastery of horsemanship and weapons.

It seemed as though more Takashi heads than Muratomo were falling. These Muratomo, Atsue recalled, had been fighting constantly in China for the last eight years. Perhaps one of the Muratomo samurai fighting now in the meadow before him was his father's killer. Whoever had actually fired the arrow, it was Muratomo no Yukio whom Atsue blamed for his father's death. One day, he had promised himself, he would ride out before a Muratomo army and call Yukio out for combat. He would take Yukio's head and bring it to his grandfather, and Sogamori would bless him for it.

The Muratomo seemed to be withdrawing, disengaging themselves from battle. Those who survived their single fights accepted no further challenges, but cantered over to the sidelines. Atsue wondered, what now? Are they about to attack us? He looked up at the white banners on the hilltop. No movement, and still no Muratomo to be seen.

A Muratomo samurai called out, 'If there are a hundred of you who are brave enough, a hundred of us will fight you in a general mêlée.'

Now I must join in, Atsue thought. He started up Tonamiyama again, followed by Isoroku. He hoped Notaro would not stop him this time.

Notaro was nowhere to be seen. Atsue put on his helmet and mounted his horse. Isoroku, on a piebald horse, was beside him. Atsue flicked his reins and the two young samurai rode down the hill together.

A Takashi officer who knew Atsue bowed him to a place in the line. The Muratomo were lined up on the other side of the meadow, too far away for their faces to be clearly visible.

There was a long silence. Atsue heard a bush warbler call in the pines. Then, from the far side of the meadow came a high-pitched scream.

'Muratomo-o!'

A samurai holding a white banner in his left hand and waving his sword in his right charged at them. Immediately behind him the whole line of Muratomo samurai pounded forward.

'Takashi!' cried the officer who had taken command on their side. Atsue drew Kogarasu from its gold-mounted scabbard and whipped Plum Tree into a gallop. He glanced to his right. Isoroku was beside him.

Atsue's heart leaped into his mouth. A dark-faced warrior with a thick moustache was charging at him. Without thinking, he held up Kogarasu to fend off the other man's blow and rode safely by him. Now he was facing the other end of the meadow, which was empty except for a few spectators on foot.

He turned his horse and saw a warrior wearing a white robe, his back to Atsue, duelling on horseback with a Takashi samurai. Should he attack the man from behind, or should he warn him before striking? He decided that it was a samurai's responsibility to guard himself against attack from the rear. He spurred the grey, aiming the point of Kogarasu at the back of the samurai's neck, underneath his helmet brim. The sword struck something hard and slid off. Atsue had thought there would be no armour there. The Muratomo whirled in the saddle, striking at Atsue with his sword. Atsue jerked back on the reins so hard that the horse stood on his hind legs.

'Back off, he's mine,' the Takashi samurai roared. Embarrassed, frightened and confused, Atsue rode a little distance away from the fighting and tried to survey the field. A samurai with a white silk cloth tied around his helmet rode at him. Atsue brought his sword up to a defensive position and stood his ground.

'I am Tezuka Shiro of the province of Toyama,' the samurai shouted. 'Who are you, sir? Declare your name and titles.'

'I am Takashi no Atsue, son of Takashi no Kiyosi, grandson of Takashi no Sogamori,' Atsue answered proudly.

'A noble opponent,' said Shiro. 'I won't disgrace your arms, either. Come on, then.'

Whispering a prayer to his father's spirit, Atsue rode forward and aimed a blow at Shiro's head. Shiro parried the slash and reached out with his free hand to pull Atsue to him. Flailing wildly, Atsue felt himself dragged from the back of his horse and pinned against the front of the Muratomo samurai's saddle. A steel and leather gauntlet smashed against his face. He felt his head being twisted around. He knew the sword blow was coming.

Then Shiro uttered a sound half-way between a grunt and a moan. He made the noise again and relaxed his grip on Atsue. Atsue fell from Shiro's horse, looking around wildly and saw the grey standing nearby. He ran for his horse and jumped into the saddle. Only then did he look back to see what had happened to Shiro.

Isoroku had just finished cutting Shiro's head off. He pulled it free from its helmet, held it up with a grin, then tied it to his saddle and remounted.

Sick with terror, Atsue rode over to him. 'I owe you my life.'

Isoroku shrugged. 'While he was busy with you I came up on his left side, pulled up his armour skirt and stabbed him twice. You and I make a good pair. Let's get ourselves another. This time I'll grapple with him while you slip up on him and stab him.'

I nearly died back there, but I didn't, and the man who was going to kill me is dead now, Atsue thought. The only way to get through this is to refuse to think. Just fight. Atsue gritted his teeth and clapped Isoroku on the shoulder. 'Let's go, then.'

One of Atsue's retainers rode up, 'Lord Takashi no Atsue, you are ordered to leave the field at once. Lord Takashi no Notaro requires your presence in our camp.'

'No.'

'Please, my lord,' said the retainer, seeing the black anger on Atsue's face. 'I'm only delivering the message.'

'You'd better go,' said Isoroku. 'Your uncle is commander of the army, after all.'

Notaro's fat face was almost as red as his general's robe. 'I told you to stay out of it.'

'Excuse me, honoured Uncle, but you told me to stay out of the single combats. This was a general mêlée.'

Notaro's eyes narrowed angrily, 'I saw what happened down there. If I have to report to my father that a Muratomo warrior took your head because I happened to be looking the other way at the wrong time, he might very well disinherit me. Now get out of my sight and don't go near the fighting unless there's an all-out battle. If you get yourself killed then, it won't be my fault.' He turned, unused to armour and clumsy, and stumped away.

Atsue spent the rest of the afternoon on the hillside watching the fighting in the valley, sunk in shame and not speaking to anyone. If only Uncle Notaro had allowed him to remain on the field, he might have redeemed himself by killing a Muratomo samurai or else have died and thereby ended his pain.

The battle in the valley remained curiously unchanged.

Though the Muratomo lost fewer men than the Takashi, they sent no new warriors down from their camp to replace those who fell. By nightfall a hundred Takashi were fighting with less than fifty Muratomo. If the Muratomo were trying to prove what formidable fighters they were, Atsue thought, they were succeeding.

It grew too dark to fight. Calling compliments to one another, the samurai withdrew up their respective hills. Servants crept out to recover the bodies of the fallen. One of those corpses could have been mine, Atsue thought. Now that it was dark he let the tears run down his cheeks. A servant came and asked him if he would have something to eat. Atsue ignored the man until he went away.

He had his flute at his belt, but he had no desire to play. He tried invoking the Buddha, but he doubted that the gentle Buddha would be interested in consoling a young man who was crushed because he had taken no enemy heads. He sat cross-legged with his hands dangling over his knees. He tried to tell himself that tomorrow he would do better. He realized that he had forgotten to take off his armour. Perhaps he would leave it on all night to punish himself for his total inadequacy in combat.

A moon the shape of a thumbnail crept above the hill where the Muratomo were camped. Atsue tried to see their white banners, but he couldn't. The forest around him was silent. Somewhere in the distance an ox bellowed.

Then there were shouts. They were coming from above and behind him. Hoofbeats crashed through the forest. Atsue sprang to his feet. There were torches flickering in the trees on the west side of the hill.

There were cries of, 'The Muratomo! Get your horses! Get your weapons!' Atsue ran up the hill to his campfire. He couldn't count the torches he saw blazing in the forest. Yukio might have as many as a hundred thousand horsemen, he remembered. They had let themselves be lulled by the gentlemanly battle the Muratomo had drawn them into. All the while the enemy was planning this.

'Run, run!' a servant cried, scurrying past Atsue. There were men on horseback, apparently Takashi, trotting around him now. He was going to be trampled if he didn't get to his own horse.

He saw Isoroku's face in the light of the campfire. A frightened servant was holding both their horses.

'Another chance to fight,' said Isoroku, as they threw themselves into their saddles.

'Where's your armour?' shouted Atsue.

'I took it off at sunset. No time to put it back on. I've got my sword.' He waved it. 'Come on, everybody's going down the hill.'

An officer galloped by, his face scarlet in the torchlight. 'Into the pass. Try to outrun them. We'll make a stand in the open country beyond the pass. Keep together.' He raced past them.

They dashed down the hill together, Atsue glancing from time to time at Isoroku to see if he was keeping up. The torchlit enemy arm seemed to be right behind them, thundering down the slope. Again he heard oxen bellowing.

He and Isoroku were in the pass now. The hills on either side of them blotted out the moon. Behind them, the pursuers had overtaken the rear of the Takashi army. They heard screams, the crash of armoured men falling, the neighing of horses. The enemy torches blazed, lighting up the trees, the struggling samurai, the tossing horns of –

Cattle.

'It's not samurai,' Isoroku called. 'It's a cattle stampede.' Now some of the Takashi were slowing down. Atsue could plainly see, at the base of Tonamiyama hill, the humped backs, the rolling eyes, the gleaming horns of the oxen.

'Let them through,' voices called. 'Just get out of the way and let them through.'

'They tied torches to their horns to madden them,' said Isoroku.

'A dishonourable trick,' Atsue replied.

Atsue and Isoroku pulled their horses to one side as a huge grey ox, groaning angrily, charged past. Sparks from the torches tied to each of its horns stung its humped back. Atsue patted the grey's neck as the frightened horse danced and threatened to rear.

There was some laughter, shaky with relief, as the samurai realized that their attackers were only a herd of cattle. The oxen continued to crowd the warriors, though, pushing them deeper into the Kurikara pass. The hundreds of torches still sizzling on the horns of the huge animals lit up the Takashi army so well that Atsue could recognize the faces of comrades half-way across the valley.

Something hissed past him through the air. A night bird? There was another whisper, and another. Thudding sounds. Someone screamed. Again there was the clang of a falling, armour-clad body.

'Arrows! They're shooting at us,' Isoroku cried.

Now, looking up, Atsue saw lanterns on the hills above and behind them. Winking balls of light, red, yellow, green, blue, white, almost like the fireflies in the distant trees, signalled to one another across the valley.

Someone near him cried out and fell. In a flash Atsue saw it all. The stampeding oxen had driven them from their secure hilltop position into the valley. The torches on the horns of the cattle made the warriors into perfect targets.

The whole valley now echoed with the shouts and screams of men and animals. There were no orders, just wild, confused cries. In a mass, with no more thought than the stampeding animals among them, the samurai urged their horses into the pass, desperately trying to escape the arrows that hummed down on them like a murderous swarm of bees.

'Forward! Hurry, hurry!' they screamed at those blocking the pass ahead of them.

But now there were cries from the front ranks.

'The valley is too narrow. Stop! We'll be crushed.'

Atsue had been expecting to see a wedge of starlit sky at the end of the pass. Instead there was solid blackness. The arrows poured down. Atsue felt himself struck many times, but the arrows glanced off his helmet and armour or embedded themselves harmlessly in its plates and padded under robe. He glanced over at Isoroku, racing his horse beside him. Isoroku lay along his horse's back and neck to present less of a target.

We left our whole camp behind, Atsue thought. They've got everything, our tents, our baggage, our armour, most of our weapons. How will we be able to fight tomorrow? That doesn't matter. How will we live through tonight? By now the packed mass of men and horses wasn't moving at all.

A man ahead of Atsue said, 'They say the valley is open at the other end, but it's only wide enough for one man at a time to go through. It will take all night for us to get out of here.'

From somewhere on the slopes above them came the pounding of drums. There were wild, high-pitched cries, like the screaming of gulls. Hoofbeats reverberated against the hills.

Something struck the western flank of the Takashi army with such force that a shock wave surged through the mass, crushing men and horses against one another.

Atsue suddenly found there was room for him to urge his horse forward. Terror had crowded those ahead even deeper into the narrow end of the valley. The screams from behind were deafening. Steel clanged. Something was biting into the Takashi army, like a shark devouring a frantic swimmer. His hands ice-cold with fear, Atsue pulled Kogarasu from the scabbard.

He caught a glimpse of big men with fur-trimmed helmets waving curved swords, lances, and axes. Their triumphant shrieks drowned out the cries of the dying. One of them struck at Atsue. Kogarasu fended off the blow.

A lance plunged into Isoroku's back, was jerked out again. He fell from his horse, his eyes fixed on Atsue, his mouth open, not making a sound.

The barbarian who had killed Isoroku glanced over his shoulder for a moment, and Atsue saw his face clearly in the light of a nearby torch. Dark brown skin, huge white teeth, mad ferocious eyes. It was a face from hell.

Screaming at himself to run, Atsue made himself jump down from his horse. 'Isoroku,' he called. He tried to find his friend in the darkness. There was no answer. Isoroku is dead, he told himself. Get back on your horse and ride out of here.

Ride where? There was nowhere to go. The torches were going out now. There were struggling men and animals all around him, but he could see nothing. He was stepping on flesh, whether animal of human he couldn't tell. There was nothing he could do for Isoroku. He couldn't even find him.

A horse bumped into him. 'Out of my way,' snarled a voice edged with fear.

'Help me, please,' Atsue called. 'I've lost my horse.'

'Takashi?'

'Yes, Takashi.' If he's Muratomo, I'm dead.

89

'Come on, climb up here.' The voice had a ring of experience and authority. Atsue took the man's hand and clambered up behind him on the horse.

'I'm a fool to do this. Two riders will slow this horse down too much. What's your name?'

'Takashi no Atsue. Why are you going this way?'

'Oho. The chancellor's grandson. I guess you are worth saving, after all. I'm Hino Juro of Ise. We're going south, back the way we came from.'

'But that's where the enemy is.' Atsue knew of Hino Juro, a veteran fighter who had distinguished himself in the battle at Uji bridge. Even though he protested, he felt safer.

'The enemy is in the pass, slaughtering our men. There's no escape that way. Our only hope is to head south.'

Sodden with despair and defeat, the Takashi samurai gathered the following morning by a bend in a stream far to the south of Kurikara pass. Notaro was among those still alive. His red brocaded robe stained with blood and dirt, he wandered dull-eyed among his surviving troops. He ignored Atsue's greeting.

'Lord Notaro, I've brought you your nephew safe and sound,' said Juro heartily. 'That ought to cheer you up a bit.'

Notaro shook his head. 'Yesterday I had forty thousand men. Today, eight thousand.'

'What happened last night, my lord?' said Juro. 'Does anybody understand it?'

Notaro grimaced, baring his blackened teeth. 'They tricked us, made us think they were going to fight like honest samurai. The bodies of our men are piled ten deep in Kurikara pass. Yukio and his barbarian monsters!'

'Where is Yukio's army now, honoured Uncle?' Atsue asked.

Notaro looked at him with dread. 'No one knows.' He shuffled off without another word.

The remnants of the Takashi, still numb with shock, began the ride back to Lake Biwa later that morning. They would have to cover the distance to the capital quickly. Even though there were fewer of them, they had already stripped bare the land through which they were passing, and they would get nothing to eat until they reached Heian Kyo.

As he rode along on a horse Juro had found running riderless, Atsue kept glancing over his shoulder. He expected to see

Yukio's army thundering down upon them at any moment. He had been at three big battles and had not won a single combat. I'm not much of a son for my father, he thought. Kiyosi must have killed hundreds by the time he was fifteen.

But then, none of the Takashi were worthy of those who had gone before them. They had let themselves be tricked and terrorized. With so few men left, how could they defend the capital and the Emperor?

What would his grandfather say? He hoped he wouldn't have to face Sogamori. As for Uncle Notaro, he would have to kill himself. How could he account for the loss of more than thirty thousand men?

Isoroku, forgive me, Atsue prayed. I failed you. Father, forgive me. I failed you, too.

They had all been so sure of themselves, so triumphant. This battle with Yukio was to be the last, the one that would secure the realm for the Takashi forever. It was now no longer a question of finishing off the last of the Muratomo. Now the question was: could anything be done to save the Takashi?

CHAPTER ELEVEN

A small, rectangular lamp illuminated Hideyori's statue of Hachiman. The war god's stern features flickered as if they were alive. Hideyori had placed before the statue a blue vase containing a cluster of handsome purple wisteria blossoms.

Bokuden and Ryuichi were both seated with Hideyori in his bare chamber when Taniko entered. The Muratomo chieftain sat like a stone, immobile, impenetrable. A scroll lay on the floor before him.

'You know my half-brother better than either your father or your uncle does. I want you to tell me what he will do next.'

Taniko bowed and knelt facing the three men. Her father looked frightened; Ryuichi, beneath his white powder, appeared bland and calm.

'That depends on what he has done lately, my lord,' said Taniko with a little smile.

91

'He has done what I could not do,' said Hideyori, almost choking on the words. 'What my father and grandfather died trying to do. He has broken the Takashi.' Hideyori described the battle of Tonamiyama to her.

She felt her body grow cold as she grasped the enormity of it. Forty thousand Takashi, the largest army ever mustered in the Sacred Islands, had gone forth from the capital. Now over thirty thousand lay dead in Kurikara pass, slaughtered by a single *tuman* of Mongols and whatever samurai Yukio had recruited. Next, she thought, there will be Mongols in the capital. Arghun, the red giant who had tried so many times to kill Jebu, would smash his way into the Imperial Palace, perhaps even capture the sacred person of the Emperor. To the Mongols no monarch was sacred, not even their own.

We should be celebrating the defeat of the Takashi, she thought. Instead, we're all frightened to death.

'He will take the capital,' said Hideyori. 'Then what? Will he proclaim himself chancellor? Will he set himself up in Sogamori's place?'

'I'm sure he won't act without orders from you, my lord,' said Taniko quickly.

'What does he need me for?' said Hideyori, a note of self-pity in his voice. 'How long will the Muratomo follow a chieftain who leads them to defeat, when they can turn to another who has won the most spectacular victory in the history of the Sunrise Land?'

It was not the Mongols that Hideyori feared, Taniko thought, but his brother. 'He does need you,' she said firmly. 'He needs you, because any legitimacy he has comes from you. He is not the son of Domei's primary wife. He is not the chieftain of the Muratomo clan. The majority of his troops are foreign. Without a mandate from you he would be nothing more than a criminal.'

Ryuichi said, 'See how much our little Taniko has learned about the way of statesmanship at the courts of China and Mongolia.'

'She has always pressed her opinions upon anyone who would listen,' Bokuden said sourly. 'Even on those who do not care to listen.'

'The words of this woman are worth the views of the entire Great Council of State,' said Hideyori flatly, not even bothering to look at Bokuden. Ryuichi stared at Hideyori with surprised approval. Bokuden quickly changed his contemptuous expression to an obsequious smile, as if Hideyori's words had enabled him to discover new virtues in his daughter.

Taniko could not help but be warmed and flattered. Hideyori was ambitious, distrustful and merciless, not at all like Jebu or Kiyosi, she reminded herself. Yet deep within him there was a vision she admired and a passion that stirred her. He needed someone to advise him. He sought such a person, without knowing it. No man could think entirely by himself. Hideyori was unable to trust any man, but he was willing to listen to her, a woman. Even though she came from Yukio he trusted her.

With Yukio's forces at his disposal, Hideyori was on the verge of being the most powerful man in the land.

A chill of excitement rippled through her. Be careful, she warned herself. Now that you feel so close to what you've always wanted, don't let yourself be swept away. She kept her eyes modestly lowered.

'These Mongols who follow Yukio,' Hideyori said. 'Why do they fight for him?'

Taniko shrugged. 'For the same reason Mongols always fight. For loot, for land, for power. Their leader, Arghun Baghadur, and his men are out of favour in their homeland and wish to fight for another master.'

Hideyori shook his head. 'From what you have told me, the Mongols are a very practical people. I suspect they are here for a more serious purpose than adventure and plunder. They are the advance guard of an invasion.'

As much as she wanted to reassure Hideyori, Taniko knew she could only earn his confidence with the truth as she saw it. 'That is possible, my lord. The Mongols do have an exaggerated notion of the wealth of our islands. The few times I talked with their Great Khan, I tried to convince him that China and the other nations west and south of it are far richer than we are. Naturally, he thought I was trying to mislead him to protect my people. Even so, I think that when his men report back to him that I told the truth, he may decide an invasion is more trouble than it's worth.'

'Is the Sunrise Land really so poor compared to China?' Bokuden asked, his eyes wide.

'Yes, Father. You were born in the wrong country.'

'If Yukio knows that the Mongols have come here to pave the way for an invasion, he is a traitor,' said Hideyori. 'If he does not realize their purpose, he is a fool. A very dangerous fool.'

'He is neither, my lord,' said Taniko. 'He does not conspire with the Mongols, and he is fully aware of the risk in bringing them to our shores. He did it because this was the only way he could have any hope of defeating the Takashi. Believe me, my lord, he fights, not for himself, but for you.'

Hideyori smiled faintly. 'I believe that you speak honestly. When I meet Yukio he will have a chance to prove his loyalty. If he agrees without objection to what I intend to order, he will pass at least one test.'

Bokuden frowned. 'What will you tell him to do, my lord?'

'I will command him to turn over the Mongol troops to me.'

Four lanterns burned around the rectangular stone tank in a shadowy room on the ground floor of one of the Rokuhara towers. In one corner two priests sat reading aloud from a huge book of the Buddhist sutras, each monk chanting a verse in turn. A pair of acolytes held the book up for them. A priest-physician beckoned Atsue forward. Atsue approached the tank and peered down into it. A stout figure wrapped in white cloths lay in the tank, panting like a beached whale. Water covered the body almost completely, except for the shining, shaven head, which was propped up on a large wooden pillow. The eyes were open, staring upwards, and Atsue automatically followed them to see the lantern light reflected from the rippling water in the tank to the ceiling.

'Hot. Hot,' Sogamori whispered hoarsely. 'Everything is going up in flames.'

Grieving and frightened, Atsue looked down at his grandfather. Since the loss of his father and his mother, Atsue had relied on Sogamori as the one indestructible person in his life. He was like that great tortoise on whose back the whole world rested. It was unbelievable that any disease could strike the old man down. Some said Sogamori's illness had been brought on by the Tonamiyama disaster. Others maintained that he was cursed because he had ordered the destruction of the

94

Buddhist and Zinja temples at Nara and the massacre of their inhabitants.

Atsue wanted to reach into the tank and shake Sogamori, demand that he come out of there and shoulder his burdens. Our army is destroyed, Grandfather, he said only to himself. The enemy is a day's ride from the capital. You can't leave us now. You must tell us what to do. He laid his hand gently on Sogamori's forehead. Instantly, he pulled it back, as if his palm had touched a hot brazier. Now he understood why Sogamori spoke of flames, why he was kept in a stone tank which was drained every hour and refilled with fresh, cold water from the well of Senshuin on Mount Hiei. The old man was consumed by fever.

At the touch of Atsue's hand, Sogamori rolled yellow-stained eyes towards him. 'I'm dying, Kiyosi-chan.'

Kiyosi. He thinks I'm my father, Atsue thought. Should I tell him who I am? 'No, Grandfather. You'll get better.'

Sogamori raised himself in the tank and put his hand on Atsue's wrist. Atsue had to break free. The heat from Sogamori's hand was unbearable.

'When I am dead, Kiyosi, do not chant sutras in my memory. Do not build temples or pagodas for the repose of my soul.' Sogamori bared his teeth, still strong and white. He had never dyed his teeth, as so many of the younger Takashi had. 'Only kill Muratomo no Yukio as quickly as you can, and lay his head before my tomb. That will be the best offering you can make for me in this world or in the next.' His eyes went out of focus and he fell back, gasping.

Atsue remained kneeling by the tank for another hour, but Sogamori did not speak again. From outside the room Atsue heard frantic cries, the thumping of boxes, the lowing of oxen and the clatter of horses' hooves. At last, giving up hope of really speaking with his grandfather, he stood up and left him.

A short time later, dressed in full armour and mounted on the dappled grey horse that the veteran samurai, Hino Juro, had found for him after Tonamiyama, Atsue was riding up Redbird Avenue, forcing his way against the crowds fleeing the capital. People kept looking to the north of the city, as if they expected to see the hills swarming with the dreaded Mongols. Once or twice Atsue was tempted to draw his sword to threaten the people blocking his way, but such a use would be beneath Kogarasu's dignity. At last he came to the main gateway of the Imperial Palace.

He ached to visit Princess Kazuko and the baby just once more, but he could not. He had spent all the time he could spare with his grandfather, and he had to join his assigned unit at the palace at once. Princess Kazuko had borne Atsue a son, Sametono, two months earlier, while the battle was raging at Tonamiyama. Following custom, the princess and the baby stayed at her parents' home, the Imperial Palace, where Atsue visited her whenever he could. His wife and child were somewhere in that complex now. They were not taking part in this mass flight. Neither was ready to travel. They would be safe enough here. Crude as the Muratomo might be, they would hardly harm an Imperial Princess and her baby. It broke Atsue's heart to leave without seeing his little family, but filial piety had demanded that he put his dying grandfather first.

He rode across the palace grounds through crowds of samurai and civilian officials as confused and frightened as the crowds in the streets. Arriving at the Pure and Fresh Hall, he joined the band of young men from the best families who had the proud task of escorting the Emperor out of Heian Kyo.

One of the young men had heard bad news. The Retired Emperor Go-Shirakawa and the Minister of the Left, Prince Sasaki no Horigawa, had both fled to Yukio the previous night.

'We're still the government, and they're still the outlaws,' said Atsue. 'We have the Emperor.'

An ox-drawn carriage rolled past, preceded and followed by Shinto priests mounted on white horses and surrounded by hundreds of Buddhist warrior monks on horseback and armed with naginatas. Lucky for the Takashi that the temples around the capital had remained loyal, thought Atsue, or we might have had to fight our way out. The carriage contained the Imperial regalia – the sacred mirror, the sword and the necklace. The Three Treasures had been given to the first Emperor by the sun goddess, and they had been the sacred symbols of Imperial authority ever since. This was the first time the Imperial regalia had left the palace in the five hundred years since the founding of Heian Kyo. Atsue and the other samurai climbed down from their horses and prostrated themselves as the cart passed.

Then the little Emperor, carried in a gilded chair, appeared on the wooden steps of the Pure and Fresh Hall. He wore the formal Imperial robes in apricot. His black cap of office was decorated with pearls, but under it he still had the shoulder-length hair of a child. Emperor Antoku, grandson of Go-Shirakawa and of Sogamori, the proudest jewel of the Takashi family, was six years old. His samurai guards all pressed their faces into the white gravel at the sight of him. When Atsue looked up again the Emperor had disappeared into the giant, gold-roofed Imperial palanquin. Atsue watched his aunt, the Imperial mother Kenreimon, a moon-faced lady in her thirties, enter the palanquin behind Antoku. The carriers raised the huge structure smoothly, and Atsue's heart lifted with pride and pleasure as he saw the golden phoenix on its roof gleaming against the blue sky. We have the Emperor, he repeated to himself. He and the other noble samurai mounted and surrounded the palanquin, and all moved off together.

After their procession left the Imperial Palace grounds, Atsue stood up on his stirrups to see down Redbird Avenue. The vast thoroughfare was an endless jumble of mounted samurai and carriages of the Takashi nobility. Dozens of Red Dragon banners fluttered as proudly as if they were going into battle instead of fleeing from it. The common people had been pushed into the side streets.

Although he could not see that far, Atsue guessed that the head of the caravan was already passing beneath the Rasho Mon. The procession stretched the entire length of Heian Kyo and even now it was not complete. More carriages and carts, more mounted warriors, more banners, would be joining the line of march.

It was late afternoon, the hour of the rooster, by the time the Imperial palanquin reached the Rasho Mon. Even with the Emperor's outriders forcing a path through the refugees, it was simply impossible for vehicles, horsemen and masses of people on foot to get out of the way quickly. The retreat was disorganized. Atsue had seen no high-ranking officers, had received no orders, for hours.

Where were they going? He only knew that they were headed south towards the sea, and from there to the western provinces. The western half of the Inland Sea had been Takashi territory since the founding of the clan. There they had won their first holdings and built their first ships. There Sogamori's grandfather had fought his battles with the pirates who then infested the Inland Sea, and thus had laid the foundations of Takashi power.

Atsue turned as he passed under the Rasho Mon for a last look at the city. Even at this distance he could see the three towers of the Rokuhara off to the east. A bright crimson flicker on the nearest tower caught his eye. At first he thought it might be the setting sun reflecting on some gilded ornament, but then he recognized fire. The Rokuhara was burning. His heart stopped for a moment, then grew heavy with sorrow. If only I hadn't looked back, he thought, as he watched the castle that had been his home for eight years enveloped in smoke and streamers of flame. Red banners on the Rokuhara to the very end. Now, over other parts of the city, pillars of smoke appeared, like the trunks of enormous trees.

'Are they burning the whole city?' he cried.

'No,' said a young man riding beside him. 'Just our palaces. Why leave them for those Muratomo dogs?'

Looking back again, Atsue saw a wall of fire and smoke rise directly to the north, at the opposite end of Redbird Avenue. A chill of horror shook him.

'Not the Imperial Palace?'

'Why not? Wasn't it ours, too?'

'But my family is there. Princess Kazuko and my son.'

The other young man's face registered sympathy and alarm. 'I'm sure they got everyone out before they set fire to it.' He patted Atsue's arm briefly and rode off, the tragedy being too much for him to respond to adequately.

There were many Takashi supporters and relatives in the Imperial Palace, Atsue thought. Surely they had evacuated the place. Still, to destroy the work of so many years in an hour was a vicious, spiteful act, and it shamed him that it was his family that had decreed it and carried it out. The Imperial Palace belonged to the Sacred Islands, to the gods, not to the Takashi family. And now there were fires in every neighbourhood. Thousands of smaller houses, as well as the mansions of the great, were going up in flames. The whole city might well be in ashes by nightfall if the fires spread. As the Imperial party passed through the gateway he heard a steady, heavy, monotonous tolling from somewhere in the distance. Looking back, he saw the pagoda of the Gion Temple in the centre of the city, almost hidden by smoke. Whether the monks were sounding the bell as a fire alarm or were ringing out a farewell to the Takashi he did not know, but in the sad sound of the bell he heard a lament for the passing of all things.

The Takashi flight followed the Shujaku Road towards the Inland Sea. They pressed on through the night without stopping, different shifts of bearers taking turns with the Imperial palanquin. At dawn, Notaro and his personal guards rode up to the Imperial party with a great fluttering of Red Dragon pennons. At Notaro's order the bearers set down the palanquin and all prostrated themselves while the yawning Little Emperor, his mother and a group of ladies-in-waiting stepped down from the palanquin and went for a walk in a nearby field. After they had once again retired behind the curtains, Notaro called together the hundred young samurai of the Imperial escort.

'Which of you is in command?' He had lost weight since Tonamiyama, and his eyes were sunk in hollows over bony cheeks. He looked nervously from one man to another, his gaze settling nowhere, like a fly trying to escape from a room.

After a pause one of the young men said diffidently, 'I don't think we have a commander, Lord Notaro.'

'How in the name of Beautiful Island Princess can you guard the Emperor properly without anyone being in charge? This should have been reported to me. Has no one any sense in this army? Must I discover everything myself?'

Notaro's glance fell on Atsue. 'You'll do. You're Kiyosi's son, after all, and you've had combat experience. You are in command of His Imperial Majesty's escort until further notice. Make these palanquin bearers run, if it kills them. We must get the Emperor to Hyogo and aboard a ship for the west.' Notaro beckoned his aide to bring his horse.

Atsue stepped closer to him to speak privately. 'Please, honoured Uncle, my wife, the Princess Kazuko, and my son Sametono were left behind in the Imperial Palace. Since the palace has been burned, I'm concerned about their safety.'

Notaro stared at him. 'Worrying about your wife? You

should be ashamed of yourself. I'm sure I have no idea where any of my wives or children are at this moment, and I'm concerned about more important matters. Are you a samurai or aren't you?'

'Forgive me, honoured Uncle,' Atsue whispered, his face burning. 'How is Grandfather?'

Notaro stared at the ground, then spoke in a barely audible voice. 'I do not want this known. The great Lord Sogamori is no longer with us.'

'No,' Atsue whispered. Even though he had known Sogamori was dying, Notaro's words were a shock. Why had everything been taken from him? The power of the Takashi was gone, Heian Kyo and the Rokuhara were gone. Kazuko and Sametono were in the hands of the enemy. His father was long dead, now his grandfather was gone. He wondered if his mother were still alive somewhere.

'Did he die of his fever?' he asked Notaro.

'I was not present.'

'When will we hold his funeral, Uncle?'

Notaro did not answer. After a moment, Atsue repeated his question.

'We do not have his body,' Notaro choked out.

'Do you mean that Grandfather's body is in the hands of the enemy?' Atsue was stunned, horrified. 'How could we let that happen, Uncle?'

Notaro shook his head and closed his eyes. Tears squeezed from under his eyelids.

'He was among the last to leave the capital. They had to find a special carriage big and strong enough to hold him and a tub of water. By the time he was prepared for travel there were only a thousand samurai left in the Rokuhara to escort him. Still, we thought that would be enough. I was at the head of the march, several hours' ride away. During the night Yukio's men attacked and cut off the end of the column just south of Takatsuki. I didn't find out that it had happened until hours later. It was too late to go back and try to rescue them.'

'Was Grandfather already dead when the Muratomo attacked?'

Notaro looked at Atsue. Never had Atsue seen such shame and anguish in a man's face.

'I don't know.'

Atsue wanted to scream. He felt a sudden, overpowering nausea. Could his grandfather have been captured alive by the enemy? Notaro should have sent the entire Takashi army back to attempt a rescue, even if rescue was impossible. To the last man, every Takashi, even the Emperor, should have died trying to save Sogamori. Hating Notaro, Atsue bit back the things he wanted to say. Notaro was his lord and leader, standing in place of his father and grandfather. To show disrespect to the chieftain of the clan now would only add a further blot to the hideously stained honour of the Takashi.

Restraining himself with a painful effort, Atsue said only, 'How sad that the greatest man of his age, after a life of many victories, should face a degrading death alone at the hands of his enemies.'

Notaro was openly weeping now. 'You don't understand, Atsue. You'll never understand. I'm the head of our family now. I have to make the plans and decisions. After Tonamiyama I wanted to take my life, but Father forbade it. There was no one else, he said, of the age and experience and seniority in the clan to take my place. I must live and lead, though I have proven that I am unfit for it.' With a jerk of his body, Notaro pulled himself away from Atsue, stumbled to his horse and rode away through the fields, the proud red banners of his escort belying the enormity of the humiliation the Takashi had suffered.

Atsue stood trying to bring himself under control before returning to the men he now commanded. But when he thought of the old man dying alone among enemies, the tears came hot to his eyes. When the Takashi were all safely in the western provinces, when Atsue could turn over responsibility for the Emperor to someone else, he would kill himself. Only that way could he protest the catastrophe, the utter degradation, that had befallen them. He would join Grandfather and Father in the next world. That was how he would mourn them.

CHAPTER TWELVE

The rice paddies south of Takatsuki were littered with the corpses of horses and men, most of the bodies sprouting clusters of arrows. Here and there lay the burnt wreck of a carriage. The Mongols had used fire arrows to light their targets in the previous night's attack. Riding along a narrow dirt road, Jebu noticed a movement in a nearby ditch. A man, pierced by so many arrows he looked like a sea urchin, was, amazingly, still alive. None of the arrows had gone deep enough or struck a vital spot. Groaning, he raised his head and reached for a sword that lay near his lacerated hand. *Tuman-bashi* Torluk also saw the man and signalled to a party of foragers who were collecting weapons and searching for any loot that might have been overlooked by the advancing troops. The Mongols fell upon the samurai, stripped away the armour that had saved him from death until now, and finished him with their short knives. Jebu turned away. A miserable death.

'This is the place,' said Torluk, pointing to a small temple half-way up the side of a terraced hill. A group of Mongols lounged at the entrance of the brightly painted Chinese-style building.

Riding abreast of Torluk, Jebu and Taitaro made an odd pair. Jebu was in full battle armour, only the headcloth he wore in preference to a helmet distinguishing him as a monk. Taitaro had on nothing but his grey Zinja robe and the white abbot's cord around his neck. Yukio had sent Jebu to ride with the Mongols as his personal representative. Jebu did not relish spending time in the company of Arghun and Torluk, but he was the only man qualified to speak to the Mongols for Yukio.

'Perhaps we can at least get a ransom out of this,' said Torluk, speaking in Mongol. 'I'll tell you, the men need some sort of reward after being told that no Mongols are permitted to enter Heian Kyo. It was we who gave Yukio the capital. Now we are forbidden to ride in his victory procession and to share in the looting of the city.'

'There will be no looting of the capital,' Jebu said. 'The capital was badly enough damaged by the Takashi as they left. Lord Yukio has traded your satisfaction for something more valuable, if you'll forgive me for saying so. His Retired Majesty, Go-Shirakawa, has given his sanction to the Muratomo. He has appointed Yukio to be Lord High Constable and Envoy of the Retired Emperor. Yukio is no longer a rebel. The task of winning support and recruiting samurai is now very much easier. In return, Yukio could do no less than agree to Go-Shirakawa's demand that no foreign troops enter Heian Kyo.'

They had arrived at the low wall around the temple grounds. As they dismounted and approached the doorway of the temple, three shaven-headed men in the yellow robes of Buddhist priests barred their way. Motioning Jebu and Torluk to wait, Taitaro stepped forward, smiling, and bowed to them.

'Is this your temple, holy ones?'

'No, sensei,' said the monk in the centre. 'This is the Takatsuki Temple of Kwannon. We found it deserted. We felt it would be the safest place to bring our great lord.' The monk motioned with his head towards the dark interior of the temple. 'We have attended him throughout his illness. His guards are all dead. We did not fight, because we carry no weapons, but if you intend to harm him you will have to kill us first.'

'Well spoken, Suzuki-shiké,' said Taitaro with a smile. 'But now that your charge is coming to the end of his journey of life, you may yield your responsibilities to us.'

Suzuki smiled back. 'Are you formally relieving me of my mission, Taitaro-sensei?'

Taitaro bowed. 'Yes.' The other two priests stared at Suzuki, then began to back away from him.

Taitaro chuckled. 'Forgive us, brothers, for having disguised a member of our Order as one of you. We felt it necessary, after the destruction of our temple at Nara, to keep a representative close to the chancellor.'

'You poisoned him,' one of the priests exclaimed.

'Not at all,' said Taitaro. 'Suzuki-shiké is an expert physician. His ministrations probably prolonged Lord Sogamori's life. I grant you, we had good cause to assassinate the chancellor, but we only wanted advance warning of any more attacks on our temples. Now, let us see him.'

Torluk waited in the doorway of the temple as Jebu and Taitaro entered the dark hall. Jebu recalled his intention of killing Sogamori at the first opportunity, to avenge the death of his mother, Nyosan. Now the man whose command had obliterated Zinja temples, whose word had been law throughout the Sunrise Land, lay panting and groaning at Jebu's feet on the polished cedar floor of an out-of-the-way, deserted temple, and Jebu felt no wish to speed his departure into eternity. Death was very close for the old man, in any case, and would now probably be a blessing. From a candlelit altar the serene face of Kwannon, goddess of mercy, looked down upon Sogamori. He could find no better place to end his days than beneath the eyes of Kwannon. He lay flat on his back, his arms at his sides, his great belly rising and falling under the wet cloths wrapped around him. Over and over he whimpered, 'Hot. Hot.' Taitaro knelt beside him, put his hand on the shaven head and drew it back quickly. Then he took a silk purse full of gold needles from inside his robe and began inserting the needles into Sogamori's bare shoulders and arms. One of the Buddhist priests cried out in protest.

'I'm not torturing him,' said Taitaro with a smile. 'This is a Chinese method of treating the sick. I am placing the needles so as to relieve his fever. I cannot save his life, but I can ease his dying.' Why in the name of the Willow Tree would Taitaro want to make Sogamori's dying moments easier? Jebu wondered. The Zinja were physicians only because a warrior must be able to treat his own wounds and those of his comrades. Now, using some powder he carried with him, Taitaro was mixing a potion in water. Drop by drop he poured it between Sogamori's thick, fever-cracked lips. Gradually the Takashi patriarch stopped moaning. Taitaro put his hand back on his forehead and let it rest there. After a moment, Sogamori opened his eyes and looked at Taitaro.

'Have you brought me Yukio's head?' he whispered.

He's still delirious, thought Jebu, but Taitaro only answered, 'It is not Yukio's time to fall. It is your time now, Lord Sogamori. All those who are great must be brought low.'

'Who are you?' Sogamori rasped. His eyes were more alert now. Taitaro's treatment was having its effect.

104

'I am the former abbot Taitaro of the Order of Zinja, Lord Sogamori.'

'A Zinja. I have forbidden all Zinja to approach me. Except, of course, for that monk Suzuki, who thinks he deceives me with his Buddhist robes. I keep him around so I can feed the Zinja false information.' Sogamori laughed feebly. Jebu smiled over at Suzuki, who shrugged and rolled his eyes.

'Listen, Lord Sogamori,' said Taitaro. 'You are going to die. I would judge that you do not have more than an hour of life left to you. I advise you to spend it well. If you wish we will withdraw and leave you to be comforted by these two Buddhist priests who stayed faithfully by you when all your guards were killed.'

Sogamori's eyes widened. He had been unconscious ever since the evacuation of Heian Kyo and had been unaware of the military situation for many days before that. Now he asked Taitaro quick, probing questions. He learned that the Takashi had lost the capital, that he was in a Buddhist temple south of Takatsuki, and that he was in the power of the Muratomo. His reaction was calm and courageous. Jebu could not help but feel admiration. Sogamori had taken the news just as a Zinja would.

'Why don't you kill me?' he asked, staring in Taitaro's eyes.

Taitaro quoted *The Zinja Manual*: 'When it is not necessary to do a thing, it is necessary not to do it.'

'True, I am about to die,' Sogamori said, 'but the Takashi will win this war. The whole realm supports us. We have the Emperor. Hideyori has only a rabble of country samurai, and Yukio's army are barbarous foreigners. We will move to the west where we are strongest. All the great samurai families will rally to us against the rebels. My grandson is the Heavenly Sovereign, and my great-grandson and all my descendants will sit on the Imperial throne until the end of time. In this world I have nothing left to desire. My only regret is that I cannot see the head of Yukio.'

Taitaro sighed. 'Lord Sogamori, do you want to go into the Void shouting lies to deafen yourself or do you want to be liberated from illusion?'

'You Zinja speak of insight,' said Sogamori. 'Can one who is not a Zinja achieve it?'

'You have your last chance now to experience insight in this life,' said Taitaro.

'Who will I be in my next life? Do you know, Zinja?'

'We do not claim to know what comes after death.'

'A year ago a saintly monk came to me and told me he had been to the kingdom of the dead in a dream. Emma-O, the king of the underworld, told him I am the reincarnation of the famous priest Jie Sojo, who lived three hundred years ago. Emma-O said that even my evil karma will help mankind. If so, I am no ordinary man, and my future life will not be ordinary.'

'The future does not exist,' said Taitaro. 'There is only the present. While I am with you, let me help you.'

'I am not afraid to die,' Sogamori whispered.

'I do not seek merely to free you from fear,' said Taitaro. 'I seek to make you an infant again, stripped of possessions, rank, kindred, knowledge, past, future, even of language itself. So that you will go into the Void as a baby goes to its mother's arms.'

Sogamori is the man who killed my mother, Jebu thought, but he was more interested in what Taitaro was saying than in his hatred of the Takashi chieftain.

'You are not Sogamori,' Taitaro went on. 'You must give up Sogamori, forget him. Sogamori was a festival mask you wore, but the dance is over now.'

'I shall take another mask for another dance.' Sogamori's voice seemed fainter.

Taitaro leaned forward and stared intently into Sogamori's eyes. 'There is no other dance. There was no dance before this. All time was, is and will be now, and you have always worn this mask, but the mask was never you. Relinquish it. Now.' He snapped his fingers over Sogamori's face, a loud, startling sound, like the cracking of a bone.

There was a silence, and then Sogamori said, 'I see.'

'What do you see?' There was eagerness in the way Taitaro crouched over him.

'I see Sogamori. I see him as a young man shooting his arrows at the warrior monks of Todaiji – at their very shrine – without fear of the gods. I see him with his son Kiyosi subduing the enemies of the Emperor. I see the Son of Heaven proclaiming him chancellor, even the Fujiwara bowing before him. I see him closing the circle that was opened when his ancestor, Emperor Kammy, was on the throne. Sogamori, Takashi no Sogamori.'

'Not Sogamori,' said Taitaro softly. 'Not Takashi.'

'Not Takashi?' Sogamori whispered plaintively. The voice was weaker still. The words slurred. Jebu knew that Sogamori was making his last slide down into fever, delirium and death. 'Not even that ? If I am not a Takashi, I am nothing. If I am nothing then I am – ' There was a long silence as Sogamori searched Taitaro's face, stared up into the shadows of the temple hall, peered at smiling Kwannon.

'Everything,' Sogamori said, and closed his eyes.

Taitaro, Jebu and the three other monks sat cross-legged and waited. From outside the temple came the cries of Mongol soldiers playing some game of chance. In the late afternoon, during the Hour of the Ape, Takashi no Sogamori died. Taitaro laid his hand on the broad, immobile chest, now cool to the touch, and nodded to Jebu. He began removing the needles from Sogamori's body. The two Buddhist priests intoned prayers, while the monk Suzuki led Taitaro to a chest in the corner of the temple, containing Sogamori's remaining possessions. The priests had rescued it from the carriage in which Sogamori had gone on his last journey. There were gold and silver cups and bowls, jade statues, bolts of exquisite silk, scroll paintings and several magnificent swords. Jebu looked for the famous Kogarasu, but it was not there. There was another sword, though, that Jebu recognized. It was very long, the blade straight in the style of hundreds of years ago. The hilt was ornamented with a coiling silver dragon on a black-lacquered background.

'This is Higekiri, the Beard Cutter,' he told Taitaro. 'The oldest sword of the Muratomo. I last saw it in Domei's hand, nearly twenty years ago, when he sent me with his son Hideyori to Kamakura. The Takashi captured him soon after that, and Sogamori must have kept the sword ever since. Yukio will be delighted to see Higekiri again.' Followed by the three priests carrying the chest, Jebu and Taitaro walked to the temple entrance, where Torluk waited for them.

'What did you do, holy man? Poison him with those needles and that drink?'

Taitaro shook his head. 'Those things were to wake him up and ease his pain, not kill him.'

'I'll never understand shamans and monks,' Torluk growled. 'Well, he's dead now and I can take his head to Lord Yukio.'

Without a word, Taitaro went back into the temple. He picked up the candles on the altar one after the other and tossed them at the paper screens and wooden walls, while the Buddhist priests screamed and Torluk bellowed at him to stop. Soon the whole interior was a whirlwind of flame and smoke.

Turluk's face was red with rage. 'If you weren't a man of religion and your son weren't Lord Yukio's companion, I'd kill you, old man.'

'I felt that Sogamori's body deserved to be burned, not mutilated,' said Taitaro calmly.

'You've burned down the temple,' one of the priests screamed. 'You're no holy man. You're a devil.' Taitaro gave Jebu a meaningful look.

'Sogamori built hundreds of temples,' Taitaro told the priest. 'The Lord Buddha and the Goddess Kwannon can spare one for him.'

'We might have had some reward if we could have brought Sogamori's head to Yukio,' Torluk grumbled. 'Now we'll get nothing.'

'Yukio doesn't need to see Sogamori's head,' said Jebu. 'The news that we captured him and he died will please Yukio well enough.' He held up Higekiri. 'He will surely reward those involved in the return of this sword to his family.'

'I will never understand what you did,' Jebu said later, as he and his father rode north along the Shujaku. Even though they could not see Heian Kyo, a grey cloud to the north told them it was still smouldering.

'An inner voice told me I should not let Sogamori be tortured, killed and mutilated,' said Taitaro. 'He seems a monster to us now, a man who destroyed his country, but perhaps it is as he told us; even his evil karma will benefit mankind. Perhaps, indeed, he was no ordinary person. There are moments in my life when our notions of right and wrong, our customs, common sense itself, must be set aside and I must act in a strange way that seems right, though I can see no reason for it. This encounter with Sogamori was such a moment. If you would understand it better, spend more time with the Jewel.'

CHAPTER THIRTEEN

Yukio urged his chestnut horse down the steep, pine-shaded path that wound over the eastern slope of Mount Higashi. It was the Hour of the Rooster, and from the top of the mountain he had seen the setting sun glowing on the rooftops of Heian Kyo. On this side, twilight had already fallen. It was cold enough now, in the Ninth Month, for his horse's breath and his own to turn to steam in the air before him. The prospect of meeting Hideyori made Yukio nervous. In childhood he had known Hideyori as someone who was big, formidable, older, who treated him with undisguised contempt. Now he reminded himself of all he had seen and accomplished since he last saw his half-brother. His victories surpassed those of any other general in the history of the Sunrise Land. Hideyori had yet to win a single important battle. If Hideyori was about to take control of the government, it was Yukio who had given it to him as a gift. I am not a child any longer, Yukio thought, I am thirty years old. Still, Yukio felt towards Hideyori as a boy feels towards a revered and feared elder brother. Why, he wondered, had Hideyori insisted in his messages that Yukio and he must meet alone, in concealment, outside the city? Why the furtiveness? He noticed a row of tumbled stones along the side of the road. Over twenty years ago, Jebu had told him, a Zinja temple had stood here. It had been destroyed by an earthquake and never rebuilt. A horse and rider stood motionless in the path ahead of Yukio. There was something ghostlike about the figure in dark armour sitting astride a pale grey horse.

Yukio climbed down from his horse and called, 'Hideyori? Brother, is that you?' There was no answer. After a moment, the armoured figure dismounted and slowly walked towards him. In the half-light Yukio saw, under a horned helmet, a stern, strong face with glittering black eyes, a face that immediately reminded him of his father, Domei. Now Yukio was sure this was Hideyori. He dropped to his knees and pressed his forehead into the earth.

'My lord. My brother. I am your younger brother, Muratomo no Yukio.'

'I know. Stand up.' The voice was gruff, the words rude. Hideyori had spent the last twenty years of his life in the uncultivated eastern provinces, Yukio reminded himself. Perhaps that was the way they spoke there. Yukio stood and smiled at Hideyori, but there was no answering smile.

'I brought you a gift, Brother. Give me leave to get it.' At Hideyori's nod, Yukio went to his horse and unstrapped a long package wrapped in green silk, which he held out with both hands. Frowning, Hideyori unwrapped it, saw the ancient sword with the silver dragon coiling around the hilt, and gave Yukio a questioning look.

'I am sure my honoured brother recognizes this sword.'

'It is Higekiri,' said Hideyori wonderingly.

Yukio told him how the sword had been found in Sogamori's baggage. 'As head of our family, you are the rightful owner of Higekiri. I am happy to be able to present it to you on our first meeting.' Yukio only regretted that the gift could not have been given at a splendid public ceremony. All Heian Kyo was eager to see and greet the chieftain of the victorious Muratomo clan. But Yukio had promised himself that he would offer the sword to Hideyori at the very first opportunity. Yukio had hoped that when he met his half-brother their common blood would kindle a warmth between them that would dispel his trepidation. But nothing, it seemed, had changed since his childhood. He still dreaded Hideyori's cold contempt.

Hideyori seated himself cross-legged on the ground and gestured to Yukio to join him. He rewrapped the sword and laid it across his knees.

'There are things we must discuss now,' he said. 'In a day or two you and I and our officers will be meeting with the Retired Emperor and his councillors. We should not disagree before them.' Yukio was overcome as, point by point, in rapid succession, Hideyori outlined his plans. Yukio, he proposed, would take to the water, seizing all the ships he could find along the coast, and hound the Takashi from their island strongholds and ports along the Inland Sea. Hideyori would wage a land war against the Takashi and their allies throughout Honshu. For now, Go-Shirakawa would reign in place of the Son of Heaven.

After the war they would choose a successor to the Takashi usurper, the boy Antoku. Clearly, Hideyori had been thinking carefully about these things while Yukio had been blundering from battle to battle. Yukio felt foolish. It was for the best that Hideyori was the older of the two of them and the head of the family.

'Do you agree to all of it so far?' Hideyori asked.

'I am a warrior, not a statesman,' said Yukio. 'I am sure your judgement in these matters is superior to mine. My only thought has been to overthrow the Takashi and win justice for the Muratomo.'

'Justice we will have in good measure, Yukio-san,' said Hideyori, a friendlier note in his voice. It warmed Yukio to be addressed as Yukio-san by his forbidding elder brother. 'You know, I had no idea what sort of person you would be or what you would want. We seem to agree on most things, as brothers should. Let us turn to the difficult question of the Mongols, then. You know, of course, that there are those who say that you have come to conquer our land for the Emperor of Mongolia, who has promised to make you his vassal-king?'

Was Hideyori going to condemn him, as so many others had, for bringing a foreign army into the Sacred Islands? 'What must I do, cut my belly open to prove my loyalty?'

'Do not suggest such a thing even lightly, Yukio-san,' said Hideyori. ''There's really a very simple way for you to show you are not an agent of foreigners. Relinquish command of the Mongols.'

Yukio was stunned. 'To whom?'

'To me, of course. No one questions my loyalty. I've never left the Sunrise Land.'

'You couldn't command the Mongols.'

'It's foolish for us to try to talk to each other in total darkness,' said Hideyori, changing the subject in a pleasant tone. 'Can you light a candle, Yukio-san?' Yukio took a tinder box and a scrap of candle from a kit at his belt. He lit the candle and set it on the box on a bed of fallen maple leaves between himself and Hideyori.

'Good,' said Hideyori. 'Now tell me what you mean about my not being able to command the Mongols.'

'Of course, they would take orders from you,' said Yukio.

'Forgive me for speaking frankly, honoured Brother, but I must give you my opinion as a soldier or fail in my duty to you. The question is, how well could you lead them? I don't think you know enough about the Mongols' special ways of fighting to make good use of them. You don't speak their language. They don't know you. A leader must be known to his men to arouse their fighting spirit.'

In the candlelight Yukio saw a dull red flush spread over his brother's face. Hideyori started to raise his hand in what appeared to be an angry gesture, then stopped himself. Gradually, the colour faded from his face. He stroked his small moustache thoughtfully.

'As you said, Yukio-san, that is your opinion as a soldier. If I had not realized that, even as you spoke, I myself would have been tempted to distrust you just as others do. If I, your brother, could suspect you, think how much easier it is for those who do not know you to believe the worst of you. You may be right when you say that I do not know how to use the Mongols as effectively as you do. Remember, though, that wars are not won on the battlefield alone. If it becomes widely believed that the Muratomo are not loyal to the Sacred Islands, the supporters we need will turn to the Takashi instead.'

There was much in what Hideyori said, Yukio realized, even though he suspected that Hideyori had other, unspoken reasons for wanting the Mongols under his control. He felt as if he had been asked to give away his sword in the middle of a battle. At this stage of the war, though, the Mongols were not as necessary as they had been when he first landed in the north. Now, just as Hideyori said, their presence might be more of a hindrance than a help in winning the war. In war, just as in go, there were fuseki, chuban and yose – opening, middle and end games – each requiring a different strategy.

'I will have to have samurai to replace the Mongols,' he said at last. Hideyori's lips stretched in one of his rare, chilly smiles.

'You shall have them, as many as you need, tough fighters from the eastern provinces, the best men in the land. From now on, though, you'll need ships more than men. We have a new shipbuilder in Kamakura, a man who studied the art in China. I will commission him to build for you. From what I know of the Mongols, they would be little use to you at sea.'

An inexplicable inner reflex of caution kept Yukio from telling Hideyori that the shipbuilder was Moko, an old companion of his. 'True,' he said. 'The Mongol homeland is far from the sea.' He was already regretting having yielded to Hideyori. He had lost his best weapon, the Mongols, and had agreed to undertake the most difficult, dangerous phase of the war – fighting the Takashi at sea. Still, heavily outnumbered, he had beaten the Takashi in Hakata Bay long ago. The vision of what he could do with plenty of ships and men began to excite him.

'One question, Yukio-san,' said Hideyori. 'I believe you have no intention of betraying the Sacred Islands, but what are the intentions of the Mongols themselves?'

Yukio laughed. 'I've always assumed that they could be spies or the vanguard of an invasion. For now, let us make use of them. When they become a problem, let us deal with them.'

Hideyori clapped Yukio on the shoulder and stood up. 'Exactly my thought. We must always remember that today's ally may be tomorrow's enemy.' He raised his arm. There was a rustling in the trees that grew throughout the Zinja temple ruins. Yukio stared about him, startled. Shadowy figures – samurai armed with bows and arrows – emerged and formed a circle around himself and Hideyori.

'You said we were to meet alone,' Yukio choked out.

Hideyori smiled. 'I told you before, Yukio-san, until now I had no idea what sort of person you are or what you would want. This meeting has gone very well, honoured Younger Brother. I look forward to seeing you in a day or two in the capital.' One of Hideyori's men brought his grey stallion forward for him to mount. With a wave, Hideyori turned and rode off down the mountain path, his men following on foot.

Yukio stood alone among the broken stones, asking himself what kind of man his brother was. A man who feared treachery, yet deceived others without a flicker of shame. Yukio felt hot anger rise within him at the thought of the archers concealed in the forest while he talked with his brother. That was why Hideyori had asked him to light the candle, to make him an easy target for the archers. What if he had refused to let Hideyori have the Mongols? He'd be lying dead on the ground right now, riddled with arrows. Yukio shivered as a deathlike chill travelled up his spine. Calling to his horse, he stepped angrily on the guttering candle and ground it out.

CHAPTER FOURTEEN

As if to show that they could be far more destructive than men, the gods chose to halt the War of the Dragons for a time with a series of natural calamities. The Year of the Hare began with blizzards, which turned in the spring into heavy rains and sudden floods. In the summer there was a drought. Many landowners and samurai deserted both the Muratomo and Takashi forces to try to save their farms. By autumn there was famine in the land. The contending clans sent most of their warriors home because they could not feed them. Hundreds of thousands of people starved to death. The dead lay unburied in the streets of Heian Kyo. A group of monks went around the city painting the character 'A' on the foreheads of corpses in the hope that they might be reborn in Amida's Western Paradise. The reported that they had found over forty-two thousand dead within the city limits alone.

The Year of the Dragon was even worse. The droughts continued, and for the second year in a row there was starvation throughout the sixty-six provinces. The weakened populace succumbed to disease, and plague swept the Sacred Islands. Then there was a great earthquake at Heian Kyo. Many were crushed by falling buildings, while those who fled into open spaces were swallowed by huge cracks in the ground. Not a structure in the capital was left undamaged, and the aftershocks continued for three months. The Red Dragon and the White withdrew into permanent camps, waiting for the time when they could begin fighting again.

At last, in the first months of the Year of the Serpent, the forces of nature showed themselves more kindly disposed, thus allowing men to resume their enmity.

The nucleus of the Takashi forces, still led by Sogamori's

eldest living son, Notaro, were encamped at a fortress called Ichinotani on the shore of the Inland Sea. The child-Emperor and his household, guarded by thousands of samurai, took shelter in a cluster of wooden buildings on the beach behind a huge log wall. Rising above the rear of the stockade were steep cliffs, a giant replica in stone of the man-made palisade. In front of the Takashi fortress was the sea, on which a fleet of three hundred Chinese-built junks and large war galleys rode at anchor out beyond the shallows and breakers, a rampart against attack from the water and a refuge in case of attack by land.

One evening in the Second Month of the Year of the Serpent, almost four years after their return to the Sunrise Land, Yukio and Jebu looked over a cliff edge, studying the defences of Ichinotani from above. Yukio had divided his force of eastern-province warriors, leaving seven thousand poised for a frontal assault along the beach from the east, while he led another three thousand along the cliffs, looking for a place to attack the Takashi from the rear. Jebu found a hunter who showed Yukio a narrow pass leading down to the beach. The path through this pass was steeper than the slope of a roof, more suitable for mountain deer than horses and men, but Yukio tested it by sending five riderless horses scrambling to the bottom. Only two of the horses fell and broke their legs in the descent. Yukio was pleased, saying that if they had had riders to guide them, the horses would have made it down unhurt. That night Yukio's three thousand camped on the cliff, the Takashi still unaware of their presence. Though it was early spring and the evening was cold, the Muratomo lit no campfires.

Word had come that day that an army of Mongols and samurai commanded by Hideyori had crushed the Takashi at Kojima, farther to the west. 'Now perhaps he won't be as envious of you,' said Jebu as he walked with Yukio back from the edge of the cliff.

'If I win victories with these eastern warriors, he can always say it was because they were his men, whom he lent me,' Yukio laughed.

As they seated themselves in the camp Yukio's eyes shone with delight. 'I've had other news, Jebu-san. These infernal disasters the land has been suffering gave me time to visit Hiraizumi last year, and the visit has borne fruit. I've just had a message that my lovely Mirusu, who helped me learn the art of war, has given birth to our son. How I wish I could be there to see the new baby instead of on this cold clifftop. I wonder why Hideyori hasn't bothered to remarry and sire some children. The Muratomo could soon be as numerous as they were in my father's time.'

Jebu was silent. A Zinja who had come down to join Yukio from the Pearl Temple near Mount Fuji had told him that Lady Shima Taniko had moved from her family home into Hideyori's castle, where she acted as a kind of hostess for the widowed Muratomo chieftain. Everyone in Kamakura assumed that Taniko was Hideyori's mistress, even though she was the estranged wife of Hideyori's ally, Prince Horigawa. In spite of the gossip about her, Taniko was known as a woman of intelligence and character and respected by all the eastern samurai. Jebu did not believe she and Hideyori were lovers, but it made little difference to him. If he lost Taniko, it would not be to another man's body, but because of her hunger for the company of the powerful and her yearning to be at the centre of events. That and the ghost of Kiyosi.

Jebu's thoughts were dispelled by the music of a flute. Someone in the Takashi stronghold was playing, unaware that he was entertaining not only his own people but an enemy army poised over their heads like an executioner's sword. The flautist was playing an air called 'Buddha Mind, Quiet as Still Water'. The melody spread like balm over the cool evening air, easing the fears of men who knew that tomorrow they might be maimed or killed.

'He plays exceptionally well, whoever he is,' said Yukio, touching his own flute, which huge in a case at his belt. 'I'd like to be able to accompany him. What lovers of beauty those Takashi courtiers are. What a pity all this is.' He lay down, pulling his cloak around him against the damp chill, and closed his eyes for sleep.

At the Hour of the Tiger, as the eastern sky paled and riders were able to see the ground at their horses' feet, the Muratomo quietly mounted. They formed their lines far back from the cliff so that the sounds of their preparation would not carry to the Takashi below. Yukio had divided them into hundred-man units, each with its White Dragon banner surmounted by a square pennant of a distinctive colour. Having commanded these countrified eastern samurai for over a year, Yukio had managed to teach them something of the mass cavalry tactics he had learned from the Mongols. Now, on a white horse, wearing his helmet surmounted by a silver dragon, Yukio trotted out in front of his formations.

'That's where we're going,' he called, pointing with his sword at the head of the pass that led to the Takashi stronghold. 'I'll show you the way.' He turned and galloped his horse straight towards the cliff edge. They may once have been Hideyori's men, but Yukio has won their hearts, Jebu thought. Otherwise they'd never follow him over a cliff. With one wild wave of his sword, Yukio disappeared below the rocky cliff edge. Thirty of his closest companions, including Jebu, thundered after him.

Jebu, his headcloth streaming in the wind, made no attempt to control his horse, but sat leaning so far back in the saddle that his head nearly touched the animal's rump. He trusted in the Self, present in his horse as in all things, to get them down the cliff safely. The first part of the descent was over sand and pebbles, and Jebu and those around him slid until the slope levelled off for a short space. Below were great mossy boulders. It looked impossible, but Jebu saw Yukio's silver dragon down there and spurred his horse on. All around him hooves clattered on rocks and riders shouted 'Ei! Ei!' to keep their courage up. Jebu saw that many of the men near him were riding with their eyes shut. So steep was the slope that the stirrup of a rider above and behind Jebu struck against his head. Then Jebu heard a shriek and a crash and jerked his horse aside just in time to avoid being struck by the tangled bodies of a samurai and his horse rolling over and over, legs flailing in the air. After the first anguished cry the rider was silent. The horse had crushed him. Falling faster and faster he hit other mounted warriors ahead of Jebu, sending two more horses and samurai crashing to destruction in an avalanche of flesh and armour.

Looking straight down past his horse's head, Jebu could see into the Takashi camp as if he were a seagull flying over it. Within the stockade the Takashi warriors, tiny figures, rushed from building to building and out to the gates to the east, where they mounted their horses. Smoke rose beyond the eastern wall of the stockade. Yukio's other seven thousand warriors had begun their attack. A rock dislodged by someone above him struck Jebu's head, dizzying him, and he had to summon all his strength to keep his seat. But the jolting and bouncing finally ended, and the hooves under Jebu pattered on the sand. Now that it was over, Jebu was struck with a sudden awareness that the mad scramble had been a wild delight. He stroked his terrified horse's neck to soothe it.

The first two hundred Muratomo riders who had landed on the beach, let out a roar that sounded more like that of two thousand men as it echoed against the cliffs. A lone Takashi archer appeared on the gallery behind the palisade, his voice and the shriek of his humming-bulb arrow sounding an alarm. A hundred answering arrows transfixed him, and he toppled out of sight. The wooden wall was low on this side and not protected by guard towers. The Takashi had thought the cliffs to be defence enough. Shouting his war cry, 'Muratomo-o!' Yukio rode up to the wall, swinging a blazing torch over his head. He hurled it, and it landed on the thatched roof of a house just beyond the wooden wall. The Muratomo gave a cheer as thick black smoke and red pennants of flame fluttered upwards. Tendrils of fire reached out to caress the palisade itself. Soon a section of the barrier would be burned away. Some Muratomo were not waiting. All along the wall men were scampering up on ropes. Someone had found a small gate further down the palisade, and now it was swinging outwards. A hundred horsemen raced for the opening, knocking one another aside in their haste to be among the first through. Drawing his sword, Jebu kicked his charger in the ribs and galloped after them.

The Takashi might have saved Ichinotani if they had rallied and put up a house-by-house resistance. They outnumbered the Muratomo three to one, but they lacked spirit and leaders. Many of the Takashi samurai were hired or impressed from Kyushu and Shikoku, with no enthusiasm for the cause they served. The nobles who might have led them in defence of the stronghold were at the eastern ramparts, fighting the other part of Yukio's army. With the Muratomo inside the walls and black smoke and flame spreading everywhere, the defenders threw open all the gates and rushed to the beach in panic, seeking refuge on the ships. Seeing the stockade overwhelmed, the Takashi fighting on the east side also fell back to the sea.

The water near the shore was filled with men wading, riding or swimming their horses to deeper water. Overloaded longboats wallowed in the waves. Jebu saw three great galleys, impossibly burdened with hundreds of armoured samurai, slowly tip to one side, then roll completely over, their keels in the air and their passengers drowning. He watched the high-ranking Takashi beat away the common soldiers trying to board the ships in the offing. They slashed with swords and naginatas at the men clinging to the rails, hacking off their arms and hands so that they fell back into the water and sank, their blood staining the sea.

The Takashi who were left behind on the beach fought with the fury of despair, their backs to the waves and their retreating comrades. Believing with Sun Tzu that to deprive an enemy of all hope is to strengthen him dangerously, Yukio had been preaching against the practice of slaughtering all captured enemies, but he had made no headway with his hardened eastern-province warriors. So these last Takashi knew the Muratomo would take no prisoners.

Atsue, his dappled grey horse up to his knees in the water, saw the fall of his uncle Tadanori, younger brother of Kiyosi and Notaro. Tadanori was a fine artist and poet, and his death saddened Atsue. Atsue knew by reputation the one who had killed Tadanori. It was the legendary Shiké Jebu, the giant, red-haired Zinja who had been Yukio's companion, so it was said, since he was a boy, the monk who had once collected a hundred swords just to show his contempt for the samurai. Atsue seethed. Again the Takashi were disgraced. The Emperor had been safely bundled aboard one of the ships, but this day was a worse defeat than Tonamiyama, worse even than the loss of the capital. Everywhere Atsue looked he saw shame. The citadel taken by surprise from the rear, the cowardice of immediate flight, his noble relatives abandoning their own troops just as they had abandoned the dying Sogamori. I was about to flee, too, Atsue thought. Why? I've resolved to die rather than bear any more of my family's shame. Today is as good a day to die as any.

The Shiké Jebu was staring across the water at Atsue. Their

eyes met. Atsue spurred his charger and drew Kogarasu from the scabbard hanging at his belt. He did not bother to call out a challenge. Warrior monks were a rabble without heritage. The Zinja sword was barely a quarter of the length of Kogarasu. Atsue could easily get in a blow while staying clear of his opponent's range. The Zinja wore no helmet, only a headcloth, so Atsue slashed at his face. The shiké flattened himself against the back of his horse, which danced in a tight circle, keeping its head towards Atsue as he rode past. Atsue pulled his horse up short and whirled, and they fenced on horseback, swords clanging together. Atsue knew that he was fighting better than he had ever fought in his life. It was as if his opponent, a consummate master of the sword, was pulling Atsue's skill up to his own level. Still, Atsue knew he was losing. Kogarasu seemed slow and unwieldy. In fighting at close quarters, Atsue was unable to swing the great sword fully. The short, two-edged Zinja blade darted in and out of Atsue's guard with ease, seeming to come at him from all directions. The enemy's face came closer and closer. The strange grey eyes were calm as incense smoke. Deep lines were etched in the sharp-boned, sun-browned face, but they were lines of experience, long journeys, hard work, not lines of rage. The dark red, drooping moustache seemed ferocious, but the thin-lipped mouth beneath it was merely concentrated, intent. It was the face of an engrossed craftsman, not a killer. What I wouldn't give to have whatever you have, Atsue thought. He cut with all his strength at the unprotected neck. Instead of parrying, the monk leaned back, caught Atsue's sword arm with his free hand, and twisted him out of the saddle. As Atsue crashed to the ground his helmet with its golden horns was knocked from his head. Instantly, the monk was crouched over him, the point of his sword at his throat. Atsue closed his eyes.

'Who are you?' came a harsh, hoarse voice from above him.

'Oh, you've done well for yourself,' said Atsue. He opened his eyes. The Zinja was searching his face, frowning in puzzlement. 'Show my head to any of your prisoners, and they'll tell you. If you let any of your prisoners live.'

'Your face is familiar,' said the shiké. 'I don't like to kill men as young as you. Please tell me your name.'

I don't want to live, Atsue thought. On top of everything

else, must I bear the shame of captivity? Torture and mutilation? No.

In a despairing voice he said, 'I am Takashi no Atsue, son of Takashi no Kiyosi, grandson of Takashi no Sogamori.'

The Zinja looked astonished. 'Atsue, the son of Kiyosi? Is your mother Lady Shima Taniko?'

'Yes. If you wish to show me a final kindness, you might try to send her word of my death. I do not know where you can find her, though. You could also send my farewell to my wife, the Imperial Princess Kazuko. She stayed behind in the capital with our son when the Muratomo captured it.' Now, he thought, Kazuko will have to find another father for Sametono.

Slowly the Zinja straightened up, the sword point pulling away from Atsue's throat. 'Please give me your sword and stand up.'

Atsue got shakily to his feet as the monk said, 'A double edge, the sharp curve that starts at the hilt, the gold and silver mountings – this must be the famous Kogarasu. Long ago I wanted to capture this sword from your father.'

'I wish you had tried,' said Atsue. 'He'd have killed you.'

'Perhaps,' said the monk with a sad smile. 'I never got very close to him.'

Atsue noticed that there were arrow shafts protruding here and there from the monk's armour. He'd been hit, but the metal strips and lacings of his armour had caught the arrows and held them harmlessly. Just as with samurai armour, though, the monk's right side was vulnerable. The front, left and rear sides of the boxlike yoroi armour were a unit, but the right side was laced on separately. Evidently the Zinja had decided not to kill him. He stood holding Kogarasu and staring out to sea. The thought crossed Atsue's mind, what glory the killer of the notorious Shiké Jebu would win. Atsue had killed a few of the enemy in small battles that preceded the withdrawal of the Takashi to Ichinotani, but he had never defeated an opponent whose death brought much honour to his arms. The Demon Monk's profaning hands held Kogarasu, but he had neglected to take Atsue's kodachi, his short sword. The monk's guard was down. Would it be honourable to attack him when he wasn't expecting it? Of course. It was the responsibility of a warrior always to be ready to meet attack, and this was no ordinary warrior, but one who had vanquished thousands of samurai. Atsue slipped his kodachi out of its sheath and took a deep breath. With a shout he leaped at the Zinja. He drove the short sword with all his strength into the crevice in the monk's armoured right side, high on the ribs, striking for the heart. His mind soared aloft on golden wings of glory.

Atsue never saw the flashing arc of Yukio's sword that swept his head from his shoulders.

'No!' Jebu screamed.

Too late. The pale young head, severed, lay in the sand, the beautiful face, in which Jebu could now clearly see Taniko's features, serene in death. The rich blood, partly hers, was staining the yellow sand. Jebu felt a hideous pain in his side, where the boy's kodachi had gone in. It was nothing to the pain in his heart. I wish he had killed me, he thought. I want to die.

'Come,' said Yukio gently. 'You're lucky I was close by and saw the Takashi spring at you.' He put his arm around Jebu's waist. 'Sit down slowly and carefully.' When Jebu was sitting, Yukio cut through the lacing of his armour with his shortsword and tore away the grey robe underneath it. 'The wound is deep, I can't tell how deep. The blood is pouring out of you like a waterfall.'

'I don't want to live, Yukio.'

'Jebu. What is it?' Yukio stared into his face. Still sitting up, Jebu swayed, already dizzy from the loss of blood. His breath bubbled in his chest. It was agony to speak.

'Please excuse me – for telling you this, Yukio,' he panted. 'That boy. He was Takashi no Atsue. Taniko's son.'

'Oh, no.' Yukio's head and shoulders sagged as though he had taken an arrow in the chest. 'Forgive me, Jebu.' He pressed his armoured sleeve to his tear-filled eyes. He knelt beside Jebu and began unlacing his armour. 'You killed the father to save my life. Now I've killed the son to save your life. Our friendship has cost Lady Taniko dear.'

'Go back to the battle, Yukio-san.'

'Not until we have cared for you.' Yukio cut a strip of white silk from the edge of his armour robe. From a pouch at his belt he took a packet of powdered herbs Jebu had given him long ago. The herbs were a Zinja secret, used to protect wounds from infection and speed their healing. Yukio sprinkled the powder into Jebu's wound, then unlaced the rest of his armour and began to bind his chest tightly.

Yukio's retainers gathered around them, some helping him to treat Jebu, others stripping Atsue's body of its armour and valuables. One of them came over with a brocade bag. Yukio opened it, then shut his eyes in pain. Slowly he drew out an ivory flute.

'This boy could have been the same one who played so beautifully last night.' Again he wiped his eyes with his sleeve.

'The sword I took from him is called Kogarasu,' Jebu said. 'It belonged to Kiyosi and is a sacred Takashi heirloom. Please send it to Taniko, along with this flute.'

'I will, Jebu-san.'

'He mentioned an Imperial Princess Kazuko to whom he was married. They had a child. He said she was at the capital.'

'I'll see that she gets word.'

Jebu thought, if Taniko had been unable to love him after learning that he had killed Kiyosi, how would she feel when she was told that he and Yukio, between them, had done Atsue to death? She would never want to see either of them again. Yukio's sword had not only cut short the life of a beautiful young man, it had forever parted Jebu and Taniko. Again and again, he thought, I learn how profoundly true it is that life is suffering. I will send a letter along with the sword and the flute, but what can I say to her? That I did not know it was Atsue. That he attacked me, not I him. I meant to spare his life. It was Yukio who killed him, not I. I am not to blame for her son's death, any more than I was to blame for Kiyosi's death. I would much rather I had been killed instead of Atsue. She will read my letter and she will understand. She will even find a place in her heart, in the midst of her grief, to feel some pity for me, but it can make no difference. She cannot force herself to love me. If only I had spoken sooner, had told the boy that his mother was dear to me. If I could have made him understand, he would not have tried to kill me. If only I had taken his kodachi from him, as any careful warrior would have done. Truly, the Zinja are devils, even as Taitaro told me long ago, if we cause such agony for those we love. I want no more of this war. I want no more of being a warrior monk. I am ready to do what Taitaro did, to withdraw

123

to a forest hut. I want to cause no more suffering. I want no longer to be a devil.

Jebu looked into Yukio's eyes and saw tiny squares of white, reflections of the sails of the fleeing Takashi ships. He tried to recite the Prayer to a Fallen Enemy, but the words slipped like little fishes through the net of his mind. Slowly a darkening sea rose around Jebu, and the pain of his wound and the anguish of his spirit dwindled with the fading of the light.

CHAPTER FIFTEEN

From the pillow book of Shima Taniko:

Hideyori has revealed to me his plan for ruling the Sunrise Land. It is an astonishing departure from our customary ways, but well suited to these Latter Days of the Law. He says that trying to imitate the courtiers at the capital made the Takashi soft, corrupt and effeminate. This notion, that softness and corruption go with femininity, is typical eastern province boorishness.

Hideyori thinks the country can only be governed well by those with the power to govern – the samurai. To escape the influence of Heian Kyo, this samurai government will have its headquarters here in Kamakura, in the field, as it were. So it will be known as the Bakufu, the Tent Government. Hideyori says he got that idea from my description of the travelling courts of the Mongol khans. He has chosen Kamakura as his headquarters because he believes the eastern provinces, especially the rice-rich Kanto Plain, are now the most important part of the realm.

In olden times, when a single general was given command of all the armed forces to meet some grave threat to the empire, he was called Shogun, Supreme Commander, for as long as the crisis lasted. Hideyori plans to take that title for himself, permanently. As Shogun he will, of course, derive his authority from the Emperor, but since the Shogun will command all the swords in the land, the Emperor will doubtless be quick to obey all his humble subject's suggestions. I, Hideyori keeps telling me, shall be at his side. If I want to be, I silently add to myself.

Hideyori has already petitioned Go-Shirakawa to make him Shogun, but to his great frustration and annoyance that wily old man replied that, being only a Retired Emperor, he lacks the authority to confer the title. This means Hideyori will have to wait until the war is over and a new Emperor ascends the throne. Meanwhile, he fears that Yukio may have learned of his request and may try to thwart him. Even though Yukio gave in to him in the matter of the Mongols, Hideyori still hates and fears him.

As for the Mongols, Hideyori has taken steps to reduce the threat from them by getting them killed off. Yesterday he told me gleefully that they have lost over a third of their original number in battles he has sent them into. He says that by the time the war is over there will probably be fewer than five thousand of them left. This is the first time I've heard of a military leader achieving his aims by being a bad general.

Good or bad, a general will rule us when all this is over, and Heian Kyo will take orders from Kamakura. When I was a girl I left my home to go up to the capital. Now the home I left will be the capital. When I first saw fires in that magical city of Heian Kyo, I didn't know they signalled the dawn of a new age. A rough, ugly age it promises to be.

—*Third Month, twenty-second day*
YEAR OF THE SERPENT

One evening early in the Fourth Month, a maidservant came to Taniko and told her Hideyori wished her to attend him in his prayer chamber. The intensely religious Hideyori had set aside a special room for meditation and scripture reading in the top of the main tower of the huge new castle he was building. Two samurai in full armour bowed to Taniko outside the oratory, and slid a pair of heavy wooden doors aside for her. The chamber was unpainted and bare except for the alcove in which Hideyori's treasured blackwood statue of the great kami Hachiman stood. A single dark red peony in a pale green vase bowed its lionlike head to the war god. Wearing a black robe with circular White Dragon crests on front and back, Hideyori was seated on a cushion, reading a scroll. Beside him was a long wooden sword box.

'What are you reading, my lord?' she asked after they had formally greeted each other and she sat down on the cushion beside him. There was no question of a screen between them. She was lady-in-waiting, in effect, to the future Shogun, and she considered herself privileged, like Imperial ladies-in-waiting, to deal with men face to face.

'This is the Lotus sutra,' said Hideyori. 'It is my favourite. It gives me great strength.' His dark eyes, when he looked up at her, seemed to search her mind. His voice was softer than usual. 'Do you have a special devotion, Taniko-san?'

'Yes, I often recite the invocation, "Homage to Amida Buddha", when I need comfort.'

'Very good. Everyone needs a way of calling upon higher powers in times of great suffering.' As she sat beside him, he gently took her hand. It was a liberty she allowed him, now that he had agreed not to try to take her to bed. 'I have news of terrible sorrow for you,' he said. 'You must bear it like a samurai.'

Jebu, she thought at once, and her heart turned to ice. Then she remembered that Hideyori did not know what Jebu was to her. Involuntarily she pressed Hideyori's hand.

'Please tell me, Hideyori-san. I can bear it.'

Hideyori picked up the long, polished cedar box and set it on his knees. He opened it and took out a sword in a gold and silver scabbard.

'You may know this sword. It is the Takashi family treasure Kogarasu.' He passed the sword to her, hilt first. It was so heavy she could hardly imagine how a man could swing it in combat. Kogarasu. Kiyosi's sword. She had supposed it went to the bottom of the sea with him at Hakata Bay. To take it from Hideyori's hands, here in Hideyori's palace, was bewildering. What was Hideyori trying to tell her?

He reached into the box again and took out an ivory flute and handed it to her. She recognized Little Branch at once. At the sight of it she could almost hear Atsue playing on it, as he had done so many times for her before Sogamori's men took him away.

Understanding flashed through her mind like a lightning bolt,

126

and with it came a torrent of grief. Atsue. She remembered the thin arms torn from around her neck, the last despairing look he gave her. She had always dreamed that one day she would find him again. She had prayed that she might see how he had grown, what sort of man he had become. Now she would never know him. She felt herself falling and leaned against Hideyori, clinging to him for support. A sob forced itself through her throat. Not my Atsue. Not my other baby.

'When a man and a woman put their pillows together, the karma relations that come of it are endless,' Hideyori said. 'How could you have known, so many years ago, that your son by Kiyosi would go to war against his mother's friends?'

'Did he die in battle? He's just a child. He has not lived.'

Hideyori's voice was strong in her ear. 'The cherry blossom falls from the tree with the first strong breeze, but we do not say that it has never lived. A bloom that lasts only a day is no less beautiful for that.'

'Homage to Amida Buddha,' Taniko whispered. She released her hold on Hideyori and sat up. She had lost so much in her life – her daughter Shikibu, Kiyosi, Jebu. Atsue she had lost twice, once long ago and now again. Sogamori had made a samurai of him and sent him into battle to be killed, just as he had done to Kiyosi. She would not let this break her. As Hideyori reminded her, she, too, was samurai. She wept silently, knowing that all the tears she could shed would leave her inner desolation untouched, a vast emptiness like the Mongol desert.

'He has fallen from the bough,' she said in a quiet voice. 'He will suffer no more. But I go on suffering. What sin have I committed, that I must trudge on from year to year, from agony to agony?'

'Perhaps you are being reserved for a higher destiny,' said Hideyori. 'The steel for the finest swords is thrust into the fire ten thousand times.'

'I have no wish to serve a higher purpose. If I can't die, let me live as a nun. My father threatened to put me into a convent the morning I left Kamakura to be married in Heian Kyo. If only he had.'

'A convent is no place for a woman as clever and beautiful as you. If you want to escape from your sorrow, turn to work. Do your duty to your family, to the Sacred Islands and to the kami.'

Taniko wrapped her arms around herself and clenched her teeth, trying with all her strength to hold herself together.

'Your son, Takashi no Atsue, is gone from this world,' Hideyori said quietly. 'You must accept it and go on.' Atsue's full name, which Taniko herself never spoke aloud, sounded like that of a stranger on the Muratomo chieftain's lips. It brought home to her again the reality of what had happened. Atsue was dead. Killed by some Muratomo samurai. She could no longer contain her grief. A long scream tore itself from the very core of her body, and she burst into a storm of weeping. She bent double over the sword and flute, convulsed by sobs. Hideyori sat silently, his face averted.

At last her anguish subsided enough for her to speak. 'Forgive me.'

'There is nothing to forgive. You have suffered greatly.'

Taniko's mind went back to that terrible time in Heian Kyo when no one dared tell her Kiyosi was dead until Sogamori's secretary blurted it out. 'I am grateful to you, Lord Hideyori,' she said formally. 'You had no duty to tell me of the death of one of your enemies. You were under no obligation to spend so much of your precious time with me to comfort me in my grief. I am obliged to you for taking this task upon yourself.'

'It might have been much more difficult for me,' said Hideyori, his glance darting sideways at her. 'I am grateful that you did not ask me how he died.'

'What do you mean?'

Hideyori looked perturbed. 'I meant nothing.'

'You have not told me everything.'

'No, no. I have said enough already.'

'I want to know all, Hideyori-san. Do not leave some ugly truth lying in wait to catch me unaware later on. Let me suffer now all that I must suffer.'

'Please, Taniko-san, do not ask me to say any more. You will regret it.'

'Did he die dishonourably? Did he commit some act of cowardice?'

'No, it was not that, Taniko. Will you force me to tell you, then?'

'Please speak.'

Hideyori sighed. 'This sword and this flute were sent to me as

128

spoils of war by my half-brother, Yukio. It was Yukio who killed your son.'

Taniko bit her lip. 'No.' Not Yukio. It could not be. Not Jebu's dearest friend. Not the smiling companion who had helped her return from China to the Sacred Islands. She felt as if she were falling into an abyss without light and without bottom.

Hideyori went on. 'Atsue was captured during the battle at Ichinotani by the giant Zinja monk Jebu, who travels with Yukio. The Zinja brought Atsue to Yukio. When Yukio learned that Atsue was Sogamori's grandson, he instantly cut off the defenceless boy's head.'

'Sogamori's grandson? But Yukio and Jebu both knew that Atsue was *my son*.' Taniko felt her body grow cold.

'Apparently that did not affect Yukio's angry mood,' said Hideyori. 'It is well known that he has a furious temper.'

'Homage to Amida Buddha,' Taniko whispered, but the Lord of Boundless Light was far from her lightless chasm. 'Was there a letter?' she asked, after a long silence in which she fought to overcome the pain.

'No. The samurai who brought the sword and the flute told me how your son died.'

'If Yukio sent these things, he must have regretted killing Atsue.'

'He sent them to me because they are Takashi treasures. Knowing I distrust him, he seeks to curry favour with me. I felt that I should give them to you.'

'Did the monk Jebu try to stop Yukio from killing my son?'

'If he did, I did not hear of it.'

'I would like to speak to the samurai who brought the sword and the flute.'

'I'm sorry, but he has already gone back to rejoin Yukio's army.'

Taniko rose to her feet, clutching the sword and the flute to her breast. 'Forgive me, my lord, but I must ask your permission to leave. I must be alone.'

'Kwannon bring comfort to you, Taniko-san.'

Knowing that everyone in the palace was constantly watched on Hideyori's orders, Taniko decided to ride out into the hills. There she would defy her karma. She would kill herself. Of course, she would be reborn to suffer more, but at least the bitter memories of this life, in which she had been so cruelly betrayed by those she trusted and loved, would be wiped away. She considered leaving a final farewell message in her pillow book, but there was no longer anyone she wanted to write to. That in itself, she thought, is a good reason to leave this world.

Soon her horse was climbing the hills along the same road she and Jebu had followed twenty-two years earlier on their first journey together. The houses of Kamakura had spread into those hills, and it took her much longer to reach the thick pine woods. The path wound to a spot from which she was able to see the whole sweep of forest, city and ocean. The blackness all around was dotted by countless tiny points of illumination, the fireflies in the trees, the lanterns in the streets and gardens below, the phosphorescence on the rolling surface of the ocean, the blazing stars overhead. The beauty of this moonless night penetrated the numbness of her grief. She decided she would follow the forest path to the top of this hill. There she would sit uner a pine with Kogarasu and Little Branch in her lap. She would take out the small dagger concealed in her kimono, and when she felt ready, perhaps at sunrise, she would cut her throat and let her blood spill over these last things she had from Atsue.

She felt a momentary surge of annoyance when her horse neared the top of the hill and she saw it was already occupied by a little temple, scarcely larger than a hut, with a thatched roof. The doorway of the small building faced east, hiding its light from any traveller approaching from the city. She had never heard of a temple on this hill, but as Kamakura grew in importance the forests around it were filling up with yamabushi, mountain-dwelling monks. Perhaps she was meant to find this temple. By saying, 'Homage to Amida Buddha,' with perfect faith one might achieve rebirth in Amida's Western Paradise where it was possible – as it was not in this corrupt world – for an ordinary person to attain Nirvana. Taniko had been invoking the Buddha for most of her life, but she had no way of knowing whether any of her prayers had enough purity to release her from the anguish of being reborn on this earth. Perhaps in one last visit to a temple she might find the wings of grace that would carry her to Amida's paradise.

The temple was very small and utterly bare, like Hideyori's prayer chamber. There was not even a statue of a Buddha or bosatsu on the altar, where a small oil lamp provided the only illumination. Taniko walked to the altar, bowed and clapped her hands to get the attention of whatever deity might dwell in this temple. Aloud she said, 'Homage to Amida Buddha.'

'A waste of breath,' said a voice behind her.

The irreverent remark immediately made Taniko think robbers must have taken over the temple. She whirled, preparing to defend her honour or kill herself here and now, if necessary, with her dagger. In the shadows on one side of the room a black-robed monk sat in the lotus position, smiling at her. He had been so silent and immobile when she entered that she hadn't noticed him. She bowed in reverence to his vows, though his words were odd for a monk.

'Why wasted breath, sensei?'

The monk had a round, cheerful face and a chunky body. Though he was utterly motionless, there was such a strength in his sitting that it seemed not even elephants would be able to budge him. His eyes penetrated Taniko's mind, giving her the feeling that he knew her because he knew the whole universe, and that he contained the universe in himself.

'Amida Buddha does not exist,' he said.

'What? Amida does not exist? What teachings do you profess, monk?'

'I teach nothing special. What sort of teaching are you looking for?' In spite of his odd words there was a kindness in his face that made her like and trust him. She needed to believe in someone. It was because she could no longer believe in anyone that she wanted to die.

'I'm not looking for teaching. I want peace, nothing else.' In a rush, she poured out her story. By the time she had finished telling the stocky monk about Kiyosi, Atsue, Yukio and Jebu, the two of them were seated facing each other before the empty altar. Though she'd had to pause several times to release the tears that seemed to fill up her whole body, the telling had eased her grief. Even so, as she admitted to the monk, whose name was Eisen, after she left his temple she meant to kill herself.

'Perhaps you were fated to come here,' Eisen mused. 'It can't be coincidence that I met and talked with the monk Jebu and Lord Muratomo no Yukio years ago, just before their journey to China. Lord Yukio did not seem to me a man who would

131

murder a helpless youth, but then, you do not seem to me the sort of woman who would kill herself because her son is dead. The Buddha himself had a son, you know.'

'I thought you said the Buddha does not exist.'

'Assuredly, a man called Siddhartha lived many hundreds of years ago, and he had a son whom he called Obstacle, because, he said, the love of a child is a great hindrance to enlightenment.'

'I would rather love my child and not be enlightened.'

'To say that shows that your enlightenment is already great. If you are willing to love, you must expect to suffer. If you are willing to suffer, you are willing to live. Your life is not yours to dispose of, you know.'

'If not mine, then whose? The Buddha's?'

'All lives are the Buddha's life, because you are the Buddha.'

At his words, there was an explosion of light within Taniko like a Chinese rocket shooting into the sky and then bursting into a chrysanthemum of glowing colour. She felt an enormous surprise. It was all so simple. She felt peace and gladness, as if she had just found the answer to all the questions that had been tormenting her for years. What she had learned or why she felt this way, she could not put into words. She looked at Eisen, amazed.

His broad smile was delighted, congratulatory. 'Some monks spend their whole lives sitting in meditation before experiencing what you have just experienced.'

'What happened to me?'

'Nothing special. The feeling will fade after a time. It is a very good feeling, but you will fall into hell if you try to hold on to it. You are a like a person lost in a forest, who stumbles across a hidden temple. Having found it once, you will be able to find your way back more easily, but do not try to stay there, because you have work to do. Work is the true Western Paradise in which we achieve salvation.'

Taniko remembered that Hideyori, the opposite sort of man from this monk, had said she could escape her sorrow through work. How strange. She stood and looked out the door of the little temple. The quiescent ocean gleamed like a bronze mirror as the rim of the sun appeared at its edge.

'May I come to see you again? I know there is much more you can teach me.'

'Life is the teacher,' said Eisen. 'Everything that happens to you is what we call a *kung-an*, a question whose answer points to the Buddha within you. Life has already set you some bitter *kung-an*. Perhaps you are being prepared for very great attainment.'

'I'll go home now.'

'Good,' said Eisen with a chuckle. 'That samurai who has been following you will be grateful. Sitting out there in the cold, damp forest must have made him quite miserable.' Surprised, Taniko looked where Eisen was looking and saw a flash of sunlight on metal in the forest sloping down from the temple doorway. One of Hideyori's men, no doubt. She wouldn't have been able to commit seppuku even if she'd tried. Angrily, she thought, Hideyori is not trying to protect me, he is trying to control me. Even this realization seemed trivial, though, beside the wondrous new feeling which made all discontent seem unimportant. As she gazed at the rising sun the light within her seemed to shine more brightly. I did not kill myself, she thought, but this night I died and was reborn.

CHAPTER SIXTEEN

It was the Hour of the Serpent. The Inland Sea sparkled in the morning light, darkening to indigo whenever a cloud crossed the sun. Jebu, in black-laced monk's armour, stood in the bow of the war junk *Soaring Crane*. With the weather so fine, the two fleets would certainly fight to a finish. Strange, how the well-being of the kami of sky and water could mean so much suffering for humankind.

Right now, the kami seemed to have sided with the Takashi. Through the play of light and shadow seven hundred ships of the Red Dragon advanced grandly from the west, borne on the tide rip flowing through the Straits of Shimonoseki. The thunder of the huge war drums on their afterdecks rolled over the waves. The Takashi had divided their vessels into three fleets. In the van came three hundred big ships led by a row of Chinese junks bedecked with red banners, sails spread like dragon wings, eyes painted on their bows glaring ferociously. Next came two hundred ships of Takashi allies, and last came the highest Takashi nobles, including the clan chieftain Notaro and his nephew the Emperor, in two hundred more.

With wind and tide against them, the five hundred Muratomo ships were hard put to maintain any sort of battle order and were driven towards the rocky islands of Kanju and Manju. Here at the narrow western end of the Inland Sea the waves beat against forbidding cliffs on the Honshu side, while the Kyushu shore was crowded with serried ranks of samurai on horseback and on foot. Supposedly, they were allies of the Takashi, but their commanders had grown independent after five years of civil war. They would join whoever won the battle at sea.

Moko, looking fierce in full samurai armour, stood beside Jebu. *Souring Crane*, like a hundred other ships that formed the heart of the Muratomo fleet, had been built at Kamakura under Moko's direction. Moko's ships were junks, propelled by sail rather than oars, but smaller and faster than the Chinese-built Takashi junks. Moko had followed Chinese models but tried to improve on them. His ships had fought in only one battle, at Yashima, where the Muratomo had taken the Takashi by surprise and won an easy victory. Today's fight would be the real test. Moko had insisted on sailing aboard *Soaring Crane* with Jebu. If his junks were defeated, he explained, he would rather go down with them than face Lord Hideyori's wrath. Jebu made him welcome, but was disappointed when Moko sadly told him he bore no message from Taniko.

'She has never talked to me about the death of her son,' he told Jebu. 'I would certainly never raise the subject with her myself. I suspect she does not want to force me to choose between you and her, shiké. She is a lady of great grace.'

The Takashi vanguard ships were crowded with archers standing shoulder to shoulder, and now at a signal they let fly volley after volley, hundreds of arrows at a time. The feathered shafts poured down like hail on the deck and hull of *Soaring Crane*. The Muratomo archers shot back, but they were at a disadvantage with the wind against them and the Takashi protected by the high hulls of their junks.

'We're going to have to board those big ships and fight the Takashi hand to hand,' Jebu told Moko. Ordering his friend below, Jebu signalled the two steersmen at the rudder to set a collision course for one of the biggest of the Takashi ships. Muratomo samurai crowded *Soaring Crane*'s rails, ready with ropes and grappling hooks. Jebu braced himself as the enemy junk bore down upon them. An arrow thudded into his shoulder plates, its impact almost knocking him to the deck. The Takashi junk swerved at the last moment, as if trying to avoid the *Soaring Crane*, but the two ships crashed together with a boom and a scream of tortured wood. The enemy's black hull loomed above Jebu like the wall of a fortress. Grapples flew through the air.

'Muratomo!' Jebu cried, scrambling up a rope. He poised himself on the railing of the Takashi ship, then drew his sword and threw himself at the nearest enemy samurai.

'Shoot Yukio!' shouted a Takashi officer splendid in red-laced armour. The Takashi would be disappointed, Jebu thought. Yukio had hidden himself elsewhere in his fleet.

Every defector who presented himself in the Muratomo camp had brought the same warning. The Takashi were convinced that Yukio was the sole cause of their many defeats. They could still turn the tide and overcome the Muratomo if only they could manage to kill Yukio. Hideyori they dismissed as a mere intriguer. Each Takashi samurai went into battle praying that he might be the one permitted by the kami to save the clan by destroying their worst enemy. But Takashi numbers dwindled steadily. Every day warriors eager to end the war on the winning side abandoned the Takashi and pledged themselves to the White Dragon. Before Ichinotani the deserters had come into Yukio's camp by tens; afterwards, by hundreds. After Yukio led his newly built fleet in a surprise attack on the Takashi stronghold on Yashima island and nearly annihilated them there, great lords of ancient lineage brought thousands of warriors to aid the Muratomo. The steward of the shrine of the kami Gongen at Kumano, appointed years ago by Sogamori, held a fight between seven white cocks and seven red ones before the image of Gongen. When the white cocks killed or drove off all the red ones, he set sail with two hundred ships and two thousand men, carrying the Gongen shrine itself in the flagship. All this he placed in Yukio's service.

Yukio welcomed the many who joined him and accepted their oaths of fealty to his brother. If today's battle went well, it would be the last. The Takashi had nowhere to go. Inexorably Yukio had driven them westwards across the Inland Sea until they were bottled up in Shimonoseki Strait. Beyond lay only the open ocean and the inhospitable, Mongol-dominated mainland. Ten-year-old Emperor Antoku, grandson of Sogamori, still in possession of the Three Treasures, ruled over an empire of wood, the decks of the Takashi ships. He was somewhere in the fleet that faced the Muratomo today, the fleet commanded by the feckless Notaro and which was now the last hope of the Takshi.

It was now almost a year since Yukio's victory at Ichinotani, since Atsue had gone into the Void. For much of that year Jebu had remained at the Zinja monastery of the Red Fox on Shikoku. His left lung pierced by Atsue's dagger thrust healed slowly. A month after Yukio's men brought him to the monastery, Taitaro arrived to nurse him. His white beard now reaching almost to his waist, Taitaro had little to say. He held the Jewel of Life and Death up for Jebu to see, when Jebu was too weak to hold it himself. Gradually, Jebu's strength came back. As soon as he could hold a brush he composed a letter to Taniko. Although he hazily recalled that Yukio had promised to write her explaining how Atsue had died, he wanted to tell her in his own words what had happened. The letter was entirely unsatisfactory, but it was the best he could do. He sent it knowing he had to send something. She never replied. With the help of his own vitality and Zinja medicine, Jebu's breathing was back to normal after six months, and he was able to resume training with the monastery masters. Nine months after being wounded he took ship from Shikoku to join Yukio's fleet, just in time to be part of the victory at Yashima.

Jebu stood over the body of the samurai officer who had called for Yukio's death and whispered the Prayer to a Fallen Enemy. The battle for the big Takashi junk had been surprisingly brief. The deck was stained red, mostly with Takashi blood. The enemy had manned the formidable ship with their least-experienced warriors, probably thinking the Muratomo would be less likely to attack the bigger vessels. Many of the dead were only boys. Each, thought Jebu, would be the object of some mother's lifelong grief, as Atsue was. The important thing now was to try to get word to Yukio that the big Chinese junks were the most negligible part of the Takashi fleet. Jebu ordered the red banners thrown over the side along with all the dead, and the white Muratomo flags run up. Yukio, he knew, was aboard the *Green Castle*, one of his smaller ships, where he hoped to avoid the notice of the Takashi. Appointing a crew for the captured junk, Jebu reboarded the *Soaring Crane* to sail in pursuit of Yukio.

The battle had moved eastwards, pushed in that direction by the wind and tide that favoured the Takashi. Smoke billowed over the water from burning vessels. At last Jebu saw Yukio's ship, grappled to a junk twice its size with the Red Dragon painted on its largest sail. That could be the Imperial ship or Notaro's flagship, thought Jebu, unless, like the junk he had just captured, it was a decoy. A Takashi sekibune, a large galley, closed in, and over a hundred warriors charged across spiked planks into the stern of Yukio's *Green Castle*. Two more enemy galleys were approaching. They must know they've got Yukio trapped, Jebu thought. He ordered the captain of *Soaring Crane* to put on more sail. They were close enough now to see Yukio, a small figure in white-laced armour at the centre of a dwindling knot of Muratomo samurai, his back to the rail. Closer and closer Jebu's ship drew. Now Yukio turned and saw *Soaring Crane* bearing down on him. He waved his sword and began cutting his way out of the Takashi ring surrounding him. With arrows and spears falling all about him, he ran and leaped across the gap between *Green Castle* and *Soaring Crane*. For a moment he tottered on the railing until Jebu seized his arms and pulled him to the deck with a thump.

'Magnificent, Lord Yukio,' Moko exclaimed. 'I don't think I've ever seen a man jump that far.'

'Fear transformed me into a grasshopper,' Yukio laughed.

'The battle is going badly for us,' said Jebu as they pulled away from the cluster of enemy galleys that had almost finished Yukio.

Yukio glanced up at the sun, which now stood almost at the zenith. 'Moko, you'd better confer the mark of divine favour on us while the wind is still blowing towards our fleet.'

'At once, my lord.' Moko went below. When he returned he

held a large wooden box cradled in his arms. Two serving men followed him carrying a stack of wicker cages on a pallet. Moko opened the box and took out a huge Chinese rocket mounted on a three-legged stand, which he set up on the deck.

'I tested this device many times in Kamakura, and it worked most times. A hundred things could go wrong, though. If all happens as planned, I truly will believe that the kami are with us.'

'What is it?' Jebu asked.

'Wait and watch,' said Yukio.

Moko lit the rocket's fuse and stepped away. A ring of curious samurai had formed around him, and they gasped and drew back as, spitting yellow sparks, the rocket leaped into the air. All heads aboard *Soaring Crane* tilted back as the blazing trail rose as high as a gull can fly and still be visible, arcing towards the midpoint between the Muratomo and Takashi fleets. There came a thunderclap and a flash of light. The noise startled the fighting men, and a silence spread over the two fleets. Now a great square of white silk unfurled in the sky. Light as a cloud, the white banner floated and rippled on the currents of the upper air, while the men below shouted in awe.

'Indeed, Hachiman has declared for us,' whispered Moko. In Moko's hand Jebu now saw an almost-invisible white string that guided the banner in its descent. Majestically the banner drifted downward towards Yukio's ship. Moko gave a signal to the men with the wicker cages. One by one they opened the cages, and a flock of white wood doves, the birds of Hachiman, whirled into the air with a drumming of wings. They circled around the white square of silk, then flew off to the north-east. Moments later the banner draped itself over the stern of the *Soaring Crane*. An utter silence had fallen over the strait.

'We could have used the exploding devices of the Chinese as weapons,' said Yukio. 'But I am already blamed for unleashing Mongols against my countrymen. At least I will not be accused of bringing another horror to the Sacred Islands.' He turned away from Jebu, leaped to the gunwale of the *Soaring Crane*, and stood with his sword drawn where all could see him. 'Nail the heavenly banner to our mast. Hachiman wills victory to the Muratomo.'

As a crewman scrambled up the ropes to the tallest of the

Soaring Crane's three masts and attached the banner there, Jebu noticed that the wind blew the flag towards the west. It was midday. The wind had shifted. Now it was behind the Muratomo ships.

Within the hour the Takashi fleet was falling back in disorder. Directed by a system of flag signals Yukio had learned from the Mongols, the Muratomo regrouped and sailed to the attack. Yukio's standing order to concentrate fire on the crewmen of the enemy junks and galleys soon had its effect. Stricken Takashi ships wallowed and spun in the powerful westwards-flowing current, the samurai on board helpless targets for Muratomo archers. Takashi ships crashed into one another, driven against the northern shore of Shimonoseki Strait below the town called Dannoura.

'When the tide ran against us,' said Yukio, 'we had all of the Inland Sea at our backs and plenty of room to run before the Takashi. Now the current is driving them into the narrows, and there is no space for them to manoeuvre.'

Some Takashi samurai beached their ships and swam to shore, but they died there under volleys of arrows fired by former allies gathered on the cliffs above them. As one ship after another in the Takashi fleet was captured, sunk or burst into flame, the balance of numbers shifted over to the Muratomo. Now an arm of the Muratomo fleet, some of the junks designed by Moko that were so much faster than those of the Takashi, outraced the enemy and blocked their escape route into the western sea.

The man who had nailed up the white banner was still aloft. Now he shouted, 'I see His Imperial Majesty. He's on a red-painted junk with gold dragons painted on the after cabin. He's just come out on deck with his courtiers around him.'

Yukio peered in the direction of the man's pointing arm. 'The Emperor is the only strength they have left. We must capture him. I see his ship.' He snapped orders to the captain of *Soaring Crane*, who relayed them to his crew. The junk plunged through the smoky chaos of ships locked in combat, relentless in its pursuit of the Emperor's vessel. Yukio gripped the rail, staring ahead, oblivious to the arrows and spears that showered down on him.

There was a cry of horror from the lookout. 'A woman has

jumped overboard with the Emperor in her arms. His Majesty is in the sea.' Jebu stared at the ship that was their objective. His mouth dropped open. From this distance it looked as it someone had spilled a basket of flowers into the water. Men and women in the brightly coloured robes of the Court were jumping to their deaths. For a moment the bright reds, greens and blues billowed out upon the waves, then the many-layered costumes soaked up water and the courtiers sank out of sight.

'His Imperial Majesty is drowning,' Yukio roared at his crew. 'Faster.' But *Soaring Crane* was already making all possible speed. When they arrived at the ship, there was no one left aboard. Even the crewmen, all Takashi samurai, had drowned themselves. A shout arose from one side of the Muratomo ship. Jebu ran to the rail. Yukio's men had sighted a woman still afloat and were pulling her in with grappling rakes. Two samurai stripped off their armour and undergarments and dived naked into the water. Soon they had the woman kneeling on the deck before Yukio. She wept bitterly as torrents of salt water ran from her sodden robes.

'Who are you?' Yukio demanded.

'My name is Takashi no Harako. I was an attendant to His Imperial Majesty's grandmother, the widow of the late Chancellor Sogamori. My husband was General of Cavalry Takashi no Mizoguchi. I am carrying his child. Now my Emperor, my lady and my husband are all dead. I beg you to let me join them beneath the waves.'

'What happened to His Imperial Majesty?' Yukio demanded.

'His grandmother told him that his cause was lost and his enemies would never permit an Emperor related to the Takashi to remain on the throne. It was time for him to leave this sorrowful world, she said. She gave him the sacred sword to hold and the sacred necklace to wear. He asked her if it would hurt to drown. She told him, 'We will find another capital beneath the waves. Grandfather Sogamori will be there, along with all Your Majesty's ancestors.' Then he said he was ready to go, and, weeping, she enfolded him in her arms and jumped over the side of the ship. They sank out of sight at once.' Lady Harako burst into sobs. 'The poor little Emperor. He was only ten years old.'

'My lord, come look at this,' a samurai called. Yukio went to the rail, followed by Jebu. The heaving waters were dotted with bobbing heads, heads that disappeared as quickly as splashes of raindrops on a pool, to be replaced at once by hundreds of others, as more men jumped from their ships. The last of the Takashi warriors were following the example of the boy Emperor and his Court and giving themselves to the waves.

'Let me drown, too,' Lady Harako begged.

'You said the sword and the necklace went to the bottom with His Imperial Majesty,' said Yukio. 'What of the sacred mirror?'

'For all I know, it is still aboard the ship.'

Sending Lady Harako below deck despite her pleas that she be allowed to die, Yukio summoned *Soaring Crane*'s priest and ordered him to board the late Emperor's ship, search for the sacred mirror and bring it back to *Soaring Crane*. Then he turned back to the rail to watch the end of the Takashi. Many of the drowning warriors had jumped into the water clutching their red banners. As their armour pulled them under, only the red squares of silk remained on the surface. It was all over in moments. The empty ships bobbed on the waves. The Takashi banners were strewn over the strait like red maple leaves on a woodland stream in autumn. A cold evening mist spread from the shore. The cries of the victorious Muratomo echoed like the screams of gulls over the dark water.

A rowboat pulled up beside *Soaring Crane*, and a man with bound arms was pushed over the railing to stand sullenly before Yukio. He was unarmoured, and his under robe, the red brocade of a general, dripped on the planking. His cheeks were hollow, his eyes sunken and lifeless. After some prodding by the samurai who had brought him to Yukio, he gave his name in a low voice.

'I am Takashi no Notaro, commander-in-chief of His Imperial Majesty's forces and son of the late Imperial chancellor Takashi no Sogamori.'

'Lord Notaro,' said Yukio wonderingly. 'How is it that all your clansmen have destroyed themselves and the chieftain alone is left behind?'

'We saw it all, Lord Yukio,' one of the samurai with Notaro said. 'All the men on his ship were jumping into the water while he hesitated. At last one of his own officers pushed him over the side. Whereupon the coward stripped off his armour and tried to swim to shore. We fished him out.'

'If I ever again hear any man refer to a son of the great Sogamori in rude terms, I will personally take his head,' said Yukio evenly. 'Lord Notaro is to be treated with all courtesy and given every comfort that we can supply. Escort him to the master cabin and move my things out of there. And untie him.'

'What are you going to do with me?' Notaro asked.

'I must send you to my brother, Lord Hideyori, for judgement.'

'My father should have killed both you and your brother when you were children,' said Notaro. 'His generosity has destroyed his family.'

'Excuse me, but it was not your father's generosity that moved him to spare my brother and me, Lord Notaro,' said Yukio with a smile. 'It was my mother's beauty.'

A rowboat carried the priest back from the Emperor's abandoned vessel. A samurai walking before the white-robed priest struck a small going to call attention to the holy object being carried on board. All on *Soaring Crane* prostrated themselves. In trembling hands the priest held a silk bag. Within, Jebu knew, was another, more worn, silk bag, and within that another, and so on to a number no one knew. Each time the outer covering of the sacred mirror began to deteriorate, it would be placed in a new one without removing any of the previous silk bags. The reflection of the sun goddess herself, it was said, could be seen in the sacred mirror, death for any mortal to look upon. The priest carried the one surviving Treasure of the Realm below to the ship's shrine.

Placing Muratomo crews aboard the abandoned Takashi ships, Yukio ordered the victorious fleet to sail at once for Hyogo. Homing pigeons were released to carry word of the victory to Shimonoseki Strait to the capital and to Kamakura. Yukio leaned on the rail and looked out at the drifting red banners receding sternwards. Joining him, Jebu saw tears on his face.

'Why are you crying, Yukio-san?' said Jebu softly. 'Is it from joy at our victory?'

'I am thinking about the Takashi, and how nothing lasts,' said Yukio slowly. 'How magnificent they were when I was a boy.

How swiftly their glory has vanished. How long will the kami permit us to enjoy our own victory?'

The following morning, as they sailed eastwards past jewel-like islands, a samurai reported to Yukio that Lady Harako had disappeared during the night.

'It is better for her,' said Moko. 'She said she was with child. Before I left Kamakura, Lord Hideyori had issued orders that all whose descent could be traced from Sogamori's grandfather are to be sent beyond. Her baby would have been torn from her as soon as it was born. Now they will sit together on the same lotus blossom in the next world.'

With a chill, Jebu remembered that Atsue had said his wife at Heian Kyo, Princess Kazuko, had a child by him. Taniko's grandson or granddaughter.

'How admirable was the Lady Harako's determination to kill herself,' said Yukio. 'How pathetic is Takashi no Notaro's clinging to a useless life. I hope I may have the wisdom to see it, when I no longer belong in this world, and have the grace to step cheerfully into the Void.'

CHAPTER SIXTEEN

The captain of the guard at the bridge over the Rokuhara's broad moat made a face of revulsion. 'It is not a pleasant thing to see children buried alive, and their mothers stabbed or strangled.'

'Who orders these executions?' Jebu asked the captain, his heart filled with foreboding.

'A tribunal presided over by Lord Shima Bokuden of Kamakura and Prince Sasaki no Horigawa,' the captain answered. 'They act as deputies of my lord Hideyori.'

Horigawa. At the sound of the name the hairs on the back of Jebu's neck prickled, and his hands itched to crush the scrawny windpipe.

'Just as I told you, shiké,' said Moko. Mounted on horses, Jebu and Moko stood side by side at the entrance to the

Rokuhara. Hideyori had commanded that the Takashi stronghold be rebuilt. It was now Bakufu headquarters in Heian Kyo. The three towers of the Rokuhara stood tall and forbidding again, as they had in the days of the Takashi, except that now the banners that bedecked the upcurving roofs were white. Meanwhile, the Imperial Palace to the north was still a blackened ruin, and no Son of Heaven occupied the throne. After the Muratomo victory in Shimonoseki Strait, old Go-Shirakawa, the Retired Emperor, could no longer delay bestowing on Hideyori the title he craved, Shogun, Supreme Commander. The new overlord of the Sunrise Land was now deciding at his leisure which of several pliable candidates would sit on the Imperial throne.

'Is the Imperial Princess Kazuko here at the Rokuhara?' Jebu asked. He had not forgotten Atsue's concern for his young wife.

'All members of the Imperial family are housed here under the protection of the Muratomo,' said the samurai captain. His right cheek was riven by a scar that ran from temple to jaw. He spoke with the harsh accent of the eastern provinces, but there was respect in his voice when he addressed Jebu, whom he recognized at once as the legendary shiké who accompanied Lord Yukio in exile and in triumph.

'Is she one of those to be judged by the tribunal?'

'Yes,' said the scarred samurai. 'It is said that her son is a direct descendant of that devil Sogamori. The child surely will not be allowed to live, but Prince Horigawa and Lord Bokuden are dealing with the easier cases first. Those involving the Imperial family require more delicate handling. What is your interest in the princess, shiké?'

Delicate handling indeed, Jebu thought, considering that the child whose execution was being prepared was Bokuden's own great-grandson. Not that Bokuden would care about putting a member of his own family to death. If Taniko knew what was happening, though, she might use her influence with Hideyori to win a reprieve. But it would take thirty or forty days for a message to reach Kamakura and the reply to be received. By that time the boy would probably be in a premature grave. It was necessary to act immediately.

'I was there when the Takashi noble to whom Princess Kazuko was married fell in battle at Ichinotani,' Jebu said. 'I promised him that I would tell the princess how he died. Where are the Imperial ladies quartered?'

The samurai indicated one of the Rokuhara's newly rebuilt stone towers, but added, 'You should apply to the secretary of the tribunal for permission to see her.'

'There is no need. It is a small matter, and I'll only spend a moment with her.'

'If it were anybody but you, Shiké Jebu, I would refuse you admittance,' said the captain. 'But I cannot say no to a hero of the War of the Dragons.'

'Thank you for your courtesy, captain,' said Jebu.

The scarred samurai bowed. 'Nagamori Ikyu, at your service, shiké.'

'Moko-san, I'll go on alone,' said Jebu. 'Do you remember the shrine of Jimmu Tenno on Mount Higashi?'

Moko's crossed eyes were wide with anxiety. 'I can never forget it, shiké.'

'Be there with your escort, prepared to travel back to Kamakura, at the Hour of the Ape.' Moko had used his new wealth to hire and equip an entourage of samurai who saw to it that he was treated with proper respect despite his lack of skill at arms.

Jebu dismounted and walked his horse across the bridge over the Rokuhara's moat, wide as a river. 'The kami grant that I see you again, shiké,' Moko called. Jebu led his mount through the maze of narrow, high-walled passages designed to foil attackers. Tethering the horse before the thick stone wall at the base of the tower where the Imperial women were quartered, he strode past guards who, like Captain Ikyu, recognized him with awe. No one stopped him until he reached the second floor of the tower. There an old dragon of a lady-in-waiting, seated at a teak table piled high with scrolls, demanded to know his business. He asked for Princess Kazuko.

'What right has a mere warrior monk to request an audience with an Imperial princess?'

Jebu was amused at her ferocity. 'As a disgraced member of the Imperial family, she is not so far above me.'

'She is not disgraced. She has not been judged.' Jebu sensed sympathy for the princess in the elderly woman's tone.

145

'You need not protect her from me. I'm here to help her if I can.'

'How can I be sure of that?'

'If I were from Lord Bokuden and Prince Horigawa, would I need permission to see the princess?'

A short time later Jebu was in a small chamber facing a shadowy figure behind a screen painted with wild roses. The lady-in-waiting sat behind him. He could hear her agitated breathing.

'I don't understand why you want to help us. You killed Atsue.' The voice was soft, melodious, the accent cultivated.

'Your husband died in battle, Imperial Highness. It was not I who killed him. Of all the Takashi, Atsue was the one I would never knowingly kill.'

'Why?' asked the gentle voice.

'Many years ago I vowed my life to the service of Atsue's mother, the Lady Shima Taniko.'

'Were you her lover?'

'Your Imperial Highness is quick to sense feelings.'

'But Atsue's father was Takashi no Kiyosi.'

'Karma has forced Lady Taniko and me to spend most of our lives apart, but that has not diminished my love for her.'

'A samurai lady and a warrior monk. How very sad and how beautiful.'

Jebu brought the conversation back to the business at hand. 'The fact that you are of the Imperial house will not save your son from death, princess. Horigawa and Bokuden have only to write the necessary decrees to make it legal and proper to execute the boy.' There was a whimper from behind the screen. The princess made a hushing sound.

'I'm sorry,' said Jebu. 'I would never have spoken so frankly if I had known the child was there.'

'I have heard that the children of the Zinja are introduced to the fear of death at an early age,' said Princess Kazuko. 'If Sametono is to live at all, he must learn to live with death. I am prepared to trust you, Zinja. If we stay here Sametono will certainly die. What do you want us to do?'

'The trick I have in mind is an old and obvious one, but it is to our advantage that they will not expect you to try to escape. After all, you have never been outside Heian Kyo. You would not even know how to speak to a common person to ask for help. You are as much a prisoner of your way of life as of the Muratomo. As for the Muratomo, their discipline is slack. They've been fighting for five years, and they want to rest.'

'But where can you take us?'

'To Kamakura, to the one person in the Sacred Islands who can save the boy's life, the Lady Shima Taniko. She is the child's grandmother and she is said to be close to Hideyori.' The words tasted bitter in his mouth.

There was a cry of horror from the old lady. 'She is the daughter of Lord Bokuden and the wife of Prince Horigawa. Why should she of all people help the princess?'

Jebu turned to her. 'She, better than anyone, knows that pair for the despicable scoundrels that they are. When she realizes that they intend to kill her grandson, she will do everything in her power to thwart them.'

'Kamakura,' the princess wailed. 'That is the end of the world. Muratomo no Hideyori is there. How can we be safe in Kamakura?'

'If the Lady Taniko can persuade Lord Hideyori to place you and your son under his protection, Kamakura will be the safest place for you in all the Sacred Islands. Can you ride a horse?'

'Certainly not.'

'A pity.' He turned again to the old lady. 'Can you find two trustworthy servants who will take her and the boy out of here in a sedan chair? She can wear the robes of a lady-in-waiting, and the boy can hide under her skirts.'

'Women of low rank enter and leave the Rokuhara regularly,' said the lady-in-waiting. 'As you say, the guards are lax. I can supply the costume she needs and find two men who will not know whom they are carrying.'

'Good. Where the Sanjo Avenue leads to the foot of Mount Higashi there is a bridge across a small stream. I will be waiting there.'

Jebu tethered his horse at the far end of the bridge, recrossed it and seated himself on a huge boulder from which he could look out over Heian Kyo. There were so many new buildings going up that the capital reminded him of Kublai Khan's Khan Baligh. The small of fresh-cut wood and the ringing of hammers filled the air. Oxen strained at wagon-loads of timber. It was a carpenter's paradise. If Moko were not already rich, and if the carpenters' guild of Heian Kyo were not so rigid about whom they allowed to work in the city, he could have made a fortune here.

It was dusk when a plain sedan chair carried by two servants emerged from the nearby Rokuhara and approached the bridge. Shouldering his naginata, Jebu stepped forward and identified himself to tue bearers. He heard the princess's frightened voice from within the chair's curtains. But at that moment the shout of warriors' voices and the clatter of hooves arose from within the Rokuhara's walls.

'Over the bridge,' Jebu snapped to the bearers. 'Run!'

Casting terrified looks at him, the men picked up the chair and ran for the bridge.

'Stop! Halt with that chair!' The voice that shouted at them was familiar. A band of Muratomo samurai raced across the moat and up the avenue towards them. Behind them, riding on the shoulders of a brawny, half-naked servant, was Prince Sasaki no Horigawa.

'Run!' Jebu called. But the bearers, looking back, recognized the prince and obeyed his order to stop. Jebu stood blocking the bridge. A circle of bystanders formed, a healthy distance from Jebu and the samurai. Jebu stared at Horigawa. The old prince's face was more withered and shrunken than Jebu remembered it, but his back was straight and the hands resting on his servant's head did not tremble.

Jebu had not seen Horigawa since that day, over twenty years ago, when he fled from the guardhouse at Daidoji. All those years he had dreamed of killing the prince, knowing all the while that to harbour such a desire went against all his Zinja training. Even the years of contemplating the Jewel day after day did not help where Horigawa was concerned. He had prayed that the prince might die during the War of the Dragons, as had so many thousands of others, so that he would be relieved of this foolish desire for revenge. Karma, it seemed, would not have it so.

Now he wanted nothing more than to plunge into the midst of Horigawa's samurai, whirling his naginata to knock the guards aside, and lop the prince's head off. He realized that, as had happened so many years before at Daidoji, he could not kill

Horigawa and accomplish his purpose. The instant he left his post at the bridge, the samurai would seize Kazuko and her son, Sametono.

'When I heard that you had visited the Rokuhara I knew some evil was in the air,' said Horigawa. 'We were not able to move quickly enough to stop this renegade daughter of the Imperial house and her tainted offspring from escaping. Her corrupt servant has paid with her death for her part in this escapade, though. Now that the princess has admitted her guilt by fleeing, she shall stand trial at once. Aside, monk, or you die on the spot.'

'If the princess is a renegade and the child is tainted, what of a prince who served the Takashi cause for a quarter of a century, to switch sides only yesterday, as it were, to the Muratomo?' Jebu could see approval in the eyes of the samurai who faced him. They would obey the prince's orders as a matter of duty, but they would do it with reluctance.

'I do not need to justify myself to a bandit masquerading in monk's robes,' Horigawa said with a sneer. 'Step aside.'

For answer Jebu took a firm grip on his naginata and set his feet wide apart in the stance called the Bear at Bay.

'Kill him,' Horigawa said.

'But, Your Highness, this monk has fought beside Lord Yukio in all the great battles of this war,' said the scarred samurai officer, Captain Ikyu, who had let Jebu enter the Rokuhara a few hours earlier.

'That war is over,' Horigawa rasped. 'It will soon be shown that our honoured Shogun's half-brother and all who are close to him are traitors to his family and the Sunrise Land. Kill him, I say.'

A samurai drew his tall bow and let an arrow fly at Jebu. With a quick, easy swing of his naginata Jebu cut the arrow in half, and it fell, harmless, at his feet. Arrow cutting with the naginata was a daily exercise for every Zinja from the age of eight. At first the arrows used were tipped with leather balls that left a painful bruise but did not pierce the body. Later the arrows had pointed metal tips and the young monks were expected to pick off as many as twelve of them fired simultaneously at close range. Now Jebu went to work with utter concentration and instantaneous reflexes. His naginata became a blur as he chopped arrows out of the air as fast as they could be fired at him. Even as they tried to kill him, the samurai cried out with admiration at his virtuosity. Horigawa's wrinkled face was red with rage.

'Shoot at the chair,' he called suddenly. 'It is the princess we must stop, not this worthless monk.'

'No,' Jebu cried as a flight of arrows whistled over his head. They rained upon the green-curtained chair and its bearers. The two servants died without a sound. There was a choking scream from within the chair. Jebu felt rage surge like lava through his body.

'Now I will kill you as I have always wanted to,' Jebu growled, striding forward into a storm of arrows, his naginata at the ready. Arrows struck his armour and wounded him, but failed to penetrate deeply, and he ignored them. Horigawa muttered a command to the brawny man on whose back he rode, and the servant turned and ran full speed down the avenue towards the Rokuhara's eastern gate. Jebu started to pursue them, but the samurai barred his way with a fence of swords.

'We don't want to kill you, Master Jebu,' panted Ikyu. 'We've done our duty, that's all.'

'That woman and her child harmed no one,' Jebu grated.

'Most of the tens of thousands who fell in the late war were innocent of wrongdoing, too,' the scarred officer answered. 'Let this end here, shiké. We do not wish to shed your blood and you do not wish to shed ours.'

'Some day I will kill Horigawa,' said Jebu. He was ashamed of the words as soon as they left his lips, but they expressed his true feelings.

'Such a desire is not worthy of you, shiké,' said the samurai leader. 'Horigawa's death at your hands would honour him, but it would do you nothing but dishonour to kill that feeble old stick of a man.'

'That feeble man has been the cause of more spilt blood in the last thirty years then the fiercest warrior who ever lived in these islands,' Jebu said. 'Still, I accept your correction.' He recalled how, years ago, he had thought of the samurai as foolish and destructive, like cruel boys. Either they had learned much in the interim, or he had, and was now seeing them differently. He bowed to the samurai leader to show his respect.

'I will guard the bodies of the princess and her son until you can send servants to take them back to the Rokuhara,' Jebu said.

'Very good, shiké,' said Captain Ikyu. 'We will also post guards at the approach to the bridge, but you may say your farewell to her in private.' The samurai marched away, and Jebu walked to the middle of the bridge, murmuring a prayer for the dead. The bearers lay sprawled in awkward positions, arrows protruding from their backs. Jebu gently drew the chair's curtain aside. A woman dressed in a plum-coloured robe sat slumped forward, her long black hair hanging down like a veil. He could see at once, from her absolute stillness, that she was dead. Two arrows had gone into her back, and her skirts were soaked with blood. He took hold of her shoulders with both hands and raised the lifeless weight. Her face, which as an Imperial princess she had hidden from the world, was round and pretty, with small features. Her mouth hung open, revealing teeth dyed in the Court fashion, like rows of tiny black pearls. She had been brave. She might have been allowed to live if she had surrendered her son to the executioner. She chose instead to lose her life trying to get the child out of the Rokuhara. Under the Princess's inert body Jebu saw a small black head and two hands clinging to her skirt. The hands moved slightly. He drew in a breath.

'I know you're alive,' he whispered. 'Are you hurt?'

'No,' the boy said softly.

'We must move quickly. I'm going to pull you out of the chair and put you on my horse. Get ready.' Jebu reached into the sedan chair with both hands, dragged the boy out from under his mother's body, and straightened up. Clutching Sametono to his chest, Jebu ran across the bridge to his tethered horse. The guards at the other end of the bridge were only beginning to react, shouting at Jebu to halt as he leaped into the saddle and set the boy in front of him. As they galloped off, arrows flew past them. Two struck Jebu in the back, but they were not strong enough to pierce his armour, though they lodged in its plates. Sametono was silent. Jebu could feel that the boy's body was rigid with fear. The horse plunged through the twilight along a pine-shaded path that wound up the side of Mount Higashi. The guards at the bridge had no horses, and it would be a long time before they could bring help from the Rokuhara. By that time Sametono would be safely with Moko and his men. Twenty years ago, Jebu thought, Horigawa killed our daughter. Now I have saved this boy from him. He exulted in the thought. It was far more satisfying to save a life from Horigawa than to have killed Horigawa himself.

'Where are you taking me?' Sametono asked. His small body had relaxed somewhat against Jebu's chest.

'To your grandmother.' Jebu knew that Hideyori might yet insist on the boy's death. And even if the gift of Sametono changed Taniko's feelings towards Jebu, that wouldn't matter if she needed her closeness to Hideyori to save the boy's life. The horse breathed hard as it climbed the steep path. A three-quarter moon, rising over the mountains east of Heian Kyo, provided Jebu and his mount just enough light to see by. It had been a full moon, Jebu recalled, the night he and Taniko had pledged to love each other forever on this same mountain. He heard a jingling of harness and a stamping of horses' hooves ahead. Moko.

Moko and Sametono both looked woeful when Jebu said he would not make the journey to Kamakura. 'I must go to Lord Yukio at once,' Jebu explained. 'Something Horigawa said just now warned me that he is up to his old trick of setting samurai against samurai. Yukio must be warned, or he may not have long to live. Meanwhile, Horigawa and Bokuden will have the Tokaido searched for me, thinking I have the boy. By the time they realize I'm still in Heian Kyo I'll be under Yukio's protection. You and your men have a better chance of getting through, hiding Sametono among yourselves. Remember that you are to take him directly to the Lady Taniko and no one else.'

'Thank you for rescuing me, big monk,' said Sametono, looking at Jebu with that calm, intelligent gaze he remembered so well in Taniko.

'You kept still until I could reach you while your mother lay dead on top of you,' said Jebu. 'You are a young man of great mental power, if you know what that means.'

'I hope I grow up to be as tall as you.'

Jebu thought, I doubt whether any of us will live to see you grow up, little boy.

CHAPTER EIGHTEEN

Hideyori pressed his hand against her breast. Taniko allowed it to remain there. A flicker of surprise crossed his stony features.

'Are you starting to find me more attractive?'

'I have always found you attractive, my lord. I only wonder what you see in such a pathetic old woman.' Gently, Taniko drew away from him and began to pour *ch'ai* from a three-hundred-year-old T'ang bowl. 'Is my lord aware that I am a grandmother?'

'You have never mentioned it before.' That was not a direct answer. She was sure he knew nearly everything about her. Hideyori seated himself cross-legged, arranging the dark robe over his knees, and sipped the foaming green *ch'ai* from a delicate, glazed cup that matched the bowl. He kept his bedchamber austere as ever, but the objects he used now were precious and beautiful enough for an Emperor.

'My grandson arrived in Kamakura only yesterday,' said Taniko, folding her hands in her lap and looking sedately down at them. This matter had to be handled with exquisite care. Perhaps it did not matter how it was handled, perhaps Sametono was doomed in any case. Taniko thought she had a proposal that would persuade Hideyori to spare Sametono, though, by appealing to the Shogun's desire to stabilize the realm. She had talked it over with Eisen the night before, after Sametono arrived. The monk agreed that her idea might work.

'But it means you must sacrifice the rest of your life,' the Zen master pointed out.

'There is no one to make the sacrifice and no future to be sacrificed,' Taniko rejoined.

'Your words stink of Zen,' Eisen shot back. Taniko knew that this was a grudging compliment to her deepening understanding. Eisen hardly ever encouraged her, believing, as he put it, that praise is poison. She did not need him to tell her that she was making progress. She knew now that you could not acquire true understanding from anyone else, and no one could give you

153

enlightenment. All you could do was increase your awareness that you already were a Buddha, an Awakened One. Only you could do that for yourself. As she moved through each day in a state of awareness maintained, enhanced and deepened by sitting in zazen meditation, she found that her decisions were right for each situation, and their consequences more beneficial to all. At the same time, she cared less about results. She did what she felt an enlightened person would do and refused to concern herself about whether things turned out as she wished.

Now, rage threatened to break through her philosophical calm. The wound left by Horigawa's murder of her baby at Daidoji had never healed. Nothing could rouse her to a more consuming anger than the thought of a child being killed. That children were being drowned and buried alive at Heian Kyo was hateful enough. That Horigawa was supervising the executions – with her own father helping him – tore that old wound open to bleed afresh. That her grandson, Atsue's son, had nearly been one of the victims left her speechless with fury when Moko told her the tale and presented the wide-eyed, travel-weary child to her.

At first her rage was directed against Hideyori himself. He, after all, had given the command for the slaughter. After a time of meditation she realized that it was useless to hate Hideyori. He had lived with fear and death since his boyhood, and nothing could change him. Now that he had achieved supreme power he felt more vulnerable and more fearful than ever. How different he was from Kublai Khan, who easily assumed that the world was his by right of birth.

'I have heard news that distresses me sorely,' she told Hideyori. 'Perhaps it would not move you, since you are a man and a warrior. I know what it is to have the child I bore torn from my arms and murdered. They are killing babies in Heian Kyo.'

For a moment Hideyori's face was blank. Then it rearranged itself into a mask of shock and sympathy. 'Who is killing babies, Taniko-san? By what authority?'

'My father and Prince Horigawa. By your orders, they say.' Taniko did not for a moment believe his air of surprise. These days, nothing went on in the Sunrise Land without his knowledge and permission.

'I have ordered the death penalty for all Takashi who threaten our peace,' said Hideyori. 'That is why I signed the warrant of execution for Notaro. I have never intended that children be killed.'

'I am happy to hear that,' said Taniko quickly. 'My grandson is a Takashi, but he is only four years old, and I am sure he has no desire to raise a rebellion against you.'

Hideyori looked away from her and was silent for a long time. This is the moment, she thought, that will decide whether Sametono lives or dies. Hideyori knows what I'm going to ask him. He will have to admit that he wants the child killed, or he will have to let the boy live with me. At last Hideyori turned to her, and she saw indecision in the dark eyes. Her hold over him was still strong.

'The blood of Sogamori and Kiyosi flows in his veins.' No more pretence that Hideyori was unaware of the boy's existence.

'The blood of Amaterasu Omi Kami flows in his veins as well,' said Taniko. 'Surely he is to be treasured for that.'

Hideyori shook his head. 'That only makes him more dangerous.'

'Besides all those illustrious ancestors, this little boy is the grandson of Shima Taniko,' Taniko said softly, 'if that means anything to you.'

'If it did not, he would be dead already.'

'If my lord could find a place in his heart for Sametono, my gratitude would know no bounds.'

Hideyori was silent. Each time she spoke, he weighed and digested her words, carefully calculating his reply. At last he gave a short, barking laugh.

'How ironic. Was this not precisely Sogamori's undoing? Was it not his lust for my father's mistress, the Lady Akimi, that persuaded him to spare Yukio's life – and incidentally mine? Shall I, for your sake, nurture a hatchling of the Red Dragon so that it may grow to devour my clan in turn?'

Now was the time to try him with her proposal. 'You have the power to change the hatchling's colour from red to white, my lord. Adopt him as your own son.' Hideyori looked amazed and angry. He opened his mouth to speak, but she hurried on. 'Forgive me for mentioning it, but it has been your karma not to have children of your own. You have no son to inherit the

Shogunate, this great title you have created for yourself. If you choose a successor from among your allies, you will make one family too powerful and all the others envious and rebellious. This boy's close kin are all dead, except for me. Make Sametono your son, and his cause becomes your cause. You never need fear that he will lead a rebellion against you. True, he is descended from Sogamori and Kiyosi, but what better way to heal the wounds of these years of civil war than by uniting the Red Dragon and the White in one family? If you do not have sons of your own blood, which is the worthiest in the land, you can at least choose your heir from the next best lineage – that of the greatest of the Takashi.'

Hideyori's frown deepened. 'Why should I concern myself with who succeeds as Shogun after I am gone?'

Taniko shrugged. 'True, you need not. If you don't, the samurai will undoubtedly turn to your younger brother, Yukio, who has a son of his own. Perhaps that would please you just as well.'

Hideyori's eyes glittered with rage, the reaction she had expected. 'Neither my half-brother nor any offspring of his shall ever succeed me.' He paused for a moment. 'Perhaps you are right. I must select my successor, and this boy may have been sent by the kami for that purpose. If I'm to adopt a son, he'll need a mother, won't he? I'll need a wife. I have desired you ever since I met you.' Hideyori clenched his hands in his lap. She knew that he burned to reach for her but was restraining himself. 'Will you sleep with me and even marry me, when the obstacle of Prince Horigawa is eliminated? What about the vow you told me of?'

'Eisen Roshi assures me that I may set aside my vow for a good enough reason. He says that the past cannot bind the present, because the present is all there is.' Actually, since there had never been any vow, she had never discussed it with Eisen, but the remark about past and present was one he had made to her once.

Hideyori shook his head. 'I do not like these teachings of the monk Eisen. I have talked with him, and he seems strange and irreligious to me. I suspect that the views of this Zen sect are not religion but a mockery of religion.'

'I have benefited profoundly from my study of Zen, my lord.'

'Your grandson is alive only because he is your grandson. Eisen has been allowed to settle here and gather disciples around him only because he is your teacher. Otherwise, I would have had him driven out long ago. I mean to bring order and discipline to that vast rabble of unruly monks that infest the Sacred Islands – as soon as I have dealt with other dangerous elements.'

Taniko knew that 'dangerous elements' meant Yukio. Ever since she had learned that Yukio had killed Atsue, she had given up pleading his cause to Hideyori. She could not believe that Yukio was as Hideyori believed him to be, a dangerous rival plotting to use his victories as stepping stones to supreme power, but it was also hard to imagine Yukio striking down a helpless, innocent boy. If he had done the one, perhaps he was capable of the other.

'Regardless of what Eisen says, I believe that your vow is binding, and I will not lie with you.' Hideyori smiled faintly. 'As you doubtless know, I do not lack for companions to share my bedchamber, even though, as you said, it is my karma to be childless. I want you because you are more beautiful and wiser than any woman I have ever known. When we are properly married, I will lie with you, not just for the pleasure of it, but to possess you utterly.' His pupils seemed to expand until they were huge black pools into which she felt herself falling. She ignored the fear that rippled through her. She was saving Sametono's life, she reminded herself.

'May Sametono live, and may he remain with me?'

'For the present. For the future, I will consider your suggestion, and I will observe the boy closely. Should his conduct even once give me cause to doubt him, he will be sent immediately into oblivion.' Taniko bowed her head in acceptance, but within she was aglow. She had won. Recognizing that the price of her victory was eventual marriage to Hideyori, she determined to press him for more concessions.

'What of the other children being killed in Heian Kyo in your name? Will you also put a stop to that?'

Hideyori smiled. 'The true samurai has compassion for the defenceless. I will order the killing of children stopped for your sake, and also because I want to be remembered in the chronicles as a man of compassion.'

Taniko whisked the green liquid in the *ch'ai* bowl to a froth and poured Hideyori another cupful. 'A handsome gesture, my lord, but it may be lost to the chronicles if all the condemned children are dead by the time your order reaches Heian Kyo. It is my father and Prince Horigawa who spattered blood on your reputation. If you were to punish them, it would show the world that they acted against your wishes.'

Hideyori stared at her, sincerely shocked. 'You advise me to punish your own father? Where is your filial piety?'

'The Sage has said that a wife shall forsake her own mother and father and give all her loyalty to her husband and his family. Anticipating our marriage, I make your interests paramount, my lord.'

'How would it be in my interest to turn your father against me? Your clan, the Shima, have always been my chief supporters.'

'That is precisely why you must not allow my father to become too powerful. He believes that he made you Shogun. He thinks himself your master, not you his. Who knows what he and Horigawa and Go-Shirikawa might be plotting down there in the capital?' The sure way to influence Hideyori was to play upon his suspicions. 'My Uncle Ryuichi would serve you better as chieftain of the Shima than my father.'

'Are you suggesting that I remove your father from the chieftainship of your clan? I sometimes think your designs are even vaster and bolder than mine. The time may come for such a drastic step. For now, I will let your father and the prince feel my displeasure, but I will not be as severe as you suggest. I am under obligation to them. Time after time when Sogamori's sword would have fallen on me, they shielded me.'

Taniko gave a cry of scorn, 'My lord, no one knows those two better than I do. Horigawa pressed Sogamori day and night to have you killed. I was at Horigawa's winding water banquet celebrating the Takashi victory over your father, Captain Domei. "Nits make lice," Horigawa said that evening, meaning you and Yukio. He changed his mind only when he realized that you could be of use to him. As for my father, I am sure he never told you this, but it was I who first put it into his mind to protect you. I wrote him a letter shortly after you went to him, suggesting that you would be more useful to him alive than dead.'

'I never knew that. I thought I had frightened and offended you that day I came to Daidoji seeking Horigawa. Why did you do that? Were you drawn to me even then?'

'To be honest, I was not, my lord.' It was Jebu and only Jebu who filled my heart in those days, she thought. 'I was simply meddling in politics. It's always been a vice of mine.'

'Vice? Hardly. Though you are a woman, you are more sagacious in matters of state than most men are. Perhaps you were an emperor or a prime minister in a previous life.'

'My incurable urge to involve myself in politics led me to arrange a rendezvous between Sogamori and Lady Akimi, Yukio's mother,' Taniko said. 'As you know, it was she who persuaded him to hold his hand from Yukio and from you as well. Horigawa was so enraged that your lives were spared that he sequestered me in the country. That is the man to whom you consider yourself obligated.'

Hideyori stared at her in surprise. 'I never knew you were so instrumental in that affair. It makes me all the more determined that you shall be the principal wife of the Shogun.'

Wife of the Shogun. Taniko's head spun with excitement. Not even an Empress would enjoy as much power.

'What of Horigawa?' she asked softly.

'To repay Horigawa for his complicity in the deaths of my grandfather, my father and so many other kinsmen of mine, he shall make a long overdue journey to the underworld. To reward him for his aid to me, which made possible the final victory of the Muratomo, I will see that his bereaved widow, Lady Taniko, is not only cared for fittingly, but exalted.' Hideyori grinned at her. 'Does that suit you, Taniko-san?'

Taniko bowed her head. She knew that Eisen would say that desire for revenge was an attachment she must break, but she could not help feeling a thrill at the thought that for her sake, the most powerful man in the realm was prepared to bring about Horigawa's death.

'It suits me,' she whispered.

'But, still –' Hideyori shook his head, 'the great-grandson of Sogamori to succeed me as Shogun? To inherit what I have created? Shall the reward of the thirty-year struggle of the

Muratomo to overthrow the Takashi be reaped by a Takashi? It is as if Sogamori had triumphed after all, in the end.'

'Who is the true father of a boy?' Taniko asked, having prepared beforehand to meet this objection. 'Is it not he who rears and shapes the child? Sametono never knew a father. He is only four years old. You will be his father, and the great Muratomo chieftains will be his ancestors. It is you, not Sogamori, who will win in the end, because you will have changed the last child of his line into a Muratomo.'

Hideyori gazed at her admiringly. 'Your mind slices like a sword into the heart of a problem. It is for this that I would make you my wife.' Then his expression hardened. 'But there is one more concession you must make to me. I know that Yukio was your companion in China and that you hold him in high esteem. You have always urged me to trust him. Now I must insist that you renounce your friendship for him out of loyalty to me. I have learned that he intends to destroy everything I have built.'

Taniko sighed. Those years in China seemed so remote. She was a different woman now. She saw Jebu again as he had looked in Kublai Khan's park at Khan Baligh that day they were reunited. Almost unrecognizable in his Mongol cap and cloak, his face gaunt, his red moustache drooping. It was Jebu who had rescued Sametono from the Rokuhara. Yet there had been no message from him, just Moko arriving with the boy.

'I have no idea what Yukio is doing now, my lord. How do you know he is plotting against you?'

'He has been in Heian Kyo ever since the battle at Shimonoseki Strait. His huge army is camped outside the city. He has begun the rebuilding of the Imperial Palace without my permission. He visits the Retired Emperor daily, and he is the darling of the Imperial Court. He has received numerous titles and honours and estates from Go-Shirakawa, including lieutenant in the Palace Guard.'

'I remember from my days at Court that most such honours bring with them no real power,' said Taniko.

'They are all ancient honours and should have been offered first of all to me, not to one of inferior birth, like Yukio. My father was captain of the Palace Guard. But these displays of Imperial favour are only the outward sign of the disease. I have learned that Yukio conspires with my enemies to take action against me and the Bakufu.'

'How do you know this, my lord?'

'I have received messages from your father.'

'It may be that the real conspirators are my father and Horigawa. Horigawa would like nothing more than to set you and Yukio at each other's throats. He has not given up his lifelong dream of destroying the samurai by pitting them against each other. He could be using my father. Indeed, Go-Shirakawa may have the same end in view. If the Muratomo quarrel among themselves, the Imperial Court gains power. Perhaps that is why the Retired Emperor shows so much favour to Yukio.'

'Everyone plots,' said Hideyori through clenched teeth. 'No one can be trusted. I can rely on men only to betray one another. Your father pretends to be Yukio's ally while reporting to me his plans and ambitions.'

'I know Yukio and I know my father. It is Yukio I trust.'

'Yukio killed your son.'

Taniko sighed. 'I can never be his friend, but I still believe him to be a man of honour.'

Hideyori's face darkened. 'You are a stubborn woman.'

His anger surprised Taniko. She realized that she was in danger, but his sharp words stung her to a quick retort. 'My lord, I am simply setting aside my own feelings about Yukio and telling you what I believe to be true. You did say, only a moment ago, that you think highly of my wisdom.'

'Yukio is my enemy.' Hideyori's eyes glittered with hate. 'From the day he escaped from the Rokuhara he has been trying to make himself chieftain of the Muratomo. While I was held prisoner here in Kamakura, Yukio was loose in the countryside, his every action a provocation to Sogamori to have me executed in retaliation. When Sogamori's son Kiyosi was killed during Yukio's escape from Hakata Bay, I was sure I was a dead man.'

Yes, yes, thought Taniko sadly, so much died when Kiyosi died.

'I would have been executed then, had not Horigawa chosen that moment to begin protecting me. Years later, Yukio returned with his army of Mongols and proclaimed himself clan chieftain, as if I were really dead. He found he could not dispose of me so easily. I risked my life to support his campaign against the Takashi, even though I was in a far more vulnerable position than he. I laboured in the shadows to found a new government, without which his victories would mean nothing. I sent him the ships he needed to win at Shimonoseki Strait. What I have done is ignored or condemned, while the land resounds with the praises of Yukio. Always Yukio, the mighty warrior, Yukio the brilliant general, Yukio the shining jewel of the house of Muratomo. I tell you, Yukio is nothing but a bandit, and his mother was nothing but a Court harlot, while mine was the daughter of a high priest. All friends of Yukio are my enemies, and I mean to destroy all my enemies. If you wish to live here with me, if you wish to adopt your Takashi grandson with my approval, you must bind yourself to me and to me alone. Do you agree to that?'

Taniko sat stunned. The wave of Hideyori's rage had crashed over her and receded, leaving a pool of despair. Much of what he said made no sense. Now she knew that Hideyori's hatred of his younger brother was a lifelong passion he would never be able to relinquish. Anything she might say to correct or contradict him could mean death for herself and Sametono. She was a prisoner. Hideyori would make use of her intelligence, yes, but for his own mad and murderous purposes. She would have no power as the Shogun's wife. She could only be the Shogun's instrument.

'I agree, my lord.' Even though she knew she must hide her feelings, she could not hold back her tears. Hideyori watched her for a moment, then reached out and took her hand.

When he spoke again, his tone was more reasonable. 'Taniko-san, I know you feel under obligation to Yukio. Perhaps you feel pity for him. I, too, have not forgotten that he and I have the same father. I fear him because in the capital his innocence can be victimized by flatterers and dangerous influences. He is the sort of man around whom rebellious forces might gather, and there are many powerful persons who oppose the new order of the nation. I simply want Yukio in a less dangerous position.'

Hideyori's sudden change of manner left Taniko even more uncertain about what he intended. In a way it was more

162

frightening than his previous rage had been. In her mind she said, homage to Amida Buddha.

From the pillow book of Shima Taniko:

It is now eight days since I agreed to Hideyori's terms. I went to see Eisen and told him of the shape my future appears to be taking. I asked his advice and he merely said, 'Show me the face you had before you were born.' Zen monks like to meditate on such strange-sounding problems as this, which their Chinese predecessors called *kung-an*, questions. Eisen had promised me a *kung-an* to study, but I hardly expected to get one instead of advice about Hideyori. Is this Eisen's way of saying I should not think so much about my problems?

'Next time you come,' Eisen said, 'bring the boy.'

Messengers have gone to the capital bearing decrees that strip my father and Horigawa of their powers as deputies of the Shogun, charging them with excessive zeal in executing women and children connected with the Takashi. My father is ordered to return to Kamakura. To think that he might have killed his own great-grandson. I am determined that he shall not enjoy power as long as I can prevent it.

Hideyori is also moving against Yukio. The day after we spoke he sent an order that no man under the Shogun's authority may receive titles, gifts or offices from anyone else without the Shogun's permission. Two days after that he followed with a letter reprimanding Yukio in insulting language for having accepted promotion to the Fifth Rank of nobility and the title of lieutenant in the Palace Guard from Go-Shirakawa, ordering him to give these honours up at once. At the beginning of the new year, he says, he will relieve Yukio of his command. It seems to me dangerous for Hideyori to offend all his vassals in Heian Kyo at the same time. Might they not band together against him? Hideyori does not think so. He says that if a ruler is going to injure his subjects, he must do all the harm at once, so that it will be over quickly, while benefits should be conferred gradually, so that men will remember them longer. He means only to frighten Horigawa and my father back into line. His attack on Yukio, though, is the first step in stripping Yukio of power. All men will realize that, Hideyori thinks, and they will abandon Yukio, leaving him alone and helpless.

Jebu, as far as I know, is still with Yukio. It has been so long since I've seen Jebu. Truly, he has washed Kiyosi's blood from his hands by his brave rescue of my little Sametono. I pray that he will not be dragged down in Yukio's ruin. Still, I cannot forgive Yukio for Atsue's death. Why has Jebu never sent a message to me? No matter, there is no future for Jebu and me. I shall soon belong to Hideyori.

Yesterday, while meditating on my *kung-an* after my midday meal, I remembered what Hideyori had said about my having been an Emperor or prime minister in a previous life. I set out at once to tell Eisen I had already solved my *kung-an*. With Sametono perched on the saddle in front of me and the inevitable pair of samurai Hideyori always sends with me whenever I leave the Shogun's palace riding behind us, I directed my favourite mare up into the hills to Eisen's temple. It now consists of three buildings. Eisen has four young monks and two elderly retired samurai studying with him. Sametono and I were admitted at once into Sensei's chamber.

'Show me the face you had before you were born,' he said without a word of greeting as soon as I was seated before him. His own face was as stern as a boulder, and I quailed a little.

'I believe now that before I was born I must have been an official at Court, or perhaps even an Emperor of olden times. This would explain why affairs of state fascinate me so.'

'Rubbish,' Eisen snapped. 'Individual persons do not pass from one life to the next. You do not understand the true meaning of rebirth.'

If I do not, I thought, then neither does Hideyori. 'Who is it that is reborn then if not the person?' I asked.

Eisen threw his hands in the air and shouted, 'Kwatz!' I was startled, even though Sensei has done this to me several times before, usually when I ask him a question about religion.

Sametono was amused. He laughed so hard at Eisen's outburst that he fell over sideways on the mat. My heart melted at the sight of that round little boy rolling on the floor. He looked exactly as I remember Atsue looking at the age of four. My eyes grew wet, but I frowned at him for behaving so in Sensei's chamber.

'This boy has more of Zen in him than many an aged monk,' said Eisen with great seriousness. 'Learn from him, Lady Taniko, and protect his attainment. Do not let his Buddha-mind become clouded over as he grows older.'

We left Eisen's temple, my *kung-an* still unsolved. All the way down from the Hills Sametono kept shouting, 'Kwatz! Kwatz!'

—*Seventh Month, fifteenth day*
YEAR OF THE HORSE

CHAPTER NINETEEN

The three bodies lay side by side on a dais. The two men and the woman were dressed in their finest robes, only their pallid faces visible amid folds of shining cloth arranged to hide their awful wounds. They had committed seppuku. First Shenzo Saburo had disembowelled himself with his short sword, then his best friend had beheaded him to end his pain. In turn, Saburo's friend had cut his own belly open and been decapitated by Saburo's son, Totomi. Meanwhile, Saburo's wife, in the women's quarters, had joined her husband in death by severing the main artery in her throat with a small dagger.

Shenzo Saburo had been one of Yukio's most trusted, respected officers all during the War of the Dragons. Now he lay dead with his wife and his friend in the main hall of his Heian Kyo mansion, and Yukio wept for one of his oldest comrades. Wiping his eyes with the sleeve of his robe, Yukio turned to Shenzo Totomi, who stood respectfully by, his face pale, his eyes huge with the solemnity of the things he had seen and done.

'Why did your father do this?'

'Out of love and loyalty for you, my lord,' said the young man. 'When the new commander Lord Hideyori appointed over your troops declared that you are a traitor to the nation and have been plotting against the Shogun, my father felt he must protest in the strongest possible way. My lord, may I present to you my father's death poem and his final testament?'

Yukio nodded, and with a deep bow the young man drew a

165

scroll from his sleeve. 'My father's last poem is dedicated to you, Lord Yukio.' Yukio read the poem, first silently, then aloud:

> On a hilltop in Yamato
> Stands a solitary pine
> Unaware of the approaching storm.

To Jebu the meaning of the poem was transparent, as it doubtless was to everyone else in the room. Yukio shut his eyes and again used his silk sleeve to wipe away tears from cheeks as pale as those of the dead. Now Saburo's son offered him another scroll, the testament. Yukio began to read it. Jebu noticed that many more men, samurai and servants, had entered the room to listen. Saburo's letter began with a recitation of the Shenzo family tree, just as if he were challenging someone on the field of battle.

Then Yukio read, 'I have tried to warn the lieutenant that he is permitting a great wrong to be done to himself, his family and his loyal followers. Honour forbids him to hear my warning. Therefore honour requires me to choose this drastic way of reaching his ear. I plead with him not to let my death and the deaths of those close to me go to waste.' Yukio stopped, unable to continue, filled to overflowing with tears. He thrust the scroll at Jebu.

Jebu found the place where Yukio had left off and took up the reading. 'My lord, your brother sat safely in Kamakura while you were in the forefront of every battle. He envies your glory and fears your prowess, and he means to destroy you. Your enemies are gathering. Your brother presumes, as did the Takashi, to give orders to the Emperor himself. Shall the Sacred Islands be enslaved by another upstart tyrant? My lord, place yourself at His Imperial Majesty's disposal before it is too late. Arise. Arm yourself. Attack.'

'Read no more,' said Yukio. 'This is treason.'

'It is you who are betrayed, my lord,' said Shenzo Totomi.

Yukio shook his head. 'I have never wanted anything but the victory of the Muratomo, and the chieftain of the Muratomo is my brother, Lord Hideyori, the Shogun.'

'Your first loyalty is to the Emperor and to the Sacred Islands, honoured lieutenant,' said Totomi quietly.

Yukio's large eyes bulged with rage. 'Do not call me by that title. I have relinquished it. Do you dare to tell me my duty?' His pale face darkened to a deep red, and Jebu tensed himself, because he had never seen Yukio become this angry without reaching for his sword. Then Yukio smiled and sighed. 'I am sorry I spoke harshly to you. I forgive your forwardness. You are the son of an old comrade, and you have just lost your father. Remember this, though. Lord Muratomo no Hideyori is the protector of the Retired Emperor and of the Sacred Islands. His every action is for the good of the Crown and the realm.'

Shenzo Totomi's eyes fell. 'My lord, there was more to the testament. My father asks you to accept me in his place as your vassal.'

Yukio put his hand on the young man's shoulder. 'It is a great gift that your honoured father and you offer me, but if I accepted you into my service now I would expose you to mortal danger. I will not do that to the son of an old friend. The day may come when I will be able to receive your oath of fealty. For now, be patient, Totomi-san. I shall see you again at your father's funeral.'

That night Jebu and Yukio sat up talking until the Hour of the Rat. Yukio was melancholy. He seemed unable to make plans or decisions, even though he agreed with Jebu's assessment of the situation. As Jebu saw it, Hideyori had decided that he no longer needed Yukio, and he feared that Yukio might become a leader for those who opposed the new military government. Yukio had only two choices. He could go into hiding or he could do what Hideyori seemed to be expecting him to do, raise a revolt against the Shogun. If he did try to flee, Hideyori would undoubtedly track him down and try to kill him. Yukio's only hope was to fight back now, while there were many who still were willing to join him.

Yukio smiled sadly. 'Have you forgotten the years of blood and fire and famine? Do you want me to plunge the country into another war, just to save my own life?' Jebu had no answer. He wished Taitaro were there to advise them. His hand stole into his tunic pocket and fingered the Jewel of Life and Death.

'If I must flee,' said Yukio, 'I can go north to Oshu where my

167

wife and children are, where my father's old ally, Lord Hidehira, can protect me from my brother's hatred.'

'You are the only man in the Sunrise Land strong enough to stand up to Hideyori,' said Jebu. 'If you run from him, I doubt that anyone can protect you for long.'

'I will not break with my brother until I have made one last attempt to convince him that I am loyal and he has nothing to fear from me. I owe that much to our father and to our family.'

Looking at his friend, Jebu felt as if he were seeing Yukio's face for the first time. Gaunt and lined, it could have been the face of a saintly abbot – Buddhist, not Zinja – steeped in awareness of the suffering and transience of all things. He did not look like a man about to lead warriors into battle.

The glory of the Takashi is reduced to a few crimson rags drifting on the sea, Jebu thought, and now the glory of Muratomo no Yukio withers before my eyes.

From a letter from Muratomo no Yukio to Muratomo no Hideyori:
. . . All my life I have wanted only one thing, to be with my family. Our father was torn from us when I was an infant, and from that day to this my mind had never been at peace for a single moment. I grew up an orphan. Now I beg you, elder brother, to be a father to me. Weeping tears of blood, I beg of you to turn your wrath aside from me. I want nothing for myself. My victories were your victories. If my success in war has made you hate me, I wish I might have died on the battlefield. I have fought for only one reason, that I might expunge the disgrace, defeat and sorrow suffered by our father. I accepted the title of lieutenant and the other honours because I thought they would bring glory to the Muratomo. You are our father's successor on earth, and I live only to serve you. All that I have done, I lay at your feet. Let me come to you and plead my innocence face-to-face. Do not spurn me, for if you do, where on this earth can I turn?

—*Second Month, twelfth day*
YEAR OF THE SHEEP

A month after Yukio sent the letter, Jebu unrolled his futon and lay down to sleep, as usual, just outside Yukio's bedchamber.

From within he heard the plaintive sound of Yukio's flute accompanying a woman's sweet voice raised in song. The singer was a young woman named Shizumi, whom Yukio had taken as a mistress upon his triumphal return to the capital after Shimonoseki. Besides having a beautiful voice, she was considered the finest dancer in the land. Jebu lit a lamp and sat cross-legged on his mat, revolving the Jewel of Life and Death in his fingers as the mournful music fell, note by note, on his ears. That men and women could take the crude clay of painful human existence and shape it into poetry, music, art and dance was, at times, all that made life bearable. Tonight was the night of the full moon, whose beauty fascinated poets and scholars. Jebu lay down and dozed, but sleep came with difficulty. He could not forget that it was under a full moon that Taniko had lain in his arms for the first time.

He was suddenly awakened by the sound of stealthy footsteps in a nearby room. For a moment he was still reliving that night nearly thirty years ago when Taniko's soft footfall had roused him from sleep. Then he came back to the present. As always when he was unexpectedly awakened, he remained motionless. To the ear of a Zinja or any well-trained assassin, there was a difference between the small sounds made by a sleeping person and those made by one only pretending to be asleep. Jebu knew how to imitate those sounds. He allowed his body to shift from time to time as a sleeper would, all the while listening carefully to the movements in the next chamber. There were two, perhaps three, men on bare feet. They had avoided the singing boards placed throughout Yukio's mansion, floorboards that would creak loudly when stepped on. That meant they had help from members of Yukio's household.

Jebu heard a screen sliding back. Clearly the intruders were not trained to make an inaudible approach. Yukio's samurai guards might not hear anything, but to a Zinja it was as if an ox were being led through the mansion. The enemy probably knew Jebu was outside Yukio's room, and now that they could see him, they would try to kill him. At that very thought, Jebu heard the faint rasp of an arrow being pulled from its quiver and the creak of a bow being drawn. When he heard the archer take a sharp breath just before he let go the bowstring, he rolled to one side. The arrow thudded into the futon. Jebu shouted an alarm, seized his naginata and sprang. The archer was still holding the bow extended when Jebu drove his stiffened fingers into the man's windpipe, crushing it.

'Wolf! Wolf!' a man cried from behind the falling archer. At that signal more dark figures crowded into the room. Jebu swung the naginata in an arc that sliced through two of the attackers. Now there was light. The young dancer Shizumi stood in a white silk robe like the statue of a goddess, calmly holding aloft a lantern as her lover, Yukio, rushed into the fray, slashing with his long sword, recklessly naked, as if he didn't care whether an enemy blade bit into his unprotected flesh. Jebu scanned the raiding party looking for a leader. It would be important to leave at least one of the would-be assassins alive, to find out who was trying to kill Yukio. All the attackers were ragged Heian Kyo street toughs, except for one who wore black armour and had the shaven head of a Buddhist monk. As Yukio's guards poured into the room and blood splashed on the floor and flecked the walls, Jebu fell upon the warrior monk and knocked him senseless with the pole of his naginata.

Moments later all the attackers except the monk had been cut to bits. The monk lay in Yukio's bedchamber, glaring sullenly as Yukio pressed the point of his sword into his throat. He was stripped of his armour and wore only his saffron under robe. According to Yukio's guards there were twelve dead raiders in the anteroom.

'Tell me at once who sent you, or I'll cut your throat,' Yukio demanded.

The captured assassin's brown eyes remained opaque, his thin lips closed. 'I'll have him talking in an hour, my lord,' said the captain of the guard, anxious to make amends for his failure to protect Yukio.

'I would rather you inspected the household,' Jebu said. 'Find out how many guards these men had to bribe or kill to gain access to Lord Yukio.' He smiled at the captive. 'You and I are going to drink ch'ai and talk together, as one monk with another.'

When the ch'ai was brought, Jebu sat companionably on a straw mat beside the prisoner, who refused even to tell his name. Jebu poured a cupful of the steaming green liquid for himself and a cup for the monk. To the monk's cup he added a white powder from a paper packet. When he held out the cup, the monk pressed his lips tightly together and shook his head. Still smiling, Jebu reached over and pressed a spot uner the monk's ear. The shaven-headed man's mouth dropped open, though he remained seated upright. Jebu put his hand over the monk's face, pinching his nostrils together and tilting his head back. He poured *ch'ai* down the captive's throat.

'Now you will join me in prayer,' Jebu said. 'Homage to Amida Buddha.' Slowly, softly, Jebu droned the invocation over and over. At first the monk sat silently. Then, as if his lips and tongue had acquired a life of their own, he joined in the prayer. 'Very good,' Jebu said. 'Continue by yourself, please.' The monk went on repeating the invocation, his voice flat, lifeless. At last Jebu said, 'Now stop.' He leaned forward, bringing his face closer to the other man's.

'What is your name?'

'Yato,' said the monk in an empty voice.

'What monastery are you from, Monk Yato?'

'The Rodojo-ji, at Hyogo.'

'That temple was endowed by the Takashi,' said Yukio. 'Hyogo was their chief seaport. This monk must have been trying to avenge them.' He was sitting on his sleeping dais, dressed now in tunic and trousers, his sword in his lap. Shizumi crouched in a corner, the dark eyes in her pale face like two inkblots on a sheet of paper.

'I doubt it,' said Jebu. 'Now, Yato. You are a holy man. You have taken the Buddhist vow never to injure any living thing. You should take up arms only in defence of your temple. Yet, you tried to assassinate this noble lord who has never harmed a holy place. You have broken your vow, have you not?'

'My abbot commanded me,' said Yato dully. 'I could not disobey.'

'So, you had to choose between your duty to your abbot and fidelity to your vow,' said Jebu gently. 'That must have been hard. You carry a heavy karmic burden. If you tell us now why your abbot commanded you to kill Lord Yukio, it would lighten your karma somewhat.'

The monk's shaven head glistened with sweat. 'I am not permitted to tell.'

'Your superiors have forfeited their right to your obedience,' said Jebu. 'You are guilty of many wrongful deaths. The men you hired to help you in this attack, the guards you killed breaking into this mansion. Their angry spirits will pursue you until you atone.'

'We did not kill any guards. We bribed those who were on duty to let us in.'

'We will have to discover and execute the guards you bribed,' said Jebu. 'You are responsible. Who instructed your abbott to send you?'

The monk's lips moved, but he made no sound.

'You must tell me, Yato.'

The cords in Yato's neck stood out as he struggled with himself. At last, in a strangled voice, he said, 'It was the lord of Kamakura.'

'No!' Yukio cried.

Now that the barrier was broken, Yato's words poured out. 'It was Muratomo no Hideyori, honoured Shogun of the Sunrise Land. He promised benefits to our temple if we did what he asked of us and said we would suffer great harm if we did not. My Father Abbot told me I would be acting for the protection of my temple.'

'This monk lies,' Yukio snarled, gripping his sword hilt.

Jebu held up his hand in a restraining gesture. 'In his present condition, he cannot lie. You do not want to see what is so, do you, Yukio-san?'

Tears sparkled in Yukio's eyes. 'It is the end of all my dreams. I've helped to rebuild this land, and now there is no place for me in it. I can't rebel against my brother. All I want to do is serve him. Why won't he accept me? Why does he try to kill me? There is only one thing left for me to do. I must go to Kamakura alone and unarmed.'

'Do you think this monk is the only assassin your brother has sent out against you? He is too careful for that.'

'The Zinja monk speaks the truth,' a hollow voice said unexpectedly. Yukio and Jebu turned to Yato.

'What more can you tell us?' said Jebu.

'My abbot said that whether our effort to kill Lord Yukio succeeded or failed, the lord of Kamakura is sending an army to seize Heian Kyo and wipe out all Lord Yukio's friends and followers. The barbarian horsemen from the Sunset Land are even now on their way.'

'The Mongols?' said Yukio, stunned. 'Have the Mongols turned against me?'

'Were they ever really for you?' said Jebu. 'You no longer have an army of your own to command, Yukio-san. You cannot make a stand here. We must gather those we trust and escape from the capital at once.' A picture of Arghun Baghadur riding at the head of his *tuman* arose in Jebu's mind. If the Mongols travelled with their usual speed, they might be here before the news of their coming could precede them.

Staring uncomprehendingly, his cheeks still wet with tears, Yukio slowly stood up. Jebu had never seen him like this. He had to resist an impulse to shake his friend. He gestured to Shizumi, who was already gathering Yukio's robes, to help him dress and went out to give the necessary orders to the household.

CHAPTER TWENTY

From the pillow book of Shima Taniko:

Hideyori tells me again and again how valuable my counsel will be to him when I am his wife, but he rarely consults me these days. Marriage seems no closer. Horigawa still lives. All my news comes from the various lords and samurai officers who flatter me by calling on me when they come to Kamakura to report to the Bakufu. I suppose they cultivate me because I am close to Hideyori, but I like to think they also find my company interesting for its own sake.

Uncle Ryuichi is particularly helpful in keeping me informed. He says Yukio has disappeared and that he has only a dozen followers left, if that many, in the whole country. Last month Yukio raised a rebellion against Hideyori. He claimed that Hideyori had sent assassins to kill him. Hideyori, of course, denied it, charging that Yukio had arranged the incident to give himself justification for making war on his brother. Go-Shirakawa was convinced, though. He gave Yukio a commission ordering him to chastize

Hideyori as a rebel against the throne and an enemy of the Court. But Hideyori had already sent the Mongols to arrest Yukio, and Yukio was forced to flee the capital. When the Mongol army got near, Go-Shirakawa withdrew the commission and sent an apology to Hideyori, saying he had issued it under duress. Yukio fled south to Hyogo with a thousand warriors.

When he sailed from Hyogo one of those great storms that the Chinese call *tai-phun* came up and wrecked his ships near Shimonoseki, the very place where he won his great victory over the Takashi only two years ago. It is said that the angry ghosts of the Takashi called up the storm. I wonder if the ghost of my beloved Atsue was among them. There are rumours among the local fishermen that the shells of crabs caught in Simonoseki waters bear the imprint of the faces of Takashi warriors.

Yukio left his mistress, Shizumi, behind at Hyogo, which probably saved her life, but she was quickly captured by Hideyori's men. Poor thing, I hear she's pregnant. Now Hideyori has his men searching everywhere for Yukio. Even though Yukio was generally loved, when it came to an open break between the brothers, almost all samurai hastened to side with Hideyori. He has lands and offices to give away, while Yukio has nothing to offer but an unprofitable struggle against injustice.

For it is an injustice, what Hideyori is doing to Yukio; even I admit that in my heart.

Insisting that Yukio is still a threat to the peace and good order of the realm, Hideyori has extorted enormous concessions from the Court. He has been granted the power to tax the rice harvest of every estate in the Sunrise Land, income which he says he needs to pay for troops to search for Yukio. He also has the authority to appoint stewards and oryoshi in every province to enforce his decrees and collect the taxes. Land, after all, is everything. Now Hideyori has control of all the land in the realm, and Yukio helped him get it. Also, at his insistence, the vacant throne is at last to be occupied by the Imperial candidate of his choosing, Kameyama, a young grandson of Go-Shirakawa. So Hideyori is now a maker of Emperors. I have known many leaders – Sogamori, Kiyosi,

Kublai Khan, Yukio – but Hideyori has started with the least and accomplished the most of all of them.

It does not trouble me that he is too busy to pay much attention to me. Another man now absorbs all my time and thought, even though he is only five years old. Of course, I could let my ladies take charge of his care and education, but I do not trust the women Hideyori has appointed to serve me. Some are doubtless spies who might report any careless remark or small act of Sametono's to Hideyori in an unfavourable light.

I am seeking music, poetry and calligraphy masters for my grandson. There was a time when it would have been impossible to find a first-rate teacher of any art in Kamakura, but now that the centre of power is here, accomplished men are drawn to the north as bees to a flower. My cousin Munetoki has agreed to teach Sametono the martial arts. And, of course, the most important part of his education is that which he receives from Eisen.

Another friend we often see is Moko. He has two children now, a thirteen-year-old son named Sakagura, who was born the year we all left for China, and a new baby girl. He is on the way to the five – or was it six? – children he claimed when Jebu and I first met him. His shipbuilding trade, he says, is prospering. Whenever he comes to call, the first question we ask each other is, 'Do you have any news of Jebu?' Neither one of us ever does, and we shake our heads together in disappointment. If Jebu is still alive he is surely with Yukio, sharing his fate.

—*Fifth Month, twenty-first day*
YEAR OF THE SHEEP

At the beginning of summer, to celebrate the destruction of Yukio and his acquisition of new powers, Hideyori gave a great feast at the Shogunal castle in Kamakura. Over three hundred kenin, the highest-ranking samurai, filled the reception hall of the castle. Most of the guests sat at low individual tables enjoying the delicacies Hideyori had selected for the occasion. While their costumes were less elaborate and confining than the dress of the Imperial Court, these new masters of the Sunrise

Land wore equally fine materials, no less handsomely adorned. The treasures that had gradually been accumulating in Hideyori's castle, gold and silver drinking vessels, T'ang dynasty porcelain, ebony and rosewood tables, statuettes and vases of jade and ivory, ancient scrolls on which Buddhist verses were painted in gold leaf, all were brought out to decorate the hall. Five groups of musicians from aristocratic families played in turn, so that there was continuous music.

Hideyori's most important vassals sat with him on a dais at the north end of the hall under a canopy of plum-coloured silk. Among them were the heads of the powerful Shima clan, the brothers Bokuden and Ryuichi, as well as Ryuichi's son, the strapping young Munetoki. With them sat the chieftains of the Ashikaga, the Hiraga, the Wada and the Miura clans. Taniko knelt just behind Hideyori, silently pouring sake and serving morsels of vegetable and fish and rice to the Shogun.

Hideyori's eyes tonight were bright and beady, like those of a crow that has just captured a tender bit of meat. He wore a black ceremonial robe and a tall black cap of lacquered silk. Midway through the banquet he clapped his hands for attention, and the hum of conversation and the clatter of eating and drinking in the hall died away. The musicians fell silent.

'I have a special treat for all my guests now,' Hideyori announced to the hall at large. 'Here is a woman reputed to be the greatest dancer in the Sunrise Land. She comes to us from the Court at Heian Kyo, where she gave much delight to our new Son of Heaven, Emperor Kamayama, as well as to His Imperial Majesty's most honoured grandfather, the Retired Emperor. As well as others who were recently at the Court.'

There were a few chuckles in the hall from those who realized who the lady was and what Hideyori meant by 'others at the Court'. Taniko sensed what was about to happen, but somehow she had not thought Hideyori would stage this kind of public spectacle.

'In return for our hospitality this lady has agreed to entertain us,' said Hideyori, pleased with himself. 'Noble lords of the Bakufu, I present the Lady Shizumi.'

The doors at one end of the hall slid back and a tiny figure was revealed in the gallery leading from the women's house of Hideyori's castle. Taniko's first sight of Shizumi wrung her heart. Yukio's mistress was a beautiful young woman with huge dark eyes and red lips. Her long black hair hung unbound past her shoulders, black locks spreading protectively over her small breasts. She held herself very straight in a trailing robe of pure white silk, tied by a white sash. She is far more lovely than I was at her age, Taniko thought admiringly. She had heard Yukio's mistress was pregnant. There was no sign of it, but it was still cruel to put her through this ordeal.

Taking small steps, her eyes cast down, Shizumi moved into an open space in the centre of the hall.

'Why are you wearing the colour of mourning?' Hideyori demanded. 'I told you to put on your finest gown.'

'Please forgive me, my lord,' Shizumi said. 'This is my best gown.' She spoke softly, respectfully, but there was a strength in her voice that was surprising, coming from such a fragile-looking body.

Six musicians in Court dress with drums, bells, woodwinds and lutes glided from the gallery and seated themselves near the dais. Shizumi looked questioningly at Hideyori, and he nodded brusquely. She bowed to the musicians, drew an ivory fan from her sleeve and spread it open. Hideyori sat back with a smile, his hands resting on his knees. To force Yukio's mistress to entertain him and his guests made his triumph complete.

The first notes the musicians struck were slow, solemn, booming, like the tolling of a temple bell. Taniko realized at once that Shizumi's choice of white robes was no accident. Her dance was as mournful as her white raiment. Her measured steps, the bending of her body like bamboo in the wind, the horizontal rippling of her arms and the droop of her fan said that all things pass, happiness turns to sadness, each of us is alone at last. This was not what these leaders of samurai wanted to hear tonight, but it was a measure of Shizumi's talent as a dancer that she changed the mood of the gathering. Every head was still, every eye fixed on the flowing white figure in the centre of the hall. In the eye of many a scarred old eastern warrior there stood a tear. The woman in white was a cherry blossom, blown from the bough by the wind, fluttering to the ground. White, those watching recalled, was the colour of the Muratomo. One day, the dance whispered, even the victorious banner of the White Dragon must fall. The music ended with the same slow, ringing notes that began it. When Shizumi was done, she sank gracefully to the floor. There was no cheering, no applause, only a sigh that rustled around the hall like the wind in autumn leaves. A far greater tribute, Taniko thought.

Hideyori alone was displeased. He gnawed at his moustache, frowning angrily.

'That dance was not suitable for this occasion,' he growled.

'Nevertheless, it was exquisite,' Shima Ryuichi said gently. Taniko's respect and love for her uncle rose. He had indeed grown braver since the days when he trembled before Sogamori in Heian Kyo. Hideyori threw an irritated glance at him, then turned back to Shizumi.

'Sing something for us now. Something more cheerful.'

'I will sing of love, my lord.'

'Proceed.' Hideyori smiled thinly.

Shizumi nodded to the musicians. She sang in a voice that was rich and sad and husky, her red lips forming a circle on certain words, as if she were offering kisses to one who was not there.

> The memories of love settle like snow
> That drifts down from the mist on Hiei's crest,
> As I sit alone and the day grows dark.
> Ah, how I grieve for the beauty we lost.

> In the cloudland under a distant sky
> He lays his head beneath a snow-capped pine.
> That strange land is an ill place for my love.
> Ah, how I grieve for the beauty we lost.

Amazing, thought Taniko. What courage this young woman has. Hideyori tries to use her to celebrate his victory over Yukio, and she seizes the moment to proclaim that she still loves Yukio and mourns for him.

> In his mansion our pillows still remain
> Side by side, though we are a world apart,
> And I will not see him before I die.
> Ah, how I grieve for the beauty we lost.

'Enough!' Hideyori shouted. He sprang up, his face suffused

with anger. The musicians faltered to a stop. The hall was utterly silent as the guests stared, amazed, at the Shogun. Yukio, Taniko thought, you have triumphed over your brother even now.

'How dare you sing such a song here in my home,' Hideyori raged. 'How dare you sing of your illicit love for a rebel and a traitor.' His fingers twitched on the dragon-adorned hilt of the heirloom sword Higekiri that hung in a jewelled scabbard at his belt.

'My lord, it is the only love I know,' Shizumi said quietly. She stood with bowed head, hands folded before her. She is ready to accept anything, Taniko thought. If he kills her, she will die happily.

Taniko was on her feet. 'My lord.' She gripped Hideyori's sword arm with all her strength. He whirled on her, his eyes so wild with fury that he seemed not to see her.

'Take a moment to think,' Taniko whispered insistently. 'Remember who you are and where you are. You would disgrace yourself if you ruined your feast by murdering this child. Everyone would say that you made her the victim of anger because you could not find Yukio.' They stood, eyes locked, while Taniko asked herself, what am I doing, why am I standing here? I have forgotten myself as much as he has.

The rage faded from Hideyori's eyes, and a look of sullen anger replaced it. 'She will be punished.'

'She must not be punished,' said Taniko firmly, wondering at her own temerity. 'She has suffered enough and deserves no punishment. What is she but a helpless prize of war? You dragged her before your guests and forced her to sing, and she had the bravery to sing of her love. If you punish bravery, my lord, what kind of samurai are you? What this girl has done tonight will be remembered. When the tale is told, will you be spoken of as the cruel lord who rewarded her fidelity with death?' They both turned and looked down at Shizumi. The young woman had thrown her head back and was staring, face flushed and eyes burning with a pure fire, directly at Hideyori.

'Get her out of my sight,' Hideyori choked.

'I will, my lord.' Hiding her hands in her sleeves to conceal their trembling, Taniko stepped down from the dais and went to Shizumi. Taking the young dancer's arm, she led her through the silent crowd towards the gallery entrance. What have I done? Taniko thought. Why did I risk Hideyori's rage when I have been so careful with him all these years? I must be mad.

Her body went ice-cold as she realized the full enormity of her action – publicly thwarting Hideyori's wrath – but she also felt a satisfaction with herself that she had rarely known before. The feeling swelled, as they came to the doorway, to an exaltation almost like satori. She had acted immediately, impulsively, without a moment's consideration. It was Zen that had inspired her to do this. Those hours of meditation followed by gruelling sessions with Eisen in which he demanded an instant response to the absurd questions he asked her – this training made it possible for her to act as she had tonight. The consequences, for herself, for Sametono, for this girl, for everyone close to her, might be dreadful, but she could hear Eisen's voice saying, 'When you do what you know you should do, the results do not matter.'

But it was not just Eisen's influence. She remembered that long ago she had intervened to help a woman threatened by a tyrant. The woman had been the Lady Akimi, Yukio's mother. Now Shizumi was carrying Yukio's child. Strange are the meshings of karma, she thought.

Tonight I, a helpless woman, stood before the most powerful man in the land and defied his wrath to protect this girl beside me. Helpless? I am not so helpless, after all. As the two women walked together into the silence outside Hideyori's hall, Taniko's flesh tingled with excitement and the blood pulsed in her head, a pounding rhythm, like the beating of a taiko drum.

CHAPTER TWENTY-ONE

Six severed heads impaled on tall poles stood out dark against the cloudy sky. At first, climbing a hill, Jebu and the men with him saw only the heads, small black ovals far away. Then, when they reached the top of the hill, they saw the fort with its brown palisade, on a ridge still half a day's walking and climbing from where they were. They could see birds swooping and darting around the heads and hear their distant cries as they picked away the remaining morsels of flesh.

Yesterday, in the foothills of these mountains on the north-west coast of Honshu, Jebu and Yukio and their men had met a party of traders coming down from Oshu, Yukio's destination. The traders told them that the soldiers in the fort at Ataka had executed six monks travelling north on suspicion that they were followers of Muratomo no Yukio attempting to escape from the Shogun's wrath.

'The Shogun is turning the country upside down to find his fugitive brother,' said the leader of the trading party. 'I advise you, holy ones, to postpone your journey and turn back here, rather than try to get past the barrier forts just now. The soldiers would rather lop off a few innocent heads than let any of the Shogun's enemies through by accident. Of course, you may have business in the north that is worth the risk of your lives.' The trader's narrowed eyes roved shrewdly over Yukio and Jebu and the eleven men with them. What he saw, Jebu hoped, was a party of yamabushi, Buddhist mountain monks. All of them had shaved heads and wore saffron robes and torn quilted coats to keep out the cold of the Tenth Month, whose teeth grew sharper than a wolf's as they worked their way north.

'Buddha will watch over us,' Jebu replied piously to the trader. With his moustache and hair shaved off, only his height and his grey eyes might give him away. 'If our time comes, we are not afraid to die as long as we are fulfilling our duty.'

'Buddha did not watch over the six monks who died this morning, and they were afraid to die,' said the trader. 'All their prayers availed them not. They begged for their lives. You seem braver. More like a samurai than a monk.' Again he cast that thoughtful look at Jebu and his men.

Jebu laughed. 'I am no samurai, honoured sir, I assure you.'

The trader shrugged. 'Who you are is no business of mine. I wish Lord Yukio no harm. On the other hand, it will be safer to travel when the Shogun's will prevails everywhere. Lord Hideyori is bringing us peace.'

Now Yukio and Jebu studied the fort that blocked their road to Oshu. It stood at the high point of a pass between two purple-black crags dusted with snow that towered like pagodas built by giants.

'Not far from here is Tonamiyama, where we first led the Mongols into battle against the Takashi,' Yukio said.

'We could try to avoid this fort,' said Jebu, his mind fully in the present as he followed the winding of the threadlike path through pines and boulders up to the entrance of the fort. 'We could climb over the peaks or work our way around them to the east or the west.'

'It would take too long,' said Yukio. 'We do not have enough provisions, and there is no food in the mountains. Besides, there are other forts to the east and the west.'

The Yukio who had led the attack at Ichinotani would leap over these mountains like a deer, Jebu thought. 'Better to go hungry for a few days than lose our heads,' he suggested.

'Remember what the trader told us yesterday,' Yukio said. 'If I die it will bring peace to the realm. Even if it does not, my sufferings will be over.'

The despair that had come over Yukio in Heian Kyo when he first realized that his brother had turned against him had grown deeper with each downward turn of his fortunes. Increasingly, Jebu was making plans and decisions for him. It was Jebu who found a Zinja monastery for them to hide in after the shipwreck in Shimonoseki Strait. The Zinja were willing to help Yukio. Though they had supported the Muratomo in the War of the Dragons, Hideyori had begun to harass and threaten them of late. While at the monastery Yukio had learned, to his great anguish, that the samurai to whom he had entrusted Shizumi had betrayed him at the first opportunity and had delivered her to Hideyori's men. The thought had driven Yukio into a fit of wild weeping.

With only a few followers remaining, Yukio had no alternative but to go into hiding. Though few would risk open resistance to Hideyori, there was widespread 'sympathy for the lieutenant', as people phrased it, remembering the title Hideyori had begrudged Yukio. For two years Yukio and his men had managed to move in disguise from one refuge to another, finding shelter in temples, the castles of friendly samurai, and the homes of commoners. Hideyori launched the greatest manhunt in the history of the Sacred Islands, sending the armies of the Bakufu into every accessible corner of the realm, conducting a house-to-house search of the capital, and even threatening old Go-Shirakawa and young Kameyama with 'certain untoward eventualities' if they did not co-operate wholeheartedly.

Hideyori used the supposed threat of rebellion as a pretext for stamping out all potential resistance to the new government he was establishing. Yukio's well-wishers were becoming increasingly reluctant to help him. The only place left for him was the far northern land of Oshu, so remote and powerful as to be almost a kingdom in its own right.

Now Jebu and Yukio stood on a mountain top in Kaga province facing a barrier fort which blocked the pass through the mountains north of them. Their men, unarmed and shaven-headed, sat down along the narrow path, part of the Hokurikudo Road, to rest. Young Shenzo Totomi, who was dressed as their porter, knelt and untied the gilt chest, a portable Buddhist altar, which he had been carrying on his back. Despite Yukio's declining of his offer of help, General Shenzo's son had not hesitated to join those rallying around Yukio when he broke openly with Hideyori. Now he set the altar on its four legs beside Yukio.

'Only with my death will this unnecessary killing stop,' said Yukio, looking at the six heads on the distant poles.

Shenzo Totomi's eyes gleamed like a young tiger's. 'Any man who dies because of you, my lord, dies well.'

Jebu said, 'Do you really believe, Yukio, that your death, or any man's death, will put an end to this kind of killing? You, like thousands of others, are deceived by Hideyori's protestations that just one more death is needed for peace. If you were dead, Hideyori would find other necessary murders. In time other warriors will arise to challenge him. When he dies, new contenders will struggle for the power he has built. Stop imagining that you could sacrifice your life to bring peace. Your duty is to try and save yourself.'

For the first time in months a merry light appeared in Yukio's eye. 'Disguise you as a Buddhist monk and at once you begin to prate like one. What must we do, then, Oh holy one?'

'Since you insist on it, we will go through the fort rather than around it,' said Jebu. 'Perhaps the very innocence of that unfortunate group of monks who preceeded us aroused suspicion, and we will be more convincing because we are more careful.' He turned and addressed the group. 'If any of you have weapons, rid yourselves of them now. They would give us away if we are searched, and they would be useless to us in that fort.

We will be greatly outnumbered.' Reluctantly, some of the men drew daggers from under their saffron robes and tossed them into the cedars that grew thickly down the hillside. Jebu turned back to Yukio. 'Yukio-san, I want you to trade places and clothes with Shenzo Totomi.'

'No,' Totomi said instantly. 'It would be a disgrace for us to make our lord do the work of a porter, even to save our lives.'

'Exactly what Hideyori's men will think,' said Jebu. 'If we dress Lord Yukio as a porter and load this altar on his back, he is far less likely to be recognized, because no samurai would adopt such a degrading disguise. As it is, he is wearing the heaviest cloak of all of us and the finest robes. He looks like our leader. If they have a good description of him, they're sure to recognize him. Indeed, there may be some who have seen him before.'

'This is intolerable,' cried Totomi.

'Do as you are told, Totomi,' said Yukio quietly. 'A samurai never does things by halves. If we are to deceive our enemies let us deceive them as perfectly as we can.'

In a few moments Yukio was dressed in Totomi's ragged robe and coat of straw. Totomi wore Yukio's sturdy new wooden sandals, while Yukio went barefoot. The men, except for Jebu, had blistered and bleeding feet because they had been mounted warriors, unused to long marches on foot.

'There is a scroll of melancholy poems in the sleeve of that robe, Totomi,' said Yukio. 'Take care of them but don't read them. It would embarrass me.'

With great reverence and gentleness, Yukio's men loaded the heavy altar on their lord's back. Bent under the weight of the altar-chest and dressed in clothing too big for him, Yukio seemed a small, sad figure. He managed a smile, a ghost of his old gaiety, and several of the samurai turned away from him with tears in their eyes. Taking up the lead, a long staff in his hand, Jebu cautioned the men to ignore their ravaged feet and try to look like true yamabushi, who had been roving the mountains barefoot on spiritual journeys all their lives. Yukio brought up the rear. He limped forward, stumbled and almost fell, then pulled himself up and trudged on with a determined expression. Totomi caught Jebu's eye and glared at him. These samurai, Jebu thought; Totomi would rather see his lord beheaded than forced to endure a few hours of pain and indignity pretending to be a porter.

The kami of the mountains chose to make their progress more difficult by sending ice-cold rain mixed with snow and hail to drum on their rice-straw hats and freeze their hands and feet. Their destination, the fort by the pass, disappeared in a grey swirl, and they could see only a few paces ahead.

Just as they reached the outpost, soaked and exhausted, the storm rolled away, chased by a howling wind that blew through their wet robes and froze the rough cloth against their skin. A silk banner emblazoned with the White Dragon of Muratomo crackled above the gatehouse. The sky was blue now, and the sun, sinking into the snow-dusted teeth of a black crag to the west, glinted on the silver helmet ornaments of six guards who slowly, sullenly formed a line in front of the barrier pole across the road. Soldiers in peacetime quickly become attached to comfort, Jebu thought. These were obviously annoyed at having to leave shelter and a warm brazier.

'More monks,' said one of the guards. 'Let's take their heads now, as we did with those others, and get in out of this wind.' He spoke with the rough accent of the eastern provinces, Hideyori's base.

'It's bad karma to kill monks,' another man protested.

'Not if they aren't really monks,' said the eastern soldier.

During this exchange Jebu stood serenely, hands clasped before him, as if he did not hear the guards discussing his possible fate. The men behind him stood patiently. It was all in the hands of the kami now, thought Jebu. After a little more talk the guards singled out Jebu and Shenzo Totomi and ordered them to go into the fort, which stood a short distance up the mountainside from the road.

'If our captain doesn't believe your leader's story, the ravens are still hungry,' the eastern warrior said to the rest of Jebu's party. With a laugh he pointed to the six almost-bare skulls on the poles above the fort's log wall. Jebu was relieved that Yukio would not be exposed to the eyes of the entire garrison. Now it all stood or fell on Jebu's ability to convince the post commander that they were authentic monks. As he climbed the steep path to the fort, Jebu felt the silent tension in the men he was leaving behind. He himself felt exhilarated, happy to be shouldering responsibility for the lives of Yukio and the others. Now, if only this young hothead beside him didn't make a mess of things.

The fort was actually a large old manor, a scattering of low wooden buildings perhaps fifty years old, in more peaceful times the mountain retreat of some nobleman. The only fortifications were the newly built log palisade and a few square wooden guard towers. The tumbling-down, one-storey halls were crowded with samurai and 'foot soldiers taking their ease, laughing and talking, gambling, quarrelling. From a distant house Jebu heard the tinkle of musical instruments and women's voices. Discipline appeared lax; some of the men were drunk. Heads turned as Jebu and Totomi were led into the central courtyard.

'A hulk like that ought to be a wrestler, not a monk,' said a voice in the crowd.

'He'll be shorter by a head when our executioner gets done with him,' said another.

The commander of the fort strode out of the doorway of the central hall. He wore a blue robe richly brocaded with silver. His face was square and hard, all bone and muscle, the mouth set in the harsh, lipless line Jebu had seen under many a samurai helmet in combat. He has the suspicious eye of his master, Hideyori, Jebu thought.

'I am Captain Shinohata. I am a kenin, a vassal of the Lord Shogun,' said the commander, his accent revealing another eastern warrior. 'And who might you be?'

Jebu knew that the high-ranking samurai known as kenin owed allegiance to Hideyori alone. They were pillars of the new Kamakura government.

'I am Mokongo, priest of the Todaiji Temple in Nara,' said Jebu in a commanding voice. In the edges of his vision he could see a crowd gathering. These idle troops, he knew, lacked amusement and would be delighted to see a monk's shaved head rolling in the dirt.

'Be careful what tone you use with me, priest,' said Shinohata with contempt. 'Six of your sort met their deaths yesterday because their answers did not please me.'

'It is a great sin to kill the servants of Buddha, bringing down terrible curses on all who share the guilt,' said Jebu, putting all the authority he could muster into his voice. A murmuring arose

186

in the crowd of soldiers around him, whether of fear or anger it was impossible to tell.

'We have our orders,' the captain replied. 'Yukio and his henchmen must be brought to justice even if a thousand innocent men have to be slain.' In spite of the merciless words, there was a note in his voice almost of pleading. This man is not comfortable with what he does, thought Jebu. He felt the excitement of one trying to lift a heavy stone, who finds the right spot to set a lever. He cast his eyes down and folded his hands piously.

'Such talk distresses me. My life has been dedicated to *ahimsa*, harmlessness to all sentient beings.'

In that same troubled tone Shinohata said, 'Agree to turn back now, Priest Mokongo, and you have nothing to fear from me and my men.'

'That cannot be,' said Jebu calmly. 'Like you, I have my orders.'

'Why must you pass this barrier, priest?'

Relying on the Self to guide him through encounters such as this, Jebu had prepared no answers in advance. Even his assumed name and temple had just come to him as he spoke. Now he remembered that the Todaiji was one of the great Nara temples that had been burned by the Takashi as punishment for supporting the uprising of Motofusa and Mochihito in Heian Kyo. Most of its monks had been killed in that catastrophe. Why had the Self chosen such an unlikely place for Jebu to claim as his temple? Then inspiration came to him.

'Know, Captain Shinohata, that the temple I serve, the Todaiji, was burned by the Takashi in the late War of the Dragons. By order of His Imperial Majesty, it is now to be rebuilt. We surviving monks of the Todaiji are going to every part of the Sacred Islands asking each to give his gift to aid this holy work. My party has been charged with travelling through the provinces on the Hokurikudo, obtaining promises of offerings. If you choose to kill us rather than let us pass, you merely release us from a life of suffering. Doubtless our martyrdom will earn us a reward in incarnations to come.'

A voice from the crowd of samurai called, 'Please let them pass, Lord Shinohata. These are no ordinary monks but holy men from one of the greatest temples in the land. If you spare them, you may balance the bad karma we brought upon ourselves by killing those monks yesterday.'

'The Takashi never won another battle after they burned the temples at Nara,' another man said. The samurai tended to be more in awe of religion than either Court aristocrats or commoners, Jebu thought. It went with the uncertainty of their lives.

'I'm of a mind to let you go through,' said Shinohata. 'If I kill every monk who comes up this road, my karma will surely be as heavy as one of these mountains. But I must be sure you are what you claim to be.' He thought for a moment. 'If you are seeking contributions, Priest Mokongo, you must be carrying a solicitation scroll to read to those whom you approach. Let us hear it, and I will judge if your mission is truly what you say it is.'

For a moment Jebu's mind went blank. Then the Self came to his rescue. He remembered the scroll of poems Yukio had mentioned. And a flood of phrases from Buddhist literature filled his mind. Part of his early training as a Zinja had included familiarization with the dominant religions of the land, and later he had often listened to sermons by Buddhist monks.

Jebu turned to Totomi, who was staring at him apprehensively, and held out his hand. 'The scroll, please.'

After a moment's puzzlement Totomi remembered, took Yukio's scroll out of his sleeve and handed it to Jebu. Jebu stepped up to the veranda of Shinohata's headquarters building and positioned himself so no one could get behind him and read the scroll. He opened the scroll and, trying to look as if he were reading, he began to speak in a resonant voice.

'Contribution roll of the Priest Mokongo, who has been charged to travel through the provinces of the Hokurikudo, respectfully begging all, high and low, to give a gift to aid the holy work of reconstructing the Todaiji of Nara: As all know, we live in that time called Mappo, the Latter Days of the Law, when men give themselves up to passion and wine, and the land is afflicted with civil war, fire, earthquake, famine and pestilence. Alas! How pitiable!

'One of the foulest deeds of these dark and gloomy times was the sacrilegious burning of this most magnificent temple, the Todaiji. Four thousand monks and their wives and children perished in the flames. Not all the cries of the sinners amid the fires of the fiercest of the Eight Hot Hells were more pitiful than their screams. Ancient works of art beyond price went up in smoke. Most shameful of all, the great bronze Buddha, the largest statue of the Sakya Sage in our Sacred Islands, was reduced to a shapeless mass of slag.

'For this desecration the Takashi paid dearly. That evil brood who hated mankind and the law of Buddha now suffer the torments of Emma-O, the king of the underworld, and his jailers. Such is the fate of all who harm the servants of the Lord Buddha.' Jebu delivered the last statement in a thunderous voice and swept Shinohata and the circle of samurai with a threatening gaze.

'The Todaiji as it was can never be replaced. We hope, even so, to build another splendid temple on its ruins. The great Buddha will be rebuilt of copper and gold with a sacred jewel in his lofty forehead.

'Even as the Buddha and his disciples went forth daily with their begging bowls, so I, Mokongo, stand before you weeping, asking your contributions. If they who destroyed the Todaiji earned bad karma, surely those who help rebuild it will enjoy good karma in equal amount according to the most true law of cause and effect. They will attain to the further shore of perfect enlightenment. As for those who hinder us, they will be cast into the fire pits, there to gibber for a thousand times a thousand lifetimes.

'A small contribution will be enough to earn the Buddha's infinite mercy. Who is there who will not give? It is said that even he who gives a little sand to help build a pagoda earns good karma. How much more he who gives something of value?

'Composed by me, Mokongo, for the purpose of obtaining contributions as stated. The Tenth Month of the Year of the Rooster.' Again Jebu gazed sternly about him. His hearers fell back under the look in his blazing eyes. He closed the scroll with a snap and handed it to Totomi, who quickly put it away.

Timidly at first, samurai in the audience began to come forward holding out small gifts – rings and necklaces, Chinese coins, carvings. Grandly, Jebu gestured to Totomi to collect the offerings.

'I did not read my solicitation scroll to obtain gifts here, only to set your mind at rest,' Jebu said to Shinohata. 'But since your

189

men seem moved to help us, perhaps you can supply us with travelling boxes to hold what they give us.'

'There is one more precaution I must take,' said Shinohata. 'I must inspect your entire party before I let them pass.' He stepped down from the porch, and with a samurai's swaggering gait led the way to the entrance to the stoackade. Reluctantly, Jebu walked beside him, followed by Totomi.

'This is distasteful to me,' said Shinohata, his harsh features softening as he spoke quietly to Jebu. 'Of course, the Lord Shogun has every right to do whatever he deems necessary to preserve order in the land. Still, I bitterly regret the turn of events that set the two great Muratomo brothers against each other. I had the honour of serving under Lieutenant Yukio during the War of the Dragons. A most gallant commander.'

Jebu glanced over his shoulder at Totomi, whose eyes bulged in a flushed face. He seemed almost ready to spring upon Shinohata's back. Forcing a casual tone, Jebu said, 'Were you at Shimonoseki Strait, captain?' Perhaps the man had not actually seen Yukio.

'Unfortunately, no. The lord I served withdrew from Yukio's army after the battle of Ichinotani. We left to help subdue the Takashi forces in the western provinces, where we fought beside the barbarian horsemen who accompanied the lieutenant from China. But forgive me, Priest Mokongo, I'm sure you have no desire to hear this talk of war.'

Jebu smiled. 'The Buddha himself was born into a family of warriors.' By this time they had passed through the gates of the fort and were among short, twisted pines, treading the steep path that led down to the place where the barrier pole blocked the road. There were about thirty soldiers following them. Another six were down below, guarding the travellers, who squatted on the ground, patient and quiet as true yamabushi.

'Yes, but the Enlightened One did not stay a warrior,' Shinohata was saying. 'Sometimes I feel ready to give up this life myself, to trade it for the serenity that you must enjoy. For now, I must faithfully carry out the order of the Shogun. Believe me, Priest Mokongo, there are those who watch everything I do.' He glanced back at the troops following them down the mountain-side. 'Much as I might wish to speed you on your way, I must err on the side of severity to be sure of pleasing the Shogun.'

'I understand, Lord Shinohata,' said Jebu, not at all easier in mind. 'We desire nothing more than peace, and perhaps peace can be best achieved when warriors remain vigilant.' Now they had reached an outcropping of jagged black rock just above the road. Shinohata poised himself there, his booted feet planted wide apart. Behind him the soldiers formed a semi-circle, holding their bows, swords and naginatas.

'Raise the barrier,' Shinohata ordered the guards blocking the road. 'Let these monks pass through it one by one.'

Jebu and Totomi scrambled down to join their comrades. 'Let's seize him now,' Totomi whispered. 'His men won't attack us if we hold him hostage.'

'He'd insist on dying, as any good samurai would,' said Jebu with an irony that escaped Totomi. Jebu ordered the false monks into line. Passing close to Yukio he whispered, 'He may have seen you before. Keep your head down.' He stood at the base of the rock from which Shinohata watched as the monks in their tattered robes trudged by.

'Have them take their hats off,' said Shinohata. Jebu gave the order, and those wearing conical rice-straw hats as protection against the elements bared their bald skulls. Yukio was tottering at the end of the procession, bent under the portable altar.

'You've got your smallest monk carrying that great, heavy altar,' Shinohata remarked.

'He's not a monk,' said Jebu. 'Just a lay brother, a porter.'

Just as Yukio, who had fallen far behind the others, came abreast of Shinohata, he tripped over a stone in the path and fell. The altar landed on its side with a booming crash. Yukio, on all fours, looked directly into Shinohata's face. Jebu heard Shinohata gasp. He saw the samurai officer's eyes fill with amazed recognition.

At that moment the Self took charge of Jebu. He sprang at Yukio, brandishing his walking staff. One part of his mind brought the stick down on Yukio's back.

'Careless monkey!' he shouted. 'How dare you let the altar of the Lord Buddha fall to the ground? Weakling! You repeatedly delay us, and now you drop our holy altar. On your feet and pick up that altar, or I'll break every one of your delicate ribs.' He thumped Yukio with the stick until Yukio crawled to the fallen altar and got his back under it. With horrified glances at Jebu, two of Yukio's men went to help him shoulder the burden.

'Get back,' Jebu roared, waving the stick at them. 'A mere porter has no right to the help of monks.' At last Yukio got the four-legged chest on his back and securely tied around him. Bent double, he staggered forward again. Shinohata looked shocked.

'I thought for a moment – ' he stammered. 'But no samurai would strike his lord as you have thrashed this porter. Not even to save his life.' He glowered at his men as if challenging them to question his thinking. The soldiers stood silent, amazed at the giant priest's outburst of anger and beating of the little porter. Also silent, staring thunderstruck at Jebu, were the other false yamabushi. Shenzo Totomi, already some distance past the barrier, appeared almost maddened with rage.

Shinohata looked back at Jebu. 'You are a remarkable man, Priest Mokongo. I am sorry that we threatened you and delayed you. I will send a runner after you with a few jars of sake, by way of apology.'

'Monks do not drink sake,' Jebu reminded him.

'Of course not. Even so, it may be permissible for you to take a drop to ward off the chill in this mountain air.' He glanced down the road at the little figure stumbling under the altar, and Jebu saw tears standing in his eyes. 'The mountains are so vast and hard, and man is so small and fragile.'

Bars of sunlight streamed from behind the black peaks to the west and gilded those to the east. The fort was hidden behind a pine-ridged slope. Jebu prostrated himself before Yukio, who had shrugged out from under the portable altar. Tears poured down Jebu's cheeks.

'Forgive me, Yukio-san,' he sobbed. 'I don't know how I could have done that. Punish me as you see fit.'

Totomi sprang forward. 'Let me kill him, lord. For striking you, he deserves to die.'

Yukio laughed. 'What will you do, Totomi, beat his brains out with a rock? Have you forgotten that the monk Jebu cleverly ordered us to throw all our weapons away? Almost as if he knew we were going to do something outrageous. Jebu, you've probably been waiting years to give me a good whack

192

across the shoulders with a stick.' Tentatively at first, then uproariously as relief swept over them, the men laughed. Even Totomi joined in at last. No one really wants to die, thought Jebu. It is one thing to be willing to die, as these men are, and another thing really to want death.

The pounding of booted, running feet echoed in the silence of the mountains. Three soldiers in tunics and trousers were hurrying along the path in the twilight. The chilling thought crossed Jebu's mind that Shinohata had sent troops after them to arrest them. Then he saw that the men were unarmed and that large sake jars were bouncing on their shoulders.

'Compliments of Lord Shinohata to your holinesses,' one man panted as they presented the wine to Jebu's party. Some of Jebu's men built a fire, and Jebu invited the three soldiers to share the wine with them. Regrettably, the soldiers agreed to stay, and so the fugitives could not freely celebrate their escape but had to keep up the pretence of being monks. Yukio, still playing the porter, served a supper of dried fish and rice cakes. Jebu felt the wine glowing in his middle like a jolly round red lantern. He was overjoyed at having survived the ordeal of the barrier and miserable at having struck Yukio. The contradictory feelings were pulling him to pieces like those horses the Mongols sometimes used to tear apart a heinous criminal. He could not sit still. He jumped to his feet, picked up his staff and held it horizontally in both hands before him. He began to dance, first stepping solemnly to the left, then hopping more quickly to the right, then whirling about. It was a young man's dance he had learned at the Waterfowl Temple an age ago. His companions stared open-mouthed, but the soldiers laughed delightedly and clapped their hands in time to Jebu's steps. Yukio produced a taiko drum and beat out a complex rhythm. Fiercer and wilder grew Jebu's dance as he poured into it everything he felt – grief at Yukio's downfall, anger at Hideyori and his minions, longing for Taniko, joy at being alive, sorrow at the tragedy that is all of life. He astounded the onlookers with a series of mid-air somersaults, then ended with side steps as slow and stately as those he had begun with.

Holding up a torch to light their way, the soldiers said good night reluctantly to this remarkably merry band of monks. When they were gone, Jebu again threw himself to the ground before Yukio and pressed his forehead against Yukio's bare foot.

'My lord Yukio. Can you truly forgive me?'

Yukio smiled sadly. 'I can forgive you the beating,' he said softly. 'That was nothing. What I am not sure I can forgive is your perpetual effort to keep me alive. When I fell and looked up into the face of the commander of that fort and knew that he recognized me, I felt a vast relief. Then you rescued me. You cannot imagine, Jebu-san, how little I desire to cling to this life.' He turned away and walked into the darkness.

Holding the Jewel of Life and Death in his hand so that the dying firelight glowed red in its crystal depths, Jebu sat where he was and wept.

CHAPTER TWENTY-TWO

Like all buildings in the Sunrise Land, the Shogun's castle was draughty and cold in winter. Taniko, Hideyori, Bokuden and Ryuichi, dining privately in Hideyori's chambers, wore many layers of clothing and kept their feet near the charcoal fire burning in the kotatsu, the square well in the floor covered with a low table.

'Taniko-san,' said Hideyori, 'you spent many years among the Mongol barbarians. I have just received word that ambassadors from the Emperor of the Mongols have landed at Hakata on Kyushu.'

Taniko's heart momentarily stopped, then began a frightened thumping. She shut her eyes, touching her fingertips to her forehead, and saw the face of Kublai Khan, huge, commanding, round and brassy as the summer sun, as vividly as if she had left his palace only yesterday. When she opened her eyes Hideyori was staring at her with a penetrating gaze remarkably like Kublai's.

'I have never seen you appear so frightened, Taniko-san,' he said softly, curiously.

'My fear is of the dreadful suffering this may bring upon our people, my lord. What message do the Mongols carry?'

'They have a letter which they insist they must deliver to His Imperial Majesty. I have ordered the Defence Commissioner for the West to detain them at Dazaifu on Kyushu until we decide what to do with them.'

'If their ambassadors are harmed, I have no doubt that they will make war on us, my lord. To the Mongols an ambassador is sacred.'

'These islands are sacred. If they invade us, the gods themselves will fight on our side.'

'Please excuse me, my lord,' said Taniko politely, 'but every nation believes it enjoys the favour of the gods. When I was at the court of the Great Khan I met a princess from a land far to the west, where they worship a god called Allah. Their spiritual leader was a holy man who lived in a mighty city known as Baghdad. He ordered the Mongol ambassadors slain when they came to Baghdad, and announced that Allah had declared war on the Mongols. He called on all the faithful to come to the aid of Baghdad. No one came. Neither god nor man could stop the Mongols from tearing down the walls of Baghdad in a few days. Because their ambassadors had been killed, they took out the people of Baghdad, men, women and children, and they put them all to death. Even babies. Ninety thousand died.'

'What of the holy man?' asked Ryuichi. Taniko's uncle had grown much fatter in recent years. He had stopped wearing white face powder, but he still dressed in trailing robes.

'They covered him with a pile of carpets, Uncle, then rode their horses over the carpets, trampling him to death. This they did to avoid shedding his blood. The Mongols' law forbids spilling the blood of a person of high rank.'

Hideyori uttered a barking laugh. 'A most lawful people. And merciful.'

'My lord, I do not suggest that we yield to the Mongols. It may be that we will have to fight them. But we should be aware of what would happen to us if we lost a war with them. Picture our beautiful city of Heian Kyo depopulated and our Son of Heaven trampled under carpets.'

Hideyori stared at her, genuinely shocked. 'Taniko, never say such a thing in my presence again. It is blasphemy to suggest that foreign barbarians could lay a hand on our sacred Majesty.'

Taniko offered no answer. Hideyori appreciated her

intelligence, or so he said, but not when her remarks verged on scepticism.

'Might not the Mongol army that is now on our soil turn against us?' asked Bokuden, stroking his sparse grey moustache with the tip of his index finger.

'There are barely three thousand of them left,' said Hideyori, his hard features relaxing in a small smile. 'They lost many in the War of the Dragons. I saw to that. They are at the opposite end of the realn. from their ambassadors on Kyushu. I have sent the Mongol army to the land of Oshu to arrest my brother.'

'Have you located the lieutenant, then, my lord?' Ryuichi asked. As if the might of Kublai Khan were not enough to frighten me, thought Taniko, now I must fear for the lives of Jebu and Yukio.

'I'm sure you are aware that title has long since been revoked, Ryuichi,' said Hideyori irritably. 'Yes, my rebellious brother has managed to escape to Oshu, where he sought refuge with the Northern Fujiwara. He managed to slip through the barrier fort at Ataka disguised as a wandering monk. I have ordered the fort commander at Ataka to commit hara-kiri to expiate for having let Yukio and his companions through. Yukio is travelling with that big Zinja monk who goes with him everywhere, and with a few other bandits. The Zinja helped us in the early stages of the War of the Dragons, but I have ordered them to withdraw their support from Yukio and they have not done so. I intend to proceed against the Order of Zinja as soon as Yukio has been captured.'

Taniko remembered an afternoon in Oshu, long ago, on a hilltop overlooking the Chusonji Temple, when a few words from Jebu had brought their happiness to an end with the suddenness of an earthquake. Now, seeing in her mind the glitter of that golden roof and the temple pillars, she felt tears coming to her eyes. I must send for Moko and tell him about this at once, she thought. At last we know where Jebu is, and that, for the moment, he is alive.

'What will the Mongols do when they catch up with your brother, my lord?' she asked.

'That depends on Yukio, of course, Taniko-san,' said Hideyori. 'What I desire above all else is to end this wrangling between us that began when he permitted the Imperial Court to turn his head. Their orders are to arrest him and bring him here to me. If he comes peaceably, we will discuss our differences. If we can come to a meeting of the minds, I will pardon him. I have sent Prince Horigawa to Oshu along with the Mongols. He acts as my personal emissary to Lord Hidehira, urging him, out of his old friendship to my family, to help make peace between Yukio and me. However things turn out, Horigawa will then proceed to Kyushu to meet with the Mongol ambassadors.' So, in spite of Hideyori's talk of marriage, Horigawa was still part of his plans, thought Taniko.

'Are you sure you can trust Prince Horigawa with such important matters, my lord?' she asked.

'Taniko,' said Bokuden reprovingly. 'Your conduct towards Prince Horigawa has shamed our whole family. You should not speak of him.'

'The question is a sensible one,' said Hideyori with a stare that crushed Taniko's father. 'The answer is that Prince Horigawa, like all who serve me, knows that he had better carry out my orders precisely if he wishes to keep his head.'

Bokuden cringed and had nothing further to say.

A cold, damp wind from the sea swept across the grey plain, blowing the white cloaks of the mourners and spurring the priests to hasten their funeral chants. The long white beard of Fujiwara no Hidehira, the late lord of Oshu, fluttered in the breeze. His body, on the pyramid of logs his people had built to do him final honour, was wrapped in a dark green robe brocaded in gold with a scene of mountain pines. Lord Hidehira's eldest son, Yerubutsu, his round head topped by a tall cap of lacquered black silk, stepped forward and held a torch to the pyre. Fed by the wind, the flames leaped from log to log, and the containers of sweet-smelling oils sizzled and released their perfumes on the air. The body on the pile of logs disappeared behind a blazing orange wall.

The people of Oshu had gathered on this plain to the west of their capital, Hiraizumi, to bid farewell to their lord, who had passed into the Void at the amazing age of ninety-six. Hidehira had ruled Oshu for so long that most of his subjects could remember no earlier lord. The masses of common people were held back from the pyre by a hollow square of four thousand warriors. The samurai wore full armour, and their helmet ornaments and naked weapons reflected a steel-grey sky. In the midst of the soldiery, Lord Hidehira's large family was gathered, headed by Yerubutsu, the new chieftain of the Northern Fujiwara and lord of Oshu, surrounded by brothers, sons and nephews. All of them looked with poorly veiled hostility at their distinguished guest, Muratomo no Yukio, who stood off to one side, dressed, as were all the others, in white robes of mourning. Towering over Yukio was the monk Jebu, who added his Zinja prayers for the departed to those of the Buddhist and Shinto priests.

Little was said while the flames crackled, sending up puffs of scented smoke to be torn to shreds by the wind before they could rise into the sky. When the pyre had burned down to ground level, Yukio approached Yerubutsu and bowed deeply, showing his reverence for his host's new rank. Yerubutsu nodded coldly.

'Now I am alone in the world,' said Yukio.

'My father commanded me to protect you and to help you to become once again the greatest leader in the realm,' said Yerubutsu, with no more enthusiasm than he had shown when Yukio sought shelter with Lord Hidehira after his return from China. 'Even as my father was a father to you, I will be a brother to you.'

'I need a brother,' said Yukio, 'my blood brother having become my mortal enemy.'

'You will always be safe with us,' said Yerubutsu, turning away and motioning his kinsmen to follow.

Before the new chieftain could move out of earshot Yukio called, 'Is it true, Lord Yerubutsu, as I hear, that an army sent by my brother is approaching the border of your land?'

Yerubutsu reddened slightly. These warriors of Oshu were not used to dissembling. With a grunt of resignation he turned again to face Yukio.

'I had intended to tell you about this army, Yukio-san, but I didn't want to worry you unnecessarily. We do not yet know who sent them, or why. In any case, it is only a small force, about three thousand. We have fifty thousand men under arms here.'

'I don't meant to sound critical, Lord Yerubutsu,' said Yukio with a gentle smile, 'but if I had been doing your scouting for you, I would have learned much more about this army by now. As you see, with no help at all I was able to find out about its existence, even though you so kindly tried to protect me from this disturbing knowledge. Perhaps you could spare me a small troop of samurai, and I could assist you in intelligence gathering?'

Yerubutsu's grin was like that of a cannibal demon in a Buddhist painting of hell. 'We are fully able to protect you, Yukio-san. You are our guest. We wish to free you from care.'

As the vast crowd drifted away from the cremation site, leaving the final burial of Hidehira's ashes to the priests of the Chusonji, Yukio and Jebu walked by themselves towards the mountains to the north.

'They want to free me from care forever,' Yukio said wryly.

'Yerubutsu has no love for you, but he would not go against his father's last wish,' said Jebu. His words rang hollow in his own ears.

'The past is the past and the present is the present,' Yukio said, repeating the old samurai saying. 'I'm finished, Jebu-san. Yerubutsu knows it as well as I do. Hideyori will have my head if he has to knock down these mountains to get to me.'

Jebu thought of his own father, relentlessly tracked down by Genghis Khan's agent, Arghun, and he felt overwhelmed by a wave of love for the small, frail-looking man beside whom he had fought for over twenty years.

'I will never desert you, Yukio.'

'I will need you at the end, Jebu-san.'

It was beginning to snow. Helmets of white formed on the dark boulders that littered the plain. Yukio pulled his thin white cloak tighter around him. They still had a long walk over the stormy ground to the castle they had been given by Lord Hidehira as a refuge. Since Yukio's arrival in Oshu ten days ago, just before Lord Hidehira's final illness, Yerubutsu had been promising to furnish Yukio and his party with horses, but the horses never came. Yerubutsu and his family rode away from Hidehira's funeral, back to Hiraizumi; Jebu and Yukio had to walk. The road they followed had been cleared by an age-old succession of travellers moving rocks and gravel to one side. The path rose into bare, black hills and began to twist and turn.

New-fallen snow partly obscured the way. The cold bit Jebu's toes through his deerskin boots.

'Yerubutsu means to betray me,' said Yukio.

'Then let's get away from here, Yukio-san.'

Yukio shook his head. 'The priests say, live as if you were already dead. I've been doing that ever since Hideyori answered my plea for friendship by sending assassins. Where could I fly to? North to Hokkaido, to live among the hairy barbarians? Back to China, to throw myself on the mercy of Kublai Khan? No, Jebu, some ways of living are so wretched that death is clearly better. I've lived like a hunted animal most of my life. That was all right when I was young and had hopes of a great future for myself and for the Sunrise Land. Hideyori has closed the door to all hope. I am too old to take up the fight again.'

'You're only thirty-eight, Yukio-san.'

'For a samurai, that is the beginning of old age. Soon my body will start to fail me. And even now I have an old man's awareness of how foolish were the visions of my younger self. Men say my victories over the Takashi were brilliant. All I ever achieved with those brilliant victories has been to inflict a far worse tyranny than Sogamori's upon my country, a tyranny that may well last a thousand years. I fought to restore the glory and authority of the Emperor, and now the Emperor has no more importance than a doll. Somewhere in heaven or in hell Sogamori and Kiyosi are laughing at me. I want to join them and laugh along with them, Jebu-san, at the futility of human hope.'

The wind stung Jebu's face with sharp, bitter-cold particles of ice and snow. 'What of your wife and children? If you stay here and fight, they will surely die when you die.' Yukio's father-in-law had sent Yukio's family over in a palanquin from his estate. Yukio's son and daughter had rarely seen their father and had no idea who he was.

'Remember what happened to the women and children of the Takashi?' Yukio said. 'I will stay with my wife and babies. I will not abandon them to be buried alive.'

The narrow path climbed the side of a cliff. Half-blinded by the huge white flakes blowing into their faces, they walked single file, Jebu in the lead, one hand on the rock wall. Whenever the wind died down, they could see the yellow, flickering glow of lanterns higher up in the mountains. They came to a cleft that offered shelter and pressed themselves into it to rest.

'You are a warrior without peer, the bravest man and the noblest soul in all the Sunrise Land,' Jebu said. 'You ought to be seated in glory at the feet of the Emperor. You, and not Hideyori, that sly, self-deluded coward, should hold the reins of power. The Order taught me to expect nothing from life but a violent death. Even so, I find what is happening to you impossible to understand.'

Long ago some pious traveller had carved deep in the cleft an image of a standing Buddha, his hand raised in blessing. With a smile, Yukio bowed towards the carving.

'If you Zinja believe in karma, as good Buddhists do, you would realize that in a past life I must have done something so evil that my present troubles are only just payment for it.'

'People believe in karma because they can't find any other idea that makes sense of life,' Jebu said.

'Life does not make sense,' said Yukio, staring impassively into the storm. 'The Buddha taught that life is suffering. The First Noble Truth. We suffer because we can't understand life. Injury and agony fall upon the virtuous and the wicked alike, without rhyme or reason. It is not only I who must fail and die. Hideyori will end in a grave just as surely. In the end life not only defeats us, it even defeats our efforts to understand it. We die as ignorant as when we were born.' Yukio slapped Jebu on the shoulder. 'Come on. It would just add to the general sense-lessness if we froze to death out here.'

They trudged on, kicking up puffs of snow. Now the storm was dying down, and the lanterns above the log wall of the castle were steadily visible. Small though it was, the castle was well placed for defence. It was set on a platform of stone overlooking a deep gorge, and the cliffs behind it were absolutely vertical. The path approaching it was so narrow, it could be defended even by the handful of men Yukio had with him. In the dim past this had been the stronghold of a tribe of barbarians of a race that no longer existed. Later, before the Northern Fujiwara unified the land, a bandit hideaway had occupied this eyrie. Lord Hidehira had known what he was doing when he turned the place over to Yukio just before he fell ill.

Now Yukio and Jebu were close enough to see a figure in a

grey fur cloak and hood watching them from the guard tower overlooking the gate. It was Yukio's wife, Mirusu, who had set the lanterns in the tower to guide them home. Jebu's feet were numb. His heart felt numb as well. A Zinja, he reminded himself, does not care whether he lives or dies. That was what troubled him. He no longer believed that he should not care. He wanted to die caring.

CHAPTER TWENTY-THREE

Three days after Lord Hidehira's funeral, at the Hour of the Horse, Jebu was finishing his midday meal of rice and fish when he heard the lookout's shout from the guard tower. As he ran to the ladder, he saw Yukio in the doorway of the hall where he lived with his family, talking to Mirusu. Yukio's hall was slightly more decorative than the other buildings in the compound, having walls of rough plaster and a tile roof with upsweeping eaves. It contained a small chapel.

Climbing to the tower, Jebu saw at once a long single file of dark, mounted figures approaching at a leisurely pace up the path from the distant plain.

'I make it about a thousand,' said Jebu when Yukio joined him. Jebu's heart boomed like a bronze bell in his chest. He had never felt the end of his life to be closer.

'More than enough to finish us,' said Yukio, peering at the line of horsemen that disappeared and reappeared as it wound its way through the hills below the fort. 'They're taller than most samurai and they have a different way of sitting a horse. Mongols, Jebu-san.'

Jebu felt a momentary surge of hope. 'Could they be coming to join us?'

'They have been riding under Hideyori's command for the last seven years. He sent them here.'

As the riders came nearer, Jebu saw that midway down the line porters were struggling to carry a heavily curtained palanquin up the steep, snow-covered path. Some high-ranking person was coming to view Yukio's death. Jebu unslung his small Zinja bow from his shoulder and made ready to fire as soon as the first of the Mongols came close enough, but they halted out of range. Only two kept coming, one holding up a heraldic pennon, both men without spears, bows or sabres.

'By the gracious Kwannon,' Yukio exclaimed. 'The one with the flag, that's Torluk, and the taller one behind him is Arghun.'

By the time the Mongol leaders had reached the fort, Yukio and Jebu were standing, unarmed, before the gate on a small tongue of stone where the path to the fort ended. Arghun had to ride behind Torluk until they tethered their horses to a crooked pine growing out of the cliff wall, and approached on foot. It was seven years since Jebu had seen Arghun, but the *tarkhan* looked little changed, except that he now wore samurai armour, a large suit with crimson lacings that must have been built specially for him. His face under the golden-horned helmet was sharp and angular as the mountains around them, his eyes as blue and inhumanly expressionless as the Eternal Heaven the Mongols worshipped. His moustache was now entirely grey. Torluk, a compact figure who still wore Mongol heavy cavalry armour, had grown a short, thick grey beard that made him look more barbaric than ever. He glowered at Yukio and Jebu with undisguised hostility.

'Well, *tarkhan* and *tuman-bashi*, have your years in the Sunrise Land been rewarding?' Yukio asked. He spoke the Mongol tongue haltingly and with a heavy accent, not having used it in years. 'I hear that two out of every three of your men have fallen in battle. You would have fared better under my command.'

'It was you who placed us under your brother's authority,' said Torluk sullenly. 'He used us ill.'

'As he uses all who serve him,' Yukio said softly.

'Even so, your samurai have learned to speak of the Mongols with dread,' said Torluk.

'You might wish to think so,' Yukio said dryly. 'I doubt it.'

'Those of us who lived have gained much wealth,' said Torluk. 'This is a poor country compared to China, but there is loot to be gathered.'

'Now you are going back to your homeland?' asked Yukio. 'After you perform this last service for Hideyori?'

For the first time Arghun spoke, his voice as heavy as the black rock beside him. He answered Yukio in the language of the Sunrise Land, which he used with more fluency than Yukio did Mongol.

'You need not die, Lord Yukio. You could be restored to your former power and glory. You could see your brother lying crushed at your feet. You could be the mightiest man in these islands. The choice is yours.'

'But there is a condition, isn't there, Arghun?' said Yukio lightly. 'You insult me, Arghun. You think I am the sort of man who would betray his country.'

'That is a foolish way to put it,' said Arghun. 'Your people will be harmed only if they resist us. If you lead them peacefully into the fold, you will be your country's benefactor, not its betrayer.' Arghun stared piercingly down at Yukio, weighing him. What he was proposing was plain to Jebu. The only thing he couldn't understand was how Arghun could have so misjudged Yukio. Argun's gaze shifted to Jebu.

'You are his friend, son of Jamuga. You are part Mongol yourself. Persuade him. A tidal wave is rushing towards these islands. Lord Yukio can ride its crest, or he can stand against it and be smashed flat. There are no other possibilities.'

'Why is this choice offered now?' Jebu asked.

'My master's thoughts move beyond China now,' said Arghun. 'He has sent ambassadors to your Imperial Court to invite your Emperor to submit to him.'

'We know that what the Court says to your ambassadors means nothing,' said Yukio. 'It is Hideyori's wishes that count. Why haven't you made this offer to the Shogun?'

'He would reject it. But even if he did agree to become deputy king of the Sunrise Land under the Great Khan, we could not be sure of him. Of all your leaders, he is the least trustworthy.'

Yukio laughed with a trace of bitterness. 'Again you insult me, Arghun. You think my brother would resist you, while I would deliver this land to Kublai Khan. I had not thought you were so stupid, Arghun.'

'Neither do I think you stupid, Yukio,' said Arghun calmly. 'Your country has turned against you. From the Emperor down to the lowliest peasant all acquiesce in your destruction. I offer you power. You and your children and your children's children could rule the Sunrise Land under the protection of the Great Khan until the end of time.'

'Do you truly expect your Mongol empire to last until the end of time?' Yukio said. 'I doubt it will be in existence a hundred years from now.'

'Then you badly underestimate us,' said Arghun. His cold eyes took on a distant look. 'Kublai Khan is the first Emperor to rule over all China in over a hundred years, and China is but one province in his empire. Doubt not, Yukio, that he can build an empire that will encompass all lands and peoples and last for all time. Your people can share in the power, the wealth, the peace and order, the arts and wisdom of the Great Khan's new empire. Of what value is the pathetic independence of your little island kingdom compared to the benefits you can enjoy as subjects of Kublai Khan?

'You know I speak the truth, Yukio, because you have seen the power of the Great Khan. That is, in part, why he wishes you to govern the Sunrise Land on his behalf. He has not forgotten that you served him faithfully and well. And even though Hideyori may persecute you now, the people would flock to you if they thought you could win out over Hideyori. You are a great general, the best among your people. You are the only one we fear. By killing you, we can assure our victory over your people, but we would prefer to have you on our side. Save yourself and your people, Yukio. Join us.'

A movement beyond Arghun caught Jebu's eye. The palanquin was rocking and bobbing towards them along the path. Warriors pressed their horses and themselves back against the cliff wall to let the gilded box and its bearers by. The person riding in it must be very lazy or very feeble, Jebu thought, to travel in such a precarious conveyance on a road barely wide enough for a horse. He wondered if armed men were concealed behind the heavy purple curtains.

'Arghun,' he said, 'whoever is in that palanquin, tell the bearers to stop right there, or this talk ends now.'

Arghun laughed, a short, harsh laugh. 'Only an old friend of yours, Jebu. Quite a harmless person.' He turned and raised a gauntleted hand, and the bearers set down the palanquin.

Yukio spoke in a quiet, thoughtful tone. 'You have lived among us many years, Arghun, but you still don't understand the Sunrise Land. I doubt that there is a single man on these islands, no matter how crude or treacherous he might be, who would give your proposal a moment's consideration. Our Emperor is a god. No mere mortal, such as Kublai Khan, could ever rule over him. Our land is the home of the gods. It could never be seized by foreigners.

'To live a long time is not important. To be exalted above other men is not important. What is important is the beauty of one's life, like the beauty of a flower that appears one day and is gone the next. To go against nature is hideous, and disloyalty is against my nature. Shake me from the tree whenever you wish.'

Arghun turned to Jebu. 'Will you say nothing? You do not share this blind devotion to the Emperor of the Sunrise Land. Your loyalty is to the Zinja, and it crosses the seas, as does the very blood in your veins. Make your comrade see that it is folly to cling to old ties when the Great Khan offers a new age of order and prosperity.'

Jebu smiled grimly. 'You once preferred old ties to the Great Khan's new age, Arghun.'

'I had the wisdom to change my views when I saw that the old ways are doomed to fail and disappear. Because I once made the same error Yukio now makes, I urge him now to follow my example.'

'Do you think Arghun is right, Jebu-san?' Yukio asked mildly.

'No, I think you are right, that he does not understand the Sunrise Land,' said Jebu. 'He does not understand the Zinja, and he does not understand you and me. Perhaps we can show him the truth. This day, let us kill so many of Arghun's warriors that he will tell his Great Khan there are not enough troops in all the world to conquer the Sacred Islands.'

The curtains of the palanquin parted, and a small figure wearing a lacquered silk cap, and swathed in shimmering grey fur, stepped out. He was alone and unarmed, but Jebu felt a chill between his shoulder blades as he recognized Horigawa. The prince advanced towards them with mincing steps, his feet hidden by the long grey coat that brushed the snow. His expressionless face was scaly and scarred with creases like a lizard's, his eyes sunk deep in his head. His tiny beard and moustache were silver white. He must be nearly eighty now, Jebu thought. He realized with surprise that if he died this day, Horigawa would outlive him. He resolved that Horigawa should die that day as well.

'I heard your words, Muratomo no Yukio,' said Horigawa in a piping voice like a child's flute. 'You said no one in the Sunrise Land would help Kublai Khan gain rule over these islands. Excuse me, but you are wrong. This aged scholar is just such a man.'

Yukio paled. 'I can't believe that. I have never heard anything good about you, Your Highness, but the Sasaki are one of our oldest and noblest families. They have served our Emperor faithfully for hundreds of years. No one of your lineage could betray the Sacred Islands and the Crown.'

Horigawa parted his lips in a smile. It was impossible to tell whether there were teeth, blackened in Court fashion, in his mouth, or whether they were all gone. What came out of that little orifice was pure venom.

'You know nothing about good lineage, Muratomo no Yukio. Those of your ancestors who were distant cousins of the Imperial family left the capital hundreds of years ago and intermarried, generation after generation, with bandits, peasants and barbarians. The few drops of Imperial blood that may remain in your body no more make you a member of the Imperial family than a few leaves tossed into the ocean could turn into *ch'ai*. You are *common*. You and your kind are useful only to do work that is too bloody and dirty for your betters. You samurai tried to rise above your station. In my lifetime I have seen first Domei, then Sogamori, and now your brother presume to give orders to the Emperor himself. I am not betraying my country, because this ceased to be my country when the samurai took control of it.

'I hoped you and Hideyori would destroy each other, but you proved too stupid and easy for him to defeat, and now Hideyori is all-powerful. To bring him down I must turn to a foreigner, the Great Khan. I did not come here to witness your death, Yukio, which is now a foregone conclusion, nor the death of this huge oaf who is your friend. I came here merely to see whether you would accept Arghun's offer, which the Great Khan insisted must be made. Had you agreed to rule the Sunrise Land as the deputy of the Great Khan, it would have been a setback for me. Fortunately, you remain stupid to the end. So I will now hasten to Heian Kyo to urge the court to submit to the Great Khan. The Mongol army will enter our land, not as invaders, but at the invitation of the Son of Heaven. Led by Arghun and Torluk and their men, who know these islands and the fighting methods of the samurai, they will crush that upstart who calls himself Shogun, and obliterate the samurai. With the Great Khan's approval I will be appointed Regent, ruling the Sacred Islands in the name of the Emperor, as the Fujiwara did of old. The tribute we will be required to send Kublai Khan will be a small price to pay for the restoration of correct and honourable government.' With a small smile Horigawa raised his hand in a parody of a bosatsu's blessing. 'Muratomo no Yukio, I bid you farewell.'

Jebu sprang. His whole attention was focused on Horigawa, who had turned away. Torluk's square, grey shape eclipsed that of the prince. Shifting the direction of his movement, Jebu checked his lunge. Grinning, Torluk drew a concealed dagger from his fur-topped boot.

'Since each finger of an empty-handed Zinja is a dagger, I thought it not dishonourable to bring my own dagger to our parley. Come on, you devil. I've always hoped I might be the one to kill you.'

'Don't trifle with me, Torluk.'

Arghun had swept Horigawa off his feet like a sack of rice and was bundling him back to his palanquin. A file of archers, arrows nocked in their bows, was trotting up the mountainside. In a moment Horigawa would be gone. Torluk, shifting the dagger from hand to hand, stood blocking the way. The Self took charge of Jebu's movements. When Torluk came at Jebu with the knife in his right hand, Jebu put out his own right hand as if to ward off the blow, and Torluk grabbed Jebu's forearm with his free hand, to pull him towards the dagger point. Jebu turned and slid past his opponent's left side, twisting and lifting his arm so that Torluk's elbow locked and he was pushed off-balance. Pulling free of Torluk's grip, Jebu threw his shoulder against the smaller man's back. The shove sent Torluk reeling over the edge of the path. He rolled down the steep incline. Faster and faster he tumbled, striking shrubs and outcroppings of rock with a force that was more than flesh could bear. At last he crashed to the bottom of the ravine, and lay still, half-buried in snow. Arghun shoved Horigawa through the purple curtains. As the bearers raised the gilded box, Arghun spoke a last rumbling word to the prince.

'The man who just fell protecting you is more valuable to me than an entire army. If he is dead, your actions in Heian Kyo had better be worth that price.'

Jebu started to rush the palanquin, but it was already too late. Six warriors stood along the path between him and Horigawa, their short, horn-reinforced Mongol bows drawn, steel-tipped arrows pointing at Jebu's chest. Beyond the palanquin more archers stood ready. His armour might be able to absorb most of the arrows, but they would surely stop him before he reached Horigawa, and he would die uselessly. Once again he would have to forgo vengeance. He stood, trembling with frustrated rage, as the palanquin bobbed off down the mountainside. Arghun ordered some of his men to climb down into the ravine to retrieve Torluk. Even if the *tuman-bashi* had survived the fall, he would not fight in this battle.

'I could kill you both now and save the lives of many of my men,' Arghun called to Jebu and Yukio. 'But I remain true to our word. Go, get behind your wall. You will die soon enough.'

As Jebu and Yukio, turning their backs on the Mongols, walked through the gate, Yukio said, 'Jebu-san, I do not want to do any killing today. I do not want to die as I have lived. I have practised the warrior's trade as best I could. I liberated the Sacred Islands from the Takashi, which, I believe, I was sent into this world to do. It has not been my karma to enjoy ease and honours. Now all that is left to me is to depart this world. I want my leave-taking to be beautiful. I want to be with my good wife and my children for a time, to read to them the Lotus sutra which has always been my favourite. Will you make it possible for me to do that, Jebu-san? Will you hold them off long enough for me to die as I want to?'

Hot tears filled Jebu's eyes. A poem came to him, a final gift from the Self. He spoke it to Yukio.

> The lone pine,
> The lightning flashes.
> The mountain top is bare.

Yukio said, 'You are the mountain top, Jebu-san.' Tears were running down his cheeks. 'Men thought me a giant, but I was always standing on your shoulders.' He gripped Jebu's arm hard for a moment, then turned away, his dark green robe swirling.

Jebu went to the samurai quarters to arm himself. Yukio's men had already put on their armour and helmets. When Jebu told them Yukio had refused Kublai Khan's offer of the kingship of the Sacred Islands, they were overcome with admiration. Several of them wept.

'To this day I have regretted that I did not kill myself when my father did, even though I was happy to serve Lord Yukio,' said Shenzo Totomi, wiping his face with the sleeve of his under robe. 'Now I am grateful that I can die with his hero – this god.'

'Let no man die until he has sent a hundred of the enemy into oblivion before him,' said Jebu. And Yukio's last army, twelve warriors strong, went out to meet the Mongols.

Alone, moving unhurriedly, Jebu began to don his suit of black armour. He tied the belt of his broad, short Zinja sword in the world-serpent knot, remembering the chant of the monks when Taitaro presented it to him on his initiation day: 'The sword is the Self, cutting through matter and time and penetrating to true insight.' He took down his naginata from the wall, a weapon so big only he could wield it. Who could withstand his naginata? Only one man, and he wasn't fighting today. As he armed himself he composed his mind, making each action part of his meditation. He repeated the statements of Zinja attitudes he had been taught as a child: I am going into battle now. I am not concerned about the outcome. I am concerned only that I fight with all the mind and strength I possess.

It is strange, though, he thought, interrupting the chain of affirmations. Even though I have entered every battle with the belief that it may be my last, I have never felt so certain that I am going to die as I do this day. He could hear the shouts of battle and the ringing of steel, but he knew there was no hurry. Today, the Mongols would not be able to use their mass tactics. They would have to come at the fort one at a time and engage in single combat, to the delight of the samurai. Let the other men have their moments of glory before I enter the battle. He took the Jewel out of the inner pocket in his robe and revolved it in his fingertips. To his surprise, instead of clearing his mind as it usually did, the heart of the Jewel showed him Taniko. She was looking right at him, with that keen, sparkling gaze that had always delighted him. The Jewel shows me what I have lost and so resigns me to death, he thought. Taniko blamed me for the deaths of those she loved, and now she is Hideyori's consort. Yukio will surely die today, and then I have no one to live for. The Zinja bound me to Yukio for so many years that he has come to mean more to me than the Order itself. It is good that I die with him today. He looked once again into the heart of the Jewel and saw there a glowing emptiness, the Void from which all things spring, not a darkness but a blinding light. His mind filled with that light, he tied his headcloth, shouldered his naginata and went out.

As he crossed the small yard to the gateway he heard, above the clangour of battle, the pure, sweet notes of a flute floating from the tile-roofed house where Yukio and his family prepared for death. Yukio had courted Mirusu by playing the flute under her window night after night. Perhaps it was she who had asked him to play now.

At the gate, six men were crowded together. Two more, in the watchtower, stood with their tall samurai bows ready.

'Each time they rush the fort, one of us goes out to hold them off,' said Kanefusa, a big northern warrior who was a cousin of Yukio's wife. 'Their archers have killed three of our men, but we've killed many of theirs.'

'Open the gate and stand aside,' said Jebu, swinging the naginata down from his shoulder. As soon as the gate was open wide enough, Jebu rushed out. There were no Mongols outside. They had taken cover from the samurai arrows behind an outcropping of rock at a bend in the road. Jebu ran down the path and around the rock. A warrior in brown stood before him, mouth fallen open in astonishment. The path was not wide enough to allow Jebu to swing the naginata in a full circle. Instead, he thrust its point into the man's throat. Shouting, the next Mongol came at Jebu with a sabre. Jebu brought the cutting edge of the naginata down on the man's shoulder, sending him tumbling over the cliff after his comrade. The attackers set up an outcry as, one after another, Jebu killed them where they stood, or knocked them into the ravine. A mounted warrior charged him. Jebu sliced into the horse's belly, and animal and rider toppled from the path together. Now the Mongols were crowding one another to get away from the flashing blade at the end of the long pole, away from the figure in black armour bearing down on them. Then Arghun, on horseback, was facing him, standing in the saddle, his bow drawn, an arrow aimed at Jebu's head. Jebu stood, staring into the empty blue eyes.

'Climb down here, Arghun, and draw your sword,' he called. 'Let's finish it now.'

'For you, it is finished,' said Arghun, and he released the arrow. A quick chop of the naginata deflected it, but a line of bowmen fired a cloud of arrows at Jebu. Several arrowheads embedded themselves in the sharkskin and steel strips of his armour, while most rebounded from it. Not one missed altogether; the archers were expert marksmen. Grinding his teeth and chopping down arrows in flight with his naginata, Jebu retreated step by step. By the time he reached the gate his armour was bristling with arrows, and one had pierced his left shoulder. Behind the gate, panting, he let Kanefusa unlace his armoured left sleeve to pull out the arrow and bandage the wound with a strip of paper.

'I do not want you here today, monk Jebu,' Shenzo Totomi said with a grin. 'Only your feats will be remembered when the chroniclers write of this battle, and the rest of us will be ignored.'

'You must outdo me,' Jebu answered, shrugging his arm back into the sleeve. 'Then we all will be remembered.'

For a time, they lost no more men. The Mongol archers could shoot at the defenders only by exposing themelves to fire from the watchtower. Thus protected, the samurai took turn single-handedly meeting the Mongol charges, striking down the attackers one man at a time. Repeatedly, Jebu charged through the gate when the Mongols attacked and rushed headlong down the path, flailing enemy warriors into the ravine with his naginata. Each of his assaults ended with his being driven back by volleys of arrows, but he was determined to break through to Arghun.

They were fighting in shadow now. The sun had crossed the narrow blue gap between the mountains above them. Jebu looked up to see bright rays stretching from their peak to splash dazzling light on the snowy mountain opposite. He heard a rumble from above. He had barely time to shout a warning. Huge rocks – grey boulders the size of houses – were tumbling down the steep slope towards them. A picture of Yukio's charge down the hillside at Ichinotani leaped up in Jebu's mind. But these were not horses and men thundering down on them. These were insensate masses of stone capable of crushing them all and sweeping the entire fort from the ledge. There was nothing they could do but throw themselves flat. With a roar like the firing of a hundred *hua pao*, the avalanche was upon them. The crashing and shaking of the earth stunned Jebu, and he squeezed his eyes shut as he waited to be smashed like an ant under a sandal. At last there was a silence, almost as terrifying as the noise that preceded it. They lay still on the ground, and Jebu realized that somehow they were still alive. He rolled to his feet. He saw the worst damage at once. The watchtower was kindling wood, the two samurai archers who had been standing in it gone. Where it had been lay a giant, jagged stone, cracked in several places from the force of its fall. Amazingly, the house that sheltered Yukio and his family was still standing. There were seven defenders left now, and no place from which an archer could provide protective fire for them. The wall itself was down in many places. Yukio had nothing between himself and his enemies but seven human bodies. One of the seven had his arm broken by a huge rock. Looking up, Jebu saw tiny figures peering down at them from a ledge far above. It was Arghun who had unleashed the avalanche.

Jebu sent Shenzo Totomi to make sure Yukio was unhurt and to report to him. Even as Totomi crossed the rock-strewn courtyard, Jebu heard the war shouts of attackers. The injured samurai ran out through the gate with his sword in his left hand and a poem on his lips. He managed to account for three of the enemy before he fell under a volley of arrows. Another samurai leaped to the top of a fallen stone and nocked an arrow with a double-bladed frog-crotch head. He let fly, and a Mongol archer screamed. The arrow had severed his hand from his wrist. The Mongols withdrew momentarily. But soon another file of them, waving sabres and spears, was running, shouting, up the path. Jebu wondered, how does Arghun get them to charge into certain death? It must be because most warriors think they will be lucky enough to survive when all around them are killed. What is called courage is often self-deception. These samurai defending Yukio, on the other hand, knew they were going to be killed. One by one they sallied forth, calmly and cheerfully, intending to keep on fighting till they were cut down. With the battle almost over, the Mongol attacks were coming faster now.

When there were only three of them left, Kanefusa said to Jebu, 'You want to be the last, don't you?'

'Yes.'

'It is your right. You were with him from the beginning,' said Kanefusa with a nod in the direction of Yukio's house. 'See to it that my cousin Mirusu is not dishonoured.' And he went out through the gate in the wall that no longer stood, to meet the next Mongol attack.

Shenzo Totomi returned from the little house, his face pale, his eyes staring as they had the night his father committed seppuku in Heian Kyo. He held a blood-dripping dagger in his hand. He seized Jebu's arm in a grip so powerful it hurt Jebu even through his armoured sleeve.

'He needs you.'

Jebu stared into Totomi's wild eyes. 'What is it? What has happened?'

'What do you think? What is the only thing that could happen? Go to him, in Buddha's name. There is no more time. Go to him, and let me die.' With a mad shriek Totomi drew his sword and charged through the gate.

Jebu turned away. The robe under his armour was soaked with sweat despite the chill of the mountain air. They had been fighting for hours, and the very bones in his body seemed ready to crack with weariness. From head to foot he bled and burned with the pain of innumerable wounds. Yet the pain was welcome, telling him that his body was still able to feel. The Buddhists were right when they said that life is suffering, but they did not acknowledge that it is suffering that lets people know they are alive.

Yukio is right, he thought. Our bodies are getting old. But an hour from now at the most this body, my body, will be destroyed; I will cease to exist. It is impossible for me to think of it. I don't want to die, do I? After all these years of being trained to kill, of facing death and dealing out death to others, I still want to live. I am not a good Zinja.

He climbed the steps to the front door of Yukio's house. There was silence and darkness within. The chapel was on the second floor. As his eyes adjusted to the gloom, he saw four rolled-up sleeping mats, with wooden pillows beside them, and a few wooden boxes containing what little clothing and possessions Yukio's family had managed to bring here. On top of one of the boxes an Empress doll sat regally, her flowing, brocaded robe glittering.

Jebu climbed the ladder to the chapel, calling hoarsely, 'Yukio. Yukio-san.' As his head rose above the chapel floor he saw, first, a tiny oil lamp flickering in front of a many-coloured porcelain statue of Kwannon, seated. Then he noticed that the goddess was smiling gently down on what appeared to be four dark bundles of clothing. Jebu felt his stomach clench as he recognized the figure lying on the polished wooden floor.

'Jebu-san?' Yukio's voice came in a whisper.

'Yukio. You are still alive?'

'Yes – unfortunately.' There was a faint chuckle. 'I asked Shenzo Totomi to advise me on the best way to kill myself. He said that all samurai down through the ages would admire me if I did it as his father had in Heian Kyo, by hara-kiri. But he did not tell me this belly-cutting would hurt so much. Or that I would take so long to die. And what is the use of it? No one will know that I died this way, suffering abominably. No one knows except Shenzo Totomi and you. He is probably dead already. You will soon be killed as well. So, who will there be to tell the world of my so-glorious end?'

'Is Mirusu – gone? And your boy and girl?' Jebu had wept before, saying goodbye to Yukio. Now his eyes were dry. The shock of this took him beyond tears.

'Mirusu gave each of them the gift of oblivion. It was her final act of love for them. Neither Totomi nor I had the heart for it. Then, not wishing to see me die, she begged Totomi to stab her in the heart. At least he yielded and ended her life. I held her hand while he drove his sword into her. Then I took the kodachi that Mirusu used to cut the children's throats, and with it I opened my belly.'

Even though it was too dark to see the terrible sight, Jebu

turned away from the shadowy figure lying on the floor before him. He was divided between anguish for Yukio and rage at his friend for being willing to inflict a mortal wound on himself, for causing the deaths of his wife and children. The Zinja code and that of the samurai were so far apart. But it would do no good to rail at Yukio now.

'Can I help you somehow, Yukio-san?'

Yukio gave a deep groan. For a long time Jebu could hear nothing but his gasping, heavy and rhythmic as ocean waves. Speech must be an enormous effort, but it was worth it, perhaps, because soon Yukio would not be able to speak at all, would never speak again.

'I will die slowly and in great agony, Jebu-san, or I will die quickly and easily. It is up to you.'

Jebu's body went cold. 'You can't ask that of me.'

'If not you, who can I ask? Totomi would have done it, but I wanted you. You knew that some day you would have to do this last favour for me, didn't you? You knew all along. Your Zinja rule lets you slay enemies by the hundreds. Surely, then, you can give death as a kindness to a friend.'

Jebu began to unlace his chest armour. He remembered that he was carrying, in a secret pocket, the one drug in the Zinja pharmacopoeia that could help Yukio now. He knelt beside his friend and took his hand. The smell of blood was overpowering.

'Yukio, I can free you from your pain. I can give you a potion. You will fall asleep at once. I will stay here with you until you have passed over. Wait a moment. I'll get some wine.'

Yukio's hand squeezed Jebu's with surprising strength, crushing the knuckles together painfully. 'No, I refuse, Jebu. I absolutely refuse to die that way.'

'Why?' Jebu's voice was hoarse with suffering. 'Must I kill you? Is that the only way?'

'I will not die in my sleep. A filthy death. I want to know what is happening to me. To die as a man. Not an unconscious piece of meat.' Yukio's words came between gasps. 'I want to feel the sword. It is the cleanest way to die.'

Jebu felt something break within him. 'All right. It will be the sword, then, as you ask.'

'You must hurry, please, Jebu-san. They will be here any moment.'

Grief was an iron ball in Jebu's chest. He had come to love this man even more than he loved his father Taitaro. He put his hand on his sword hilt and began to slide the blade from its scabbard.

'I do this only because I know I won't have to suffer long,' he said. 'No matter how terrible the load of sorrow I bear, it will be but for a moment. Outside the chapel Arghun and his men wait to give me peace.'

'We will meet again in another life, Jebu-san,' Yukio whispered.

'We Zinja do not believe that men and women are reborn after they die. Nirvana is death.'

'Warriors like us are not worthy of Nirvana. We will see each other again. Strike now, Jebu. You will be as much a bringer of mercy as the goddess there who watches us. Your steel will end my agony.'

Once again a poem made its presence known in Jebu's mind, a last verse to share with Yukio. Now he was able to weep. His eyes burned as the tears flooded them.

> Together we roamed,
> Braved the roaring ocean waves,
> The hot desert sands.

Faintly, but promptly, Yukio's voice came back with lines to complete the poem:

> Together our swords in hell
> Will send its guardians howling.

Why must such a mind, that could compose the ending of a poem in an instant, be obliterated in an instant? Jebu still could not relinquish his belief that life, even on the worst terms, was preferable to death. But there was no more time to deliberate. He drew his short, heavy sword from its sheath and knelt beside Yukio, so he could see his friend's exposed neck in the dim light. He avoided looking at the dreadful wound below.

'Strike,' Yukio whispered, 'and burn this house down.'

Many times Jebu had gone into a trance in battle and had killed without knowing what he was doing; later he was unable to remember how he had fought. This moment was not like that. Just as Yukio wanted to be aware of death, so Jebu refused to draw his mind away from his task. Never had he lived so utterly in the here and now. This room, his friend's body, his sword, all seemed to glow with the same fire he had seen often in the depths of the Jewel of Life and Death. Still on his knees, Jebu raised his arms over his head and brought the sword down. The Zinja sword fell truly. Muratomo no Yukio was dead.

Jebu stood up quickly. He had not expected to feel this strange relief, this sense of lightness. For nearly twenty years he had fought beside his friend, feared for him, rejoiced in his victories, wept with him, worked to strengthen him, tried to protect him, planned for his future. Now Yukio's life was ended, and Yukio's servant was dismissed. For good or for evil, the terrible task was over. At the same time, he knew that without Yukio to give it meaning, life was impossible for him. He felt this lightness because he was empty inside, a hollow tree, dead and ready to fall before the first wind.

What were Yukio's final words? 'Strike, and burn this house down.' The command made Jebu think of the verses of the Lotus sutra: 'In the Three Worlds there is no rest; it is even as a house that has taken fire.' He picked up the little oil lamp that burned on a table before Kwannon's statue and tipped it, spilling a thin trail of burning oil along the polished wood floor to the plaster wall. The swirling orange flames leaped up, and the chapel was brightly lit. Jebu saw clearly the lavender and pale blue robes of Yukio and Mirusu and their children, the eight scrolls of the Lotus sutra spattered with blood, the sweet white face and pink cheeks of Kwannon. The goddess was the only living thing left in the room. A shame to let her be destroyed. Jebu picked Kwannon up and, cradling the heavy porcelain figure in his arms, climbed down the ladder to the first floor of Yukio's quarters. I have only a few breaths of life left to me, he thought.

He emerged from the building to find himself staring into a ring of surprised Mongol faces. They expected me to commit suppuku in there with Yukio, Jebu realized. A strange sight I must look, in bloodstained black armour with arrows sticking out all over me, and instead of a weapon, I hold a statue of the goddess of mercy.

The blunt tip of an armour-piercing arrow struck the statue squarely. With a ringing sound the porcelain goddess vanished. His arms were empty and a thousand white shards lay at his feet. She was gone, irrevocably, just as Yukio was gone forever. The devastating realization of the loss of Yukio struck him with the force of a spear thrust. He staggered backwards. Ignoring the arrows that bounced off or stuck in his armour, moving neither slowly nor hastily, he turned and went back into the burning building. His naginata was leaning against a wall where he had left it. As soon as he held it, he felt a sensation of enormous power coursing into his hands, through his arms and shoulders, spreading throughout his entire body, as if a superior being were taking him over. Not Kwannon, but Hachiman, the god revered by all the Muratomo. He came out of the house at a run, swinging the naginata in a circle, feeling it bite through leather armour and flesh and bone, hearing screams.

He gave himself over to the forms and movements of battle that he had been practising from the time he was old enough to stand upright. The warriors surrounding him fell back before the whirling blade. They were veterans enough to read the face of the giant advancing upon them; they had seen men possessed by battle madness before. They knew that no ordinary soldiers, no ordinary weapons, could bring down a man in that state. They were cautious, because this was the last enemy they had to finish. None wanted to die this close to victory.

A lucky blow of a battle-axe cut through the staff of Jebu's naginata, and the Mongols shrieked in triumph as the blade clanged to the ground. Jebu drew the sword that had killed Yukio and rushed his opponents. They tripped over one another, trying to escape, and many fell to the sword that looked so small in the hands of the huge man who wielded it. Steadily, sword in one hand, naginata staff in the other, Jebu drove them back past the ruined palisade to the narrow path where their numbers were useless to them, forced as they were to come at him one at a time. One at a time, they died.

Jebu was aware that some had slipped past him and were behind him in the ruins of the fort. He glanced over his shoulder and saw them hurrying in and out of the blazing building where Yukio had died. They're after Yukio's head, he thought. He wanted to return to the fort and stop them, but he could not turn his back. What happened to Yukio's head no longer mattered, anyway. Nothing mattered now. Jebu was beyond wanting or not wanting. He felt a peace and a bliss beyond comprehension. His mind was filled with a pure, endless white light that blotted out every individual thought or feeling. At the same time, the world around him, its sights and sounds, its feel and its smells, was more vivid then it had ever been at any time in his life. In the midst of the howling Mongols he was perfectly happy, incredibly happy. There would never be a better time for him to die.

He had become the Self. In battle he could make no mistake. He *was* his opponents, and he *was* the sword in his hand. Time stretched towards infinity. The Mongols attacked him ever so slowly, as if wading through water. It was no trouble at all to drive his sword past their clumsy defences. There was even time for him to say the Prayer to a Fallen Enemy for each opponent who joined the pile of bodies in the ravine. This was the state Jebu's masters in the Order called ultimate insight, that ecstatic condition in which the individual achieved complete union with the Self and could see the universe through the eyes of the Self. A single instant of ultimate insight, he had been taught, was worth a hundred lifetimes of ordinary consciousness.

The Mongols were backing away from him now, not attacking, and only their restricted position prevented them from running in panic. Each knew this superhuman being was going to kill him. Jebu was almost to the bend in the path now. It was growing darker. In winter, night fell in these mountains at about the Hour of the Ape. If he lasted until darkness was total, there was actually a chance of his escaping. At night, in these mountains, it would be nearly impossible to track down a single man. The thought disappointed him. He no longer wanted to live.

The intrusion of desire into his mind was enough to bring him down from the peak of ultimate insight. It was an ordinary warrior, sad, wounded, tired, who rounded the outcropping shielding the main body of Arghun's troops from him. Beyond the rock the path was empty. The roadway curved in a long, concave arc, and at the other end of that arc, shadowy in the twilight, a line of mounted bowmen stood up in their stirrups, eyes narrowed, arrows unwaveringly pointed at him. At the head of the line sat Arghun on a stocky black Mongol pony, his deep red cloak rippling in the wind.

'Kill me!' Jebu roared, and held his arms out wide.

His face hard and immobile, Arghun raised a gauntleted hand and brought it down in a sweeping motion. Bowstrings thrummed in unison, a deep musical note that echoed from the rock walls. Arrows whistled and shrieked across the ravine. His arms still outstretched as if to gather the arrows in, Jebu felt their impact all over his body. There was no pain, only uncountable numbing shocks. He saw Taniko looking at him with her bright eyes, just as he had seen her in the heart of the Jewel earlier today. His last thought was; the Jewel. I should have thrown it away. Now Arghun will get it. Then he lost consciousness as he began the long fall into darkness.

PART TWO

THE BOOK OF TANIKO

> Those who hold rank and power
> claim that the gods have set them up
> to rule over the people. In truth,
> rulers become rulers by tricking the
> people with just such stories as this,
> and by using force to make them
> submit. Whoever says the gods are
> responsible for the privilege of the
> few and the oppression of the many,
> slanders the gods.
>
> —*The Zinja Manual*

CHAPTER ONE

From the pillow book of Shima Taniko:

The wisteria blooms cluster like purple clouds among the pines. The cherry blossoms on the grounds of the Shogun's castle are a delight. The sweet songs of the bush warbler beguile the ear. In the hills the creeks have become rivers, and the frozen silence of the waterfalls has turned to thunder. The roads to the north-west are open again. Already parties of samurai have set out in the direction of the land of Oshu. All this winter I have buried my dread under a calm exterior, even as the land lay buried under snow.

There has been much to occupy me and help me to keep calm. Continuously, I work on my *kung-an*. Driven by fear of Eisen's mockery and scolding, I try to *become* the face I had before I was born, for I dread going to him without an answer. The chapel Eisen built himself in the woods above Kamakura has become part of the landscape. Pine seedlings grow from the roof tiles, and moss is spreading over the walls. Sametono, who is now officially my foster son, always goes with me to see Eisen. These two have a way of talking to each other that has nothing to do with speech. It is all winks and growls and gestures and strange cries. They greet each other with shouts of 'Kwatz!'

My cousin Munetoki has become Sametono's kenjutsu master. Hideyori's suspicion is like a drawn bow pointed relentlessly at our hearts, and I fear for Sametono's life, should he show that he has his father and grandfather's proficiency with the sword. Still, he must learn the way of the warrior, unless he is to end up as a monk.

Hideyori has said nothing to me at all about Oshu. He busies himself with his two favourite occupations, statecraft and religion. The Bakufu is now as highly organized and has as many officials as the court of Kublai Khan. Whenever weather permits, Hideyori rides to the temple of Hachiman Dai-Bosatsu, where he is building a stupa, a holy tower, dedicated to his mother. I never met the lady, who died in exile after Domei's insurrection, but Hideyori insists that she was a saint. I am sure his hatred of Yukio must arise, in part, from the rivalry between his mother and Yukio's mother, my friend Lady Akimi.

—*Third Month, twentieth day*
YEAR OF THE DOG

Visiting Taniko in the women's hall of the Shogun's palace, Ryuichi and his burly eldest son, Munetoki, accepted *ch'ai* from her with courteous compliments. When, she asked herself, had she seen that uneasy expression, a strange mixture of sorrow, shame and apology, on Uncle Ryuichi's face? Long ago she had seen it, so long that she could not place it, even though the sight of it filled her with terror.

Where was Sametono? She wanted to draw him close to her.

'That is very handsome handwriting,' said Ryuichi politely, gesturing with his cup towards the alcove where Taniko had hung a large sheet of pale green paper. On it, Sametono had written a verse of the Diamond sutra, suggested by Eisen as a calligraphic exercise:

Though we speak of goodness, the Tathagata declares that there is no goodness. Such is merely a name.

Taniko lowered her eyes modestly. 'It is the poor work of my unworthy son.'

'Sametono, madame, may grow up to be one of the finest swordsmen the Sunrise Land has ever seen,' said Munetoki fiercely. The epicene Ryuichi could hardly have produced a son more unlike him than Munetoki. Munetoki's voice was always on the verge of a parade-ground shout. He sounded angry even when he was at his most benevolent. His eyes blazed and his thick moustache bristled. Seated on cushions in Taniko's chambers, he had the air of a resting tiger. Since Taniko's father, Bokuden, had no sons of his own, Munetoki was heir apparent to the chieftainship of the Shima clan. Sametono adored him.

'I am happy that my son's efforts please his sensei,' said Taniko softly. Then she looked up quickly and fixed Munetoki's piercing brown eyes with her own. 'I would prefer that you not praise the boy too highly or too publicly, Munetoki-san. It might prove embarrassing.'

Munetoki glowered at her as if she had said something outrageous. 'Madame does not realize that there are samurai in the western provinces who would cheerfully give their lives for her. There are such men all over the Sunrise Land.' Taniko remembered the old samurai in the capital, years earlier, who had died defending her and Atsue from Motofusa's retainers.

She dropped her eyes. 'The first loyalty of all samurai is to the Shogun and the Bakufu. The Shogun in his vigilance against threats to the peace of the realm finds it hard to forget that Sametono is the last of Sogamori's line, or that we Shima are a branch of the Takashi. I do not wish the Shogun to be unnecessarily vexed.'

'Concerning the peace, Lord Hideyori has less to fear now,' said Ryuichi with that same expression of sorrow. Now she recognized his look. It was the same he had worn the day she learned Kiyosi had been killed.

'My honoured uncle and cousin did not visit me to admire my son's calligraphy and praise his swordsmanship,' Taniko said, fear tightening its cold grip on her heart.

'Taniko-san,' Ryuichi said slowly. 'Long ago I failed you by allowing you to hear terrible news from the lips of a stranger. I vowed that if the occasion should arise, I would not play the coward again.'

Taniko put her hand to her heart. 'Tell me quickly, Uncle.'

'The monk Jebu and the Lieutenant Muratomo no Yukio are dead.'

The cup Taniko was holding crashed to the floor. Munetoki's hand was on her arm instantly, steadying her.

'How clumsy of me,' Taniko murmured as she wiped the pale green liquid from the polished floorboards. 'What were you saying, Uncle?'

Ryuichi went on. 'I know that you cared deeply for both men. I wanted to be the one to tell you.'

'Please tell me how Jebu – how they died,' Taniko whispered.

Munetoki answered her, his voice softer than usual. 'Most heroically, as the story is told. The Lieutenant and twelve followers, among them the giant monk Jebu, held out for half a day against a thousand Mongols. The Zinja in particular performed superhuman feats in battle. At last Yukio and his men succumbed; but not before they had killed over three hundred Mongols. Yukio and his wife and children all committed seppuku. The story will be told down through the ages.'

I can't believe Jebu is dead, Taniko thought. Aloud, she said, 'With so many against so few, might not one or two have slipped away unnoticed?'

'They were trapped in a fort on the side of a cliff,' said Munetoki. 'An easy place to defend, but impossible to escape from. They are certainly all dead.' He spoke with some satisfaction. By Munetoki's martial standards, if any of Yukio's men had got away, it would have tarnished the glory of the event.

'Besides, the heads of Yukio and Jebu have been identified,' said Ryuichi sadly. 'As soon as the snow melted in the passes, Lord Yerubutsu of Oshu sent a delegation of his warriors with the heads of Yukio and Jebu preserved in black lacquer boxes filled with sake. When they arrived here, the Shogun was occupied with the rites dedicating the new stupa to his mother. It would have been unseemly for him to inspect severed heads. So he delegated my honoured brother, Lord Bokuden, to go and see the heads. Then they were burned on the beach.' His face took on an even more miserable look. 'I'm sorry, Taniko-san.'

I will not scream, Taniko told herself. I will hold myself

together. This has happened to me before, and I have lived through it. I will live through it this time. I will not scream.

'Do you know Moko the shipbuilder, Uncle? Please send him to me. He was devoted to Jebu and Yukio. I want to do the same service for him that you did for me – make certain he does not get this news from a stranger.'

'A common carpenter is your friend, Cousin?' said Munetoki with a puzzled frown.

'A very old and dear friend,' said Taniko, feeling a sob swell in her chest until it threatened to tear her apart. 'I need to be alone now. Will you excuse me?'

After they left, she sat still for a long time. A maid came to remove the *ch'ai* service, but Taniko waved her away. Alone, she poured water into the brazier under the pot to extinguish the coals. Thus life ends – a little fire that is suddenly overwhelmed and snuffed out. The windows of her room faced south, and bars of sunlight streamed through the lattice. Whenever I saw the sun, she thought, it always comforted me to think that wherever he was, the same sun was shining on him. It shines on him no more. Cut his head off and put it in sake, and then burn it on the beach! Oh no, no. Yukio's wife killed herself to die with him. Where is the girl Shizumi? I must try to get word to her as well as to Moko. She will probably want to kill herself, too. If only I could have died with Jebu. And yet I have only myself to blame for being apart from him. I held Kiyosi's and Atsue's deaths against him. I felt I couldn't live with him. I was a fool. Perhaps if I had stayed with him he would not have been killed with Yukio. Oh, Jebu, Jebu. I never knew how much I loved you until now.

She stood, holding her fists clenched at her sides, and screamed his name, so loud and so hard that it hurt her throat. Then she collapsed like a bird, arrow-shot in flight. She lay curled on the floor, weeping violently. Her maids rushed in. With little cries of pity and dismay they washed her face with cold water and put quilts over her. Not knowing what was wrong, they wept along with her even so, pressing their flowing sleeves against their faces. Taniko was unable to speak to the women, but part of her mind was clear. She was surprised at the sharpness of her grief, the violence of her reaction. She had thought that Zen somehow protected a person from the suffering of life. Eisen seemed so resilient, so calm and cheerful, that she had expected Zen would make her that way, too. That she hurt so much seemed almost a betrayal.

She lay helpless, tortured by a grief that would not let her eat or sleep or talk to anyone. Sametono came and tried to talk with her and ran out of the room crying when she could not answer him. He did not come back, and one of the maids, who realized that Taniko could hear and understand even though she did not speak, told her that her Uncle Ryuichi and Aunt Chogao had taken the boy to live with them for a time.

For four days she remained in that condition. Then she fell into a deep sleep, dreamless, almost a coma. When she woke, the first thing she saw was the terrified face of a maid, saying that Lord Hideyori was on his way to see her.

She felt beyond fear. She remembered Hideyori's rage when the dancer Shizumi publicly avowed her love for Yukio. How must he have felt on learning that Taniko, the woman he wanted to marry, was prostrate with grief at the news of Yukio's and Jebu's deaths? Having no idea of what had existed between her and Jebu, he would think, of course, that her grief was for Yukio. And some of it was. She had come to like Yukio, in China, and next to the Order, he had been Jebu's whole life. She might have given Jebu a reason to go on living after Yukio's death. But she had not. Jebu died believing that she did not love him. She began to cry again. It was thus that Hideyori found her, when he hurried into her chamber before the maids could give her warning.

Despite the suddenness of his entry, sliding back the shoji screen with his own hand, he looked unhappy rather than angry. He wore billowing white silk robes of mourning with a taboo tag, signifying that he was bereaved and was to be left alone, dangling from his black cap. No sword hung from his belt.

Taniko pressed her forehead to the floor. 'Forgive me, my lord, for being so poorly prepared to receive you.'

He knelt before her, seizing her hand in a powerful grip. A fire seemed to burn in the black depths of his eyes.

'Do you hate me, Taniko-san?'

'I? hate you?' For a moment the question bewildered her. Then she understood. He was, after all, the man responsible for the deaths of Jebu and Yukio. Why didn't she hate him? Because, she realized, this grief left her no room for vengefulness. Now she could see how the loss of Kiyosi and later, of Atsue, had embittered her, turning her against the man she had loved most in her life. Now, she understood, it did not matter who had killed Jebu. It was her karma that the men she loved must die in battle, and it was foolish to hate those who killed them.

Hideyori said, 'I realize that it was Yukio who rescued you from the Mongols and brought you back safely to the Sunrise Land. You owed him a great debt of gratitude. I also owe him a debt for doing that. Otherwise I would never have met you again. I spoke violently against him to you. But that was only to use your wisdom to test my fears about Yukio. You were the only one who would argue with me.' He gestured down at his white robe. 'Like you, I mourn him. I swear to you I did not want him killed. Do not blame me for his death, because now I need you more than ever, Taniko-san.'

I suppose I need you, too, Hideyori, Taniko thought. At least, I need your good will if Sametono, who is now all I have left in the world, is to live. How amusing that Hideyori expected me to hate him, and I expected him to hate me. But how can he mourn Yukio? How can he say that he did not want him killed? What a horrible world this is. When Sametono reaches manhood, if he lives that long, I will kill myself.

'Do you truly regret your brother's death, my lord?' she asked.

'By the Three Buddhas, I swear I gave strict orders to Arghun not to harm him, only to arrest him and bring him to me. Yukio was a good soldier who did not understand how the courtiers were using him in their intrigues against me.'

'I'm sure he would have come to you any time you sent for him and promised him safe conduct.'

'He would have come with an army, Taniko-san. How could I have stood against him?' Hideyori's eyes widened with candour. 'You know I'm not half the general he was. He would have overthrown me, taken over the country, and then not known what to do with it. Under his administration, the Sunrise Land would have fallen to pieces. I am building a nation to last forever. But now that he is dead, I can admit that I would not be where I am were it not for him. When they brought his head to Kamakura along with that of his friend, the mighty Zinja, I made an excuse that viewing the heads would defile the rites I was performing for my mother's memory. Actually, I was too heartbroken to look at my brother's head, or that of Jebu, the Zinja. He saved my life once, long ago. I was told that even your father, Lord Bokuden, was moved to tears when he opened the black boxes and gazed upon the pitiable contents.'

I will not believe that, Taniko thought.

'Who does not grieve over Yukio's death?' Hideyori went on. 'He was beloved throughout the Sunrise Land, so my reports tell me. Even though his life ended in failure, the people admire him. They think of me as a coldhearted murderer when I was only trying to do good. I must punish Arghun and Yerubutsu, to prove that I did not want Yukio to die. I must avenge him, Taniko-san.' Unease flickered in his eyes. 'I fear his angry ghost.'

'His ghost?'

'Yes, his and the monk Jebu's. Such powerful spirits are not easily put to rest. I must avenge them, to placate them.' He clenched his fist. 'Yerubutsu will be dealt with when the time is ripe, but Arghun's rampaging through this country must be stopped at once. His army puts the whole nation in jeopardy.'

'Because of the Great Khan's designs?'

Hideyori bowed his head in agreement. 'Immediately after the death of Yukio, Arghun and his troops rode in haste out of Oshu. They are now somewhere in the mountains of Echizen province, only a few days' ride from the capital. Prince Horigawa, your husband – ' he made a wry face – 'hurried on ahead to Heian Kyo by the Hokurikudo Road. Shortly after his arrival in the capital, the Imperial Court invited the Mongol ambassadors at Dazaifu to come to Heian Kyo and present their Great Khan's letter to our Emperor. I had expressly ordered that they not be allowed to come to the capital. This would not have happened if Go-Shirakawa were still alive. There are no wise heads in Heian Kyo now.' The wily old Retired Emperor had left the world late last year, in the same month as Lord Hidehira of Oshu.

'What does the Great Khan's letter say?' Taniko asked.

'I have not seen a copy yet.'

It was good to have something to think about besides her grief. 'It must be a demand that we submit to the Great Khan.'

Hideyori eyed her narrowly. 'And if it is, how do you think we should reply?'

'That may be the most difficult decision you will ever have to make in your life, my lord. As I have warned you before, those nations who have resisted the Mongols have been destroyed utterly.'

'Then you think we should yield?'

'There is no salvation in that course, either. I have seen what Mongol rule does to nations. If we give in to them without a struggle, they will end by plundering these islands from end to end and taking all our men to fight in their wars. They will impose their laws on us in everything from religion to the way we dress. We who called ourselves the children of the gods will cease to exist as a people.'

'But if we do decide to resist, how should we answer this letter from Kublai Khan? Should we be conciliatory and try to gain time?'

'I think not, my lord. That would only create conflict and confusion in our own ranks. If you intend to fight the Mongols, send for their ambassadors. Have them come to Kamakura and present their letter to you. Then have them publicly beheaded. There will be no turning back after that. To the Mongols, the killing of an ambassador is unforgivable. The whole country will have to unite behind you to fight the invaders, because the only alternative will be our total annihilation.'

Hideyori took a deep breath and let it out slowly. 'That is very drastic advice, Taniko-san.'

'My lord, we are threatened by the greatest power the world has ever known. The Great Khan has hundreds of thousands of troops and hundreds of huge oceangoing ships. The whole country must be united as one man, or we are surely doomed.'

'I shall offer up many prayers to Hachiman, asking his help in making this decision,' Hideyori murmured.

'Prince Horigawa is obviously in league with the Mongols, my lord,' Taniko went on. 'He always has been. He will intrigue on their behalf with the Imperial Court. You must kill him.'

'And rid you of an ardently undesired husband?' said Hideyori with a small smile. 'Well, I do not wish him to remain your husband, either.' His eyes darkened. 'I have promised myself and you that you will be my wife. I need you at my side. I must make decisions that will determine the future of the Sunrise Land for all time. You can help me.'

'I only tell you what must be obvious to any person of sense, my lord.'

'This talk has been a great relief to me, Taniko-san.' Hideyori stood up. 'I have dreaded seeing you ever since I learned that Yukio and Jebu were dead. I am happy to see that you bear your grief with wisdom and patience.'

After he was gone she shed more tears for Jebu. That was a wound she would carry with her to the grave, one that no one would know about. Yet, how puzzling that Hideyori had not only permitted her to grieve, but had even mourned for Yukio himself. How odd that his need for her seemed to override every other consideration.

She was hungry. She called a maid and asked for food. She was coming back to life. She still had Sametono. She had to see him through to manhood. Then, as she had decided, she would commit seppuku. There was one other thing, the Mongol threat. She would not leave this world of her own volition until she had done what little she could to help defend the Sunrise Land.

Sametono came to her later that day, and she tried to explain to him, in part, the cause of her sorrow.

'Do you mean that the big warrior monk who saved me from the Rokuhara was killed?' Sametono's small face was stricken. Tears streamed down his round cheeks. 'I have often dreamed of him. I want to grow up to be just like him.'

To comfort the child and herself, Taniko went to the cedar chest that held her most precious belongings. Sametono's eyes widened as she brought out a sword wrapped in silk. She removed the covering and slowly drew the gleaming, ancient blade part-way from its scabbard.

'This sword is called Kogarasu,' Taniko said. She told him its history. 'Some day when you are grown you will be able to wear it. For now you may come to me and secretly visit Kogarasu from time to time. But you must never let Lord Hideyori know about this. If he ever sees you carrying Kogarasu, that will be your last day on earth.' She held the hilt out to him and he drew the two-edged sword all the way from its scabbard. Even though it was as long as he was tall, he held it up with the ease he had already acquired through kenjutsu practice.

'One day with this sword I will protect the nation.'

Two days later, Taniko was well enough to visit Eisen. For once she went without Sametono. This time she wanted to unburden herself of a private grief. She told the monk of Jebu's death, and he listened, unsmiling.

When she was finished he asked, 'What has this taught you?'

'Taught me? It has left me with a question, sensei. I have been studying with you for years. I expected my work in Zen to make me stronger to bear sorrow. When I heard the news of Jebu's death I screamed and collapsed. I have made up my mind, once my last duties are fulfilled, to put an end to my miserable life. Why doesn't Zen help me?'

Eisen smiled. 'There was an abbot who saw deeper into realization than any person of his day. He was a living Buddha. One day this holy man was travelling on a pilgrimage and robbers set upon him. His screams as they stabbed him to death could be heard six provinces away.' Eisen looked piercingly at her. 'Do you understand?'

'No, sensei.'

'When you understand, my child, you will see the face you had before you were born.'

CHAPTER TWO

Standing on the parapet of the outer wall of the mighty castle Hideyori had built for himself, Taniko watched the approach of the procession bringing the Mongol embassy from the Tokaido Road into Kamakura. A row of samurai stood on the wall a respectful distance behind her. Tears stung her eyes as she remembered how she and Jebu, when she was a young girl, had ridden out of Kamakura to the Tokaido. Beside her, just barely able to see over the stone ramparts, Sametono squeezed her hand excitedly.

'Are those Mongol soldiers, Mother?'

'No, Sametono-chan. Ambassadors do not travel with their own troops. Those are our samurai, sent to escort the emissaries.'

Messengers riding ahead of the diplomatic party had brought disturbing news from Heian Kyo. The Imperial Court Council of State had met with the Mongols. The councillors were deeply grieved by the barbarous, contemptuous, well-nigh sacrilegious letter from Kublai Khan, which had claimed divine right to the title Son of Heaven, but, as Kublai had doubtless foreseen, its threat of annihilation should they fail to submit had thrown them into a panic, and they had decided to yield to the Great Khan's demands. A letter would be sent by the seven-year-old Emperor Kamayama acknowledging Kublai Khan's authority over him. The Emperor would send the tribute required. And the Imperial Court would permit a Mongol army to enter the country and set up a garrison near Heian Kyo.

Undoubtedly, Taniko thought, Arghun and his veterans of five years of warfare in the Sacred Islands would form the nucleus of that occupying army. The courtiers neither knew, nor would they have cared, that the samurai and the common people who had got wind of the capitulation were furious. One reason Hideyori had sent five hundred horsemen and two thousand foot soldiers to escort the ambassadors and the Court officials accompanying them was to protect them from the outraged populace. Only Hideyori himself knew what he would do when he met the ambassadors. He had asked Taniko's advice, but had not confided his plans to her. He might elect to do nothing at all. Officially, this visit by the ambassadors was just a courtesy call on the Supreme Commander of the Emperor's armed forces. Instead of speaking for the Sunrise Land, as Taniko had hoped he could, Hideyori was expected merely to ratify the decision of Heian Kyo. The Imperial Court had chosen to give in to the Mongols without consulting him.

From the height on which Hideyori's castle was built, Taniko could see the entire procession winding its way in from the Tokaido. The din of drums, gongs and flutes grew even louder. Now the first foot soldiers, running rhythmically, were crossing the bridge over the wide moat, passing through the heavily fortified main gate of the castle, which was only opened for ceremonial occasions like this. Rows of white Muratomo banners on the walls waved at similar banners strapped to the backs of officers in the escort. Many of the people lining the streets of Kamakura held smaller white flags. They cheered for the samurai as they passed, but watched in sullen silence the heavily curtained, gilded palanquins bobbing along in the midst of the parade.

When the palanquins had passed through the main gate, Taniko and Sametono went down the steps from the walls. Inside the wall there was a succession of lovely gardens meant to resemble those on the grounds of the Imperial Palace at Heian Kyo. These gardens, however, had a second purpose. They were cleverly arranged to form a maze in which any attacker would get lost and could easily be trapped. As Hideyori's officers led the embassy through this circuitous route, Taniko, Sametono and the samurai escorting her hurried through a secret shortcut to the central hall. Taniko was anxious to see the Mongol ambassadors; she wondered if she would recognize any of them from her days at Kublai Khan's court.

Through a narrow gate she entered the courtyard before the Shogun's central hall. She did not expect that the first dignitary she would see descending from a palanquin, stepping on the back of a prostrate servant, would be Prince Sasaki no Horigawa. Surrounded by a ring of samurai in armour, they stared at each other across an expanse of white gravel. The little eyes in the wrinkled face sparkled with malice as Horigawa gave her a mocking bow.

'How many years has it been since I had the pleasure of meeting my esteemed wife? You have aged gracefully, lady.'

A few years ago, had she encountered Horigawa, she might have tried to kill him with the handiest weapon. Now the fire of that hatred only smouldered, like a cooling volcano. Showing that she was unperturbed, she decided, would be the best response to this creature. But she could not resist a word of contempt.

'Long ago you delivered your wife into the hands of barbarians. Now, it seems, you intend to do the same thing to your country.'

Horigawa smiled. 'That will be my country's good fortune, if it is treated awell by those barbarians as you were. Ah, but I nearly forgot to extend my sympathies. The Zinja monk with whom you were so initimate long ago has at last passed into oblivion. I saw him shortly before his well-deserved death. He tried to kill me. My friend Lord Bokuden tells me that he has seen that red head pickled in sake. A fitting end for such a violent fellow.'

Horigawa befouled Jebu's memory by speaking of him. Now she did want to seize a sword from one of her samurai escorts and run the prince through, to avenge Jebu. Instead she forced herself to smile.

'All of us eventually meet the fate we deserve, Your Highness.'

Horigawa stared at her, puzzled, annoyed by her equanimity. 'All of us do meet our proper fate, my lady,' he agreed in his piping voice. 'Perhaps I will have a hand in determining yours, once the affairs of this realm are settled.' He turned away and started up the stairs.

'Give me the order and I'll cut him in two,' a voice growled at her ear. She turned and looked up to see Munetoki standing behind her.

'Thank you, cousin, but that will not be necessary,' she said. 'Such a breach of the peace would be a disservice to the Shogun.' She discovered that she was trembling. Only then did she realize what an effort it had cost her to maintain her self-control.

'Who was that man, Mother?' Sametono asked. 'He said you were his wife. Is he really your husband?'

Taniko took a deep breath and let it out to relax herself. 'He is no one, my child. No one at all.'

It was evening when Hideyori and the high-ranking samurai of Kamakura gathered in the Great Audience Hall of the Shogun's castle to meet the Mongol delegation. Ceremonial etiquette required Taniko to observe the gathering from behind a screen on a dais a short distance from where Hideyori would sit. The chamber itself was a huge room, lit by hundreds of oil lamps, with rows of White Dragon banners hanging from the beamed ceiling. Over five hundred vassals of the Muratomo and officers of the Bakufu were seated on cushions. Whatever Hideyori intended, he wanted plenty of witnesses.

When Hideyori entered, stately in his black sokutai robe, the assembled samurai bumped their foreheads on the floor. His face stony, Hideyori seated himself without a word. On the dais to his right and left were his chief councillors, Bokuden, Munetoki, the chieftains of the great clans and the heads of the Bakufu

Secretariat, the Samurai Office and the Judiciary. Hideyori nodded peremptorily to the guards at the rear of the audience chamber, and the large doors slid back.

Three envoys came into the room, a portly, bearded Chinese wearing a red and blue robe brocaded with gold dragons, and two tall Mongols in cloth-of-gold coats trimmed with fur. The Mongols wore sabres in jewelled scabbards. Behind the ambassadors walked Prince Horigawa with five other court officials from Heian Kyo, all in silk robes of varying shades of pearl grey and light green, appropriate for spring. There followed a long exchange of diplomatic courtesies, with the Chinese diplomat speaking for the delegation in the language of the Sunrise Land. He introduced himself as Mon Lim, assistant secretary in the Great Khan's Office of Foreign Affairs. The two men in gold were Prince Gokchu and Prince Belgutei, grandnephews of Genghis Khan, princes of the most exalted blood in the Mongol empire.

'Where did you learn to speak our language?' Hideyori asked gruffly.

'Your eminent Prince Sasaki no Horigawa was kind enough to teach it to me, sir,' the Chinese replied with a smile.

'I have already read your Great Khan's letter to our Emperor,' said Hideyori. 'For the benefit of these honoured warriors, I ask you to read it now.'

Mon Lim drew a scroll from his sleeve, unrolled it and began to read the Great Khan's letter. Angry mutterings rose around the room at the arrogance of the Great Khan's claim that his victories in warfare were proof of his 'mandate from heaven' but Mon Lim went on without hesitation until he came to the phrase, 'offer of union between our great empire and your little country.'

'Enough!' Hideyori shouted suddenly. There was a murmur of approval from the assembled samurai, who also had heard enough.

Mon Lim looked up, surprised. 'There is only a little more remaining, sir.'

'I wish to hear no more. This letter insults His Imperial Majesty. How dare you bring such a blasphemous document to our Sacred Islands? Your Great Khan must be an ignorant barbarian. Such a letter deserves no reply at all.'

'Good!' shouted Munetoki from Hideyori's right, unable to contain himself. He smacked his fist into his palm.

'I do not understand, sir,' said Mon Lim.

'I do not expect you to understand,' said Hideyori. 'The Chinese people have surrendered to the Mongols and you yourself have chosen to serve them. We do not intend to submit.'

'A truly civilized people turns to war only as a last resort,' said Mon Lim calmly. 'You, sir, are the chief general in this land. My master would be most kindly disposed towards you if you were to help bring peace between our two nations.'

Hideyori bared his teeth in a tigerish smile. 'Does the Great Khan reward you well for your services to him? Do you have a fine palace in your own country? A vast estate yielding much rice? A strongroom full of treasure?'

'The Great Khan has deigned to show me such kindnesses, which I little merit,' said Mon Lim with a modest smile.

'I hope for your sake you have enjoyed those possessions thoroughly,' said Hideyori, still grinning, 'because you will never see them again.'

The ambassador's face paled. 'Sir, you can't mean that.'

Hideyori rose to his feet and strode to the edge of the dais, his black robe swirling around him and his hand on the hilt of Higekiri, the Muratomo heirloom sword. 'Translate what I say so your two princelings will understand. In coming to this land of the gods with this message, you have descrated our country and insulted the sacred person of our Emperor. Only death can atone for this sacrilege. Only the death of his messengers is a fitting reply to the one who calls himself Great Khan. I sentence you to be taken to the execution ground on the beach north of the city and beheaded. Let this happen tomorrow at sunrise, that Amaterasu Omi Kami may see you pay for your blasphemy against her son.'

Mon Lim had begun to murmur a translation for the Mongol princes, but as he grasped the full import of Hideyori's words, he fell silent and his mouth hung open. At last, in the tense silence that followed Hideyori's sentence, he spoke.

'Sir, your Emperor has already agreed to our terms. It is not we who are offending him. It is you who are disobeying him.'

'His Imperial Majesty has agreed to nothing. Illegal agreements were made by rebels and traitors in the Imperial

Court.' Hideyori glared meaningfully at Horigawa and the other officials from Heian Kyo, who stood shocked and silent behind the Mongol ambassadors. The Chinese diplomat hastily finished translating Hideyori's speech for the two Mongol princes. At once, the one called Gokchu reacted. His sabre flashed as he rushed at the dais, knocking Mon Lim aside. Hideyori stood rigid and motionless, like a guardian statue before a temple, the knuckles white on the hand that gripped his sword. Taniko felt her heart stop. Draw your sword, she thought. Draw your sword.

With a leap and a shout, Munetoki was between the Mongol prince and Hideyori. He seized Gokchu's upraised sword arm with both hands and twisted it violently, stepping into the Mongol at the same time and throwing him to the floor. Taniko heard the muffled snap of a bone breaking. Straddling the fallen Mongol, Muntoki unsheathed his long sword and lifted it high over his head.

'No,' called Hideyori. 'Do not shed blood here. Let him be killed tomorrow at the public execution ground as I have already commanded. But, for drawing his sword against the Shogun, let him be executed, not by beheading, but by being cut to pieces starting with his feet.'

The other Mongol prince spoke rapidly to the pale, trembling Mon Lim, who turned to Hideyori and said, 'He warns that if you do this to us, every man, woman and child on these islands will die for it. Every city and village will be levelled. Your country will cease to exist.'

Hideyori spoke in a calm, measured tone. 'If the Mongols should conquer us, which I doubt our gods will permit, the people of these islands will die willingly. To us death is always preferable to surrender. But we will not line up to let our throats be slit like the animals that the Mongols herd. We are a warrior race, the children of the gods. Each of us who dies will take many, many Mongols into the Void with him. In any case, you will not see the outcome. Take them away.' Hideyori's guards marched the three envoys from the room. They would be held in a cellar till dawn.

Munetoki jumped lightly back to the dais and bowed to the Shogun. 'Forgive me for drawing my sword in your castle, my lord,' he said politely. As was customary, Hideyori offered no thanks to the young warrior for saving him from assassination. Munetoki had simply been doing a kenin's duty. Instead, Hideyori addressed the assembly.

'Do any doubt whether our warriors are a match, man for man, for the Mongols? See the ease and skill with which Shima Munetoki disarmed and disabled that barbarian.' Cheers and shouts of approval came from all parts of the room.

'Now,' Hideyori said, seating himself. 'Let Prince Sasaski no Horigawa and those officials who accompanied him from Heian Kyo be brought forward.' Taniko realized that Hideyori had rehearsed all this in advance. At his words, guards sprang to the sides of each of the six noblemen. Taniko's heart beat faster. After all these years of hating Horigawa, she was about to see his downfall.

'Prince Horigawa,' said Hideyori, 'even before the overthrow of the Takashi you were making overtures to the Mongols, encouraging them to cast covetous eyes on our Sacred Islands. It was you who invited these ambassadors to Heian Kyo and you who persuaded the Imperial Court to yield to their demands. We could have delayed the ambassadors. We could have kept up negotiations for years, giving us time to prepare for an invasion. I had no wish to kill those men. They are simply serving their master. But because you persuaded the Court to show weakness, you made it necessary for me to take drastic action to demonstrate our resolve. You have served your country and your Emperor so badly that it is plain you are a traitor to both.'

Horigawa's eyes narrowed. 'There was a time, Muratomo no Hideyori, that you wet your sleeves with tears of gratitude because I befriended you. Have you forgotten that you owe your life to me?'

'My life?' Hideyori's face was as cold as a shark's. 'Yes, I owe you my life, but only because you wanted to use me as a weapon against the Takashi. I also owe you the death of my grandfather, executed at your urging. I owe you the deaths of my father and my elder brothers, driven to rebellion by Sogamori's excesses, which you encouraged. I owe you the years of oppression and shame suffered by the Muratomo after my father's uprising was put down. If I am under any obligation to you, Prince Horigawa, it has been washed away by blood.'

Horigawa's lips drew back, baring teeth that gleamed like tiny black pearls in the lamplight. 'Samurai.' He spat the word as if it were a curse. 'A servant who steals his master's place. Apes, pretending to be human beings. I did my best to use your bloody-mindedness to destroy you. I failed because, like lice, you grow fat and multiply on blood. You destroyed the world I loved, and the world you have made holds no delight for me. If you end my life, Muratomo no Hideyori, you could do me no greater service. My only regret is that I will not live to see Kublai Khan sweep you all away like so much chaff before the wind.'

He means it, Taniko thought. Where such a man is concerned, revenge is impossible. He will even turn his own execution into a triumph of sorts.

Hideyori smiled at Horigawa. 'Twenty-four years ago my father sent me to kill you. Now at last I can carry out his order. I have searched my mind for a death that would be as long and horrible as your life has been, but no such thing is possible. You are an old man and will go quickly, no matter how careful we are. Yet, beheading is a samurai's death, and you do not deserve it. So, I have decided that tomorrow you will be taken to the place of public execution and drowned in the sea. Your body will be left there. Your bones will be nibbled by fish and crabs when the tide covers them, and they will bleach in the sun when they lie exposed. It is too merciful by far for you, but I can think of no way to punish you properly.' He laughed without humour. 'I am not cruel enough.'

Taniko thought, it is more appropriate than you realize, Hideyori. He will drown, as my little Shikibu did. Why am I not more delighted? Why, instead of joy, do I feel only this sad emptiness? Because his death will not bring my lost loved ones back.

Horigawa thrust his head forward like a striking snake. He spat at Hideyori's feet. Munetoki roared with rage. Without turning, Hideyori held out his hand in a restraining gesture.

'Do not stain your sword, Munetoki-san,' Taniko called from behind her screen. Hideyori motioned to the guards, and Horigawa was led from the hall.

The pale, moon-faced Heian Kyo aristocrats who had come with the embassy cowered as Hideyori's dark gaze turned next towards them. 'As for you officials of the Court,' he said, 'you are also guilty of trying to surrender your country to the Mongols, but I will assume that you acted out of ignorance and cowardice, rather than, as Horigawa did, out of deliberate malevolence. Therefore, I merely sentence you to return to the capital.' The powdered faces brightened with relief. After a pause Hideyori added, 'On foot.'

A howl of anguish went up from the noblemen and a shout of laughter from the samurai. One fat aristocrat fell to his knees. 'My lord, such a journey will kill us.'

'Nonsense,' said Hideyori. 'It will make you stronger and wiser. See something of the country you were so eager to give away to Kublai Khan.' Again he paused, while the courtiers stared at him, appalled. 'Of course, I shall respectfully point out to His Imperial Majesty that you are not fit to hold the ranks and offices you now enjoy. You and all others at the capital who had a hand in this decision to surrender will be sent into honourable retirement.' Hideyori waved away the stout men in their subtly shaded robes.

Now he addressed his clansmen and allies. 'We have already sent out two armies, one to the land of Oshu to punish Yerubutsu for killing my brother Yukio against my wishes. The other pursues the Mongols under the *tarkhan*, Arghun, now lurking in Echizen province and threatening the capital. All Mongols are our enemies now. We must prepare the nation for war.'

The samurai cheered until they were hoarse, shouting the old battle cry, 'Muratomo-o!' over and over again. Tears ran down Taniko's cheeks. She wept for these samurai and for all the people of the Sunrise Land. They did not know, as she did, the enormity of the disaster that threatened them. Even to Hideyori, this crisis with the Mongols was more an opportunity than a danger. He had used the occasion to assert the supremacy of the Shogun and had put down an attempt by the Court to decide a question of war and peace. Now he would destroy the independent lord of Oshu and Arghun's army. Then there would be no one in all the Sacred Islands not subject to his will.

Hideyori turned away from the cheering assembly. A moment later he was behind Taniko's screen, looking down at her with a smile. 'Of all who advised me, your advice was the soundest.

Together we will face the worst the Great Khan can send. After tomorrow, you will be free to marry me.'

Taniko was unable to speak. Vengeance, she had found, was empty. All victories were hollow. Whether she looked to the past or to the future, all she could see before her or behind her was destruction and death. Only with an enormous effort of the will could she hold down a sob. For some reason she found herself remembering Eisen's story of the Zen abbot who had died screaming.

CHAPTER THREE

Taniko lay awake all that night, thinking of the men somewhere else in the Shogun's castle, waiting to die. They, too, must be awake, she thought. How could anyone spend the last night of his life sleeping? She did not want to be nearby when they – especially Horigawa – were led out to the beach to be executed. Some time during the Hour of the Ox, with dawn two hours away, she called on her maids to help her dress for a journey into the hills, to see Eisen. Sametono refused to wake up. She had him wrapped in a quilt and carried down to the courtyard where her horses waited. With a maidservant and a samurai guard, who held the sleeping Sametono propped before him on his saddle, she rode up the familiar path into the pine-covered hills north of Kamakura. The sky over the great ocean to the east was already growing noticeably lighter. By the time she had arrived at the monastery, there were great ribbons of crimson unfurling like Takashi banners in the eastern sky.

'Why are you crying?' Eisen wanted to know. 'Are you mourning Horigawa and the Mongol envoys?'

'I am crying because I am partly responsible for their deaths through my advice to Hideyori.'

'A samurai should never feel regret at causing death,' said Eisen firmly. 'Killing is what a samurai does.'

'There is no end to it,' said Taniko, wiping her face with her sleeve. 'What have we human beings done to deserve so much pain, sensei?'

'If a man is shot with a poisoned arrow, he does not bother to ask whether he deserved it. He pulls out the arrow and applies the antidote as quickly as possible.'

'What is the antidote to all this suffering?'

'Show me the face you had before you were born,' said Eisen fiercely.

Her mind a blank, Taniko shrugged helplessly. She still had not solved the *kung-an*. Their talk turned to her coming marriage to Hideyori. As the wife of the Shogun, she would be the most powerful woman in the land.

'You will be able to accomplish much,' said Eisen

'Yes, through Hideyori.' She shook her head angrily. 'Sensei, I want to do things in my own right, not just because some powerful man like Kiyosi or Kublai Khan or Hideyori has decided he wants to go to bed with me.' Eisen laughed softly.

She and Sametono took their midday meal with the monks. By now, she thought, feeling the tension drain out of her, the condemned men must all be gone. This evening she could return to Kamakura and it would be behind her. The past, said Eisen, did not exist. In the afternoon, at the Hour of the Sheep, she and Eisen walked in the temple's garden.

Their conversation was interrupted by a messenger from Hideyori, a breathless young samurai who bowed to the monk and the lady in the temple garden. 'The heads of the Great Khan's ambassadors are on their way back to him. As for Horigawa, he has survived the morning high tide. When I left the Shogun's castle he still lived. Lord Hideyori thought you would be pleased to know that he is still suffering.'

'What are they doing to him?' Taniko asked, horrified.

'There is a cliff that drops down to the sea near the execution ground,' said the samurai. 'The executioners have hung Prince Horigawa from that cliff by a rope tied around his chest. As the tide goes in and out, they raise and lower him so that his head is always just above the water. The waves dash continuously into his face, the cold is intense, and his body is bloody from being repeatedly thrown against the rocks. At times they allow him to be submerged for a moment and he comes close to drowning.' Taniko fell to the ground and put her face in her hands. The young samurai stared at her, puzzled. Eisen sent him away.

After he was gone Taniko said, 'Hideyori thinks it may please me to know that Horigawa is still alive and in pain. In the name of Amida Buddha, what does he think I am?'

'There is a part of you that wants Horigawa to be tormented. That is why you are feeling so much pain.'

In the evening Hideyori's samurai messenger returned to tell her that Horigawa yet lived. He was raving and babbling now in three languages, the young man said. The exquisitely educated mind was unravelling.

Taniko stayed at the monastery that night. She did not want to go back to Kamakura as long as Horigawa was still being tortured. Long before daylight she rose and put on a hooded cloak and went to the meditation hall to sit in zazen with the monks.

At the Hour of the Dragon that morning, Hideyori himself arrived at the monastery and sent for her. He was waiting with a small group of horsemen just outside the gate, sitting astride a skittish, pure white stallion that had been a present from Bokuden when he assumed the title of Shogun. A retainer held the horse's head and stroked its nose to keep it calm. When he saw Taniko, Hideyori dismounted. He took a gleaming black box from a servant. Taniko knew what she was going to see and she wanted to run away, but she forced herself to look as Hideyori opened the box with a self-satisfied smile.

The white stallion screamed and reared at the sight, almost kicking the man holding him. Horigawa's dead lower lip hung open, showing his blackened teeth. His face was even more wrinkled than it had been in life, and there were bruises on his cheeks and forehead. She felt an enormous relief that it was all over. She turned away and put her hand over her eyes. Hideyori closed the box lid with a bang and handed it back to his servant. In just such a box as that Jebu's head lay, she thought.

'That man was harder to kill than a centipede,' Hideyori said with a smile. 'He survived until just before dawn this morning. He screamed all through the night. I went out to listen to him. I am sorry that you could not bring yourself to be there. I hope his execution pleases you.'

She must give him some reply. 'Thank you, my lord, for giving me this satisfaction,' she said quietly.

'You are free of your vow now,' said Hideyori. 'When may I come to you?'

Was she to acquire another husband so quickly? She felt frightened, walled in. Well, it was the way she could be most useful to the Sunrise Land and could best protect Sametono.

'You will adopt Sametono, my lord?'

'Yes, yes. He will be my foster son. He will be treated as an Imperial prince is. If he shows himself capable, he may even be Shogun himself some day, as well as chieftain of the Muratomo.'

And as the mother of the Shogun-to-be, she, and not her father, would be the most important member of the Shima clan.

'When may I come, Taniko-san?'

'Please understand, my lord. I am upset by all that has happened.'

'I can be patient a little while longer. But when?'

'Come to me in the Fourth Month on the night of the full moon.'

'Will you have a baby?'

'I'm too old, I think.'

'But isn't that what happens when people get married?' Sametono, like everyone else in her family, saw Taniko's new position as the Shogun's primary wife in the light of his own concerns. He was anxious that he might be supplanted in her heart by a new baby. Bokuden was nervously deferential and not pleased that his daughter would nightly have the ear of the most powerful man in the land. Uncle Ryuichi and Aunt Chogao felt themselves vindicated. Taniko's first marriage, which they had helped arrange, had been such a disaster that this one, according to their simple view of the law of karma, must be a great success.

'Now you've got a real man,' Aunt Chogao had bubbled as they soaked together in a hot tub. 'You deserve some good luck, Taniko-chan.'

It doesn't feel at all like good luck, Taniko thought later, as she lay on her futon in her dimly lit room, waiting for Hideyori's first-night visit. It simply feels like another turn of the wheel of birth and death.

Her screen slid back. Hideyori was not even making a pretence of secrecy. Beyond him, in the corridor, she could see two guards trying to suppress grins. Hideyori shut the screen and turned to her. He wore a plum-coloured kimono, a departure from his usual sombre tones. He looked unhappy and nervous. I'm the one who should be nervous, Taniko thought. It's been years since I've been to bed with a man, while he, from what I hear, has a different courtesan every night.

'Will you have sake, my lord?' She poured a cup for him and held it out. He seated himself awkwardly, drained the tiny cup in one quick sip, and held it out for more. Twice more she filled it and twice more he drank. She hoped he was not going to drink so much that he would be unable to enjoy his visit. That would be embarrassing for both of them. As for herself, she might as well have been discussing the Confucian classics with an old scholar, for all the desire she felt.

He praised the vase of tulips she had set in a corner of the room. Abruptly, he took a rolled-up sheet of rose-tinted paper from his sleeve. 'I wrote this in praise of your great beauty.' The scroll was tied with a long blade of grass. Taniko opened it and read the verse.

> The bamboo grasses
> Bend their backs in the autumn wind,
> Dancing in the sun.
> But when the wind does not blow,
> They point straight to the heavens.

A lovely poem, thought Taniko. Of course, it's two hundred years old, at least. She remembered that Horigawa had offered her an old poem as his own creation, too. She told herself firmly that she would not think about that marriage. The past did not exist.

She praised the poem.

'I copied it from an old book,' said Hideyori glumly. 'I am no courtier, Taniko. I do not know how to make love as they do in Heian Kyo.'

'I myself am a simple woman of Kamakura, my lord,' said Taniko. She picked up her samisen and played, 'When the Silver Moon Sets'. Then she blew out the lamp and raised her outside screens. The evening air was pleasantly warm. She sat beside Hideyori, and they looked at the full moon just rising above the black castle walls. She played two more melodies for him and gave him more sake. She had expected him, after his long wait to make her his wife, to be more ardent.

At last he put his arms around her. He stroked her face and her hands and began plucking at her robes. She moved to help him open her clothing, feeling at last a tingle of anticipation. It had, after all, been a long time, and Hideyori was, in his way, attractive. They fell back together to the quilts which she had already unrolled. Now his hands, the soft hands of a man who did no labour and no fighting, were gently awakening sensations in her body. Sighing, she stroked the ivory column he pressed against her and she opened her thighs. For a moment Hideyori was above her, blotting out the moonlight. Then he gasped and stiffened as if arrow-shot. He dropped to one side, breathing heavily. Taniko waited for him to take her, but instead he rolled away from her and lay staring out at the moon. Unsure about what to do, she began massaging his back. She ran her hands inside the collar of his kimono and rubbed his neck and shoulders. His muscles were stiff, unresponsive.

'Don't I please you, my lord?' she said at last.

'Don't be ridiculous,' he said gruffly, keeping his back to her. She was stung by his rudeness. What was the matter with the man?

'You are too forward,' he said suddenly.

Nettled, she answered, 'I can't believe that a man as experienced with women as my lord is would find anything unusual in my conduct.'

'I seem to have been mistaken in you,' Hideyori said, sitting up. He was going to leave her, she realized. She was not going to be the Shogun's bride after all, and Sametono would never be Shogun after Hideyori. The whole future of the Sunrise Land was going to be different because of some mysterious thing that had gone wrong in the last few moments. Should she try to placate him, try to persuade him to lie down with her again, or was it too late? She sat up also, and as she did so her fingertips touched a wetness on the quilt that told her everything. How stupid of me, she thought. I should have known at once. But it had never happened to her before. Other women had told her about being with men who reached their peak too soon, but all agreed that it was very rare. Hideyori was, no doubt, ashamed. He probably felt she doubted his manhood. The quarrel he had started was just a pretext to escape further embarrassment. She knew what to do to help Hideyori, from conversations she'd had with women over the years. But would he permit her?

'Forgive me, my lord,' she said softly. 'I realize I haven't been all that you hoped for. But if you leave me now, the whole castle will know it. Let me amuse you with more songs and warm you with more sake. I beg you, at least pretend you find me pleasing for this one night, or you will make me a laughing stock.'

'Very well,' said Hideyori, doubtless realizing that he, too, would be a target for humour if he left her now. He sat down again, and Taniko relit her lamp. She put a jar of sake over the brazier to warm it, and took up her samisen. She played and sang a series of songs. The first was romantic, but they became progressively more comical and salacious. Hideyori actually broke into a grin at the last and most uproarious. The songs and the sake were doing their work. He was much more relaxed. She moved closer to him and began caressing him. His kimono was still open, and she stroked his bare chest first, then his entire body. She gently pressed him back on the quilt while she continued to touch him. Soon she was exclaiming at the magnitude of his arousal while he grinned, pleased with himself. When she judged the moment to be right, she lay back and whispered that she wanted him to enter her. He took much longer to achieve the mountain top this time, because he was less sensitive than he had been before. In fact, he took so long to satisfy himself that she unexpectedly reached the sublime moment three times before he finished, for which she was very careful to express her humble female gratitude. When at last he lay back with his eyes closed, his face serene and relaxed, she quietly breathed a sigh of relief.

'You are a wise and understanding woman, Taniko-chan,' Hideyori murmured contentedly. He turned his head towards her. 'Your face as you look down at me now reminds me of the face of Kwannon I saw in a temple my mother took me to as a child. There was a time when I was very young that I thought the statues of Kwannon were statues of my mother. I feel as if I should worship you, Taniko. Please forgive me for speaking so harshly to you before. Be my Kwannon, be merciful to me.'

'There is nothing to forgive, my lord.' What a strange, strange man this is, she thought.

'I want you to visit the great stupa I built at our family shrine to Hachiman to honour my mother. I am sure it will please you.'

After a time he fell asleep. The moon was now high in the sky. She lay looking at his face in the moonlight. In repose, it seemed just the ordinary face of an ordinary man, not the face of a man who had conquered the Sunrise Land and was now about to embark on another war with an enemy vastly more powerful than any he had yet encountered.

'Let me alone, Yukio,' Hideyori moaned in his sleep. Yukio lived inside him, she thought, as Hideyori shifted his limbs and whimpered. You can never truly kill anyone. She settled herself down to sleep, propping her head on the worn wooden pillow that had been her lifelong companion. Past and future might not exist, but their traces in the present were eternal.

The next morning before he left her, Hideyori made her promise that she would tell her relatives he had kept her awake all night. His morning-after letter arrived at the Hour of the Serpent. It was simple, but seemed sincere. There was no poem with it. Even so, Ryuichi and Chogao were delighted. Two more night visits and a holy man's blessing, and the Shima, the Takashi and the Muratomo would be united in the persons of Taniko, Sametono and Hideyori.

CHAPTER FOUR

The wooden walls of the dojo, the martial arts practice hall in the Shogun's castle, rang with youthful cries and shook with resounding thumps. Seven boys, aged eight to fourteen, and an instructor, all dressed in loose-fitting white jackets and calf-length trousers, threw themselves at one another ferociously, somersaulted in mid-air, and twisted each other's arms and legs in vicious locks that, with a bit more pressure, would have broken them. Shima Munetoki sat at one end of the long, bare room, sternly watching everything and saying nothing. Invited by Munetoki, Taniko observed the class from a screened gallery. It was Munetoki's first visit to the dojo in over six months, and the young students, all sons of leading eastern-province families, were prepared to kill each other and themselves to show their sensei that they had made progress while he had been off fighting the Mongols on Kyushu.

Munetoki strode into the midst of the students, his thick moustache bristling as the corners of his mouth turned down. 'Attack me,' he commanded. The seven boys and their instructor formed a half circle around him. Sametono, as the Shogun's foster son, had the honour of being first. He flew at Munetoki with a wild scream. Hardly seeming to move, the big Shima samurai sent the eight-year-old boy spinning through the air. Taniko's heart leaped into her mouth. Sametono hit the woven grass mat with his shoulders, rolled and bounced to his feet with a grin. At least he falls well, Taniko thought. Singly, then together, the boys went for Munetoki, who tossed them in all directions. The young instructor was the last to charge. He threw a punch at Munetoki's head, twisting his fist as his arm shot out. Munetoki threw him almost the length of the room. Then, at Munetoki's order, the class knelt in two rows facing each other while he stood at the end, hands on· hips, and surveyed them. Having learned from Eisen that neither praise nor criticism truly helps students, he simply glowered at them. At last he pointed at Sametono. 'What are you thinking about?'

Sametono looked his burly cousin fearlessly in the eye. 'Sensei, I was wondering if you'd honour us by telling us what happened in Kyushu. Please excuse my impertinence.'

'Indeed, you are impertinent, young Sametono,' said Munetoki gruffly.

'Please, sensei, it would inspire us to do better,' said Sametono. Emboldened by Sametono's outspokenness, the other students added a chorus of eager pleas to his.

'Sit in silence and listen respectfully, then,' said Munetoki. 'I will tell you of the bravery of the warriors of the Sunrise Land as they faced the barbarian invaders.' He seated himself cross-legged on the floor. Taniko was delighted. Hideyori had kept her informed of the progress of the war with the Mongols, but she wanted to hear about it from someone who had actually taken part.

'We knew that Arghun's army of some three thousand horsemen was lurking somewhere in the mountains north of the capital,' Munetoki began. 'In the Fourth Month, therefore, Lord Hideyori sent an army of five thousand from Kamakura. I, unworthy as I am, had command. From the Fifth Month on, we camped north of the capital. At the same time the Shogun sent twenty thousand men into Oshu to punish Fujiwara no Yerubutsu for the murder of Lieutenant Yukio.

'Fearing that the Mongols might take us by surprise unless we caught them first, we at last began to move cautiously into the mountain country. All we found were smouldering villages where the Mongols had come and gone. Not a soul alive. Thus they left a twisting and unpredictable trail of death drawing us deeper into the mountains. After two months of this, fortune turned in our favour. Down from the far north came our army from Oshu, victorious. Oshu had fallen with surprising ease. When old Hidehira died, something went out of that country. The warriors did not want to fight for Yerubutsu. One of his own men assassinated him and brought his head to our army. Of course, Lord Hideyori ordered that the traitor in his turn be beheaded. One should never violate his oath to his lord.

'Now that we had ten times as many men as the Mongols, we pressed them harder, chasing them through a maze of mountain passes. Then, at the beginning of autumn, they stopped circling around in the mountains and began to move southwards. We knew where they were headed. Word had reached us that the Great Khan's invasion fleet had left Korea and was sailing towards Kyushu. And now Arghun's army began a long march through our western provinces towards the Inland Sea. When they reached the ports at the western end of the Inland Sea, they fell upon them like a forest fire, destroying everything and killing everyone except the crews of the boats they needed to cross to Kyushu. By the time we landed on Kyushu, Arghun and his men had already fought their way through to the Great Khan's invasion army at Hakata Bay.'

Taniko recalled the shock she had first felt on learning that the beachhead of Kublai Khan's invasion had turned out to be at Hakata Bay, where Kiyosi had died and Yukio and Jebu had embarked for China so long ago. Perhaps Kiyosi's spirit still lived there, protecting the Sunrise Land.

'When we arrived at Hakata Bay we found the Great Khan's fleet anchored offshore. The ships were Korean, pressed into service by the Mongols. There were over a thousand vessels of every description, from small coastal galleys to seven-masted ocean junks carrying as many as a hundred men and their horses. The enemy army was camped on the shore. It was evening when we arrived and the first day's fighting was already over. From their campfires we estimated that there must be thirty thousand invaders. The Kyushu men had nearly been overwhelmed.

'The following day I met the Mongols in battle for the first time. It was hot, dirty fighting. The enemy were armed with machines that threw big stones at the earthworks. They had giant crossbows that fired arrows the size of spears. And they had a terrible weapon called *hua pao*, that cast iron balls that burst among our warriors with a noise like thunder, shooting fire and deadly iron fragments in all directions. Their *hua pao* rained down thousands of the fire balls on our men. Our troops were maimed and killed and our horses stampeded, and the things gave off a black smoke that stank like the Eight Hot Hells. Knowing nothing about Mongol methods of fighting, many of our noblest warriors rode out to challenge the Mongols to single combat. The Mongols slaughtered them from a distance with arrows. They also used poisoned arrows that killed our men by the hundreds.

'Again and again the Mongols massed and charged at this place or that, trying to break through our lines. With stones and *hua pao*, they battered holes in our earthen walls. We filled the gaps with our bodies, rushing madly from place to place to hold the invaders back.

'At the end of the second day's fighting we were exhausted and in despair. Our only course, as far as we could see, was to keep on fighting until we were annihilated, in the hopes that by then reinforcements could be raised. We prayed that night. The priests passed to and fro among us all night long, carrying their portable shrines, chanting and dispelling the odour of the *hua pao* with the sweet smell of their incense.

'There was another smell in the air that night, the smell of rain. The air gew cold and damp, and we wrapped our quilts around ourselves and shivered behind our dirt walls. Lightning flickered in the clouds and thunder rumbled like Mongol fire balls. The rain began near morning at the Hour of the Tiger. It quickly became a drenching downpour, but the Kyushu men welcomed it with shouts of joy. We eastern warriors did not yet understand why. The wind began to rise, shrieking like a hundred thousand humming-bulb arrows.

'There was no dawn that day. The dark of night extended far into the morning and not until the Hour of the Dragon was there enough light to see by. Even then we could not see much beyond our own walls. The wind blew harder and harder until it was tearing trees to bits and knocking men in full armour flat on their backs. Timbers from houses along the shore flew over our heads. I saw the tile roof of a temple in Hakata ripped loose and sailing through the air like a kite until it fell to pieces. The sea came roaring up the beach to our fortifications, throwing spray into the air higher than the treetops. At times the wind and rain died down enough for us to see the shore and the bay. The waves reared up as high as Fuji-san and tumbled in all directions. The invaders and their horses were huddled in small groups here and there along the beach. Their tents and their great machines had vanished. We were more frightened of the storm than of the enemy, and we crouched against our crumbling walls and prayed that we would not be drowned.

'The storm was gone by next morning. So were the Mongols and their fleet. The waters of Hakata Bay were full of broken timbers and planking. All along the curving beach we could see broken hulls of junks that had been thrown up on shore. With a shout of joy we ran down to the water's edge. We found a remnant of the invaders hiding in the ruins of Hakata and the other towns around the bay. Before we put them to the sword we questioned them. The Korean shipmasters had warned the Mongol commanders that this was one of those great storms the Chinese call *tai-phun*, and that they would be safer in the open sea than in the harbour. We learned later that most of the fleet had been sunk at sea and thirteen thousand Mongols drowned.'

Munetoki stopped speaking and sat there, hands folded in his lap, lost in recollection of the awesome sights he had seen. The boys remained silent, eyes on the floor. On the smooth cheeks Taniko could see the glistening tracks of tears.

Sametono was the first to speak. 'Sensei, do you think the Mongols will return?'

'They will certainly return,' said Munetoki gravely. 'It may be next year, or it may be some years from now, but I believe they will be back in greater numbers than before. We must be ready

for them. Thank the gods for our great and wise leader, the Lord
Shogun Muratomo no Hideyori, who will mobilize the nation to
defend itself.'

'I hope that when the Mongols come back I will be old
enough to fight them,' said Sametono eagerly. Taniko's heart
sank, even though she knew that as a samurai mother she should
be proud.

Munetoki stood up, towering over the little group of
students. He turned suddenly to the instructor.

'They aren't bad, these boys, all things considered. Keep
them at it.' The instructor's face glowed like a temple mirror.
Bowing to Taniko, Munetoki turned and strode out of the dojo.

CHAPTER FIVE

From the pillow book of Shima Taniko:

Can it be seventeen years since I last saw Heian Kyo? The
capital has suffered so much in those years – civil war, fires,
earthquakes, plagues, famines. Over half the buildings have
been destroyed and rebuilt. It is not the fairytale city I came to
so long ago with Jebu. But the girl who saw it that way no
longer exists, either.

The Mongols having been driven off, Hideyori decided to
make a state visit to the capital. We travelled down the
Tokaido with three thousand mounted samurai and twice
that many on foot. I would have preferred to travel on
horseback myself, as I did so long ago, but Hideyori insisted
a screened palanquin is the only proper conveyance for the
wife of the Shogun. He himself rode that nervous white
stallion, Plum Blossom, though he is as much at ease on a
horse as I would be on the back of an elephant. But the people
lined the Tokaido to see the Shogun, and Hideyori felt he
should show himself, looking like a warrior. Sametono did
not come with us. He begged to be left behind, and I did so,
knowing too well how he dreads the Rokuhara.

Hideyori's visit has upset the Imperial Court no end. From
the Regent on down, he has removed members of the

Fujiwara and Sasaki families from office, replacing them with men of less ancient lineage whom he considers more trustworthy. He has also moved against the warrior monks, persuading the Great Council of State to pass an edict forbidding the Shinto and Buddhist monks to bear arms and ordering the Zinjas to disband altogether. No wonder he chose to travel with an army.

My lord seems more fearful of ghosts, though, than of living warrior monks. Since we've married, I've spent very few nights in peaceful sleep. Again and again he wakes up screaming and covered with cold sweat. It seems his whole family is pursuing him through his dreams, not just Yukio but his father, Captain Domei, his grandfather, his uncles and various illustrious ancestors. Hideyori believes these are not just dreams, but ghostly apparitions. I find it hard to understand why his family would persecute him when he, of all people, has brought the Muratomo clan more power and glory than they ever had before. After one of these dreams, only the union of our bodies restores his peace of mind. I must add, though I dare confide it only to my pillow book, that all too often he is unable to accomplish his desires with me.

Through my personal network of samurai and servants, I've learned that Shizumi, Yukio's brave mistress, has retired to a convent only half a day's ride from here. I must find out why she left Kamakura so suddenly.

Also, as Horigawa's widow, I've inherited not only most of his possessions, but his private papers as well. His family placed them in the keeping of the Kofukuji monastery in Nara, and I have sent for them. The thought of reading documents written in Horigawa's own hand makes my flesh crawl, but there is doubtless much to be learned in those papers, as well as some fascinating and scandalous stories.

—*Third Month, twentieth day*
YEAR OF THE PIG

The nunnery of Jakko-in was in the Ohara hills, north of Heian Kyo. For appearances' sake, Taniko allowed herself to be carried there in a sedan chair. The temple itself was an ancient building with a broken tile roof, set beside a pond surrounded by dignified trees. In the hills sheltering the temple, small huts nestled in the shadows of pines and oaks. Taniko felt nervous coming here. Many of the women here who had retired from the world and taken vows were ladies of the Takashi family. Such women might resent someone like herself who had benefited conspicuously from the same turn of the wheel of karma that brought them low.

She paid her respects to the large wooden statue of Amida, the Buddha of Boundless Light, in the temple. Then she presented herself to the abbess, inquired after Shizumi, and was directed up a flight of stone steps spiralling to a grassy slope. Before long Shizumi, a basket of mountain azaleas on her arm, appeared.

Taniko followed Shizumi to her hut. It was a single room on bamboo stilts. Pinned to the shoji were coloured papers bearing verses from the sutras which Shizumi had copied out in a calligraphic hand that reflected her dancer's spirit. Shizumi herself had aged. Her face was gaunt, her hair lank – she had not yet shaved her head – and the edges of her patched robes were threadbare. The one valuable object in her hut was a samisen hanging on the wall.

'Do you play often?' asked Taniko.

'The dampness has ruined it, I'm afraid,' said Shizumi with a rueful smile. 'But I keep it because of the love and art that went into making it.'

'Why did you leave Kamakura without a word to me?' Taniko asked. 'You could have stayed with me.' Through the mist of time Taniko saw again the fragile, beautiful young woman who had danced in white robes before Hideyori.

'I would have brought ruin to anyone who tried to protect me. I was carrying Yukio's son.' Fear gripped Taniko's heart as she asked a question she did not want answered.

'What happened to your baby?'

'I don't want to talk about it, my lady. Please forgive me.'

Taniko seized both the young woman's hands in a crushing grip. 'You must tell me. You must.'

'My baby was nothing to you, my lady. Please don't concern yourself.'

'Shizumi, my firstborn child, my daughter, was torn from my arms and drowned. I care about what happens to children.'

Shizumi's thin shoulders shook with sobs. 'I ran away from the Shogun's castle when I knew my time was coming. I fled to a cave along the beach. I was alone and it was horribly painful, but my son was born alive. A group of samurai came riding up to the cave entrance. They must have heard the baby cry. One came and took the baby from me.' Her weeping choked her for a moment. 'He held him by his ankles and swung his head against the cave wall.'

'Oh no, oh no.' Taniko took Shizumi in her arms and cried along with her. 'Do you know who did this?'

'I'm sorry, my lady, I don't want to tell you.'

'I insist that you tell me, Shizumi-san. Whoever he is, I'll see to it that he is punished. I'm not helpless, Shizumi. I am the wife of the Shogun.'

Shizumi looked at her with haunted eyes. 'Forgive me for telling you, my lady. I am under obligation to you, and you have insisted. It was your husband. The Shogun.'

Taniko felt as if she had been struck in the heart with a hammer. 'Not Hideyori,' she said weakly. 'He doesn't kill children.'

Shizumi squeezed Taniko's hand. 'Forget what I told you, my lady. It won't do you any good to brood about it. It would be much better if you didn't believe me at all.'

Taniko shook her head. In the midst of her shock and pain, she felt fully convinced that Shizumi was telling her the truth. Sogamori had let Hideyori and Yukio live because they were so young, and the two boys had grown up to destroy the Takashi family. Hideyori would not make the same mistake. Taniko wiped away her tears with her sleeve.

'You have been very helpful to me, Shizumi-san. It is never an injury to tell someone the truth.'

She sat talking with the pale young woman until the tolling bell of the Jakko-in signalled sunset. Then she said goodbye to the dancer. She called her attendants and had them carry her back to the capital. Back in her quarters at the Rokuhara she ordered ten robes from her own wardrobe to be sent to the nunnery for Shizumi. Then she turned to the chests containing Horigawa's documents.

Horigawa's papers had been brought to Taniko by a priest of the Kofukuji, a temple that had been heavily endowed over the centuries by the Sasaki family. She had not yet told Hideyori that the papers had come into her hands. Having heard Shizumi's story, she now decided she would tell him nothing. Tonight he was meeting with the military commanders of the Home Provinces to discuss the defence of the capital against another Mongol attack. The meeting would probably last till nearly morning, and it was unlikely that he would send for her. She lit her lamp and told her maid she did not want to be disturbed.

Six red-lacquered cedar chests, decorated with sprays of sagittaria leaves painted in gold, lay in a row before her. She decided to start with the box on the far right. To pick up one of Horigawa's scrolls felt like touching poisoned food, but the fragrance of cedar helped her overcome her revulsion. She quickly became absorbed in details of Horigawa's life and work stretching over the past seventy years. Most of the papers were written in Chinese, the literary language of the old nobility. Taniko found memoranda to other government officials, copies of poems, reports from spies, genealogical tables, lists of flowers and roots to be judged in Court contests, trading contracts and inventories of Horigawa's lands, possessions and wardrobes. There were threatening letters phrased with the utmost courtesy from other nobles to whom Horigawa owed vast quantities of rice and many bales of silk. It became apparent that Horigawa had been deeply in debt before his marriage to Taniko. Crops had failed on lands he owned far from the capital, and the lavish entertaining he had done to advance himself had required heavy borrowing. Shima Bokuden, as she had always suspected, had rescued the prince from debt, receiving in turn the friendship of the Sasaki and the Takashi and a titled husband for his third daughter. Her father's letters to Horigawa were disgustingly obsequious.

Some of the papers Taniko found would have caused a scandal if their contents had become known. A series of letters revealed that Horigawa and Chia Ssu-tao, the chancellor of the Sung Emperor of China, had been dealing secretly with the Mongols, each betraying his country for his own reasons. The letters showed that when Horigawa had visited Kublai Khan's camp and abandoned her there, he had been acting as a go-between for the Chinese chancellor, who wanted to surrender the Sung empire to the Mongols. One letter told Chia Ssu-tao that among the gifts Horigawa was presenting to the Mongol leaders there would be 'an accomplished and experienced courtesan from our capital, a beautiful young woman. She is also faithless and bad-tempered, but the Mongol officers enjoy taming wild creatures, I am told.' Taniko clenched her fists and restrained herself from tearing the scroll to bits.

It was long after midnight that she struck real treasure. On a scroll dated 'Year of the Dragon' she read:

Eighth Month, twenty-fifth day.
   The gods have delivered the Muratomo into my hands. After all the heads have fallen, only Domei will be left. Sogamori will be my weapon against Domei.

She unrolled the scroll eagerly, her eyes racing up and down the columns of characters in Horigawa's precise, rather cramped hand. The diary, a pillow book like her own, but terser in style, was written in the language of the Sunrise Land, in which, no doubt, Horigawa found it easier to express his private thoughts.

She dug through the scrolls, foraging for the ones that looked most recent. At last she came upon what must have been the last scroll Horigawa had written. It began over five years ago, with the prince gloating over Yukio's impolitic involvement with the Court, his acceptance of the ancient office of Lieutenant of the Palace Guards, and Hideyori's rage when Horigawa reported it to him. Sadly Taniko traced the downfall of Yukio and the success of Horigawa's efforts to intensify the enmity between the brothers. Horigawa recounted Yukio's flight from the capital, his shipwreck and disappearance, and his subsequent emergence in Oshu. The came an entry for the Year of the Rooster that made Taniko gasp:

Eleventh Month, fourteenth day:
   Attended upon the Shogun in his castle. He ordered me to go to the land of Oshu and persuade Fujiwara no Yerubutsu to permit the Mongol general Arghun to cross his borders and kill Yukio and his remaining followers. 'Tell Arghun that Yukio and all with him are to be killed on the spot and their heads sent here for identification,' he said. I asked him, 'Would it not be easier to arrest Yukio and bring him here to Kamakura for trial so that all might know the justice of your case against him?' He rejected my argument. 'There are many

who sympathize with Yukio and whose feelings would be aroused against me by a public beheading. Let him die obscurely in a far-off part of the country and he will soon be forgotten.' So will end the one general who might be able to stop the Mongols.'

Taniko stared at the scroll in the flickering lamplight. Hideyori had said his order to Arghun was to arrest Yukio. But there was no reason for Horigawa to lie in a diary intended for his eyes alone. The next entry had been made here in Heian Kyo and bore a date in the Second Month, after Yukio and Jebu were already dead. Taniko began to cry as she read the details of Horigawa's final encounter with Yukio and Jebu on the mountainside in Oshu:

... Truly, though Arghun has spent years in our country he does not understand how the samurai feel about their Emperor. As soon as Arghun suggested that Yukio might supplant the Emperor, he lost him, for which I am thankful. It was the greatest delight of my life to see the frustrated rage on the face of the monk Jebu, as he tried to come at me barehanded and was stopped by Arghun and Torluk. If there was anyone in the world whose death I desired more than I want life for myself, it is that obnoxious Zinja. On my way to the capital a messenger brought me news of his death. He fell, pierced by innumerable Mongol arrows, into the gorge below Yukio's fort. The men of Oshu collected his head, as they did that of Yukio, and sent them to Kamakura. Good riddance at last.

Taniko sat back, eyes shut, trembling, as she was swept by waves of rage and grief. She had thought she hated Hideyori for killing Shizumi's baby. This was far worse. She saw now that she had deceived herself about what Hideyori was. Out of her yearning for safety for Sametono and power for herself, she had blindly bound herself to Hideyori and believed what he told her. She was furious with herself now. She sobbed and fell to the floor, pounding it with her fists. A maid, heavy-eyed and confused, jolted out of her sleep by Taniko's cries, peered into the chamber. Taniko screamed at her to go away. Lying there in her agony, she saw with clarity that there was only one way to extricate herself from the trap in which she had caught herself. She must face Hideyori and tell him everything she knew. It would be unbearable to try to maintain a pretence of ignorance to preserve their marriage.

Surprised at her sudden resolve, she asked herself, how could I know so easily what to do? Even though I have not achieved enlightenment, those years of meditation have changed me. The knowledge of what to do comes from the face I had before I was born. For a moment she thought she had solved her *kung-an*, but when she groped in her mind for the insight, she could not recapture it or put it into words.

'What you told me about the way my son died – I suppose that was a lie, too.'

'It happened as I said. I did leave out one detail. After Jebu captured Atsue, the boy stabbed him with a dagger when Jebu wasn't looking. Yukio killed Atsue to save Jebu, and he didn't know he was your son until after he was dead.'

That was the crossroads, Taniko thought, desolate. That was when I broke in my heart with Jebu. That was what drove me to Hideyori. And it was all a lie. Hideyori's voice was calm, careless, as if he were reporting an anecdote of no importance. Taniko covered her face with her hands. She stood on a stone path in the middle of a Rokuhara garden, her back turned to Hideyori. They had chosen this open spot to avoid being overheard. Hideyori put his hand on her shoulder and she wrenched free.

'You used my son's death to turn me against Yukio and Jebu. You lied about not wanting the Takashi children killed. You killed Shizumi's baby with your own hands. You lied about ordering Yukio and Jebu killed. Why have you done all this to me?' She whirled to face Hideyori, letting him see her ravaged, tear-streaked face. His black eyes were opaque.

'You would not have married me if you had known it all.'

'Did you think I would never find out?'

The cold, bottomless eyes reflected her image back at her. 'You are my wife now. My destiny is your destiny. My well-being is your duty. I have done nothing that was not necessary. I expect you to see these things as I see them.'

She was stunned. 'You thought that my obligation to you as your wife would stop me from hating you?' Her voice rose to a shriek on the last words.

His tone remained calm. 'I thought that by being married to me you would learn to understand me. You told me to kill Horigawa, and you did not condemn me for having it done. Yet I killed him for the same reason I killed all the others whose deaths upset you so. He was my enemy, and so were they.'

'Horigawa actually betrayed you. What harm did Yukio do you, or any of those children?'

Hideyori took her shoulders in his hands and stared into her eyes. It was like looking into a night sky that had lost all its stars.

'Their mere existence threatened the security of the realm,' he said. 'That made them my enemies.' He was mad, Taniko decided. Or, at least, in this belief, which had already driven him to kill hundreds of innocents, there lay the seeds of madness.

'Anyone at all might become a threat to the realm,' she said.

He laughed. 'Don't be absurd. Millions of people make up the nation, but those who threaten it are like a handful of rice out of a whole year's harvest. Taniko-san, think how many people, from the lowliest peasants to the nobles of the highest rank, lost their lives in the War of the Dragons. If killing a few people will prevent another war like that from breaking out, is not the sacrifice justified?'

She did not answer him. Hideyori's fingers toyed with the silver-mounted hilt of his long sword. He turned and gazed down into the pebble-lined bottom of the goldfish pool in the centre of the garden. The frightening thing about him, Taniko thought, is that he doesn't seem at all mad. He is talking calmly and quietly as if he makes perfect sense. And what is even more terrifying is the possibility that if I listen to him long enough it will begin to make sense to me.

'No wonder,' she said at last, 'your family haunts your dreams.'

He turned and faced her, his air of cold assurance turning unexpectedly to anguish and fear. 'Only you know how I suffer night after night for doing what was necessary to preserve the realm. Only you can comfort me. I thought you, of all people, would understand. You have known many rulers. You understand affairs of state. Why do you look at me like that now?'

Taniko held out her hands in a helpless gesture. 'There are many ways to be a ruler.'

'Every time I killed, or ordered someone to be killed, it seemed the only way to me. Surely you can see that.' His expression changed again, his face twisting in anger. 'I know what is clouding your mind against me. It is the warrior monk, the Zinja, Jebu. He was your lover, was he not?'

Taniko lowered her head and pressed her sleeve to her face as she felt the tears come. 'Yes,' she whispered.

Hideyori looked off into space. 'Even among the Zinja no other monk has become a legend as he has. He could have been very valuable to me. But his Order assigned him to Yukio, and he became Yukio's friend and companion. So, he had to die with Yukio. And now in the night he, too, comes to haunt my sleep.'

'You never told me that,' said Taniko, thinking that it was the least of the things he had never told her.

'For a very good reason. I have always suspected that you still love him. I know what there was between you. Horigawa told me, even about the baby he killed. That's why you fly into a rage every time a child's life must be taken, isn't it? Just as I could not marry you while Horigawa lived, I could not marry you while Jebu lived, knowing what he was to you.'

Because of this man's suspicion, and jealousy, and madness, Jebu had died. Taniko felt hatred blaze out from the centre of her body and spread to her very toes and fingertips. Now Hideyori came close to her, took her chin in his hand and raised her head so that she was looking into his eyes.

'Come, Taniko-san. At my side you rule over the whole Sunrise Land. Surely you aren't going to throw that away over an illicit affair with a half-barbarian monk.'

She tried to pull her head away, but he held her chin tighter. He brought his face down to hers until she could feel his breath. Hatred overflowed in her. She brought her foot up and reached down to take off her satin slipper. Before he could stop her she slapped him across the face with it. He sprang away from her and his hand flew to his sword. In a land where cleanliness was part of religion, there was no worse insult than to be struck by a piece of footwear. The sword was already half-way out of its scabbard before he stopped himself, trembling.

'If I killed you now, I would have to answer to your family. I still need the support of the Shima, and even a coward like your father can only be pushed so far. I will consult with him before taking action against you. Consider yourself under arrest. You are forbidden to leave your quarters. When I return to Kamakura I will decide what to do with you. And with that Takashi whelp you persuaded me to adopt.' He slammed the sword back into its scabbard. 'If you meant to make an enemy of me, you succeeded. We will no longer live as man and wife. I do not give those who insult me a chance to make amends. I thought you were very wise, Taniko. Now I see that you are stupid. You have lost everything.'

She held herself erect and stared up at him as he rubbed his cheek with the sleeve of his black gown. 'You do not know me at all, Hideyori, if you think I could regret anything I've said or done. I would rather not live than submit any longer to you.'

His eyes narrowed. 'I forbid you to kill yourself. As your lord, I have the authority to say whether you shall live or die.'

She reached into the bosom of her kimono, drew out the small dirk she carried there and held it up. 'I could have killed you instead of hitting you with my slipper, but I chose not to. If I do not kill myself, it is also because I choose not to.'

He turned pale for a moment, then smiled. 'If you do kill yourself, I will see to it that Sametono dies. Painfully.'

That left her shaken. She warned herself to say no more to him. The satisfaction of besting him in a contest of words might cost greater suffering for those she loved. As it was, she felt no fear, nor did she reproach herself for what she had done. Instead, she felt an amazing joy and freedom. For many months now she had been a puppet, her every word and action controlled by another. Her life was hers again. She recalled that cry of 'Kwatz' that Eisen and Sametono were always bandying with each other. She felt now as if she had shouted, 'Kwatz!' at Hideyori and all the power of his Bakufu and his tens of thousands of samurai. Walking away from him, she felt the fire of her hatred transmuted into a glow of triumph.

CHAPTER SIX

Now that they were back in Kamakura, Taniko felt very near to death. She stood at the head of the long flight of stone steps that led to the Hachiman Temple, under a great gingko tree said to be five hundred years old. Hideyori had finished his visit to the god and now was descending the steps. He had dressed in warrior's gear for the occasion. He wore white-laced armour and a helmet with the White Dragon badge of the Muratomo hanging from the sides and back. A quiver of twenty-four arrows with black and white falcon feathers was slung over his shoulder, and he held a tall rattan-bound bow in his hand. At his side was the Muratomo heirloom sword, Higekiri. A sword he had never carried on the battlefield, Taniko thought. His face was still suffused with fear as he left the temple. The visit to the ancestral shrine had not helped him. He had no one to tell his dreams to now. He had reached his life's pinnacle, but he tortured himself more than ever with fear.

It was the Hour of the Hare, and an early-morning mist obscured the landscape. From the temple entrance Taniko could see down the steps to her waiting palanquin and Hideyori's white stallion stamping his feet as a retainer held him. A small escort of warriors bowed as Hideyori reached the bottom of the steps. The main body of the army waited outside the precincts of the temple to begin the triumphal march into Kamakura. After that, life would end for her. Her only sorrow was that Sametono would inevitably be the next target of Hideyori's suspicion and hatred. Perhaps, though, it would be better for the boy's life to end now, a cherry blossom, while it was still beautiful. Growing up under Hideyori could destroy Sametono's spirit.

She started down the steps after Hideyori, two maids holding up her train and sleeves so they would not trail on the mist-dampened stone. Hideyori levered himself into the saddle so stiffly that two young guards reddened and looked away, suppressing their laughter at the all-powerful Shogun's awkwardness. Your rule will not be absolute as long as we can laugh, Hideyori, she thought. Settled in the saddle, Hideyori turned to look at her. In his eyes there was a mixture of resentment and yearning. So, your feelings for me cause you pain, Hideyori? Then surely you will not let me live long. Hideyori waited, jerking his horse's reins angrily to keep him under control until Taniko had descended the steps and was in her palanquin. He had ordered her to accompany him here, declaring that for the time being he wished to maintain appearances in public. When her bearers raised her palanquin, Hideyori raised his gloved hand in a signal to begin the procession to the temple gate. A long avenue lined with plane trees stretched before them, the trees veiled in white cloud and the distant gate, a great torii, invisible. The sound of horses' hooves and the thud of sandalled feet on the pounded earth roadway sounded flat and dull in the misty air.

Taniko was staring at the small White Dragon banner fluttering from a staff attached to the back of Hideyori's senior guard. A movement on the roadway caught her eye and she leaned forward and parted the curtain before her to see better. A man had stepped out from behind a tree to block Hideyori's path. She gasped and her body went cold as she thought, *assassin*. But the man's hands were empty and he wore no weapons. He raised his hands in a gesture that was at once command and invocation. He was very tall and thin and wore a grey robe. With his long white hair and beard he seemed a creature that had materialized out of the mist. But she recognized him at once, and the shock of recognition shook her to the very core of her being.

Jebu.

One moment her bearers were still carrying her along towards the gaunt figure in grey. In the next moment, without any transition, the palanquin was on the ground and she was lying crumpled among its cushions. She must have fainted. She looked out through the curtains and screamed. The white stallion, whinnying in fear, had reared up on his hind legs and was pawing the air with his front hooves. Hideyori, arms and legs flailing, was toppling out of the saddle. Still Jebu stood with upraised arms, wild-eyed but motionless. Hideyori fell backwards over the horse's rump. The samurai guards who had nearly laughed before at his awkwardness stared in open-mouthed horror. He crashed to the ground, landing on the back

266

of his head and his shoulders, his chin crushed into his chest. His limbs sprawled with a clanging of armour plates, then lay limp, in odd positions like those of dead men on a battlefield.

The bodyguards, who would have reacted instantly to the sight of a weapon, had Jebu been carrying one, sat on their horses as if paralysed. Now, tentatively, one man drew his bow from its saddle case. Jebu's head turned towards her. She looked into his grey eyes, but could read nothing in them. His face was all bone and deep shadows, as if he had been starving. Despite these changes and his white hair and beard, she had had no trouble recognizing him. Her eye went to a bit of bright blue on his chest. It was the embroidered Willow Tree emblem of the Zinja. Slowly, he lowered his arms. He looked at the fallen Hideyori for a moment. Without haste, he turned and walked back into the mist.

Taniko had climbed out of her palanquin by this time and had run to Hideyori, who lay without moving. Now she began to be aware of sounds all around her, the cries of her maids, the shouts of the samurai.

'Don't let that monk escape!' ordered the guard with the Muratomo banner on his back.

'Never mind that,' Taniko snapped. 'His lordship needs your help here.' Could Jebu be alive? The thought made her heart flutter, but she put it out of her mind. With Zen-trained concentration, she turned to what she had to do here and now. Where was that wretched horse? She heard the stallion galloping through the mist somewhere to her left. She knelt beside Hideyori, remembering that to disturb a man with a neck or back injury could kill him outright. Hideyori himself had not moved at all. She gently touched her fingertips to the right side of his throat. There was a faint, irregular pulse. She put her hand over his nostrils and felt air move against her palm. An age later, it happened again. With her index finger she carefully pushed back his eyelids. His eyes were rolled back into his head.

'He's alive,' she said. One of the maids, frightened, began to sob.

'Can we take his helmet off?' a samurai asked. 'He'd breathe easier.'

'Moving his head might kill him,' she said. She stood up and swept the ring of samurai with a gaze that she hoped was commanding. 'I don't know how badly the honoured Shogun is hurt, but this was an accident, and there is no point in chasing after culprits. The most important thing to remember is that for the time being, no news of this must get out. No one is to enter or leave the temple unless I authorize it.' The warriors bowed acknowledgment. Taniko pointed to one man. 'Go tell the chief priest that our lord is injured and we need priests trained in medicine.' The man leaped into the saddle and galloped off. Taniko next pointed to the senior officer with the Muratomo banner. 'Ride to the temple gate and get General Miura. Make sure no one can overhear you. Tell the general what happened and say that I respectfully invite him to attend upon the Shogun with a few carefully chosen officers. Now. Some of you catch our lord's horse. If he gets away, people will realize what happened. If you should find the monk we saw standing in the Shogun's path, he is to be brought to me, unharmed, for questioning.'

Waiting for the priests to arrive, she knelt again at Hideyori's side, her hands folded in her lap as if she were in the zendo. She took a deep breath and let it out again. She felt a surface calm, but she knew that in the depths of her mind powerful emotions were churning that would need her attention when she had time. There was silence all around her except for the murmuring of the maids and a few samurai repeating the invocation to Amida. Taniko was pleased that she had given orders without hesitation and that everyone had obeyed her. Evidently, she was the only one on the scene of this accident who had any idea what to do.

Four Shinto priests arrived on the run, their white robes flapping. Taniko stood aside to give them room. Two immediately began chanting prayers to Hachiman and other deities while the others examined Hideyori. After a time more priests brought a large wooden panel and placed it beside the Shogun. With infinite care they pushed the panel under him so as not to disturb the position of his body. They lifted the panel from the ground and slid it into Taniko's palanquin. Waving the bearers aside, the priests themselves shouldered the palanquin and walked slowly down the roadway. They carried Hideyori to a large, thatch-roofed building just off the road, the house of the high priest of the Hachiman shrine. He greeted Taniko himself, showed her the room where they were laying Hideyori and introduced her to the priests who would treat him. Doubtless, she thought, this holy man saw her as a grief-stricken wife threatened with widowhood, and she tried to play that role. No one had any idea that before Hideyori's fall he had planned to be rid of her. Now she was doing everything she could, little as it was, to keep Hideyori alive.

After the priests had carefully lowered the Shogun to a sleeping dais, General Miura Zumiyoshi arrived, looking stunned. He was a member of one of the great clans that had allied itself with Hideyori early in the War of the Dragons, a tough, eastern-province warrior with a peasant's manners. As head of the Samurai Office, he was one of the leading figures in the Bakufu. After examining Hideyori he led Taniko into an adjoining room where he politely asked her, as the one closest to the Shogun, what she wished done.

'I would suggest that you post a hundred of your most trustworthy men to seal off the temple grounds,' Taniko said. 'Give it out that my lord Hideyori has decided to spend more time in prayer before Hachiman and has postponed his formal entry into Kamakura. Disperse the rest of the troops. The last thing we need right now is large bodies of armed men hanging about in Kamakura. Then assemble the chief officers of the Bakufu here to decide what is to be done next.'

'Very sound suggestions, my lady,' said Zumiyoshi with a bow. 'We need time to plan the orderly transfer of power.'

'Transfer of power?'

Zumiyoshi lowered his eyes and spoke with much greater formality than was usual for him. 'Lady Taniko, I'm sorry to tell you that in my opinion our honoured Shogun is going to leave us shortly. I've seen injuries like this before. There is no healing such a hurt. He can neither move nor be moved. In a few days his lungs will fill up with fluid and he will be taken into Paradise. If he were one of my own men I'd have him mercifully helped on his way. Unfortunately for him, he is the Shogun and he must pass on without assistance, so it cannot later be said that there was a conspiracy to shorten his life.'

The temple priests agreed with General Miura's estimate of Hideyori's condition. Gravely, they told her she must expect the Shogun's death. She warned the chief priest to be prepared in the next few days for the comings and goings of many officials of high rank. Then she sat beside Hideyori and stared down at the pale, immobile face. Surprisingly, she felt a pang of sorrow for him. A murderer, partly mad and deadly to those close to him, he was also a man whose powers of mind equalled those of Kublai Khan.

Working with exquisite care, the priest-physicians removed Hideyori's helmet and armour and bathed his face and body with cool water. Pairs of priests took turns ministering to him and chanting in the room where he lay. The chief priest assured Taniko that the temple was saying its most puissant prayers for the Shogun's recovery or happy passage into the next world.

Seated beside Hideyori, lulled by the monotony of the priests' voices, Taniko wondered what had really happened. If any spirit were powerful enough to return to earth after death, that spirit would be Jebu's. But she had never before seen a ghost, and that made it harder to believe that the apparition that had frightened Hideyori's horse came from the spirit world. There had been nothing ghostly in the monk's appearance. It had seemed solid, breathing, fleshly, albeit aged and emaciated. But if it had been a ghost, would it not have taken the form of a younger, healthier Jebu? The more she considered it, the more certain she became that Jebu must be alive. The thought made her head swim. Yet, there was the report of his death in the mountains of Oshu. Her own father, Bokuden, had identified Jebu's head. What should she believe? What others told her, or what she had seen with her own eyes? But how could Jebu have survived?

One person might know – Moko. He had disappeared after learning that Jebu was in Oshu. When she had made inquiries, his family had said he had gone to supervise the building of warships in Nagato province. He had not come back until long after Jebu was reported dead. Perhaps he was hiding something. She must talk to him as soon as possible. Her mind spun dizzily as it tried to absorb the sudden reversal of her position. Early this morning Hideyori was triumphant, Jebu was dead, and she expected to be killed. Now Hideyori was dying, Jebu might be alive and she was, for the moment, safe. It was as Eisen was always saying; it was foolish to be certain of anything. The evil she had heard about Jebu, about Atsue's death, had turned out to be a lie. She could love Jebu again. She looked down at the dying Hideyori and apologized to him in her mind for the joy she was beginning, uncertainly, to feel at his deathbed.

More pressing problems demanded her attention. What would Hideyori's death mean to the future of her family? She realized that she was no longer just a woman who had no control over what happened to herself. She was the widow of the Shogun and foster mother of the Shogun's heir. She could command attention. Her first and most important consideration must be to make sure of Sametono's claim to the Shogunate. But the boy was only nine years old. Just as the Emperors in Heian Kyo had Regents who governed in their name, so a Regent would have to be appointed to head the Bakufu in Sametono's name. She couldn't hold that position herself. Not for centuries had a woman held any high office in the Sunrise Land. Who then? With sinking heart she realized that the probable choice was Shima Bokuden. The Shima had been Hideyori's earliest and strongest allies. As Sametono's senior male relative, Bokuden would be the boy's official guardian. Bokuden, that crafty, greedy, mean-spirited man whom she had despised ever since she could remember, would be the real ruler of the Sacred Islands. But Bokuden could never hold together the coalition of powerful, wilful warrior chieftains Hideyori had built to overthrow the Takashi and set up the Bakufu. Bokuden was the right sort of man to be Hideyori's second-in-command, utterly without scruple, but such a man did not command enough respect to lead the nation. His inevitable failure could mean another civil war. And that, with the Mongols gathering their armies just over the horizon, might destroy the Sunrise Land forever. Still, there was no way for her to prevent Bokuden's appointment as Regent. She would have to accept it and be ready for whatever developments might come afterwards. As today had proved, it was impossible to plan for an ever-changing future.

By afternoon the leading officers of the Bakufu, shocked and solemn, had assembled at the Hachiman shrine. Each went first to offer condolences to Taniko and stare down at the nearly lifeless Hideyori and make a silent estimate of how long he had to live. Then they held a brief meeting. Later, Ryuichi told her what had been decided.

'Forgive me for saying it, but it makes it easier for us that the Shogun is so obviously about to die,' said Ryuichi. 'Who would dare propose a successor for Lord Hideyori if there were a possibility of his recovering?'

The Bakufu's leaders had agreed, as Taniko hoped they would, that Sametono must be the next Shogun. He was the only candidate whom all could accept without dispute. Next they decided, as Taniko had expected, that there must be a Regency until Sametono was old enough to govern, and that Shima Bokuden was the only possible choice for Regent. He would preside over a council of Bakufu officers.

'Hideyori did choose intelligent subordinates,' said Taniko. 'Lesser men would have bickered for a month over so many important decisions.'

'Their intelligence in choosing my brother as Regent escapes me,' said Ryuichi. 'No one respects him.'

'When strong men cannot find a leader whom everyone respects,' said Taniko, 'they are better off with a leader whom no one respects.'

Now the Bakufu officers publicly announced that Hideyori had been badly injured in a fall from his horse and was unconscious. Even then they did not add that the Shogun was likely to die. They sent for Sametono, who came from the Shogun's castle in an ox-drawn carriage like an old noble of Heian Kyo. The people of Kamakura lined up to watch the stately vehicle pass, knowing that the future of the realm rode in it. Taniko had not left Hideyori's side all day, and she was still sitting there when Sametono entered. The boy's round face was serious but calm. He looked thoughtfully down at Hideyori for a long time, then recited the invocation to Amida. From his sleeve he took a scroll.

'I wrote a poem for him. If I read it to him, do you think he'd hear it?'

'Perhaps,' Taniko said wearily. 'We never know what unconscious people can hear.'

Sametono nodded and read his poem:

> Beholding the stars,
> I know that one day
> They will fall from the sky.
> If even stars must vanish,
> Why mourn the shortness of life?

'That's very beautiful, Sametono-chan. And it was kind of you to think of it.' Sametono took the flute, Little Branch, from its silk case at his belt. At the sight of the flute that had belonged to Kiyosi and Atsue, Taniko felt tears come to her eyes. To think, Hideyori would probably have killed this boy. Sametono sat on cushions at Hideyori's feet and began to play soft, soothing airs, many of them well-known musical settings for the sutras. The priests in the corner of the room stopped chanting and listened with beatific smiles. Without apparent fatigue, Sametono played on for over an hour.

Hideyori opened his eyes. He blinked. The dark pupils focused on Taniko. His lips twitched. They were dry and stuck together. Taniko wet them with a damp cloth, and he licked his lips thirstily. She helped him sip water from a cup. A whisper crackled in his throat. She leaned forward, holding her hair back from her ear.

'Yukio is here. I can hear his flute.'

'That's Sametono, your son. He is playing for your pleasure.'

'I never had any children. Karma. Get the priests to drive Yukio's ghost away.' The fluttering lids curtained the dark eyes.

'What did he say, Mother?'

'He thanks you for your playing. He asks you to let him sleep now.'

That night she and Sametono slept side by side on pillows and quilts the priests set next to Hideyori's bed. Somewhere in her dreams the pious chanting droned on. She woke many times during the night, listening to Hideyori's laboured breathing, staring at his motionless face. There was a bubbling sound coming from his throat and chest. He's going to drown, she thought, just as Horigawa did.

Sametono remained beside her the following morning, occupying himself by reading poems he had brought with him. Every so often he would read one aloud to her and the unconscious Hideyori. Taniko's only fear was that Hideyori might waken and say something dreadful to Sametono that would hurt the boy. During the Hour of the Sheep Hideyori did manage to wake up again. She leaned forward to catch his words.

'What happened to me?'

'You fell from your horse.'

273

'I remember. A ghost. The Zinja.' His eyes widened in terror. 'I can't move.'

It was her duty to help him prepare himself, but she could not bring herself to say the words. Then Sametono was beside her.

'Father, you are dying. Ask all the gods and Buddhas to be merciful to you.'

'Pray for me,' Hideyori murmured, fear and anguish in his face.

'The whole realm prays for you,' said Sametono.

'I was only protecting myself,' Hideyori whispered. 'I have never wanted to die.'

Feeling an urge to comfort him, Taniko said, 'I will see that the great Buddha you spoke of is built at Kamakura. It will bring you an abundance of good karma.' While at Heian Kyo, Hideyori had ordered the restoration of the great bronze statue of Buddha at the Todaiji in Nara, which had been burned by the Takashi. He had remarked to Taniko that he dreamed of erecting an equally large Buddha for Kamakura.

The black eyes fixed on hers. 'Have mercy on me, Mother, I'm afraid of them.'

Sametono turned to her, open-mouthed. 'What did he mean by that? Mother?'

She sighed. 'Your foster father was very attached to his mother.'

That evening the chief priest of the shrine came to visit them. 'There are strange stories going about the city, my lady. People are saying that the ghost of Muratomo no Yukio caused the Shogun's horse to throw him.'

In case Jebu was alive, Taniko shaped her answer to protect him. 'I was too upset to see anything clearly. Those who have sympathy for the lieutenant might say his ghost took its vengeance on my husband. Perhaps it's true. I don't know.'

Taniko and Sametono fell asleep early that night, exhausted by the long hours of sitting and waiting. Suddenly she felt a hand gently shaking her shoulder. She opened her eyes. Sametono was standing over her.

'He's gone, Mother.' Tears were trickling down Sametono's cheeks. Even for such a man as Hideyori, she thought, there was someone to weep.

CHAPTER SEVEN

The tall, four-panelled screen was painted on both sides with an identical scene of mountains, waterfalls, pines and temples. On one side the landscape was bathed in sunlight, on the other drowned in moonlight. Fittingly, the night side was turned towards Taniko, hiding her from her father, who was talking to Ryuichi and Munetoki in Ryuichi's central hall. Only Bokuden, she thought, would be stupid enough to call a secret family meeting without first looking behind all the screens in the room. Not that Bokuden was a trusting soul. Next to Hideyori, he was the most suspicious man she had ever known. It was arrogant carelessness of the sort that would ruin the Sacred Islands if Bokuden were long permitted to govern them. Just now he was gloating over his cleverness in acquiring a shipment of copper coins from China.

'But, honoured Uncle,' Munetoki protested, 'it is forbidden to trade with China now that it is mostly in Mongol hands.'

'Since I am the senior member of the Bakufu Council, the Bakufu's regulations do not bind me,' said Bokuden airily. 'The information I gather from the Chinese traders is worth breaking the law for.'

Insufferable as always, Taniko thought. How long would the other samurai clans put up with Bokuden's enriching himself by violating regulations he himself had helped draw up?

'The traders were anxious to exchange the last of their bulky valuables for smaller and more portable amounts of gold and gems,' said Bokuden. 'They told my agents that the Mongols are about to take Linan and capture the Sung Emperor. Once the conquest of China is completed, Kublai Khan will turn his attention to us again. The traders say he has set up an Office for the Chastisement of Ge-pen, headed by one who knows our land well -- Arghun Baghadur.'

'We destroyed them before and we will destroy them again,' said Munetoki.

'What is even more distressing,' said Bokuden, ignoring his

275

nephew, 'is that the Shogun, the commander-in-chief of our armed forces, is a child.' Now he was getting to the point of this meeting, Taniko thought. He wants Sametono out of the way.

'My honoured cousin the Shogun has you to rule in his behalf, Uncle,' said Munetoki.

'That would be fine if I could truly rule, but I cannot,' said Bokuden. 'I am not free to issue orders as I think best, but must have the approval of the Bakufu Council. My position is also untenable because I govern in the name of Sametono, and Sametono is not suitable to be Shogun.'

'Surely there is no one more suitable,' Munetoki bristled.

Munetoki was simply incapable of guile, thought Taniko. He and Ryuichi had agreed before the conference that they would seem to agree with whatever Bokuden said, in order to draw him out. But Munetoki couldn't stop himself from arguing.

'Lord Hideyori laid down no regulations about how the next Shogun was to be selected,' Bokuden pointed out. 'Surely it would be ridiculous to say that Hideyori's family holds office by decree of the gods, as the Imperial line does. Even if the Shogunate does somehow belong to the Muratomo by divine right, Sametono is really a Takashi, not a Muratomo. Are we to let a direct descendant of Sogamori pluck like ripe fruit the power for which generations of Muratomo fought and died?'

'We Shima ourselves are Takashi,' Munetoki pointed out.

'Yes, Brother,' mused Ryuichi. 'I wonder if your zeal for the Muratomo cause is so great because you are only recently converted to it.'

Taniko held her hand over her mouth to keep from giggling.

'Furthermore,' Bokuden went on, 'this boy Shogun listens only to my daughter, never to me, his official guardian. She cannot but be a bad influence on him.'

Behind the screen, Taniko smiled to herself.

'Our little Taniko is an intelligent, well-travelled lady of strong will,' said Ryuichi. 'What is more, she is very religious.'

'Her will is not strong, it is perverse,' Bokuden snarled. 'Ever since she was a child she has been disobedient. She is an adulteress many times over. Well-travelled? Yes, she spent years among the Mongols. The gods alone know what secret links she may yet have to them. As for being religious, she is an adherent of that foreign Zen sect whose doctrines sound like the ravings of madmen. If she is so religious, let her be packed off to a nunnery where she can do no more harm.'

Munetoki's voice trembled with anger. 'I have the honour to be the young Shogun's teacher in martial arts. No one knows him as well as I do. His character is perfectly pure. There is no sign of any bad influence anywhere about him.'

Ryuichi spoke with uncharacteristic sternness. 'Munetoki, be silent. I forbid you to contradict your uncle, who is chieftain of our clan as well as acting head of the Bakufu. You forget yourself. Apologize to Lord Bokuden.'

There was a long silence. When Munetoki spoke again, it was in a firm voice that Taniko knew was the result of rigorous self-discipline.

'Please accept my apologies, honoured Uncle,' he said. 'I am ashamed of myself.'

'That's better,' said Ryuichi. 'Now, Lord Bokuden, you have pointed out some of the boy Sametono's shortcomings as Shogun. But to whom else could the office be given with confidence?'

'There is the son of my oldest daughter, who is married to Ashikaga Fukuji. The Ashikaga are a branch of the Muratomo. There is also the son of my second daughter, who is married to the chieftain of the Nagoya Muratomo. With Hideyori and Yukio dead, the Nagoya Muratomo are now the senior branch of the clan.'

'Excuse me, honoured Brother,' said Ryuichi, 'but why would these other grandsons of yours be more suitable than Sametono?'

'They are Muratomo by blood, not by adoption,' said Bokuden. 'And they and their mothers would obey me in all things.'

'Of course,' said Ryuichi. 'Still, there are many serious objections to both those young men. For instance, the Nagoya Muratomo fought on the Takashi side almost until the end of the War of the Dragons. And to choose a Shogun from the Ashikaga would arouse the envy of the Wada and the Miura. Surely these points have occurred to you. Do you have any other candidates to put forward?'

'If there are too many objections to any other candidates I can only, in all humility, offer myself.'

There was a long silence. Even Taniko was shocked. She knew her father had a high opinion of himself, but she had no idea that his vainglory verged on madness. His hold on the Regency was precarious enough, and now he wanted to reach higher still.

'There is no impediment that excludes me from consideration,' Bokuden went on. 'And there is much that qualifies me. I am head of the most powerful family in the realm. I am the late Shogun's oldest and staunchest ally. Without me, he could never have overthrown the Takashi. Finally, I am a man of advanced age and much experience.'

'Indeed, you are superbly qualified, Brother,' said Ryuichi. 'But there is one stumbling block. Just as there is no rule for choosing a Shogun, there is no legal procedure for removing a Shogun from office.'

'We will have to eliminate him, of course,' said Bokuden blandly.

'Kill Sametono?' cried Munetoki, shocked into speaking again.

'We cannot permit him to survive as a rallying point for opposition forces,' said Bokuden. 'Many of the other families will be envious when the Shima step forward to take the Shogunate. Rival claimants to high office must be eliminated, no matter how young and innocent. I have been thinking, Nephew, that since you are the boy's teacher you might be in a good position to arrange an accident for him. It would be better if it did not appear to be an assassination.'

'Munetoki,' said Ryuichi sharply. 'You will listen to your uncle and obey him in whatever he tells you to do.'

'Yes, Father,' Munetoki muttered, his voice shaking with suppressed rage.

'The extent of your devotion to the nation amazes me, honoured Brother,' Ryuichi went on. 'That you would actually sacrifice your own great-grandson for the security of the realm fills me with awe.'

'Every tree benefits from pruning,' said Bokuden sententiously. 'Besides, the boy is not a true Shima anyway. Munetoki, you may be reluctant to help Sametono into the beyond, but remember that you would be my heir. I have no sons, after all. Look here, Ryuichi, we've seen the Fujiwara, the Takashi and the Muratomo each rule the land in their turn. All this time we've just been supporters of the great families. Isn't it time the Shima had their turn at ruling? Think of how rich we could make ourselves.'

Taniko stood up and stepped out from behind the screen. 'It is not the Shogun who needs deposing, but the Regent.'

Bokuden, looking like a large, malicious insect caught in a granary, stared at her. Moon-faced Ryuichi rose and backed away from his brother with an expression as if Bokuden gave off an unpleasant odour. Munetoki stood towering over his uncle with a grin of satisfaction. His fingertips stroked the hilt of the dagger hanging at his right side.

'I'm not surprised at your willingness to murder your great-grandson,' Taniko said. 'A lizard has more love for its offspring than you do. What does amaze me is that you have actually deceived yourself into believing that the great clan chieftains, generals and scholars my lord Hideyori gathered together here in Kamakura would be willing to take orders from you.'

Bokuden managed a ghastly smile. 'So. The three of you intend to try to bring me down? I should have known you would all put personal ambition before family welfare. This is very foolish of you. I am still Regent as well as head of this clan.' He tried to stand up, but age made him stiff. Munetoki helped him to his feet. Then he pulled his arm away.

'You are Regent and clan chieftain only until we can gather the Bakufu Council and charge you with plotting to murder the Shogun,' said Taniko.

'You think to bring charges against the Regent?' Bokuden laughed shrilly. 'It is you who will face charges for rebelling against me. Out of my way.' He hobbled to a window and slid back the screen covering it. 'Guards!' he shouted. There was no response from the courtyard outside the window.

Munetoki spoke quietly. 'Sorry, Uncle, but we took the liberty of disarming your escort and locking them up. Sad to say, none of them wanted the privilege of dying to protect you. In case any of your other retainers should feel differently, this mansion is now surrounded by three thousand samurai chosen for their loyalty to the Shogun and the Shogun's mother.'

'The Shogun's mother!' Bokuden spat. 'You are responsible

for all this, Taniko. You have always been a disobedient, ungrateful daughter.'

Taniko laughed bitterly. 'All my life you have looked upon me as a piece of goods to be traded when it suited you. Should I be grateful for that? Should I be grateful to you for plotting to murder Sametono? Being a woman, perhaps I am not capable of understanding the principle involved.'

'Kill me,' said Bokuden, 'and a father's curse will follow you through the Nine Worlds.'

'We want to see you praying, Father, not cursing,' said Taniko with a smile she knew would infuriate him. 'We hope you will live a long time. We feel no need to kill you. We do not fear that you will become a rallying point for those who may oppose us. You are not the sort men rally around. You have spent over seventy years of your life absorbed in the affairs of this world. Now we would like you to enter the cloister, shave your head, and turn your thoughts to the next world. Your worthy nephew Munetoki volunteers to take on the burdens of the Regent's office.'

Bokuden's face reddened with fury as he glared at his daughter, his brother and his nephew. After so many years of scheming and plotting, Taniko thought, it must be unbearable to have the ultimate prize snatched away by your own family.

'I made our family first in the realm,' Bokuden sputtered. 'Your ingratitude will bring you a terrible karma.'

'Excuse me, Brother, but it is karma, not your efforts, that put our family in this position,' said Ryuichi. 'You were merely just carried along, as a piece of driftwood is lifted to the crest of a wave.'

After Bokuden had been ushered off to a guarded chamber in Ryuichi's mansion, Taniko's uncle said with a smile, 'He is right in holding you responsible for our effort to depose him, Taniko-chan. If you were not as clever and resolute as you are, I would have preferred to send you and Sametono into hiding and let my brother have his way with the Regency and the Shogunate.'

'That would have led to disaster, Uncle,' said Taniko. 'In six months he would have infuriated the other great military families and they would have rebelled against him. And they would doubtless have felt compelled to kill of all the Shima for the usual reasons. This will keep the Regency in our family, but Father will be out of the way.'

Ryuichi laughed. 'With no father or husband to rule over you, you are now the real chieftain of our clan, though I will now take the title. I shall ask that you be invited to meetings of the Bakufu Council, as the former Shogun's widow. Such things are not unheard of. Right now the Sung Empire – what's left of it – is ruled by the boy-Emperor's mother, the dowager Empress. And among us samurai, it has always been the custom for a wife to take over her husband's duties if he is killed or too badly hurt to manage his own affairs. So now, behind our little Shogun will stand his cousin, the Regent, and behind the Regent will stand the Ama-Shogun – the Nun Shogun.'

'I am far from ready for the nunnery, Uncle, regardless of what my father said,' Taniko answered, thrilled, but casting her eyes modestly down. But without those years of study and meditation with Eisen, I would never have been ready to seize this moment. I would not have known how to protect Sametono from assassination and save the Sunrise Land from the disaster of Bokuden. Just in time, too. The Elephant will undoubtedly be sending an army to wipe us off the face of the earth. And I know more about the Mongols and their Great Khan than anyone in the Sacred Islands.

Except for one other person, she thought, who knows more than I do about how they make war. But how can I find him?

CHAPTER EIGHT

'I think you know more than you admit about the late Shogun's demise,' said Taniko.

Moko looked surprised and anxious. 'I had nothing to do with your husband's death, my lady.'

Taniko observed the heavily brocaded Chinese robe that Moko wore. Many stories of daring raids on the ships and coasts of Mongol-dominated China and Korea had filtered back from the west coast to Kamakura. If Moko hadn't gone on such raids, he had surely supplied ships to the raiders and been rewarded for it. He also wore the long and the short swords of the samurai. Hideyori had consistently refused to award samurai status and family names to commoners, no matter how worthy. Taniko felt that the samurai class should be opened up to bring in new blood and men of merit. Moko was one of a number of men whose services had been especially valuable to the Bakufu and who had been granted, along with their families, samurai status by Sametono, now that he and Taniko and Munetoki were securely in control of the Bakufu. Moko now wore his hair in a topknot, carried swords which he had no idea how to use and had a family name, Hayama, taken from the town where he had built his main boatyard.

'Everyone agrees that Lord Hideyori's death was caused by his horse's shying,' said Taniko. 'The poor animal was sent to the slaughterers to satisfy those who felt someone must be punished. But surely you heard that Jebu was seen that day.'

'I heard many tales, my lady.' The crossed eyes were not as amusing as they had been once, Taniko noticed. They were the eyes of a man who had seen much and had done much thinking. The heavy lids were outlined by deep wrinkles. Well, we're all getting on, she thought. Can I actually be forty-five?

'I saw him, Moko. He looked very aged. Moko-san, besides Yukio and perhaps some of the Zinja, you're Jebu's closest friend. I know he is alive. You must know it, too.'

'I am not worthy to be called his friend,' said Moko, looking sadly down at his broad, worn woodworker's hands. 'My lady, you blamed the shiké for Lord Kiyosi's death and for the killing of your son, Atsue. Now you want to blame him for the Shogun's death as well.'

'Moko-san, the Shogun was planning to kill me. If he hadn't died when he did, I wouldn't be alive now.' She told Moko how she had learned that Hideyori had deceived her, and how she had hated him after that.

'I promised the shiké I would tell you nothing,' he said hesitantly.

'Then he is alive!' she exclaimed. 'You've talked to him. Moko, tell me. Tell me everything, I beg you.'

He sighed. 'I can't break a promise.'

'Yes you can, for the sake of a greater good. Would you have me live out the rest of my life in loneliness and despair?'

For a long time Moko did not speak. Finally he sighed again and said, 'Please understand, I don't mean to make too much of my part in it. It was just luck that I was there. What the priests call karma. You gave me the idea, my lady, if you remember. It was you who told me that Lord Yukio and Shiké Jebu had been discovered in Oshu, that Horigawa and the *tarkhan* Arghun were going there to arrest them, and that Fujiwara no Yerubutsu had secretly promised to betray Yukio. I never believed that Lord Hideyori wanted Lord Yukio brought back alive. He was not the sort of man who gives his enemies time to defend themselves.'

'I wanted very much to believe that he intended to spare Yukio.'

'It is a woman's duty to think well of her husband. I don't know what madness possessed me, but I thought somehow I could help the shiké, warn him if nothing else. I did not tell you because I did not wish to compromise you with the Shogun. I packed various items into travelling boxes and hired a crew for my fastest kobaya, an open ship with twenty rowers. I sailed north along the coast from Kamakura. When my kobaya reached Kesennumo, near the capital of Oshu, I learned that Horigawa and Arghun and the Mongol army had already arrived at Hiraizumi, and that Lord Yerubutsu had given them permission to attack Yukio. I had just time enough to don the Mongol cavalryman's armour I brought back with me from China ages ago, trade some gold pieces for a horse, and ride off after them. My years among the Mongols helped me to join Arghun's troops without attracting attention. The greatest risk I ran was that I might be sent into the fight and be killed by one of our own people, or even by Lord Yukio or the shiké. But no Mongol officer recognized me as one of his men, so none gave me orders to attack. And so it was that I saw Lord Yukio's last stand, my lady.'

'Moko-san, much as it will hurt me, I want to hear what happened. No one has been able to tell me the whole story of that battle.'

'It will be painful for you, my lady, but I'll try.' He described Arghun's parley with Yukio and Jebu, Jebu's attempt to kill Horigawa, how he threw Torluk over the cliff edge, the heroic deaths, one by one, of Yukio's followers and Jebu's final charge as the chapel burned behind him.

'He stood there, my lady, like the god of war himself, an enormous figure in black armour. He held out his arms and shouted, "Kill me!" The Mongols tried to kill him, pouring arrows into him. Still he stood, leaning on the broken staff of his naginata, and he did not fall. He had killed so many of them by this time that they were afraid to venture closer to him. At last one officer rode close to him, brandishing a sabre. The shiké seemed to lunge forward, and the Mongols shrieked that he was attacking again. But it was just that the breeze from horse and rider had knocked him over. It had only been his armour and the staff holding him up. He crashed to the ground, then rolled over the cliff edge and tumbled down the steep mountainside into the gorge. There he lay, half-buried in the snow.

'I scrambled down the hillside at once. I didn't care whether they found me out, whether I lived or died. I had some mad notion of saving the shiké's body from any further indignity. The Mongols would have to kill me, too, I told myself, before I would let them cut off my beloved Shiké Jebu's head. I got to the bottom of the gorge. There were soldiers there, but they were busy rescuing wounded comrades and retrieving their dead. I had just found the shiké's body when the officers above shouted orders to retreat. I dragged the body behind a big rock. It was heavy as a boulder itself – I don't know where I got the strength. I heard the Mongols calling something about being attacked, that they had been betrayed, then they were gone, with that eerie Mongol way of vanishing instantly. They even left some of their dead behind. I was alone with the shiké, weeping over his body.

'But not for long. I was just beginning to think of gathering wood for a funeral pyre when I heard the footfalls of an approaching horse, muffled by the snow. A figure on horseback came riding up the ravine. To my amazement, it was the Abbot Taitaro.'

'Taitaro!' Taniko exclaimed. 'I had no idea he was still alive.'

'He does seem very old, my lady. You have the feeling he was there when the world was created and knows all the secrets of heaven and earth. When he saw the shiké's body, all he said was, "If only you could have outlived me." Then he explained to me that the Zinja always know the whereabouts of their own. Now that Shiké Jebu was gone, the old abbot had come to get his body and dispose of it according to Zinja rites. The old man did not weep, nor did I expect him to, knowing that the Zinja do not consider death an evil. He thanked me for saving the body. "Now his urn will not be empty," he said. He lit a pine torch and sat staring at the shiké's still face for what seemed an hour.

'Then he gave a little start of surprise and bent forward. He whispered to me that he had seen a little wisp of vapour above the shiké's nostrils. He began to examine the shiké carefully, touching him here and there, removing his helmet and some parts of his armour that were not pinned to him by the arrows. He made me hold the shiké's wrist, saying that he feared his emotions might trick him into finding signs of life that weren't there. But I felt it, too, a faint pulsing under my fingertips. Somewhere in the centre of that great, motionless, armoured form riddled with arrows, something lived. The old man warned me, though, that the shiké would probably be dead within the hour. "Even so," he said, "we ought to do what we can for him." I could tell he was trying hard to control his own eagerness.

'"The Self is not ready to drop the mask that is Jebu," the old man whispered into the shiké's ear. Out of pockets in his robe he began to take vials and folded papers. He blew a pinkish dust into the shiké's nostrils. He trickled the contents of tiny porcelain tubes between his lips. He kept whispering Zinja incantations to the shiké. Once I thought I heard the word "devils". We started to remove the arrows, which had been driven through every part of his body. The abbot asked me to cut away the shafts of those that had not penetrated vital areas, leaving the heads embedded. Those that were close to Shiké Jebu's heart and lungs and stomach would have to be taken out now, lest they stab him to death when we tried to move him. I held the torch high while the old abbot cut into the deep wounds and gently drew out the heads of the arrows. He plastered over the wounds with medicated papers and cotton cloths. He must be three times my age, but his hands were steadier than mine have ever been.

'The night grew darker and colder around us. Abbot Taitaro explained to me that the cold was helpful. It slowed down the life processes in the shiké's body so that he did not need as much strength to survive, and it would keep his many wounds from becoming diseased. He said that a slowing of heart and breathing and all other bodily activities was taught to all Zinja and was a state into which they could put themselves at need, sheltering their life energy within a seemingly dead body, as a fire may hide itself in the heart of a blackened coal. We wrapped the shiké's body in robes and made a pallet of spears and quilts to carry him.

'Before we left the ravine we found a dead Mongol with reddish hair who was about the shiké's size, and we dressed him in the shiké's armour. The abbot said that Lord Hideyori's men would undoubtedly be looking for proof that Shiké Jebu was dead, but to them, one Mongol would look much like another. By the time the head was carried to Lord Hideyori, it would have deteriorated so much it would be impossible to say whose it was. Thus, the head that your father identified as Shiké Jebu's was that of some unknown Mongol.'

'Was the other head truly that of Yukio?'

'Yes, sad to say. Before the Mongols left the scene of the battle they managed to save Lord Yukio's head from the burning building in which he had committed seppuku.'

'Why did the Mongols leave so hastily?'

'Their scouts told them Lord Yerubutsu's army was on its way to attack them and had already engaged their rearguard. Arghun didn't hesitate for a moment, and the Mongols dashed off without even taking time to collect the heads they had been sent to get. Lord Hideyori outsmarted himself. He arranged for Arghun to kill Yukio and then for Yerubutsu to attack Arghun, after which his Kamakura army would destroy Yerubutsu. Yerubutsu's attack on Arghun did not leave Arghun time to take Shiké Jebu's head, and it gave Abbot Taitaro and me time to rescue the shiké. The Oshu men fought and pursued the Mongols all that night, and by the time they came to the scene of the battle the abbot and I had left with the shiké's body. They sent what they thought were the right heads to Kamakura, for which Lord Hideyori rewarded them by invading and conquering their country.

'It was a dreadful journey we made through the mountains of Oshu. Our destination was the Black Bear Temple of the Zinja, near Oma on the northernmost tip of our island of Honshu. For many days we trudged through snow-covered valleys between black crags, clambered over boulders as big as the Imperial Palace. We tied one end of the shiké's litter to the abbot's horse and we took turns walking with the other end. The shiké managed to live through all this. It's the nearest thing to a miracle I've ever seen. The Zinja medicines the old abbot carried helped, of course. His potions fed that tiny flame of life in Master Jebu as oil feeds a lamp. And they helped us, too. A certain powder we took with our meals of dried fish and rice cakes gave us new strength to push on. That powder even made me cheerful, despite the tragedy I had witnessed and the ordeal we were going through. If I could get some of that powder for my shipyard workers, I could build a navy as big as the Great Khan's in a year.

'At last we came to a family of woodcutters, and the abbot paid the eldest son to ride ahead to the Black Bear Temple for help. Two days later we were met on the road by a party of Zinja monks with horses and a palanquin, and the following day, we were at the temple. I was so exhausted I had even stopped worrying about whether Shiké Jebu would live or die.

'He was still fearfully close to death. Our long trek through those cold northern mountains, with winter coming on, had nearly killed him. After they put him to bed in the monastery they removed all the arrows from his body, cleaned and dressed all his wounds with powders and papers and ointments and cotton cloths, and kept murmuring invocations over him. The abbot explained to me that these prayers would penetrate to his deepest self, which never sleeps, and call forth the shiké's inner energies to speed his recovery. Along with these words, of course, went potions and such nourishment as they could get down his throat. But after a few days at the monastery he developed a fever, and we almost lost him again. Abbot Taitaro and I took turns sitting with him day and night. I watched the fever burn his flesh away until it seemed there would be nothing left of him but a skeleton. After several sleepless days and nights for us, his fever began to cool. It was then I noticed that all the red hairs had fallen out of his hair and beard, and those that were left were quite white.

'He lay unconscious at that temple for more than a month. The heavy snows came and buried all the temple buildings. When I was not at his bedside, which is where I spent most of my waking hours, I was talking with the Zinja monks. I learned that among the brothers of his Order, even though the Zinja discourage hero worship, the shiké is thought of as the greatest warrior of these times.'

How strange that Hideyori falls from a horse and dies, Taniko thought, while Jebu is riddled with arrows, falls from a cliff and lives. He's alive, he's alive, her heartbeats seemed to shout, as Moko told his story.

'Shiké Jebu started to stir restlessly one evening, an hour or so after the monastery cook had managed to get an entire bowlful of soup, drop by drop, down his throat. I watched him eagerly. His eyes opened. He looked at me and I started to weep for joy. I wanted to jump up and call Abbot Taitaro and the other monks, but I couldn't bear to leave the room for an instant. I waved my hands helplessly and jumped up and down and stammered. He stared at me, puzzled. I realized that his last memory was of Mongol arrows tearing into his body on a cliff in Oshu. He might be thinking that this was Paradise and that the Buddha bore a most peculiar resemblance to his old servant Moko.

'At last he spoke – just one sentence. "Will I never find peace?" Then he fell back on his quilt and closed his eyes again.

'Now I ran for Abbot Taitaro. He and I sat there until dawn, waiting, but he said nothing more that night. The following day he woke again and greeted me and his foster father and asked where he was and how he got there. He wept a long time for Lord Yukio. The old abbot told him they would hide him, because the Shogun would certainly want him dead. I expected him to react with rage at the mention of Lord Hideyori but all he said was that Muratomo no Hideyori was the most tormented man he had ever known.'

How true, thought Taniko. And how he tormented everyone around him. But if Jebu did not feel any hatred for Hideyori, why had he come to the Hachiman shrine?

'Now that Shiké Jebu was on the mend, I was anxious to get back to Kamakura. But by then the coast was surrounded by ice and the snow made the roads impassable, so I stayed and watched him grow stronger and learned more about the Zinja. Abbot Taitaro brought him a strange crystal with an intricate design carved upon it, which they call the Jewel of Life and Death. The shiké spent hours staring into it in a silence so profound an earthquake wouldn't have jolted him out of it. He let me look at it a few times, but all it did was hurt my eyes. That sort of otherworldly thing is not for me.

'As spring approached, the shiké's strength returned and he was able to take walks in the temple grounds. I wondered what he would do now. Years ago the Zinja had assigned him to serve Lord Yukio, and he had spent more than half his life at Yukio's side. What would help him survive this loss? I could not stay to find out. I had fulfilled a duty to Shiké Jebu. Now I had obligations to others. For months my family and those who worked with me in the boatyard had no word whether I was alive or dead. Time I returned to them. I said goodbye to Shiké Jebu, Abbot Taitaro and the other monks, and eventually made my way home.

'Now I have told you everything I know, my lady. I don't know where the shiké is now. I have no idea how he came to be at the Hachiman shrine when his lordship the Shogun paid his unlucky visit there. I do know that when I left Shiké Jebu he seemed calm enough, except for the words he spoke when he first awakened − "Will I never find peace?" Those words have haunted me. Was he − is he − truly so unhappy that he longs for death? I had always thought he was living just as he wanted to live, a privilege few men enjoy.'

Of course he is unhappy, Taniko thought. She ached to see him again and hold him in her arms. I know why he is so sad, and perhaps in all this world I alone can help him to be happy.

'One thing you haven't told me, Moko,' she said with a smile. 'Did he speak of me at all?'

Moko hesitated. 'He wanted to know if you were well. If you had kept the boy Sametono with you.'

'That's not what I want to know, Moko. How did he seem to − to feel about me?'

Moko looked at her sadly. 'I really couldn't say, my lady.'

'Please tell me what you think.'

Moko sighed. 'My lady, he particularly charged me not to tell you that he is alive.'

'Why would he make you promise such a cruel thing?'

'Must I tell you, my lady?' Moko seemed to be in acute pain.

'Don't do this to me, Moko.' She was almost screaming at him, and she had raised her voice only once or twice before in her life, even under the most trying circumstances.

Moko squeezed his eyes shut in anguish. 'My lady, he said, "She has tortured me too long. May I leave this world before I see her again."'

If Moko had driven a dagger into her stomach he could not have hurt her more. She covered her face with her sleeve and wept bitterly. Moko sat sad and silent, unable to offer comfort.

At last, when her sobs had died down he said, 'Now you have heard the worst, my lady. You cannot suffer any more than you are suffering now.'

She looked into those strange, inquisitive eyes that seemed to be staring everywhere but at her. 'You're right, Moko-san. Now that I've heard the worst, things can only get better. And you can help. There is something only you of all the people in the world can do for me.'

CHAPTER NINE

Even before Muratomo no Hideyori's death, the Bakufu made no attempt to enforce the decrees forbidding monks to bear arms. Now that Hideyori was gone, his effort to suppress military monks was entirely forgotten. The Zinja Pearl Temple west of Mount Fuji, only a few days' journey from Kamakura, was thriving. Since there was little fighting to do at the moment, the monks of Pearl Temple spent their time training in the Zinja arts of combat and teaching them to the local samurai families. It was here, after making discreet inquiries, that Moko found Jebu.

They stood together on the parapet of the monastery's stone wall. The cone-shaped peak of Fuji, gilded by the afternoon sun, towered above ranks of low green hills. It was a year since Moko had seen the shiké. He looked ravaged still, but no longer skeletal. His white hair and beard were long, but seemed cared for.

'I heard you were present at a certain tragic event in Kamakura, shiké,' Moko began tentatively.

The bony, brown face was grim. 'I did not want Hideyori to die. I did not go there to kill him.'

'You had every reason to, shiké'

In the afternoon light Jebu's eyes were a pale grey, and his gaze was distant. Moko realized that he did not know this man at all. This was a man who had lost everything in life that he valued, had died and been brought back to life, was changed beyond imagining. Moko's heart sank. How could his words persuade such a man?

'I went to confront Hideyori because the Order sent me,' said Jebu. 'Our Council of Abbots realized that it would be useless, with a man like Hideyori, to plead that he reconsider his decree suppressing the Zinja. They decided to apply pressure at his weakest point, superstition. So I appeared before him at the Hachiman shrine.'

'A dangerous game, shiké. If you had been blamed for the Shogun's death, the samurai would have attacked every Zinja temple in the Sacred Islands.'

'If Hideyori's decree had remained standing, they would have done the same.'

'Lucky for you and for the Zinja that Lady Taniko put a stop to the talk that a Zinja monk caused the Shogun's death,' said Moko, thinking that it might help his cause to point out that Jebu owed some gratitude to Taniko.

Jebu shrugged. 'She has no reason to wish to harm the Zinja.' He sounded as if he were talking about a stranger.

Moko took a deep breath and plunged in. 'Shiké, there are very few people alive in the country today who know anything about the terrible foe we face. It may be that the most tragic thing about Lord Yukio's death is that we lost the one general who could have led us to a victory over the Mongol invaders. Of all the survivors of Lord Yukio's expedition to China, you and Lady Taniko could best advise our military leaders. You mustn't bury yourself in a monastery, shiké. Lady Taniko sent me to tell you that she needs you in Kamakura.'

'The most tragic thing about Yukio's death is that in the end, only twelve men were willing to fight for him.' Turning away, though not before Moko caught a glimpse of tears in the grey eyes, Jebu looked out over the domain of the Pearl Temple. It was appropriately named, being hidden like a pearl in a secluded valley. The monastery buildings were all long and low with thatched roofs connected by covered galleries. Nearest the gateway were the men's and women's quarters and the guest-house. A little further off were martial arts practice halls and stables, and beyond that the long, narrow lagoon for swimming and the archery ranges and bridle paths. The temple precincts also included rugged, heavily forested hills laced with streams where students trained under field conditions. On the highest hill of all was the temple building, as simple in construction as all the others, with a zigzag flight of steps leading up to it. On the far side of the temple, facing Mount Fuji, was a torii, a symbolic gate consisting of two posts and a lintel with upsweeping ends. Nowhere did Moko see banners or military display, and just now there were not even any training activities. It was a peaceful-seeming place, not at all the sort of setting where anyone would imagine the deadliest arts known to man were practised with ferocious intensity. It frightened Moko precisely because it was so calm, clean and quiet.

'Lady Taniko did everything she could to help you, shiké,' said Moko. 'She repeatedly tried to persuade Lord Hideyori that his brother was not his enemy. For a long time she believed that he did not want you and Lord Yukio killed. When she found out that it was he who ordered your deaths, she broke with him at once. He would probably have murdered her if he hadn't died when he did. She never really turned her back on you and Lord Yukio, shiké, not for a moment.'

Jebu shook his head angrily. 'How could anyone believe Hideyori wanted us to live? Whatever else she may be, Taniko is not stupid.'

'She was Hideyori's prisoner, shiké. He wove a net around her and nothing passed through without his permission. She had not talked to you or had any message from you in years.'

'I sent her a letter after Atsue was killed.'

'Hideyori must have kept it from her. She always cared about you, you know that. It was because of her I went looking for you in Oshu. She sent for me secretly to tell me she had learned you were still alive. She fairly glowed with happiness but she was also terrified at the peril you and Lord Yukio were in.'

Jebu smiled and put his hand on Moko's shoulder. 'Seldom has karma manifested itself so clearly, Moko-san. Over thirty years ago I spared your life, and now you have saved mine.'

'It was Lady Taniko who urged you to spare my life, shiké.

We three are bound together by what began under that maple tree on the Tokaido Road. You must not leave her out.'

Jebu gripped the battlement with his large, bony hands, the knuckles turning white. 'Moko, I have loved Taniko ever since that journey we took together down the Tokaido. I have loved her without hope. Again and again she refused my love. I am a warrior and a monk. I can be nothing else, but she blames and despises me for what I am. Now she wants to see me again. It is too late for that. She could never forgive me for Kiyosi and Atsue. I cannot forgive her for Yukio.'

'She did nothing to hurt Lord Yukio, Master Jebu.'

'She married the man who murdered him. All her life she has sought to link herself with powerful men. Horigawa, Kiyosi, Kublai Khan, Hideyori. I do not seek power, Moko. And that finally is what has always come between Taniko and me. Now she has power. She's ousted Bokuden from the Regency. Her uncle is chieftain of the Shima, her cousin is Regent and her foster son is Shogun. I hear the samurai are calling her the Ama-Shogun. In a real sense she is the Empress of the Sunrise Land, more powerful indeed than any Empress or Emperor could be nowadays. She may find it is easier to get power than to know what to do with it when she has it. She will get no help from me. The woman who married Hideyori can get her guidance from Hideyori's ghost. The land that let Yukio die does not deserve to be protected from Kublai Khan.'

Moko, his heart filled with despair, held out his hands to Jebu. 'Shiké, you cannot be so unforgiving towards the woman you love or towards your country.'

Jebu turned with a swirl of his grey robe and strode towards the steps leading down to the monastery courtyard. 'I'm glad you came when you did, Moko, even though I had to refuse you,' he said briskly. 'We are to hold a ceremony here after sunset. There are three circles in our Order – monk, teacher and abbot – and tonight a monk is to be tested for entry into the circle of teachers – myself.'

'You are to be honoured by your Order, shiké? That is wonderful.'

'We do not consider it an honour but an added burden. No monk wants to be removed from the outermost circle. The difficulty of living as a true Zinja, of achieving insight and remaining in contact with the Self is much greater in the inner circles. I pointed out to my brother monks that I would not still be alive if it were not for you and urged that they grant you the privilege of attending tonight. I must warn you that Zinja ceremonies can be frightening.'

'Did I not say I would follow you anywhere, shiké?'

All that afternoon Moko waited in the guesthouse of the Pearl Temple, bemoaning his failure to win Jebu over for Taniko and worrying about tonight's ceremony. He had lived at Zinja monasteries, but he had never before been invited to witness one of their rites. All the rumours he had heard rose up in his mind, that the Zinja worshipped devils, practised human sacrifice, blasphemed against the Emperor, engaged in unclean sexual practices. That last might be all right, he supposed, but he hoped none of the other things turned out to be true.

It was the beginning of summer and the shutters and blinds of his apartment were open to the outside. Every so often a grey-robed Zinja wearing a white rope around his neck would enter at the gate and be ushered ceremoniously into the monks' quarters. Obviously these were the teachers and the abbots. Their faces were austere, expressionless. They frightened Moko. Over the years, through his travels and his studies of the crafts of carpentry and shipbuilding, he had learned to regard most religion as empty show, but there was something terribly convincing about these Zinja.

From where he sat Moko could also see some women of the Zinja washing laundry in a small stream that ran past their building. Smoke from a cooking fire rose from a nearby shed. Moko was curious about the Zinja women, but he had always been too afraid of the monks to ask questions about them.

The shadow of the temple hill crept across the compound until it enveloped the room where Moko was sitting. As the sun disappeared, his heart quailed, as if he were bidding goodbye to an old friend he might never see again. A monk in a grey tunic entered behind him, startling him, though he managed to retain enough dignity to keep from crying out. The monk lit an oil lamp for him and silently gave him a black cotton robe which Moko put on over his kimono. It had a deep hood and a black silk cord that went around the waist. Moko seated himself on the floor again, though in his nervousness he ached for something to do. He supposed if he were really a monk he'd meditate. How do you meditate? he wondered.

Twilight deepened to evening. A crescent moon, yellow as a boar's tusk, rose above the monastery gate, taking Moko's breath away. He wished he could see the moon rising behind Fuji-san. That would be a spectacle. Amazing how a moment of beauty made a man forget he was frightened. No wonder the samurai devoted themselves to painting and poetry.

His fear returned when a hooded monk came up to the veranda and beckoned. A procession of abbots and teachers, heads and faces shadowed, was slowly ascending the narrow stone steps. They carried no torches. The crescent moon gave faint but sufficient light. Moko's escort led him to a line of Zinja in grey robes who made room for him. They began to climb the steps.

When he entered the temple, Moko was struck by its simplicity. It was a bare room with a polished floor of dark stone, and walls and ceiling of rough-hewn wood. A rectangular stone block served as the altar. The floor descended towards the altar in a series of shallow steps, each broad enough to accommodate a row of seated monks. The rear of the temple, beyond the altar, was open to the night. Out there were the great torii and Mount Fuji, but it was too dark to see either. With slow, monotonous rhythm, a monk with a heavy stick was striking a hollow log suspended from the central roof beam, sending resonant booms through the temple.

The emptiness of the place seemed utterly strange to Moko. All the Buddhist temples he had seen were adorned with gold, crowded with statues painted in dazzling colours. Shinto temples, bare as they were, were palatial in comparison to this. Only Eisen's meditation hall was as plain, and even that had a statue of Daruma, the founder of Zen, for trainees to contemplate. The Pearl Temple was nearly filled when Moko entered. The white robes sat in front, grey robes in the rear. Moko sank down near the rear and waited. The hollow booming continued, and behind him he could hear the shuffling of sandalled feet as the rest of the monks entered the temple.

Abruptly, there was silence. Abbot Taitaro and Shiké Jebu came from behind the altar. The shiké was naked. His body, all bone and stringy muscle, was pocked and criss-crossed with scars. Nakedness in a temple? That startled Moko, reminding him of the rumour about unseemly Zinja practices. Taitaro wore his white abbot's robe.

Father and son faced the assembled Zinja. Taitaro began a long incantation that Moko found impossible to follow. The old abbot called upon the sun, the moon, the stars, the earth and various forces of nature to witness and bless what they did this night. The invocation was partly sung, partly spoken in a weird high-pitched keen, and it went on for a long time. Taitaro's voice in recent years had lost resonance and was frail and reedy.

At last the old abbot said, 'Monk Jebu, most deeply do we regret that we must call you from your life of action in the outermost circle of our Order. Are you willing to teach others even though this may deprive you of the opportunity for greater attainments?'

Jebu's voice was clear and firm, a startling contrast to the feeble voice of his father. 'It is time for me to try what I can accomplish in a different circle of the Order.' Moko sensed that both Taitaro and Jebu were reciting lines from an ancient ritual. The aroma of incense filled his nostrils, a scent different from any he had ever smelled, somewhere between cedar and *ch'ai*. He felt himself relaxing.

'Once before, the Order asked you to undergo an ordeal that might end in your death,' Taitaro said. 'This is required of you again.'

'I am willing.'

Taitaro raised an arm. 'Let him be bound and threatened.'

Threatened? That gave Moko a little start. He watched with growing horror as two monks in grey came forward and laid Jebu on his back on the altar and tied his arms and legs with ropes to iron rings in the stone. Then, standing on the altar, one of the monks attached a long, heavy spear to a rope coming down from the roof beam, so that the point was directly above Jebu's chest. Should the spear fall, it would pierce his heart. This is madness, thought Moko. Had the shiké come through the ordeal of Oshu only to be killed by his own people? He wanted to cry out against this folly, but fear paralysed his tongue.

'You may refuse this trial now,' said Taitaro. 'If you elect to go on, it will be as when you were first initiated into the Order.

You will either prove yourself adequate, or you will cease to exist.',

Tell them you won't do it, Shiké Jebu, Moko urged silently. Why risk death for something that isn't even an honour? Why give up your life for the sake of these madmen? But then he remembered that Shiké Jebu, whom he admired above all other men, was himself one of the madmen.

'I will go on,' said Jebu in a strong voice.

'At certain times in each person's life, an all-important decision must be made,' said Taitaro. 'Such a decision will determine the entire course of one's own future and may affect countless other lives as well. We call these decisions life-problems. Monk Jebu, we know that you are facing a life-problem now, which you must solve to settle your own destiny as well as those of others. To be admitted to the circle of teachers, you are required to answer two questions. First, what is this life-problem you are facing now? Second, what will you do about it? Your answers must show these assembled teachers and abbots of the Order that you have attained a level of insight that qualifies you to be a teacher. You are given all this night. You will be questioned just before sunrise.'

The old monk turned away from the altar where Jebu lay bound and naked with the gleaming steel spear pointing at his heart, and took his place in the front row of white robes. The booming of the stick against the hollow log began again, and the monks raised a chant in some strange, long-lost language. The temple reverberated with their deep droning.

Moko wondered, are we actually going to sit here until dawn? He recalled, from what he had learned in China about heavenly bodies, that this particular night of the Fifth Month was the shortest night of the year. Of course, he wanted the shiké to have all the time in the world to find the right answer to old Taitaro's strange questions, but this stone floor was going to be awfully hard by morning. It was painfully hard now. The incomprehensible chanting went on and on, and Moko lost all track of time. He found himself nodding off to sleep. He heard the rustling of robes about him and looked up to see that many of the monks were pacing around the temple. Some of them were conversing in low tones and others were even leaving the building. How could they just stroll about and chat when a man lay bound to that altar stone in peril of death? Those who remained in their places kept up that devilish chant.

After a time, feeling a little ashamed of turning his back on the shiké, but realizing that his simply suffering through the night or falling asleep in the temple would do Shiké Jebu no good, Moko stood up and shuffled outside. It was a relief, after the sweet incense, to breathe unscented night air and to watch fireflies twinkling like earthbound stars.

'What do you make of this, Moko-san?' said a voice beside him. Moko started and turned. It was Abbot Taitaro.

His bewilderment and indignation bubbled to his lips. 'Holiness, forgive me, but this seems like utter lunacy. I know you love your son. I was with you in the mountains of Oshu when you nearly died yourself, struggling to keep him alive. How can you encourage him to risk his life just so the other Zinja can call him teacher, when it doesn't seem to mean anything as far as I can make out?' A suspicion suddenly dawned in his mind. 'Or, isn't he really risking his life at all? You wouldn't let him be stabbed by that spear, would you?'

'Oh, yes,' said Taitaro. 'If his answer lacks true insight, I myself will cut the rope with a stroke of my sword, and the spear will fall and kill him.'

'Why, holiness? What drives you to this?'

'The belief that only a certain kind of life is worth living.'

'I don't know what that means, holiness.'

'Do not seek to understand everything about an Order whose lifelong members do not always understand it, Moko-san.'

'But why kill a man for failing to answer a question?'

'For Jebu the problem might lie, not in knowing the correct answer, but in admitting that he knows it.' Moko felt Taitaro's hand give his a light, friendly pat, and then the old abbot was gone.

With a twinge of fear Moko remembered Jebu's first plaintive words, which only he had heard, on waking up at the Black Bear Temple. Now he understood the test the Zinja had imposed on Jebu. They were offering what he had wished for. Peace. All he had to do was give an answer that would cause the spear to fall. Moko prayed that Shiké Jebu would want to live.

Moko went back into the temple and took his place among the seated monks. In spite of his anxiety, the chanting and the incense and the booming of the hollow log lulled him, and he allowed himself to drift into sleep. There was nothing he could do for Shiké Jebu except be here. Now he was on a ship, racing over bright blue ocean waves, leaving the Sunrise Land far behind. He was being carried to the sea coast of Persia. His ship plunged like a wild horse, without sail or oar to propel it. The bow smashed upon great, green, transparent rocks like giant emeralds. The Persians were naked women, and they lived in circular towers of polished white stone without doors and rode about on the backs of giant birds. Brandishing sabres, long legs flashing in the sunlight, they came running down to the shore. They surrounded him and raised their swords. They were going to cut him to pieces and feed him to their great birds. He screamed in terror, 'Help! Help!'

A comforting hand shook his shoulder gently. The echo of his screams still reverberated in the incense-heavy air of the temple. Monks were staring at him. His face burned with shame and he bowed his head to hide his embarrassment. They honoured me by inviting me to their ceremony, and I fell asleep and disturbed it, he thought. I have disgraced Shiké Jebu. If I were of noble blood I would commit seppuku, but I am not even worthy to do that.

Taitaro's thin voice cut into his agony. 'The time has come for you to speak, Monk Jebu.'

There was a long silence. With a chill Moko thought, he's not going to answer. That would be the shiké's way. He would not wish to answer the question incorrectly. He would rather let his silence announce that he had chosen death. Moko stared down at Jebu's naked form stretched out on the altar stone, silently imploring the shiké to speak. Beyond the altar, seen through the open end of the temple, the sky was growing light. The skeleton of the great torii and the cone of Fuji were black silhouettes against an indigo sky.

'Just now I heard a cry for help.' Jebu's voice was loud enough to hear but easy, casual, as if he were conversing with a few friends. 'Earlier today I heard another cry for help. I refused it. The Order taught me when I was a child never to expect anything but pain in life. I am now almost fifty years old. I have loved, and love has brought me torment and loss. I have seen the woman I loved married to my enemy. I have had to kill the man I loved with my own hands. Death brought him peace. I held out my arms and fell into the embrace of death, and I awoke later and found that even death had abandoned me.

'I am not obliged to fight any more, but the woman who leads this country, the woman I formerly loved, has sent for me. This is the life-problem you question me about, Father. I know there is no correct solution. If I die on this altar, it is correct. If I remain in this temple and refuse to leave, it is correct. If I go to Kamakura to help the lady who sent for me, it is also correct. I have made my decision. It is the right choice for me because *I have made it*.' He paused a moment. 'I will be a teacher, but not in a Zinja monastery. I will go to Kamakura.'

A blinding glow appeared beyond Jebu, above the tip of Mount Fuji, almost as if the volcano were exploding. It was the edge of the rising sun. Moko held his breath as Taitaro strode forward, sword upraised. He wanted to scream, but his throat was constricted by terror. Taitaro's sword flashed down, cutting the ropes that held Jebu to the stone table. Moko's scream came out as a sigh of relief. The old abbot backed away from Jebu, sheathing his sword, and knelt.

'In this decision, the Self is manifested,' he said in a barely audible voice. Slowly he bent forward until his forehead was pressed to the floor. Row by row the other monks did the same. Moko bowed too, rejoicing, realizing that not only was Master Jebu's life saved, but he was going to return with him to Kamakura to help Lady Taniko fight the invaders. For a long time Moko kept his head down, while his heart danced with joy. He heard movement around him and looked up at last. The sun had risen fully and looked like a red disc balanced on the black point of Fuji-san. The torii framed sun and mountain perfectly. The man who had lain bound on the altar all night was now standing, his arms outstretched in a kind of benediction. Moko realized that the temple and the torii had been placed to provide, at the dawn of the longest day of the year, this view of the sun centred over Fuji, and that it was no accident that this ceremony had been held on this particular night.

Taitaro helped Jebu don a long grey robe. 'The robe of a teacher is the grey of emptiness,' he said.

'At the heart of knowledge is the Void,' the monks chorused.

Taitaro placed a white rope tied in a complex knot around

Jebu's neck and said, 'The universe is bound by one cord tied with one knot.'

'The cord is the Self, and it binds the Self,' the monks chanted.

Now another monk stepped forward and handed Jebu a thick book bound between wooden covers. 'Take *The Zinja Manual*,' said Taitaro. 'It holds that part of our wisdom that can be written down. Read it daily and impart its treasures to those who are worthy.'

The monks chanted, 'Insight is a flame that turns written words to ashes.'

'Let us welcome our new teacher into the Order,' said Taitaro, and to Moko's amazement the monks threw away all decorum as they scrambled to their feet, laughing and shouting, hurrying forward to crowd around Jebu, to cheer and embrace him. Moko had never seen behaviour like this among monks. But the exhilaration of the moment swept him along, and in a moment he, too, was in the clamouring circle around Jebu.

When Jebu saw him, he reached out with a smile and took Moko by the shoulder. 'Here is the one who brought my life-problem to me.'

Moko ducked his head, embarrassed. 'Please, shiké, I don't want to be stared at.'

Taitaro said, 'Those made use of by great destiny are often humble people.'

Moko turned to Taitaro. 'Did destiny have a hand in this, holiness? Or might things have gone otherwise?' He wanted to believe that the shiké had never been in real danger, but he also wanted to believe there was a good reason for his fear.

'Tonight's test might well have had a different outcome,' Taitaro said. 'I could not have predicted how Jebu would choose. But I see a great pattern in these events, a pattern of destiny, if you will. I will tell you about it as we travel to Kamakura.'

'Then you're coming with us, holiness? How marvellous!'

'I will go some of the way with you,' said Taitaro with a smile. Jebu turned and stared intently at the old abbot.

'Shiké,' Moko said, 'are you not glad now that you made this decision?'

Jebu kept his eyes on Taitaro. 'I do not expect to be glad about it, Moko. No matter what path we choose, it leads in the end to sorrow. And on this road, sorrow may come out to meet us.'

It suddenly occurred to Moko to wonder whether the shiké had ever known a moment of unalloyed joy. Moko found himself aware of an emotion that made him acutely un-comfortable. It was disgraceful for one so humble to feel pity for one so exalted.

CHAPTER TEN

Hundreds of banners of the Shima family bearing the clan crest fluttered in the breeze from the great ocean all along the seemingly endless line of samurai snaking down the Tokaido. In the centre of the procession a silver palanquin bobbed, preceded and followed by officers on horseback with golden-horned helmets that gleamed in the light of the setting sun. A cousin of Regent Munetoki was travelling to Heian Kyo to occupy the Rokuhara and represent the Bakufu at the capital.

Three men on foot, travel boxes strapped to their backs, stood on the landward side of the road to let the parade pass. Two were bearded Zinja monks in long grey robes, the third a short, cross-eyed man in a handsome brocaded scarlet jacket and trousers. Behind the travellers a broad plain divided into rice paddies stretched to the distant mountains. In the nearest paddy a row of peasants standing in water up to their shins transplanted rice sprouts to the beds where they would grow to maturity. Ignoring the gorgeous procession of the Shogunal deputy, they were racing against the setting of the sun to get all their plants into the earth before dark. In just the way that the foot soldiers tramped down the road to the beat of drums, the backs and conical straw hats of the peasants rose and fell in unison as they pushed the tender roots of the rice plants into the mud to the age-old chant of 'Yattoko totcha, untoku na!'

'Those peasants are lucky not to get a whipping or worse for failing to bow to that great lord,' Moko whispered.

'The great lord ought to get down from his palanquin and bow to them,' said Taitaro. 'There is more nobility in planting a rice field than there is in leading an army. The lives of these peasants are tales of misery that have never been written. They and their children eat wild roots so they can pay their tax of rice. Millions of them labour to feed the thousands of warriors and rulers who consider themselves so important. The peasants are truly the nation.'

He pointed to a high, forest-covered hill some distance up the road, overlooking the sea. 'With this army in the way we will get no further before sunset. That hill seems as good a place as any to spend the night.'

Jebu was in no hurry to get to Kamakura. He was sure he was more serene now than he would be when they arrived. By the time they had climbed the hill and enjoyed the soup and rice he cooked over a small fire, the rumble of the army had faded into the south, the peasants had gone home from the rice paddies, the stars were appearing over the boundless ocean to the east. The seaward side of the hill on which they were sitting was a sheer cliff, dropping straight down to a jumble of spray-wet rocks. The rhythmic boom of the waves was soothing, reminding Jebu of the peasants' chant.

The lines in Taitaro's face were deeply etched by firelight. 'Jebu,' he said, 'tonight I want to tell you and our good Moko here a few things. Final things. Please bring forth the Jewel of Life and Death.'

The same sense of foreboding Jebu had felt three days ago, on the morning of his initiation, gripped him now. Several times Taitaro had seemed to be hinting at some serious illness. Yet, aside from looking very old – Jebu was not sure of Taitaro's age – the abbot seemed in good health. Jebu took the Jewel out of a hidden pocket in the sleeve of his new robe and held it up.

'Let your mind drift and your body relax,' said Taitaro. 'Let sleep overtake you. The Jewel is an instrument like a mirror, that reflects another world. In that world dwells a kami, a great spirit. In contemplating the Jewel, one can at times become one with this kami.'

I felt I had become one with a kami, thought Jebu, when I stood on that cliff in Oshu, protecting Yukio from the Mongols. Now the Tree of Life appeared in the tracery on the Jewel, expanded, entered into his eyes and seemed to be growing in his mind. A complex tracery of drooping branches formed a structure around him.

'Listen to me, Jebu, but do not hear me,' the old abbot went on in a soft voice that seemed to grow out of the muffled roar of the breakers. 'Sink into the world of the Jewel. Go where I send you.'

Jebu saw Moko's wide eyes, staring through the branches of the Tree, full of concern, the crossed brown pupils reflecting the fire. Then Moko was transformed into a fur-clad giant with green eyes and a red moustache that drooped past the corners of his mouth. Jebu had seen this giant once before in a vision and had not known him. Now he knew that the red hair and light-coloured eyes were the stamp of the Borchikoun, that strain of Mongol men and women from which his own father, Jemuga the Cunning, had sprung. And this was Genghis Khan, founder of the Golden Family, grandfather of Kublai Khan, he who had sent Arghun in pursuit of his father and himself. The giant smiled his merciless smile and extended his vast arm. They were on top of a mountain, standing with their feet buried in snow. Below, in all directions, Jebu could see the countries and people of the world as clearly as if he were on a high hill looking down at peasants in a rice paddy.

As he had seen once before, armies of men on horseback, doll-sized from this height, galloped over the Great Wall and rampaged through China, burning cities, slaughtering the masses of troops sent against them. As the horsemen completed their conquests they seemed to change. Their arms and armour became more elegant, and they were joined by hundreds of thousands of Chinese infantrymen, as well as contingents of special troops with fire-spitting *hua pao*, great siege machines, and elephants. The conquering army was now many times larger than it had been. The troops piled up at the edge of the sea. They boarded Chinese junks and crossed the barrier of water to the Sunrise Land. Jebu wept and cried out helplessly as he saw the samurai overwhelmed, first Kyushu taken, then the Home Provinces. The Mongols burned Heian Kyo, put all its people to the sword, and drove the Emperor into the east, just as the Takashi and their Emperor had once been driven into the west. The last stand was at Kamakura. Jebu watched in agony as Taniko herself stood on the battlements of the Shogun's castle, shooting arrows into the waves of invaders. When it was hopeless she turned and threw herself into the flames consuming the stronghold.

The leader of the conquerors, Arghun Baghadur, turned his craggy face towards the mountain where Jebu stood and held out his arms, offering up his triumph. Looking up, Jebu saw that the giant beside him was now his old master, Kublai Khan.

Now the defeated people of the Sunrise Land began to work for the Mongols. New cities appeared on the ruins of the old. Ships were built, sailing ships after the Chinese manner but bigger and more seaworthy. They set out from the ports of the Sunrise Land, and from China and Korea. With *hua pao* mounted on their decks, they were able to demolish enemy fleets from a great distance, just as Mongol horsemen destroyed enemy armies with clouds of arrows. The huge new vessels transported the Great Khan's armies to the shores of the islands and jungle kingdoms to the south. Where mountains or jungles impeded the onslaught of the Mongol cavalry, the Great Khan sent forth troops adept at other styles of fighting, experienced with other kinds of terrain. A new generation of samurai now fought under the banners of the Great Khan, devastating his enemies. The flotillas turned westwards, attacking and conquering lands and peoples of whom Jebu had only vaguely heard.

'My cavalry of the sea,' Kublai Khan rumbled.

Wonderingly, Jebu turned and looked in the Four Directions. The world was no longer a patchwork of countries. Ruled by the Great Khan, the Central Kingdom was now the centre of an empire stretching from ocean to ocean, and the oceans were patrolled by the Great Khan's ships.

From above Jebu a metallic voice said, 'All people everywhere exist to serve and enrich the Golden Family.' Jebu turned and looked again and saw that on the mountaintop with him was a giant statue of gold, dressed in the voluminous, stiff robes of a Chinese Emperor. The eyes and lips and hands moved, but the rest was frozen metal. All the people of the earth were walking to the foot of the mountain. There they knelt in their millions and pressed their foreheads to the ground, worshipping the no-longer-human thing towering above him.

'And now, Jebu, return to us,' said a voice that seemed to come from the golden statue. Then the face became Taitaro's face, close to his own, the brown eyes, sparkling between wrinkled lids that were almost shut, peering into his. Gently, the thin old fingers drew the Jewel of Life and Death from Jebu's hand.

'What did you experience?' asked Taitaro.

'A terrible dream. I've had such dreams before. I remember having many during the time I was nearly dead with wounds.'

Taitaro smiled. 'Dreams tell you what you already know. But in this vision I added my knowledge to yours to help you see what would happen if the Mongols overrun the Sacred Islands.'

Taitaro turned and tapped Moko's hand with bony fingers. 'Moko-san, I told you there was a great pattern in the events we have all lived through. The War of the Dragons was necessary. Without the samurai and the Shogunate, who would there be to meet a Mongol invasion? An Emperor who is a holy puppet . . . a venal government knowing nothing of the real world . . . an army made up of untrained courtiers and frightened conscripts. If the Takashi had ruled unchallenged until now, the condition of the country would not be much better. They were rapidly growing soft and corrupt as the Sasaki and the Fujiwara. We Zinja helped prepare the nation for a Mongol attack, first by helping Yukio get to China where he and other samurai learned the fighting methods of the Mongols, then by helping Yukio and Hideyori win the War of the Dragons.'

'Was Yukio's death necessary, too?' Jebu asked bitterly.

'Not at all,' said Taitaro calmly. 'To unify the Sunrise Land both Yukio and Hideyori were needed. Yukio was a general but no statesman. Hideyori was a statesman but no general. It is unfortunate that Hideyori was the sort of statesman who is afraid of everyone around him and eventually destroys anyone he is afraid of. But that was something we could not control. We could only work with the material available to us.'

'I had no idea my mission was part of some larger plan,' said Jebu.

'And I did not realize your Order had such power,' said Moko.

'We are not so powerful, Moko-san,' said Taitaro, shaking his head. 'In sheer numbers we are weak and growing weaker, because we have sacrificed our bodies to affect the course of events, as a man might throw himself into the path of a runaway carriage to turn it aside from others. Our only strength lies in the fact that we go a long way back in time and are spread throughout the world.

'We are called by different names in different lands. Here we are known as the Zinja. In China we were once the *Ch'in-cha* and are now the secret White Lotus Society, which works against the Mongols. Among the Mongols themselves we were formerly shamans. Indeed, it was shamans of the Order who guided and aided Jamuga the Cunning in his rebellion against Genghis Khan. Now we are represented by Tibetan lamas who have the ear of great Kublai and who will have tamed the Mongols in a few generations. In the far western countries we have such names as Hashishim and Knights Templar, which no doubt sound incomprehensible to you, Moko-san.

'What all branches have in common is the effort of each member of the Order to achieve direct contact between his or her own consciousness and the entire universe, which we call the Self because each of us *is* the entire universe. Fundamentally we believe in no superior beings, no supernatural or magical powers, not even rules of good and evil. We believe that one day humanity will rise above civilization and live as the earliest people did, without priests or kings or warriors. We believe that ordinary mortals are all that ordinary mortals can rely on.'

'That's not so different from some of my own ideas, holiness,' said Moko. 'Respect the gods, I say, but don't depend on them. Still, how can we hope to get along without rulers and religious teachers and warriors? Surely you're not suggesting that we stop worshipping our sacred Son of Heaven. And you're both a religious teacher and a warrior. So is Master Jebu. Frankly, holiness, most people don't want to learn the martial arts and fight in their own defence. I've never wanted to.'

Taitaro's little bow of acknowledgment was barely visible to Jebu in the dying firelight. 'True, Moko. The ordinary man lets the warrior protect him, and soon the warrior has made a slave of the ordinary man. The Order's answer to this is to produce trained, dedicated military monks who can be trusted not to enslave their fellow human beings.'

'Excuse me, holiness, but a warrior who doesn't want power is like a shark that doesn't eat.'

'We do not desire power because we are engaged in a far more satisfying pursuit, the achievement of insight.'

307

'Do you mean what the Buddhists call enlightenment, holiness? I have never understood what that is.'

'Insight is the same as enlightenment,' Taitaro agreed. 'It is that contact between one's own consciousness and the Self which I spoke of earlier. It is impossible to describe fully in words. It is the discovery that everything you have been doing all along is the activity of the Self.

'We think that the earliest people did not need rules of right and wrong. They believed that everything happens as it should, even one's own death. It is said that some of them could even decide when to die. They would say goodbye to their loved ones and sit down peacefully and let go of life. It is even said that there have been great masters who did this among those who studied the ways of the old ones.

'We believe that there is a spirit of perfect action which exists in all people even now. It is often at odds with the rules of lawgivers and priests. It prompts slaves to rebel against harsh masters and warriors to show compassion for the helpless.'

'You Zinja observe very strict rules, holiness,' said Moko. 'And though you talk of liberating all men, I know that the Zinja follow the orders of their superiors in all things. It seems you do not live according to your beliefs.'

The fire had gone out, and Taitaro's voice coming out of the darkness was almost a whisper. 'We follow the rules of our Order freely, because they help us maintain the state of insight we wish to cultivate. It is just as a samurai avoids drinking the night before a battle, not because drinking is evil in itself but because it would interfere with his fighting ability. We may appear to be disciplined military monks, but the reality of our Order is total liberation.

'Our Order tries to blend in wherever it goes, keeping our knowledge alive and sharing it with those who seem ready for it. We have found that it serves us well to present ourselves in the guise of warrior monks, similar to those of the Buddhist and Shinto temples. We are permitted by custom a certain degree of secretiveness. By training as warriors we have the means of protecting ourselves from suppression. And we can prevent the profession of arms from being the exclusive privilege of a warrior class. Anyone – farmer, craftsman, trader – can join the Zinja and train in self-defence. We must blend in because our ideas are wicked, utterly foreign to the people of the Sunrise Land. People have been killed for saying openly some of the things I have said here tonight. That is why there are those who say we Zinja are devils.'

The Zinja are devils. Jebu, lounging in the darkness on a soft bed of pine needles, sat up with a start. Was that what it meant, then, that deadly secret Taitaro had imparted at his initiation so long ago? If the Zinja beliefs and their ultimate aims were known, the people around them would think them devils and try to destroy them. And only by knowing that they would appear to be devils could they be kept from the supreme arrogance of trying to impose their beliefs on people not yet ready for them. It was the ultimate protection from the temptation of power and therefore the Saying of Supreme Power.

Jebu lay back again, turning this new idea over in his mind as he listened to Taitaro explain the Order to Moko. He could hear the weariness in the old man's voice and he wished he would stop and rest. Jebu's mind wandered. He let his thoughts go back to that time with Taniko just after Kublai Khan had released her to him and before he told her how Kiyosi died. Even if he hated her now, there was no harm in remembering a happier time.

It was very late when he heard Taitaro talking about things he had never discussed with Jebu before, and he began to listen again.

'Our ideals require a way of life so strenuous that there cannot ever be many Zinja. And lately it seems to have been our Order's karma to dwindle even more. During the War of the Dragons many of our monasteries were destroyed and more of our men and women killed than we can replace. There are now less than a thousand of us, men, women and children, and we have only six monasteries in all the Sacred Islands.

'So we have decided to disappear, allowing it to seem that we have become extinct. It is a strategy we have resorted to in other parts of the world where the Order's position seemed too precarious.

'You, Jebu, will be one of the last to be known openly as a Zinja. In the future the Order will exist in secret, in the midst of other organizations such as the Zen monks, whose beliefs are in some ways similar to ours, the schools of martial arts and the families who call themselves Ninja, the Stealers-In, whom the samurai use as spies and assassins. Members of our Order have already joined these other groups to prepare the way for our absorption into them. Our most important work will be among the samurai. We hope to teach them to be something more than professional killers. We will share with them the Zinja ideal of the way of the sword as a ladder to the sublime.

'The world is entering a new time in which new knowledge will spread faster among the nations. The Mongol conquests have speeded this process by breaking down boundaries all across the great continent to the west. And the barbarians of the far west have sent their armies eastwards on religious wars, and their warriors have brought new knowledge home with them. People are on the move everywhere. Through this exchange of ideas the day will come when humanity will have a better understanding of the universe and be ready to hear the teachings of the Order.

'The Mongols will not conquer the world. It frequently happens that after defeating every opponent an expanding empire comes up against some little, fierce, stubborn nation far out on the edge of its territories, and this little nation inflicts on the empire a stunning defeat that puts an end to its spread. It can happen here and now. If any warriors can stop the advance of the Mongols the samurai can. They are the finest fighting men in the world.'

Jebu looked out at the dark ocean to the east. The horizon was visible now, and the stars were fading in a sky more purple than black. Taitaro sounded exhausted, Jebu thought. They had, as he had feared, stayed up all of this short night talking. He did not want Taitaro to use up any more of his strength.

'There is one last thing I have to tell you, my son,' came the thin whisper from the old man seated opposite him. 'The Jewel of Life and Death. It was never really necessary. I might just as easily have given you a crow's feather to meditate on.'

Jebu was shocked. Just when he had thought nothing more could surprise him, he heard this.

'I don't understand, sensei. How can you tell me now that the Jewel has no special power?'

'It is no different from a man who looks up at a cloud and sees the shape of a bird or a fish. The shape is not in the cloud. The man's mind puts it there. I told you that by contemplating the Jewel you could enter another world and become one with a kami. That other world is your own mind, and that superior being is yourself. Let go of the Jewel now, my son. Keep it as a memento of your father, if you like, but do not cling to it for spiritual power. The meaning of the Jewel of Life and Death is that life and death have no meaning, except what we put into them by the way we choose to live and die.'

'Is my father saying that the Tree of Life and all the other visions I saw were only in my mind?' Jebu asked, feeling that he had lost something infinitely precious.

There was amusement in the fragile voice coming from the figure in white. 'Why do you say *only*, my son? Is it not a marvellous mind that has such visions in it?'

It was almost dawn. 'Let us watch the sun rise,' said Taitaro. 'Entering and exploring the miraculous worlds of our minds.'

Clouds piled on the horizon turned a glowing pink. The first blinding radiance of the sun burst over the edge of a calm sea. Jebu thought, how beautiful it is. Then he saw that the beauty was not there in the sunrise, but in the mind of him who beheld it.

'I am going to die now,' Taitaro said softly.

The words were a fist striking straight at Jebu's heart. 'Father, no. What is it? What's wrong?' I knew I shouldn't have let him exhaust himself talking, Jebu thought.

'Nothing is wrong. I have decided that today is my day to die.'

'No!' Jebu cried. He did not doubt for a moment that Taitaro could die whenever he wished.

Moko was on his feet, standing over the old man who sat staring serenely ahead, his long white beard blowing in the breeze from the sea. The carpenter reached out to Taitaro, as if to hold him back from the Void, but he drew his hands away before touching the old man, as if Taitaro were already a corpse and therefore taboo.

'Holiness,' he wept, 'of all the Zinja madness I've seen in the last few days, surely willing yourself to die is the maddest of all. You can't leave us now. We need you.'

'It is my privilege to die when I choose to,' said Taitaro calmly. 'I have earned it, and some day you and Jebu may feel as I do today. Jebu-chan, I have transmitted to you everything I can tell you. I have freed myself from all attachments to this world. Even better, I have freed myself from all the foolish fears that beset the elderly. My choice of death is right for me, Jebu, just as your choice of going to Kamakura and the Lady Taniko is right for you. You no longer need me, any more than you need the Jewel. If you want counsel, go to the Zen monk Eisen, whose temple is just outside Kamakura. You met him once, and he was one of us long ago.'

With a sigh Taitaro stood up and climbed a few paces to the pinnacle of the cliff where they had camped the night before. He looked out at the waves and the rising sun. After a moment he sank into a cross-legged seated position with his hands folded in his lap. He is looking at the last sight he is ever going to see in this world, thought Jebu. It was too much for him. He threw himself to the ground. The first few sobs forced themselves through clenched teeth. Then the tears began to run freely from his eyes, and he opened his mouth wide and let out a wailing cry of pain and protest.

Taitaro turned and looked down at him calmly. 'Come, come, is this any way for a man almost fifty years of age to behave? A Zinja monk, at that?'

'You are the only person I have left in the world to love,' Jebu sobbed. 'Do not abandon me now, I beg you. You gave me the choice between life and death a few days ago, and I chose life. Will you make a mockery of my choice?'

'What you say about love is foolish, my son. The world is full of people whom you love. One is right beside you. As for mockery, I would indeed mock your choice if I refused to make a choice of my own when one is called for. Life and death are the same to a Zinja. The resolve is all. This old body of mine is worn out. The Self is ready to drop it. Accept, accept. All happens as it should.'

'I don't want you to die,' Jebu wept.

'Your passions are a gale, my son, always threatening to blow away everything we've taught you. You know that freedom from the fear of death is the key that unlocks humanity's chains. Yet you treat my passing as a fearful, sorrowful thing. You disturb the calm of this moment with your ignorant wailing.' For a moment the gruff strength Jebu remembered from his childhood came back into Taitaro's voice. 'Be silent now.'

312

Jebu climbed to his feet and stood with bowed head, ashamed, realizing that his father's admonition had the weight of Zinja teaching behind it. Yet beneath the stern tone he heard love. His father wanted him to be calm, invulnerable, a true Zinja. He also wanted him to be human, and to be human he must suffer.

'I'm sorry, Father,' he said. For the first time he heard a strange sound beside him and realized it was Moko, bent double, muffling his sobs. Jebu put a comforting hand on Moko's shoulder.

'Sit and meditate with me, Jebu and Moko,' Taitaro said. This brought a moan from Moko, but at the gentle urging of Jebu's hand on his shoulder, the carpenter sank to the ground. The sun was now well above the grey-blue sea, and its radiance was blinding. Jebu felt himself wanting to ease Moko's sorrow, and in that wish his own pain lost some of its sharpness. For a long time they sat in silence.

Taitaro said almost in a whisper, 'This mild wind blowing from the sea will carry me off. I will become the Self. No longer will there be any separateness at all. I will return when needed, and I will bring the wind with me. I have always loved my Sacred Islands. Truly they are a gift of the gods to the world.'

Jebu seemed to forget time and death as the sun gradually rose higher, warming him with its summer heat, while the soft sea breeze dried the tears on his cheeks. After a while there was a stillness about Taitaro that made Moko and Jebu turn questioningly to each other.

'Let me look,' Moko said, the tears running down his cheeks like a waterfall. Jebu bowed, though he already knew what Moko would find. Moko stood up and climbed to the pinnacle where Taitaro sat with his back to them. He peered into the abbot's face, then turned to Jebu a face full of woe.

'He has left us, shiké. He has truly left us.' Moko fell into a crouch beside Taitaro, sobbing.

As if it were a parting gift from Taitaro, Jebu suffered no longer. He felt utterly serene. Some time during the long meditation, as Taitaro's breath went out of his body, the sorrow had drained out of Jebu like poison being drawn out of a wound. He had done his mourning while his father was alive.

'We will build a pyre for him here and scatter his ashes in the sea,' he said. And in time an empty urn would move into its place in some Zinja monastery.

Now Jebu made himself go up to the top of the cliff and see his father's dead face. It was like that of a porcelain monk. Taitaro's eyes were lightly closed, his head was sunk on his chest, his hands were clasped together in his lap. Jebu lovingly touched his father's shoulder, and Taitaro's body started to slump forward. Moko and Jebu lifted the body, light as a doll's, and carried it back a little way from the edge of the cliff.

They plunged together in silence into the forested slope leading up from the Tokaido Road. Moko, as always, was carrying with him his box of carpenter's tools, his Instruments of the Way. Even though he now wore a samurai sword, he never went without the tools of his original trade. Each of them took a saw and began cutting down small trees. By noon they had made a waist-high platform of crossed tree trunks and bamboo poles, the spaces between them filled with pine boughs. They laid Taitaro's body on it and built a thick canopy of poles and branches over it, peaked like the roof of a shrine.

At the Hour of the Ape the sun was in the western sky, and they were ready. Moko lit a branch with flint and tinder and handed it to Jebu. Jebu walked around the pyre and in five places set fire to the boughs at its base. Swiftly the flames, almost invisible in the bright sunlight, curled up around the wood and met in a peak above it. It had been a dry summer, and the pyre burned with a fierce hissing, sending up thick white smoke. The wind had shifted during the day and now blew from the land towards the sea. The smoke stretched out in a long white plume over the waves. Jebu and Moko stood back from the shimmering air around the fire.

'The smoke reminds me of his beard,' said Moko sadly. He was calmer now, having emptied himself for the time being of tears for the old abbot.

Jebu slowly recited aloud a prayer he had been taught long ago, the Prayer to a Dead Zinja. 'Death is not the enemy of life. Life is the mountain, death is the valley. As the snowflake that falls on the mountaintop is carried at last to the river, so your self has at last rejoined the Eternal Self. I congratulate you, Brother, on a life well lived. You have seen all the arrows fly, you have seen all the swords fall. You will remember nothing and you at last will be forgotten. But in remembering the Self, we remember you. The Self never forgets.' For the first time Jebu realized that this prayer, like other Zinja prayers for the dead, was not addressed to the one who, after all, had ceased to exist, but to the one who spoke the prayer.

'Homage to Amida Buddha,' Moko declared, as if both prayers were part of the same ritual.

It was late afternoon by the time the fire had burned down to the blackened rock. Moko, weeping again, used his Instruments of the Way to perform the final office of pulverizing the skull and remaining pieces of bone. Then, with pine branches, they swept the ashes from the cliff edge. The wind caught them and carried them down to the sea.

Jebu stood looking out over the ocean as Taitaro had only this morning, feeling on his back both the warmth of the setting sun and the cool wind blowing from the west. Long shadows purpled the waters below. The wind reminded him of the battle of Shimonoseki Strait. Yukio and Taitaro, the two men dearest to him, both gone. They had melted back into wind, fire, earth and water, of which all things are composed. Yet it was impossible not to think that their spirits were somehow still intact, that Yukio and Taitaro could still watch and love the Sacred Islands and could, as Taitaro had said, return at need.

He looked down at the ocean and thought, we appear, run our course, and vanish again, like waves, while the ocean remains. How sad we are, wishing we could go on forever. Some people manage to attain a spirit of accepting death, but others are cut off before they even have time to do that. The young samurai try to learn acceptance by comparing themselves to cherry blossoms. The life of a blossom is only a day, but it is complete. Atsue, I think, must have known that kind of acceptance. But Yukio, young as he was, lived fully. He did the greatest deeds possible, and wanted to die when the time finally came. And my father Taitaro – if ever I have seen a life ended in the fullness of days, it was his. Men like Yukio and Taitaro are not blossoms, they are golden fruit, falling in ripeness. If it were not that all partings are sorrowful I could almost say that the death of my father was a happy occasion, as I know he wanted it to be. Teach the samurai, he said. I must teach them what is best and truest in the way of the samurai, their own way. We do not have to win wars, we have only to achieve insight and liberation. I must help them understand this.

He heard heavy feet pushing through the woods below. He looked down and saw movement and the flash of metal among the pines. Armed men. Uneasily, Moko moved to stand next to him. A few moments later three samurai of the lowest rank, foot soldiers armed with spears, emerged from the forest. Their bearing was respectful when they saw they were dealing with a monk and a man who appeared to be a well-dressed samurai, albeit not of very military bearing.

'What's happening here, shiké?' one of them asked. 'We saw your fire a long way off. It was too big to be just an ordinary campfire.'

'My father, Abbot Taitaro of the Order of Zinja, died here this morning,' said Jebu. 'We have been performing funeral rites for him.'

The samurai frowned. 'Things aren't done that way any more, shiké. You don't just dispose of your dead in the wilderness. You're expected to report a death to the proper authorities.' He turned to his comrades. 'We'd better take them to the general.'

Moko spoke up grandly. 'The highest authorities of all require our immediate presence in Kamakura. You'll regret it if you delay us.' Though he was not samurai by birth and had never drawn the sword that hung at his belt, he knew he outranked these three.

'General Miura will sort things out, sir,' said the samurai, forcing himself to be polite. 'Please come with us.'

Taking a last look at the spot where Taitaro had died, Jebu shouldered his travel box and started down the hillside. Moko pointed out his own box to one of the warriors.

'I have had to make this journey without servants, but there is no reason for me to carry luggage when there is one of lower rank to do it for me. Since you force me to go out of my way, you may carry my box.' The samurai Moko singled out responded with a murderous look, but after a gesture from his superior he reluctantly strapped Moko's box to his back.

A small company of foot soldiers and cavalry was lined up on the road at the base of the hill. Moko and Jebu were led to their splendidly-dressed general, a black-bearded man who sat on a brown and white horse. Over his armour he wore a light blue cape bearing a white disc, the badge of the Miura family.

'You're the two I've been sent to fetch,' said General Miura Zumiyoshi when they identified themselves. He spoke in the accents of an eastern warrior. 'What were you doing starting fires up there in the hills? Surely you know that's dangerous in dry weather like this.'

Jebu explained the funeral pyre and apologized for not having followed proper procedures. 'We monks are not always aware of new regulations. The world passes us by.'

'I'd believe that if you weren't a Zinja,' Zumiyoshi laughed, his teeth flashing white in his beard. 'In any case, shiké, my sympathies. I know what it is to lose a father.'

'If there's nothing else the honoured general wishes, we should be getting on our way,' said Jebu. 'We are expected in Kamakura.'

'Indeed you are,' said Zumiyoshi. 'And I've come to speed you on your way. Be good enough to mount the horses we've provided. We'll travel by torchlight. I'm to take you at once to her ladyship, the Ama-Shogun.'

CHAPTER ELEVEN

From the pillow book of Shima Taniko:
The Ama-Shogun. I both like and dislike that nickname. To be thought of as Supreme Commander of the samurai even though I am a woman – what woman has ever achieved so much? There have been Empresses who ruled alone, but they inherited the title, and they ruled so badly that no woman will ever be permitted to occupy the throne again. So the historians say. Of course, the historians are all men.

How well I and my family rule will soon be tested. The people and the samurai are strong enough, and the gods are surely on our side. What it comes down to is whether we, who happen to be leading the country now, can lead well during this coming invasion. It is hard to believe, but there are moments when I miss Hideyori's cleverness in matters of state.

Our agents in China and Korea report that the southern Sung capital, Linan, has surrendered to the Mongols without a struggle, and the child who is Son of Heaven has knocked his head on the floor in homage to Kublai and has been carried off into captivity. I'm glad Linan surrendered. It would have been a horror beyond imagining if that magnificent city had been destroyed and its millions slain.

But some Chinese fight on. The war party has crowned the younger brother of the captured Emperor, and they still occupy the coastal provinces. They have a huge navy. The longer they hold out, the more time we will have to prepare for our own ordeal. A naval war between the Mongols and the Chinese will destroy many ships Kublai could use against us.

But, the Nun Shogun? I am far from being a nun. I know that now more than ever, as I tremble with anticipation at seeing Jebu again. He must come. I have sent Moko after him to the Zinja Pearl Temple, and I sent Zumiyoshi with troops and horses after Moko. Jebu may be here at any moment. Here. At last, after all these years, with all barriers between us gone. My love for him has arisen like the phoenix and soars in the heavens.

Someone knocks at the door of my chamber. Perhaps Jebu is in the castle even now. I feel all the eagerness I should have felt, but did not, on either of my wedding nights.

—*Fifth Month, twenty-fifth day*
YEAR OF THE RAT

It was late in the evening when she received them in her personal audience chamber, the Lilac Hall. She wondered if anyone had told Jebu that name and if so, whether it would mean anything to him. As etiquette required, she sat on the dais behind a screen. It was a warm night. She had ordered the shoji panel on the east side of the room opened, permitting a glimpse of the moon floating among the branches of pine trees, as if caught by them. A double row of councillors in red and green kimonos lined the length of the room, seated under the murals of lilac bushes that gave the hall its name. Even though no one could see her except the one lady-in-waiting who relayed her signals to the servants, she had dressed with care in a white silk outer jacket printed with the red Shima crest, shades of green showing at her neck, sleeves and hem. In her hair was her mother-of-pearl butterfly, the lucky ornament that had gone with her to China and back. She needed luck tonight, she thought, feeling a hollow in her stomach. She signalled to the lady-in-waiting that she was ready.

Miura entered first, his helmet tucked under his arm. Then came Moko in his rich robes. Her eyes leaped to the tall figure beyond them. Her first sight of him struck her like a physical blow, and she gasped. He looked splendid in his long robe. The skin of his hands and face was a rich dark brown against the grey cotton. He dropped to his knees beside the others, and all three pressed their foreheads to the polished wood floor. Jebu sat back, eyes cast down, hands folded in his lap, waiting. One advantage of a screen, Taniko thought, was that she could avidly drink in the sight of him and no one need know. Her heart was hammering furiously in her chest, like a prisoner trying to escape. He was so near, for the first time in over ten years. Other than that strange, brief glimpse of him at the Hachiman shrine, this was her first look at him in all that time. There were many more wrinkles around his eyes, whose grey she could not see because he kept them determinedly fixed on the floor. His white hair was parted in the middle and fanned out stiffly to his shoulders, giving him the look of a lion in a painting. The ends of his moustache hung down to his white beard. Anyone looking at him would see a fierce-looking middle-aged monk, but to her the young man she had met the day she began her first journey down the Tokaido was clearly visible.

She spoke at last, first thanking General Miura and Moko for bringing Jebu safely and quickly to Kamakura. Moko's eyes flickered nervously back and forth between Jebu and the screen behind which she was sitting.

At last it was time to address Jebu. The mere thought of saying his name aloud intimidated her. She hoped there would be no quaver in her voice.

'My most profound gratitude to you, Master Jebu, for your willingness to leave the peace of your temple. You must find this military capital a noisy, discordant place after the quiet of monastic life.'

Now, for the first time, he lifted his eyes, and again she felt as though she had been struck by a club. He was looking straight through her screen, as if he could see into her eyes, even though she knew he couldn't. She almost felt like fainting, as she had at the Hachiman shrine. The eyes were impenetrable as granite. There was not a trace of feeling in them. They saw into her and told her nothing – and thereby told her everything. Oh no, she thought. The hollow in the pit of her stomach turned to a sinking iron ball. The joyless grey eyes told her that he was not happy to be here, that he hadn't wanted to come to her, that he hated her.

He spoke now, thinly masked disdain curling his beard and moustache back from his teeth. 'My lady, a summons from one as exalted and powerful as you honours this lowly monk.' The voice was hoarser than she remembered it, but softer. The sound of it made her shiver. 'I cannot seem to find peace anywhere in this world, and I am more used to the ringing of steel on steel than the chiming of temple bells. For every night that I have slept in a monastery, I've spent a hundred nights on the ground. As for this capital of yours, it is a strong, fierce city, worthy of samurai. Of all its edifices, the grandest is this residence of yours, my lady, the Shogun's castle. The Shima family mansion, where I left you long ago, before I joined Lord Yukio to fight at his side during the War of the Dragons, was an admirable palace. But this castle dwarfs it utterly. My lady has risen far in this world.'

He had never forgiven her for being ambitious. The other men in the room were all staring at Jebu. He had committed an offence by mentioning Yukio, whose reputation was still under a cloud here in Kamakura. She was sure it was Jebu's way of reminding them that he had fought for Yukio to the end and did not regret it.

'My lady, we're worn out from travelling such a great distance in such a short time,' Moko stammered. 'We have not eaten all day. Might it not be better to meet again when we're fresh?'

Dear Moko was trying to protect Jebu by blaming his

320

discourtesy on fatigue. It made her want to laugh in spite of her sorrow.

'Don't be absurd, Moko. We've only begun this conversation,' she said.

'My apologies, Lady Taniko,' said Jebu, still staring steadily at her screen. 'Of course the name of Muratomo no Yukio should never be mentioned in this castle.' That implied she had approved of Yukio's persecution and death. She could not answer the accusation in front of her councillors, because that would require her to criticize Hideyori, whom she was obliged as a respectable widow to defend. But she could not let the charge go unanswered.

'I accept your apology, Monk Jebu,' she said in the pleasantest tone she could muster. 'Your loyalty to your friend and lord of so many years is commendable.' She chose her next words carefully. 'The dispute between my lord Hideyori, the late Shogun, and his brother Lieutenant Yukio, was a great sorrow to me, and I never understood the reason for it. Now that both are gone, let the quarrel be buried with my husband's ashes at the Hachiman shrine, where karma took him from me. Let both lords be remembered only as two of the greatest heroes of the Muratomo clan. With the passing of time we forget the reasons for our bloody quarrels. We remember with respect all the great warriors of the Sunrise Land, even the mighty ones of the Takashi family, as well as those who slew them. If only all our heroes were alive today we would not have to fear the most terrible enemy our nation has ever known.' There, she thought, that message was clear enough: *I, too, sympathized with Yukio. See, I publicly call him lieutenant, the title Hideyori forbade. Let us forget all past grievances. I do not blame you for the deaths of Hideyori or Kiyosi or Atsue. I need your help.*

Jebu smiled, a smile without humour or kindness. 'I quite agree, my lady. Yesterday's enemy, today's friend.' Meaning. *You are no better than all the other samurai, with their ever-shifting loyalties.* The answer bitterly disappointed Taniko. She had hoped to have his love to sustain her. Instead, if she wanted him near her, she would have to live with his contempt. She felt as if an earthquake had split the ground open and she were falling into the fissure. This situation was impossible. They must come to terms of some kind, even if he could no longer love her. She realized that she owed him much for the years of suffering she had inflicted on him by sending him away after he confessed to killing Kiyosi, and that she should be patient now. She could endure his scorn for a little while. Perhaps if they talked alone, she could make a peace of sorts with him.

'The Zinja honours the samurai by quoting an old saying of ours,' she said. 'I am hoping that Zinja and samurai knowledge combined will help us to win this war. I would like to discuss this further with Shiké Jebu. I will not hold the rest of you.' With formal salutations to Moko, Zumiyoshi, her councillors and most of her court women, she cleared the Lilac Hall. For appearances' sake she remained behind her screen and kept an elderly lady-in-waiting, whose discretion she trusted, sitting at a corner of the dais.

'Come closer, Jebu,' she said. 'Now that we are alone there is no need for you to sit so far away.' He rose fluidly, halved the distance between them and dropped to his knees again. No man moves so gracefully, she thought. He made the samurai look like waddling ducks. Her hunger for him was actually physically painful. She could not take her eyes off his long brown hands.

'What does my lady require of me?' he asked in that hoarse, soft voice that made her spine tingle.

She forced her mind to the business at hand. 'We know the Mongols will attack somewhere along the west coast. The Bakufu generals are preparing our defences. You can help them by teaching them whatever you can remember from your years of fighting among the Mongols. You can tell them how to train our men. You yourself can set up a school in which samurai can be taught new tactics. Scattered all over the Sacred Islands there must be surviving samurai who fought under you and Yukio in China and Mongolia. You must find them and make teachers of them.'

'There will not be many of them, my lady,' said Jebu coldly. 'Only about three hundred came back with us from China. Many of those were killed during the War of the Dragons. More died when your noble husband made war on those who remained loyal to Lord Yukio.'

'Well, you will tell all who supported Lord Yukio that the past is done with and their nation needs them now,' said Taniko, despairing as she saw that Jebu was not going to let the subject of Yukio alone. 'If the rules of your Order permit, I wish you also to train our men in the Zinja martial arts. By this I mean the Zinja philosophy as well as the specific techniques. From what you told me of it long ago, I believe the Zinja philosophy could be most valuable to the samurai.' She gave Jebu what she hoped was a winning smile, momentarily forgetting the screen between them and then cursing it when she remembered.

'Perhaps you can also help our officers with planning,' she went on. 'The Mongols could attack anywhere along the coast of Kyushu or Honshu, and that is a terribly long line to defend. Our forces will be spread so thin that a Mongol attack will be like punching through a paper wall.'

'Then I suggest you build a wall of stone,' said Jebu.

'A stone wall all along the coasts of two islands? Impossible.'

Jebu shook his head. 'It will only be necessary to build it around Hakata Bay. That is where the Mongols will land.'

'How can you possibly be sure of that?'

'They need a very large harbour to accommodate a huge fleet. The harbour must be as close to their ports of embarkation as possible, so that their ships, already overloaded with men and horses, won't have to carry provisions for a long voyage. The landing site must also be close enough to the heart of our country that the Mongols will not have to fight their way across the whole island of Kyushu or down through the mountains of Honshu to get at the Home Provinces and Heian Kyo. There is only one harbour that fulfils all those conditions, Hakata Bay.'

'If we put all our troops and defences there, the Mongols are sure to learn of it,' said Taniko. The conversation was going much better now. The bitterness was gone as they discussed the problem that faced them.

'They will still land there, even if they know we are waiting for them. They will be confident that they can overwhelm us. A shrewd strategist would try to land at an undefended place, but when a man has conquered as vast an empire as Kublai Khan's he expects to win by throwing all his troops against all the enemy's troops in one tremendous encounter. Such a man feeds his overly exalted notion of his own power with adventures like that.'

Taniko saw the smiling face of Kublai Khan in her mind. A

man before whom nations had trembled from the time he was a small boy. A man who could dream of building his own green mountain with one tree of each kind in the world on it. Jebu was right; such a man would probably land his troops at Hakata because it suited his convenience, even if every warrior in the Sunrise Land was waiting there for him.

'Do you think we can possibly win, Jebu?' she asked anxiously. 'You are the only fighting man, of all those around me, who has any idea of the Mongols' real power.'

'They have never failed in any war they have undertaken,' said Jebu. 'Still, Kublai Khan is attempting the most difficult and hazardous of all military operations, an invasion across a wide ocean. His ability to send reinforcements will be limited, especially if his fleet is forced to remain at anchor on our shores. If we can hold his army to the water's edge, they will need their ships as a base to operate from. They won't be able to send the ships back to ferry more troops across. That is why I suggest a wall. As to whether we can win, no one can say. There are too many uncertainties. We Zinja believe in throwing ourselves into the struggle with all our energy, without concerning ourselves about who wins or loses.'

'If they win, I do not intend to live,' said Taniko.

'I know,' said Jebu with a smile. 'You will take a bow and arrows in your own hands and die fighting.' The moment was almost companionable. Thinking of the wall he had suggested, she remembered the half-ruined Chinese Great Wall, where they had stood together and looked north, into the wind, at the land that bred the Mongols. The lamps in the Lilac Hall burned low, and the lady-in-waiting who was there for respectability's sake seemed to be asleep.

'Oh, Jebu, when you spoke of a wall, I could not help remembering the time you and I saw the Great Wall in China together. We had just been reunited after so many, many years apart, and I have never been happier, before or since. You must remember. This is happening again now. We're together again. We can be happy.'

Her voice faltered. There was a long silence as Jebu stared at her. Beneath the granite eyes she sensed volcanic fires. The brown hands resting on his thighs were tense.

At last he spoke. 'I am prepared to serve you, my lady, but

only in this war. I do not think it accomplishes any purpose to discuss a past that no longer exists.'

She cringed back, glad of the screen between them that hid from him her look of dismay. 'Why so fierce, shiké?' she pleaded. 'From the moment you entered this hall, I have felt your anger. I do not think I have done anything to deserve such hatred. Whatever the reason, I beg you to forgive me. How else can we work together? Surely you would not have come here if you hate me as much as you seem to.'

Jebu's reply smashed her hopes. 'There are many reasons why I am here, but the most important is Yukio. He was my life. I am doing what he would want me to do if he were alive. He would be in command of our defences now if he had not been murdered by the man you married — my lady.' He spoke through bared teeth.

I do not have to humble myself before anyone, she thought, much less this rude monk. I am the mother of the Shogun. Samurai by the tens of thousands would die to defend me. The Regent turns to me for advice.

'Thank you for explaining yourself to me so clearly, Shiké Jebu,' she said in a steely voice. 'Please leave me now. This audience is ended.'

'My lady.' He stood up, bowed, and backed out of the room with an elaborate display of courtesy.

She sat with her fists clenched. I will not let that man have anything to do with defending the Sunrise Land, she thought. Let him go back to his monastery. I hate him.

CHAPTER TWELVE

At noon the next day Taniko sat in the moon-viewing chamber, a room on the top floor of the highest tower in the castle, which she often used for meditation. The sun was bright on the lower rooftops nearby, their gold dolphins reflecting a blinding radiance. Her feelings were more divided than ever. She had to accept Jebu's help, now that she had asked for it. The good sense of his plan to build a wall around Hakata Bay proved how useful he could be. And in spite of his anger at her, she could not get his face out of her mind.

Then there was the problem of what to do about the sword presentation. Ever since Hideyori's death she had kept the Muratomo heirloom sword, Higekiri. She thought it fitting that it go to Sametono, and was planning to give it to him in a ceremony at sunset today. She had intended Jebu to be a guest and to meet Sametono and Munetoki. His presence at the presentation would symbolize the reconciliation of the Shogunate with the followers of Yukio. But since she and Jebu could not be reconciled, it might be better to hold the ceremony without him. She both wanted, and did not want, him to be there. After so many years, her need to be near him was so great that she wanted to see him despite his hatred. She thought of asking Eisen's advice. He would be invoking the blessing at the ceremony. But Eisen did not know Jebu. Moko did. She quickly wrote a note asking Moko to come to the castle immediately and sent one of her guards off to his house.

Moko came to Taniko's private chamber at the Hour of the Sheep. He was perspiring under layers of kimonos, each more heavily embroidered than the next. Being old friends, they met without either screens or ladies-in-waiting to protect Taniko's virtue. Taniko's quarters were as austere as they had been when Hideyori was alive. The principal decoration in the room was the calligraphic copy of the verse from the Diamond sutra Sametono had made years ago, which she had mounted on a scroll and hung in her personal altar. Today there was a vase of white roses beside it. As usual, Moko took a moment to admire Sametono's artistry and to read the verse.

'No such thing as goodness,' he said. 'You know, the old sage Taitaro said something like that just before he died.'

'Taitaro dead?' Taniko was shocked. 'Jebu didn't say a word to me about it. That wonderful old man. Oh, how sad!' Taitaro's appearance in Shangtu long ago had given her the first ray of hope that she might one day be rescued and return home. Taitaro had seemed like a father to her – a real father, not like Bokuden – during her sojourn with Jebu in China. Tears sprang to her eyes. How could Jebu have failed to tell her that? Did he hate her that much? 'Homage to Amida Buddha,' she whispered in Taitaro's memory. 'How and when did he die, Moko?'

Moko told her of Taitaro's almost miraculous departure from this world.

'The Tokaido,' said Taniko, wiping her eyes with the pale green sleeve of her outer kimono. 'So much that is important to us has happened along the Tokaido. Do you remember how you swore you would always be the messenger between us, Moko-san?'

'I do, my lady.' Moko's eyes were large and liquid with sadness.

'Moko-san, you saw how he spoke to me at the audience last night. I feel that I should never have sent for him. What do you think?'

'My lady, I am sure Master Jebu still loves you. His rages prove it. He is a man who has been learning all his life to accept calmly everything that happens to him. Yet, towards you he is an earthquake, a tidal wave, a *tai-phun*. Even a fool like me can see that he loves you.'

Encouraged, Taniko stopped crying. 'What about the sword ceremony, Moko? Shall I invite him?' Amazing, she thought. The leaders of the nation turn to me for advice, and I turn to a cross-eyed carpenter.

'Let me take your invitation to the shiké, my lady. I will persuade him not to behave like a bear in springtime.'

'Oh, Moko, how can I thank you enough?'

'I have another reason for doing this, my lady. Since your son was gracious enough to raise my family to samurai class, my eldest son must now carry our new family name, Hayama, into battle. I want him to be trained by the shiké. I can think of no better way to ensure that he comes out alive.'

The Great Audience Hall of the Shogun's castle was hung with the banners of the great families that supported the Bakufu. On the top level of the dais, wearing a jewelled head-dress amd almost buried in crackling, gold-embroidered robes, was the ten-year-old Shogun, Muratomo no Sametono. Behind him hung a huge silk cloth bearing the embroidered Muratomo White Dragon. At his side was the hilt of a gold-mounted sword which many in the hall recognized, some with reverence, some with indignation. Kogarasu. It was the first time Sametono had openly worn the Takashi sword. At Sametono's left sat the Regent, Shima Munetoki. The lower levels were occupied by the principal officers of the Bakufu, by the great clan chieftains and, behind a tall folding screen, Taniko. Even though she had arranged and planned the ceremony down to the last detail, Taniko was expected to remain behind the screen throughout.

She could see Jebu and Moko on the floor of the hall, near the dais. She had broken protocol to seat Jebu there, where she could look at him. Eisen stood up now and recited a blessing. Munetoki spoke from his seated position beside Sametono, telling the history of Higekiri and the tragic way it came into the possession of the Shogun's widow.

'She who next to the Empress herself is the most highly honoured lady in our realm now chooses to present this treasure to her exalted son, our Lord Shogun, Muratomo no Sametono.'

Munetoki rose and went over to Taniko's screen and received from her the sword box, a work of art in itself with mother-of-pearl birds in flight inlaid on gold lacquer. Reverently, Munetoki carried the sword box across to Sametono, kneeling and bowing as he held it out to him. Sametono took the box and opened it. He took out the sword and held it up so that people could admire the black-lacquered scabbard wrapped with bands of silver and the hilt with its silver dragon. He drew the ancient straight blade one third of the way out of its scabbard as was customary for sword viewing, studying the perfectly polished steel and its wavering, shadowy temper line.

'I have written a poem for this occasion,' Sametono said, putting the sword back in its box. His ten-year-old voice, as he recited, was boyish, but firm and strong. Taniko's heart soared with love and pride.

> Two souls at war,
> Duelling in a single breast
> To capture the heart.
> But one mind will persuade both
> To turn against the true foe.

There were polite cries of appreciation from the guests. Everyone understood that the 'souls' were the two swords,

328

Kogarasu and Higekiri, the sword being traditionally the soul of the samurai. These two 'souls' contended for the heart of Sametono, whose heritage combined Takashi and Muratomo. 'Mind', with which Sametono would put an end to the conflict, was the awakened mind, the Buddha nature, which Sametono, like many young samurai, was cultivating in his Zen studies. Through the search for enlightenment the country could put past feuds behind it and unite itself against the invaders. For a ten-year-old, thought Taniko, it is a brilliant poem. She looked at Jebu and saw that he was sitting with his spine rigid, weeping unashamedly. If only he and I could have had such a son, she thought. In a way, this is our son. Jebu rescued him from death and gave him to me.

Sametono made a little speech thanking his mother for the gift of Higekiri and expressing his hope that he would be worthy of the long line of ancestors who had worn it. 'But the time will soon come for both the honoured Higekiri and the noble Kogarasu to be retired among our national treasures. The holy monk Eisen, with us today, is collecting subscriptions for the rebuilding of the Todaiji, the great Buddhist temple at Nara which was tragically burned to the ground during the War of the Dragons.'

Sametono did not mention that it was his great-grandfather, Takashi no Sogamori, who had caused the burning of the temple. Listening to Sametono but unable to take her eyes off Jebu, Taniko noticed that he was now looking at the boy with an ironic smile. She wondered what special meaning the Todaiji had for Jebu.

Sametono continued, 'I propose, after we have been victorious in this war, to donate both swords to Eisen Roshi, to be kept among the most precious objects in the Todaiji. I take this occasion to humbly ask that the monks of the Todaiji, as well as all other people of high and low rank, pray unceasingly to the Buddha, the saints and all the gods and goddesses for victory.'

Again there were loud cries of approval from the warriors and officials gathered in the hall. Taniko looked at Jebu and saw that he was weeping again. He did not bother to wipe his eyes with his sleeves, as most people did, but let his tears flow openly down his hard brown cheeks and into his white beard. If he cares that much for Sametono, she thought, can he not find a place in his heart for Sametono's grandmother?

Now the guests rose and formed a line to present themselves to the Regent and the Shogun. Taniko could have left the hall, but she stayed behind the screen, watching Jebu, who towered over all others in the room, patiently waiting his turn.

Finally Jebu knelt and prostrated himself to Munetoki, identifying himself. 'Welcome,' Munetoki rumbled. 'I have heard much about you, shiké, from my honoured cousin, the Ama-Shogun.' Taniko watched Jebu eagerly for a reaction to Munetoki's mentioning her. The white-bearded face remained mask-like.

'Shiké Jebu!' Sametono exclaimed before Jebu could kneel to him. The boy Shogun stood up and, in spite of his eight layers of robes bounded down the steps to throw his arms around Jebu's waist. There were gasps of astonishment from all over the hall at this unseemly behaviour. Taniko noticed that Eisen, who stood nearby, beamed approvingly.

Munetoki, as Regent, stood in place of father to Sametono. 'You must return to your place at once, Your Highness,' he said in a reproachful voice.

'I am Supreme Commander of the samurai,' said Sametono. 'I do as seems best to me, not as ceremony dictates. Cousin Munetoki, this good Zinja monk saved me from being murdered years ago. I told him I would never forget it, and I won't. Come up, Shiké Jebu, sit on the dais near me.' There was wonder and a little anger among the other guests at a Zinja monk's receiving this unusual honour. There was even more murmuring when Sametono added, 'You, too, Uncle Moko.' Only a few people knew that Moko was a close friend of Taniko and that Sametono had known him very well for years. Jebu and Moko seated themselves a little uncomfortably on the dais below Sametono. The boy now conducted a disjointed conversation with them while greeting other guests. This Zen spontaneity that Eisen encourages in his students could go too far, Taniko thought, but she recalled how Kublai Khan did whatever he wanted, without fear of censure. If a leader couldn't make his own rules, how could he truly lead?

'Not only do I owe you my life, shiké,' said Sametono, 'I owe both these swords to you.'

330

A cloud passed over Jebu's face. 'I should ask your forgiveness, Your Highness, considering how I came by the swords.'

'My honoured mother told me about the death of Takashi no Atsue, Master Jebu. I know very well that war makes enemies of people who should be friends.'

'Your mother is most kind,' said Jebu, glancing over to the screen where Taniko sat, sending her heart whirling upwards like an autumn leaf caught in the wind.

Sametono said, 'It's true that the blood of three great Takashi gentlemen flows in my veins, but in my own humble person I represent the union of the contending clans, wouldn't you agree?'

'Bosh,' said Eisen, a twinkle in his eye, having come up to the Shogun. 'Sametono is Sametono. Takashi and Muratomo are names and nothing more.'

Sametono laughed, a clear, metallic sound. 'No matter how high I climb on the ladder of Truth, Eisen-sensei is always above me.'

'Look up at my rump,' said Eisen, 'and you'll see the face of the Buddha.' He turned casually to Jebu, ignoring the shocked stares of Munetoki and Moko and said, 'We meet again, Monk Jebu.'

'My father recommended that I see you, sensei,' said Jebu.

'How is the aged, honoured Taitaro?'

'Dead,' said Jebu flatly.

Eisen smiled. 'The tide rises, the tide falls. We must talk when there is more time, Monk Jebu.' He patted Jebu's hand, bowed to Sametono and turned away.

'There's something I've always wanted to ask a Zinja monk,' said Sametono. 'I've heard that you Zinja monks can kill at a distance just by pointing a finger at an enemy or shouting at him. Can you really do that? Could you teach it to me?'

'Those are old stories that go all the way back to the martial arts schools of China, Your Highness,' said Jebu with a smile. 'We Zinja train very hard, but we can't kill by magic.'

But he looked at Hideyori, Taniko thought, and Hideyori fell off his horse and died. Sitting behind her screen, watching Jebu in conversation with Sametono, Taniko felt a surge of hope. Jebu was his old self, kindly and intelligent. The day before, when he had entered the Shogun's castle for the first time after Yukio's death, he must have felt he was putting himself in the hands of his enemies. Now he knew that all here were his friends, anxious to have his help. Perhaps, next, he would relax a little towards Taniko herself.

So, let us try again, she thought. She would invite him to have *ch'ai* with her in her chambers tonight. One more conversation might not rekindle the love he had once felt for her, but at least it could put an end to hate, and that would be a beginning. With her invitation there must, of course, be a poem. As she stared longingly at Jebu she began to compose one in her mind:

> Lonely waterfowl
> Lilac branch bare of blossom,
> Together again.

He came to her chambers just before midnight, escorted by a giggling maidservant. As she looked into his face her heart sank. Even though there was now no screen between them, his eyes were as cold and hard as they had been this morning. After he had stared at her for a moment his eyes fell, and he sat there as if alone. The silence seemed to stretch on endlessly. She watched him hungrily, thinking that if he would not talk to her at least he could not prevent her from enjoying the sight of him.

But at last she could stand the silence and the yearning no longer. 'Jebu. Why did you come to Kamakura if you hate me so much?'

The grey eyes were watchful, unsympathetic. 'I do not wish to hate any person. It is not the Zinja way. I came to Kamakura because to refuse to help in this war would be a betrayal of all Yukio fought for.'

She did not know how to answer this. A silence fell again, which she filled by preparing *ch'ai*. As she handed his cup to him, she noticed with anger at herself that her hand was trembling. She saw him looking at her hand as he took the cup from her with polite thanks. He leaned back on the elbow rest beside him and drank.

Although he seemed perfectly at ease, the intimacy of the chamber, which she had hoped would draw them together, was making her oddly uncomfortable, as if she had disrobed to seduce him. She looked at the verse Sametono had inscribed on green paper years ago, which now hung on a scroll above her private altar: 'Though we speak of goodness, the Tathagata declares that there is no goodness. Such is merely a name.'

What would Jebu make of that if he noticed it? Probably that she was a wicked person who did not believe in goodness, which was apparently what he thought of her already. More than anything else in the world she wanted him to love and respect her. And here he was, so close, but he despised her. The need for him was unbearably insistent; for it to be thwarted was intolerably painful. If only he would talk about the reasons for his hatred of her, instead of sitting there in that dreadful self-contained silence.

'You think what I did was a betrayal of Yukio, don't you?' she said at last.

He glared at her. 'Must we speak of this? I'm here. I've agreed to help. Let the rest of it alone. Don't write me any more poems.'

How could he be so cruel? 'I can't help it. I love you.' She was close to tears.

He stood up instantly. 'This conversation must end now. To continue will only cause great pain for both of us, perhaps make it impossible for me to serve you.'

She held out her hand. 'Wait. At least let me hear from your own lips what it is you hold against me. Give me a chance to defend myself.'

He sat down again. 'Very well. If nothing else, perhaps hearing it will convince you to leave me alone. I will tell you what you have done to me, and you will send me to Kyushu, where we will never have to see each other, and you will never again be so foolish as to mention love to me. Love? Apparently you were able to forget that love for ten years.'

He paused as if collecting his thoughts and took a deep breath. Then he began to speak in a hollow voice, as if he were describing ancient history. He began with their parting, which had happened at her insistence. He reviewed everything that had happened since then, as he saw it. Finally he said, 'What you really love is rank and power. When you saw a chance to get them, you forgot about Yukio and me. You did nothing to help us. When Hideyori began to draw his net about Yukio there was no help, no word of friendship, no warning from you. There was only the news that whenever Hideyori appeared in public, you were always at his side. Out of blind ambition you married the man who murdered Yukio and tried to murder me. Can you see now why it is painful for me to be near you? I ask you respectfully, if you want my help, to send me somewhere far away from you.'

By the time he had finished speaking, sobs racked her. Her tears were as much for him and what he had endured as for herself. But she was also astounded at how different his view of events was from hers. He seemed to have the notion she could have left Hideyori any time she wanted to.

'You have no conception of what a woman's life is like,' she wept. "We are not permitted to go anywhere, to see anyone, to know anything. After you left me here I was virtually the prisoner of my father and Hideyori. I encouraged Hideyori's interest in me because it was the only protection I had from my father. Once Hideyori had me in his power, I was forced to view the world through his eyes. He surrounded me with his spies and agents. When Moko brought Sametono here, I was so grateful to you I could have walked the length of the Tokaido to tell you. But I couldn't get a message to you. I dared not try. From then on, Sametono was my life, and the only way to protect Sametono was to give in to Hideyori and to believe, or try to believe, everything he told me. Yes, I married him. I married him because I was completely alone in the world, because he agreed to adopt Sametono, and because he had Horigawa killed so that he could marry me. Judge me if you must, Jebu, but only after you have tried to feel how I felt then, how helpless I was, how desperately I wanted to protect my grandson.

'I always thought he was lying to me about some things, but it was not until we journeyed together to Heian Kyo that I learned he had lied to me about everything that really mattered to me. He admitted it all with a smile. He said none of it should be important to me, since I was now the most powerful woman in the Sacred Islands. See, he had the same low opinion of me that you do. He tried to embrace me. Knowing what I knew by then, I would as soon be touched by a giant spider. I took off my slipper and hit him in the face with it.'

Jebu looked amazed. 'Your slipper? You hit Hideyori in the face with your slipper?'

334

Taniko smiled bitterly. 'Who has more right to strike the Shogun than his wife? He would have cut me down on the spot if he had not been such a cold man.'

'You struck him with your slipper,' Jebu repeated, as if that, of all the things she had told him, was the most astonishing. 'The courage that must have taken! You are a true samurai.'

'It took no courage,' she said curtly. 'I was angry, and I acted without thinking.'

'It's all very different from the way I thought it was,' said Jebu, his grey eyes troubled.

'Just as the truth about what you did after we parted was very different from what I thought,' she agreed. 'Oh, Jebu-san, there was so much beauty between us. Why couldn't we have believed in each other?'

'Because we suffered too much to think wisely,' he said. He sat lost in thought, his eyes wandering around the room. They drifted to Sametono's verse, moved past it, then stopped and returned. She watched curiously as he read it to himself in a whisper, frowning. Suddenly a sun seemed to rise in his face. She shivered as she watched his transformation.

'Yes,' he said. 'Yes. There is no such thing as goodness. Exactly.' She wanted to ask him why the verse affected him so, but she held her tongue. It was obvious that something profound was happening to him, perhaps the moment of discovery Eisen called satori. She was even more sure of this when he started to laugh.

'It's so obvious,' he said. He turned to her suddenly, a glowing smile on his face. 'Where did this come from?'

'Sametono wrote it,' she said. 'The Zen monk Eisen suggested it to him as a calligraphic exercise.'

'Eisen,' he said thoughtfully. 'Of course, of course. Who else would select a verse in which the Buddha himself says there is no such thing as goodness? If there is no such thing as goodness, then we must all be devils, mustn't we?'

'I don't understand,' she said, bewildered by his glee. 'What is it you learned?'

'Nothing new. I've just rediscovered something I already knew. So Sametono studies under Eisen?'

'He and I both do,' she said. 'You already know Eisen, don't you?'

Jebu told her of his first meeting with Eisen, at the Teak Blossom Temple. 'Before my father died, he told me something about Eisen.'

'What is that?'

'Let us say that it does not surprise me that Eisen would assign a student that particular verse as a calligraphic exercise. And, now that I know you are a student of Eisen it doesn't surprise me as much that you struck Hideyori with your slipper. Without thinking, as you put it.'

At Jebu's mention of his father, Taniko said, 'I was desolate at the news that your father died, Jebu. He was a wise, kindly man. The kind of man a father should be, not like mine.'

'There is no cause to grieve for Taitaro,' Jebu said. 'He decided to die.'

'Yes, Moko described his death to me,' she said. 'How strange and beautiful. What a marvellous man the old abbot was. You can't imagine how happy I was to see him in Shangtu, the night Kublai had himself proclaimed Great Khan. It gave me hope for the first time since Horigawa took me to China. The only time I was happier in China was the day I found you again.'

Jebu nodded. 'How odd that one of the happiest times of my life should have been in a foreign country. You and I had been through terrible things. We had no idea that even worse was in store for us. But we lived in our *yurt* and were content.'

'I was happier cooking and washing in a *yurt* than I am today living in a castle with hundreds of servants.' Her heart beat faster. His anger had vanished and his mood was warm, peaceful. It had something to do with the slipper and with Sametono's verse. There was hope.

'When you mentioned the Great Wall last night, that brought it all back to me,' he said. 'Our excursions into the Chinese countryside. That ruined temple where I tried to teach you that love of the body is holy. I thought then that one day you and I might be married and live together in a Zinja monastery somewhere. I remember my father even said that it would please him greatly.' She was amazed to see tears coursing down his cheeks, brown as carved hardwood.

The sight of him crying made her own eyes grow hot and blurred with tears as well. 'Jebu, Jebu. It's all my fault,' she sobbed. 'We could have stayed together. But I had to go on

336

blaming you for Kiyosi's death. How different things would have been if I'd never left you, instead of coming here to Kamakura. Oh, Jebu, ten years lost because of my foolishness.' She threw herself down on a cushion, her face buried in her arms.

'Don't blame yourself,' said Jebu. 'Taitaro showed Moko and me the pattern in these events. Things had to happen as they did.'

'Karma?'

'Not karma. It has nothing to do with being punished for wicked acts and rewarded for virtue. It's just a pattern. Besides, you would have been quite bored, living in a monastery. I'm sure you've been happier as the Shogun's wife.'

She laughed through her tears. 'It was like being married to a mamushi, a poisonous snake. It is a dreadful thing to say, Jebu-san, but I'm much happier as the Shogun's widow. From what I've heard about the monks and their women in the Zinja monasteries, I don't think it would have been boring. Oh, my wild waterfowl, if everything had to happen as it did, then please stop judging me. Stop hating me. Accept me as I am.'

'"There is no goodness. Such is merely a name." We are two faces of the same Self, I told you that long ago. How can I judge you? I would simply be judging myself. Many of my own acts won't bear judging. Taniko, when I look into your eyes I want to become one with you. That's why I've been so angry. Being cut off from you is too painful for me, as if I were being cut in two. I did hate you, Taniko, and for that you must forgive me. I hated you because I love you. I don't accept you, I love you.'

At those words Taniko felt a melting warmth spread through her body. I never thought I could still have such feelings at my age, she thought. I feel the same hunger for him, and it feels just as new and strange and wonderful as it did that night when I was thirteen years old and he was seventeen and I lay with this man on Mount Higashi, looking down at Heian Kyo. Oh, Jebu, are we going to be lovers tonight? Oh, please take me in your arms, Jebu, crush me with the weight of your body. But, how can he want me when I am a hag, with a face full of lines, sagging belly, sagging breasts, wrinkled hands? Perhaps if I can get the lamp put out in time he won't notice how age has ruined my body. She reached for the small bronze oil lamp that burned beside them.

His lean, long hand reached out and seized her wrist. A thrill ran up her arm and through her body. His skin, so brown, against her white skin – beautiful.

'We want light, don't we?' he said softly. She sighed with delighted anticipation. He did want to lie with her.

'Darkness creates the illusion of beauty,' she said, her eyes downcast.

'I want no illusions. I want you, exactly as you are.' His face was very close to hers, and she reached up and stroked the stiff hairs of the white beard with her fingertips. 'We are beyond judgment now, you and I,' he said. 'Judgment of good or evil, beautiful or ugly, young or old, that's all behind us. Such worries are for youngsters.'

She relaxed with a sigh and lay back, her mouth yielding to the pressure of his mouth against hers, his rough hands massaging her breasts. Indeed, she didn't care whether her breasts looked old and sagging or not. They were able to give pleasure; that was evident from the gentle, lingering movement of his hands on them. And they were very much able to receive pleasure, she thought, drawing in a shivering breath. And they were her breasts, and therefore he wanted them. He wanted her body as it was, and not any other woman's. She now felt sure of that.

As their love progressed she made another delightful discovery. Somewhere in the years between thirteen and forty-five she had lost all shame. Even that beautiful first night on Mount Higashi had been alloyed by fears of what the world would think if they were suddenly discovered. Now, she thought, if all of Kamakura walked in here and saw us lying in this embrace, our clothes open, our bodies touching everywhere, I would let them watch. I think I might enjoy being watched. I am proud of this. Proud that I can excite this man, this warrior, and draw his passion into me. The years with Kiyosi, with Kublai Khan, in China with Jebu, even with Hideyori who needed so much coaxing – all that experience had taught her a great deal about the art of love. I am as much a master of this flowery combat as Jebu is a master of the sword, and I wish that the whole world could see us.

She stood up, taking his hand, and drew him with her to the sleeping platform, the untied cords of her mauve silk robe hanging loosely by her side. As she turned to pull him in through the curtains she looked closely at his body under his grey robe, which had fallen open. She gasped, shocked. There were scars everywhere. His neck and chest were covered with large and small marks, slightly paler than his brown skin. She pushed back his robe and saw that his shoulders were also scarred. She stroked the scars with her fingertips, feeling their thickness and roughness. Then she leaned her head against his chest and began to cry.

'My darling, what have they done to you? How you must have suffered.'

'I never felt most of these wounds,' he whispered. 'You have caused me far more pain than any of these cuts and gashes.'

'Don't say that, Jebu.'

'You could not have hurt me if I had not loved you.'

'I will give you pleasure that will more than balance the pain.'

'You can give me more than pleasure. You can give me happiness.'

'You have known so much pain,' she murmured. 'Your body is so scarred, so toughened. Can you still feel my touch?'

'I may look to you like an old oak at the end of winter,' he whispered, laughing softly. 'But, miraculous as it may seem, life surges within.'

She pulled him down to the bed beside her. Their movements together were like those of swimmers, graceful and rhythmic. Together they were gliding through a sea of pleasure, a warm sea without a shoreline, rising and falling with the waves. She forgot where she was, she forgot time and age, she forgot that she was the Ama-Shogun and he was a Zinja warrior monk. She was a woman enjoying the body of a man. Nothing more. But nothing less.

When at last they lay side by side, exhausted in a blissful semi-trance, she patted her old wooden pillow. 'I'll have a good story to tell my pillow book tomorrow.'

'You keep a diary? You never told me that.'

'It's my deepest secret. I've never told anyone before this. Perhaps I'll read to you from it, if you stay with me for always.' The thought brought reality painfully back. 'Jebu-san. What are we going to do? How are we going to live?'

Jebu pursed his lips. 'There was a time when we might just

have run off together, not concerning ourselves about what is correct. But we can't do that now. Your first duty is to the Sunrise Land. To have it openly known what we are to each other would damage your prestige. We must go on meeting in secret.'

'When I sent Moko to bring you to Kamakura, I wanted this. I never thought beyond the moment when we might be united in body and spirit after so long a time apart. I never thought about what it would mean to my position. I never thought about how we could live as lovers.' She took both his hands and stared deep into his eyes. 'Jebu, I swear to you – if you wish it, I will give up all this right now. I will go with you wherever you want to go. I will never, never let anything come between us. Let us leave this castle tonight, if you want. I will be your wife or your consort. I will live with you in a temple or a farm or a mountain hermitage. You need only tell me.'

He propped himself up on his elbow and his grey eyes stared into hers for a long time. 'I wish – ' he said. Then, 'No. That is not the way for us.'

'Why not, Jebu? The Sunrise Land can fight this war without us. Surely we deserve happiness in the years remaining to us.'

'That is not the way to insight. That is the way to lose it.'

'I don't understand.'

'You said you would go anywhere with me. Then I ask you to stay here, and we will manage to be together as often as we can, and we will go on with the work we must do.' He smiled. 'I imagine countless great ladies and lowly monks have had to surmount this very problem in the past. You remember the story of Empress Koken and Priest Dokyo? She took him for her lover, wanted to marry him and make him Emperor, until the god Hachiman himself intervened, declaring, "The usurper is to be rejected," and put a stop to that foolishness. We must be discreet, my lady Ama-Shogun. I will accept no titles or offices. I will be just one of many military advisers attached to the Shogun's Court. Whenever you send for me, I will come to you. Moko will be very happy that his mission to the Pearl Temple turned out so successfully. We must find a way to tell him without anyone else finding out.'

Taniko laughed. 'Everyone will know about you and me, Jebu-san. It is impossible to keep secrets in these paper-walled chambers where there is a servant behind every shoji. The best we can hope for is to be discreet, as you said, and not make a public scandal. Everyone in this castle is loyal to me. They may talk about me among themselves, but they will protect my reputation.'

'Good. Then we can tell Moko at once. He's been very unhappy ever since you and I quarrelled at that audience last night.'

'Not at all,' said Taniko, twining her fingers in Jebu's white beard. 'Moko was always confident that you'd come round. He told me this morning that you loved me. Otherwise, he said, you wouldn't have been so angry at me.'

'The fellow knows me too well. And reveals my secrets. I should have cut off his head the day I met him. You stopped me from doing that.'

'You wanted me to stop you.'

'Indeed I did. And my instinct was right. Ah, Taniko-san, how sweet to lie here with you and summon up the past. Almost as pleasant as what we were doing a little while ago.'

'I enjoy conversation much more than that other,' she said teasingly.

'Well, then, there's no need for us to worry about discretion,' said Jebu with a laugh. 'From now on I'll come openly to your rooms. You can have your ladies-in-waiting present, and we'll just talk. In fact, why not dress ourselves and call them in right now?'

'For all I know, they're hiding just beyond my door, laughing at us,' she said.

She turned towards him, her small white hand stroking his scarred chest. She could hardly believe this was happening. One night after he arrived they were in each other's arms, after being apart for ten years. She could hardly remember at this moment what it was that had separated them for so long. She was not even sure they had ever been separated. Now that they were reunited, though, she wasn't going to let him go so quickly. She kept him there in her chamber till dawn.

CHAPTER THIRTEEN

From the pillow book of Shima Taniko:

Our own Great Wall is finished at last. It has taken us nearly five years with many setbacks, including earthquakes and terrible storms. But a message from Jebu tells me it is done, and it is time for me to inspect it. From Kamakura to Hakata is a long journey, but I've been anticipating this news and have been packed since the last full moon. It's been six months since I've seen Jebu, and at this rate I'll soon lose interest in life. I just turned forty-nine last month. Next year I will be half a century old. That a woman my age should be carrying on in secret with a warrior monk is absolutely scandalous.

I'll see dear old Moko, too, while I'm at Hakata Bay. He has helped design and build a fleet of kobaya, fast little war galleys carrying from fifteen to fifty men. They will go out and attack the Mongol ships and try to sink them before they can land any troops. Many of the kobaya will be captained by men who served with Yukio at Shimonoseki.

The new spirit of the Sacred Islands delights me. I've never seen our people so enthusiastic, so willing to work together. They even pay taxes cheerfully. They contribute their share of labour on defence works and then do more than is asked. The samurai eagerly volunteer for duty at Hakata, each hoping he will be the first to take a Mongol head. Individual quarrels, even feuds of long standing, are forgotten. It is a shame that it takes the threat of national destruction to draw us together like this.

—*Eighth Month, sixth day*
YEAR OF THE DRAGON

There had been an autumn rainstorm that morning and the yellow grass on the hillside near the town of Hakata was wet. A hundred officers in plain kimonos stood on the slope with Jebu, looking down at the great stone wall. The Hakata Bay wall formed a vast circle following the shoreline of the huge harbour, one day's ride in length. It was topped by watchtowers and battlements facing the sea. Its seaward side presented a sheer, smooth face over twice the height of a man. On the defending side, sloping stone ramps enabled the samurai to ride their horses to the top of the wall.

Near where Jebu and the officers were watching, a group of several hundred samurai with white surcoats over their armour, half of them mounted and the other half on foot, were lined up behind the wall. A long way down the beach, at the water's edge, an equally large group, all cavalrymen wearing bright scarlet coats, awaited Jebu's signal. They looked from this distance like a bloodstain on the sand. Standing with Jebu and the samurai officers on the hillside was a man holding a large yellow banner with the characters for 'Training Is Endless', painted on it in black. Jebu had chosen the slogan to remind these officers that they did not already know everything about warfare, as most of them thought they did.

He pointed to the bannerman, who waved the yellow standard back and forth slowly. The red-coated cavalrymen charged down the beach with shrill, ululating cries. They sounded exactly like Mongols, as they should, since many of them were samurai who had fought in Mongolia and China and would remember the terrifying sound of Mongol war cries till their dying day. As soon as the charge began, the samurai behind the wall rode up the stone ramps nearest them, followed by the men on foot. Removable wooden ramps on the other side of the wall let the defenders sally out on to the beach.

The samurai in white raced down the beach, waving their swords and shouting. A small band of leaders soon outdistanced the rest. The Reds, the samurai impersonating Mongols, slowed their charge, while the White leaders rode on, challenging them to send out their best fighters for individual combat. The Reds replied with a massive volley of arrows. The challengers fell to the sand, all killed.

The main body of White horsemen, enraged at the unchivalrous slaughter of their leaders, came roaring down the beach. The Reds turned and fled. When they had drawn their pursuers about two hundred paces down the beach, they stood in their stirrups in unison and shot arrows over the backs of their horses. Half the White samurai fell from their saddles. The attackers wheeled and bore down on the remaining samurai with sabres and spears. In moments all the White horsemen were lying dead on the beach and some of the Reds were rounding up their runaway horses. The White foot soldiers, who had been unable to keep up with the horsemen, found themselves half-way between the wall and the Reds, unprotected. They set themselves to meet a cavalry charge, but the attackers kept their distance, showering the foot soldiers with arrows. Archers among the Whites brought a few of the enemy down, but not enough to make much difference. Finally the surviving foot soldiers broke ranks and ran. The red-coated horsemen rode them down and finished them before any could make the protection of the wall.

'Very good,' said Jebu, and the man beside him signalled again with the yellow banner. The casualties scattered along the beach and the grassy dunes began to pick themselves up, and foot soldiers went out to collect the arrows, all of which were tipped with large leather balls stuffed with cotton. Jebu hoped none of his demonstration troops had been hurt. In the three years he had been staging these mock battles, only one man had been killed and six seriously injured. There had been a number of broken arms and legs from bad falls, many teeth knocked out – and a few eyes. He turned to address the officers who had been watching the demonstration.

'This is what happens when samurai fighting in the usual way come up against Mongol tactics. I saw it again and again in China until we learned to employ the Mongols' methods against them. Samurai tend to fight as individuals, each man seeking glory for himself. Mongols are only interested in winning as quickly and easily as possible so that they can enjoy the fruits of victory. They are organized and trained to manoeuvre and fight in large masses, not as individuals. If you ride out to meet them seeking a worthy opponent for single combat, the only opponent you'll meet will be a cloud of arrows.'

Jebu analysed the demonstration in detail, pointing out how each instance of customary samurai fighting behaviour was less effective than the corresponding Mongol tactic. He noticed many of his listeners growing restless and annoyed. He enjoyed provoking that reaction.

An eastern samurai with a scar down his face suddenly spoke up. 'May I say something, shiké?'

Jebu recognized the scarred samurai as Nagamori Ikyu, who had been in charge of the guards at the Rokuhara the day Jebu rescued Sametono. 'Certainly, Captain Nagamori.'

'Excuse me, shiké,' said the samurai with a twisted smile. 'Lieutenant Nagamori, if you please. I let a prisoner escape from my custody many years ago and was demoted.'

'I'm sorry you were demoted, lieutenant. What is your question?'

'Don't feel sorry, shiké. I am very happy that particular prisoner escaped. And at least I wasn't ordered to commit hara-kiri as other officers were who fell victim to your tricks.' The samurai standing around Lieutenant Nagamori stared at him curiously. 'What I want to say is, when you stage a battle for demonstration purposes you can set it up to prove whatever you want. It could just as easily be arranged to have those impersonating the Mongols play dead and the samurai appear to be victorious.'

'Quite true,' said Jebu. 'But I was not trying to prove anything to you. What you saw was a re-enactment of what happened here six years ago when the Mongols attacked, as well as many battles I witnessed in China between our samurai and the Mongols.'

'How would you have us fight them, shiké, if not in the manner we are accustomed to?' an officer asked.

'Our strategy must be to avoid meeting them head on. When they land, we will stay behind the wall and our bowmen will shoot them off their horses. When they advance, we will retreat and draw them into traps. We will not attack them, we will simply try to hold them to this beach until they decide it is too costly to stay here. If they lose enough men and horses and ships they will withdraw, and that will be victory.'

'A poor sort of victory,' said Nagamori. 'Any true samurai would be ashamed to fight by feigning retreats and hiding behind walls.' Some of those around him muttered agreement.

Jebu smiled and said, 'It is painful to be told that one's preferred style of fighting is not effective.' He stopped smiling and stared hard into the eyes of each of the officers facing him, especially Nagamori Ikyu. 'You enjoy the privileges of samurai because you have accepted the duty of defending this land and its people. In decisive moments, to be unwilling to use the necessary means is to invite disaster. It is to betray those you are pledged to protect.'

The words sank in and they stared back at him solemnly. 'Please understand, honoured sirs, I am not here to give you orders on how to fight. My superiors – our superiors – have asked me to teach you certain ways of fighting that are different from those you are used to. The Shogun, the Regent, the Bakufu and their generals will decide what tactics to use. I am no general.'

He could tell by looking at them that his frankness and simplicity had impressed them. The initial resistance displayed by Ikyu and those who agreed with him was typical of the first day with a new group. He had been training samurai officers in Mongol tactics and Zinja fighting methods and attitudes for the past five years, and he felt he knew how to overcome that resistance. In different parts of the Sacred Islands he had set up nine other schools like this, staffed by Zinja martial arts masters and veterans of Yukio's China campaign. Each school took one hundred samurai officers through a gruelling, intensive course of training lasting two months, running from sleep to sleep every day and through some sleepless nights as well. Most of the samurai hated it, undergoing the training only because their lords told them to. Jebu had managed to put over twenty thousand through the course. The highest-ranking and most promising samurai studied under Jebu himself at Hakata Bay.

Now that he had this group's respectful attention, he could speak of deeper things. He opened his heart to them and shared with them some of the Zinja principles that had been part of his way of life since boyhood.

'Get rid of the fear of death. Being afraid to die will not keep you alive in battle. It may even kill you.

'Warriors who rise to eminence, as you have, honoured sirs, may think they have earned comfort. This temptation can ruin you. Hardship and danger make warriors strong. Comfort and safety spoil them. In my Order the older monks are treated more harshly than the younger ones. If you would be good officers, you must discipline yourselves more rigorously than you would the rawest recruit.

346

'Practise, practise, practise. Practise constantly with all your weapons. Practise until the sword is part of your arm. Become one, not only with your bow and arrows, but with the target. Learn to react instantly with all weapons, without having to take time to think.

'Remember that anything can be a weapon. We Zinja are trained to fight and kill, when we have to, with any object that comes to hand – a monk's walking stick, a parasol, a fan, even a teapot.

'Since you're officers, the unit of troops you command is your chief weapon. Practise long hours every day with them, drilling them in the tactics you are going to use.

'Remember Muratomo no Yukio. Not his unhappy final days, but his great victories. Tonamiyama, Ichinotani, Shimonoseki. In China, Yukio led the defence of the city of Kweilin against a Mongol force many times the size of ours. We held out for six months and the Mongols eventually left the city unconquered.

'Yukio was a master of all weapons. I am honoured to say that the first time we met he trounced me soundly. And he was only fifteen at the time.

'He was cheerful and courageous. He was merciful and just. In all things, Yukio is a model you can hold up to your sons. Never forget him. He is watching us as we fight.' Jebu felt tears coming into his eyes, and he saw tears on the cheeks of many of the men listening to him.

'Enough talk,' he said. 'Now our samurai and our "Mongols" will show you how the warriors of Kublai Khan can be defeated.'

The Ama-Shogun and the last of the Zinja walked together in the garden of the military governor of Kyushu at Dazaifu. She carried an oiled-paper umbrella to conceal her face, should anyone spy her walking at night with Jebu. There was a mist in the air, and rain was threatening. They followed a winding path past clusters of black bamboo full of fireflies and bell cicadas. The lagoon occupying the north side of the garden was intended to be a small replica of Lake Biwa. Some former governor of Kyushu, his heart in the Home Provinces, had built it. A garden house on a little island was a miniature replica of Lake Biwa's shrine to the goddess of Chikubushima. Jebu picked Taniko up

347

in his arms. She felt light and tiny. He carried her over the stepping stones to the island.

A faint light from the lanterns scattered artfully around the garden filtered in through the windows of the little house. Jebu looked down at Taniko's upturned face, loving her delicate bones, her fine skin, her large eyes. He touched her cheek lightly with his fingertips, then bent to kiss her greedily, like a warrior slaking his thirst during a respite in battle. They sank to the floor, Jebu drawing Taniko down into his lap. Facing each other, they kissed for what seemed endless moments. They had made love in this manner many times before. He reached around behind her, untied her obi, then began to part her robes. It fascinated him that, considering how many layers women wore, it was always easy to get through the clothing of one who was willing. His own simple robe and the fundoshi, the loincloth underneath, were never a barrier. Joining their bodies, they went into a near-trance of mental and physical bliss. They barely noticed the patter of rain on the wood-shingled roof of their shelter. As in meditation they paid no attention to the passage of time. They sought no climax in their union, the state of arousal and the ecstasy to which it lifted them being the main object of their desires. They were no more anxious for completion than they would have been if listening to beautiful music.

When she felt like speaking again Taniko asked, 'Will you ride with me when I inspect the wall tomorrow?'

'I'll be near you.' He leaned back against the wall of the little house. She lay with her head on his chest.

'Jebu,' she said abruptly, 'I don't like the idea of being carried along the wall in a sedan chair. It would make me happier, and I think would please the samurai, too, if I could go on horseback.'

'I have no say in the matter,' said Jebu.

'It's Munetoki,' she said bitterly. 'He takes my advice in everything, but he insists that I hide myself like a leper. It makes no sense. We're prisoners of rules in these islands. Not just the women, but every one of us from the Emperor down. That's why I fear for us. The Mongols will do anything to win, while with us it's all honour and ceremony.'

'Yes,' said Jebu. 'Exactly what I've been trying to teach the officers who are sent to me.'

'When the Mongols come I intend to show myself to the

348

troops as the Ama-Shogun. I will not hide myself. Jebu, how much more time do we have before Kublai's fleet comes?'

'It will come next year,' he said with certainty.

Last year, the Year of the Hare, the Mongols had completed their conquest of China, destroying a Chinese fleet in a great battle off the southern coast. The last Sung Emperor, a boy, had disappeared beneath the waves, like the child-Emperor Antoku at Shimonoseki. And so the Mongols are already a sea power, Jebu thought with foreboding. Agents on the mainland reported that the Mongols were ruthlessly driving both the Koreans and the Chinese to prepare for the invasion. Chinese soldiers and ships, only a short time ago fighting against the Mongols, were now being rounded up to fight for them. Arghun Baghadur, head of the Office for the Chastisement of Ge-Pen, had left Khan Baligh and journeyed to Korea, where he spent a month and then sailed on to the fallen Sung capital, Linan, the largest port in China. Arghun would waste no time. They would come next spring or early summer and try to break through the coastal defences before the autumn storms.

Her nails dug hard into his scarred chest. 'What is it, Taniko-chan?'

'I dread the Mongols. So many times they nearly killed you. So many times I have lost you. I don't want to lose you again.'

'You must not think of the future. The future does not exist.' And yet, as he stroked her long hair, which had not turned grey despite her age, he thought, you may very well lose me, my love. There are so many things I have to do. And there is so much for you to do, as well.

CHAPTER FOURTEEN

A letter from Kublai Khan to Shima Taniko:

Since you have shown a predilection for chopping off the heads of my ambassadors, I send this letter to you by a more indirect route. By the time you receive it, the lama who placed it in the hands of one of your ladies-in-waiting will have disappeared. If the seal on the letter is broken, I suggest you chop off the lady's head, since she will have learned far too much about you. That you may not doubt the authenticity of this letter, let me remind you that the name 'Elephant' was known only to the two of us.

Do not allow the failure of my last expedition to your islands to raise false hopes. It might well have succeeded, but for the accident of a storm. Also, that time we sent only a small army, the greater part of our troops being occupied with ending the resistance of the southern Sung. This time we will come with all our might, together with the power of China and Korea, which are now ours to command.

I remember well your wisdom and strength of character. That is why I released you those many years ago. I knew that you would, even though you are a woman, rise to a position of influence in your own country. You have gone even further than I expected. You can tell your countrymen what you have seen of me and my power. Tell them that to resist me will lead to their destruction, whereas your small nation can reap incalculable benefits by becoming part of a greater whole. I am even prepared to overlook the execution of my ambassadors, since he who ordered it is now dead. I do not understand a people who would turn their backs on their most able general, Muratomo no Yukio, my former officer, and submit to the rule of a man who got himself killed falling from a horse . . .

I know that your people are proud. All nations believe they are descended from gods, but you seem to believe it with more passion than most. Do not let pride drive your countrymen to destruction.

You know me well, Lady Taniko. Perhaps you would like to renew your acquaintance with the splendours of Khan Baligh and the companionship of the Great Khan. Nothing would please me more than to welcome you back. This will become possible after your countrymen have been persuaded that honourable submission is their wisest course.

You know that I have the will and the power to do whatever I decide to do. I can move mountains and change the course of rivers. Do you imagine that I will let a little people on the world's edge resist my authority? You claim you live in the place where the sun rises. I tell you that from the rising of the sun to its setting all nations must bow to the one Great Khan. Eternal Heaven wills it.

—written and sealed at Khan Baligh
First Month, fourteenth day
YEAR OF THE SERPENT

Angrily biting her lip, Taniko rolled up the letter and held it over the brazier that heated her room. How insulting that he should have thought her capable of betraying her country, eager to return to his harem. Unbidden a vivid memory of their love-making in his huge bed flashed through her mind, and she felt herself stirred. This only made her more furious, and she thrust the remainder of the scroll viciously into the fire, almost burning her fingertips. He hadn't seen her in years and years. He would never want her in his bed now. Didn't he realize she knew that? Or that she still had Jebu? Yes, I know him, she thought, but he does not know me. He does not know my people. Whatever we may be, children of the gods or ordinary human beings, we cannot be subject to any other nation. We must rule ourselves or not exist at all.

It was late in the Fourth Month when a small junk with a red mainsail was sighted approaching Hakata Bay from the north-west. The junk and its coloured-sail signal had long been awaited. At once a messenger was despatched to western defence headquarters at the town of Dazaifu, inland from Hakata, with the simple message that the Mongol fleet had set sail from Korea.

Jebu ordered a fifteen-man kobaya to carry him out to the approaching vessel. As he looked out at Shiga Spit, the sandy islands on the north side of the mouth of Hakata Bay, he recalled the day Yukio and he had watched that line of ships flying blood-red Takashi banners rounding the same island.

As Jebu's little ship crossed the mid-point of the harbour, the junk with the red sail came into view. An hour later Jebu was aboard it, embracing Moko.

'You act as if you are relieved to see me, shiké,' said Moko with a smile. 'You know I'd do nothing to endanger myself. We simply hovered around the mouth of Pusan harbour with the sea gulls, fishing and trading, claiming to be friendly Chinese. When we saw the Mongols embark on the Korean ships we came back here at once.'

'What are they sending against us?' asked Jebu.

Moko's smile disappeared. 'There are two fleets coming, shiké. From Korea there are nine hundred ships carrying fifty thousand Mongols and Koreans, and their horses and siege equipment.'

'That's about as many as they sent against us last time,' said Jebu.

'Yes,' said Moko. 'But before that fleet arrives here, it is to be joined by a second fleet, known as the South of the Yang-Tze Fleet, coming from Linan. In that fleet, shiké, there are four thousand ships. It carries one hundred thousand warriors and even more machines and fire-spitting devices. If I believed that the gods would help us, I'd have some hope, but if we must depend on what mere mortals can do, then it is certain that we will be overwhelmed.' He searched Jebu's face as if hoping to find some comfort in it.

'Remember what mere mortals did at Kweilin,' Jebu said.

'Yes, shiké. Please excuse my cowardice.' Some of the anxiety went out of Moko's eyes. This man calls himself a coward, Jebu thought, yet he sailed into the jaws of the enemy to bring back information we need.

Jebu tried to visualize four thousand ships spread out over the sea. The reality would be too large for a single pair of human eyes to take in. He wondered, how can we ever hold out against them? He brought himself up short. I should not ask myself that question. My spirit must be untarnished by the lust for victory. I must try to help all who fight beside me to feel the same way.

'Sensei, I have never killed a man.' They sat facing each other as they had so many times before, cross-legged on woven grass mats, in Eisen's cell. As always, Sametono felt peace and certainty looking at the monk's rock-hard yet kindly face. Only to this man could he confide his fears.

'Are you afraid that you will not be able to kill, my son?' said Eisen with a smile.

'No, sensei. That I might be able to kill too easily. The Buddha teaches that we should harm no living thing. How can I remain a follower of the Buddha and at the same time do my duty and wage war?'

Tomorrow he and Mother Taniko and Munetoki would offer prayers at the Hachiman shrine. They they would set sail for Ise. Arriving there a few days later, they would worship at the grand shrine of the sun goddess, asking her help against the Mongols. Thence they would journey to Hakata Bay, making the last part of the trip by land, because the western coast of Kyushu was already under attack by the Great Khan's ships. And then he would be at war. The truth was, it was not the teachings of Buddha that provoked his present dilemma. His revulsion at the thought of killing lay deeper than any religious teaching. It was somehow connected with his memory of the arrows striking his mother's body as she tried to shield him from Horigawa's samurai. That was killing. That was what he did not want to do. To him it seemed that a horror of killing was as much a natural part of being human as was his newly discovered yearning to hold a woman in his arms. Yet it was his duty to kill and to lead the nation to war.

'You are samurai,' said Eisen, narrowing his eyes sternly. 'To be a samurai is to be willing to face death. Whatever work we have been given to do in life by karma, that work is the practice that will lead to our enlightenment. We must do our work correctly to the best of our ability. That is true both for the peasant and for the Shogun. For you to fail in your duty would deprive you of an opportunity to realize your Buddha-nature. But, to be willing to kill does not mean you have to love killing. As a follower of the Buddha you should hate killing. You do it only because it is your duty. It is the same with waging war.'

The smell of incense drifted in from the meditation hall near Eisen's chamber. The scent hung heavily on the damp afternoon air. Sametono realized he was sweating and wiped his forehead. Eisen's domelike head was free of sweat and looked cool.

'If I were to retire from the Shogunate and become a priest like you, it would no longer be my duty to kill, sensei.'

Eisen nodded. 'But the right time for a man to enter a new life is when he has truly finished his work in the previous stage. Of course, such a decision is ultimately yours to make. Prince Siddhartha abandoned his position and his family as a young man to go into the forest to seek enlightenment, and he became the Buddha. Each man is different and must find his own way. We do whatever, in our judgment, is most likely to lead to our discovering our own Buddha-nature.'

The perspiration on his forehead, Sametono realized, was not brought out merely by the wet warmth of this spring afternoon, but by his struggle with this, the most difficult and important problem he had ever had to resolve.

'I was in touch with my Buddha-nature before I even heard the word "Buddha",' he said. 'What I fear is that I may lose this awareness if I take the life of another.'

Eisen hunched forward, his eyes burning into Sametono's. 'What you are asking is, can a samurai have the Buddha-nature? Long ago the great Chinese Zen master, Joshu, was asked whether a dog has the Buddha-nature. What do you think his answer was?'

Sametono did not answer immediately. Eisen's questions, though they were never mere trickery, always had unexpected answers. Sametono wanted to please Eisen by finding the right solution to this one. He sorted through a number of possible answers, and at last, frustrated, gave up. Perhaps the obvious answer was correct.

'Every being has the Buddha-nature, sensei. So a dog must have it, too.'

Eisen laughed. 'Joshu's answer was, "Mu." No. Why do you think he said, No?'

Sametono felt himself becoming exasperated. Here he had presented Eisen with a question that affected his whole future life, a question of flesh and blood, and Eisen's answer was to play with words. Well, Sametono knew how to play, too.

'Kwatz!' he cried. He sat back on his haunches and grinned at the bald monk. He felt much better.

Eisen, too, laughed. 'Is it kwatz, then? Do you roar like a lion? And will your lion devour Joshu's dog? Be a lion, then, and meet the Mongols with your roar and your teeth and claws.'

Very clearly now Sametono saw it. I must be what I am. I am a lion, and must eat flesh. A vast relief and pleasure swept over him as he felt his problem solved.

'But.' Eisen held up a finger. Sametono's heart sank. When you studied with Eisen, no problem was ever solved. One layer

354

was peeled away like the skin of an onion to reveal another layer of mystery underneath.

'Yes, sensei?' he sighed.

'If you were truly enlightened, Sametono-chan, you would be able to tell me why Joshu said that a dog does not have the Buddha-nature. Whenever you have a spare moment, think about Joshu's No. What does Joshu's No mean to you? Try to hold No in the back of your mind constantly. Love No. Become No. When you know why Joshu said that a dog – or a lion – does not have the Buddha-nature, you will know what to do with your life.'

The sense of relief was gone. Eisen had given it to him and taken it away again. Perplexed, feeling heavy and awkward, Sametono pressed his forehead against the mat, bidding Eisen goodbye. His armed escort snapped to attention and the monks bowed, but Sametono, lost in thought, did not notice. A monk brought his horse, and he vaulted into the saddle without being aware of what he was doing. Feeling deeply discouraged, he led the way down the mountain path back to the castle in Kamakura. Then it occurred to him that when he had gone to Eisen that day he had been afraid. Now he was just puzzled. That was an improvement. No, No, No. What did Joshu mean by that No?

CHAPTER FIFTEEN

Shogun Sametono, his family and his generals, had barely arrived at Hakata Bay when lookouts reported the sails of a great fleet off Kyushu. Munetoki called a meeting of officers at sunrise, six days after the full moon of the Fifth Month. Before the camp at Hakozaki, northernmost of the three towns around the bay, a pavilion had been built on the beach. Over three hundred samurai of the highest rank, all in full battle dress, sat facing it. These men would lead the defence forces. In the pavilion Munetoki, Sametono, and Miura Zumiyoshi met with the commanding generals. Jebu, who held no official rank, sat in the front row of warriors facing the pavilion.

Scouts had reported a portion of the enemy fleet sailing towards the coast of Honshu, but the leaders agreed this was only a diversion, and that the main body of Mongols would land here at Hakata Bay. Sametono, dressed in general's armour with white lacings, gave a short speech, and the officers bowed low to their Shogun and then gave a cheer for him. Munetoki gave an even shorter talk in down-to-earth eastern province style, promising rewards for all, especially those who distinguished themselves in battle. Jebu kept glancing beyond the leaders at the distant grey line where sky met sea, knowing that some time today or tomorrow the first enemy sails would appear there.

A horse-drawn carriage surrounded by riders in full armour carrying both the Muratomo and the Shima banners rolled up the hard-packed sand of the beach and into the space in front of the pavilion. Guards stepped to the rear door of the carriage and placed a little stepladder under it.

Taniko emerged from the carriage. The first sight of her was dazzling. The sun had just risen above the hills behind the bay, and its early morning light flashed on her head-dress of lacy gold set with jewels, pearls and coral. She wore gold necklaces and an embroidered lavender outer robe. She carried a large folding fan made of thin strips of carved ivory. Jebu, who had spent part of the night with her, was as surprised as anyone at this apparition. She had sent him away at the Hour of the Ox without explanation. She must have spent the remainder of the night dressing for this occasion. She had not given Jebu a hint of what she was planning and neither, judging from the dumbfounded expressions on the faces of Munetoki, Sametono and the others, had she told anyone else. Jebu wished Moko could be here to see Taniko as she was today, but he was out on the sea with a scout ship, watching for the Great Khan's fleet.

With a bearing that was a marvel of stateliness for a woman so small, Taniko mounted the dais under the pavilion. The lords hastily made room for her, and she took a seat between Sametono and Munetoki. Jebu heard the whispers scurry through the ranks of kneeling men around him: 'The Ama-Shogun.' One by one the awed samurai bent forward and touched their hands and foreheads to the sand. Now Jebu understood why Taniko had come here. Until now this had been a gathering of military men, nervous on the day before a battle, discussing an unknown enemy. Her presence raised the occasion to the level of a rite, and the pavilion had become a shrine.

But not everyone was pleased. 'My lady, it is not seemly for you to present yourself, without any shield or screen, in a gathering of men,' Munetoki growled. 'Consider your reputation.' He tried to speak softly, but his drill-ground voice inevitably carried out to the first few rows of samurai.

'Much more than my reputation is at stake today, Lord Regent,' said Taniko in a clear voice that, though much lighter than Munetoki's, was perfectly audible. 'We are beginning a struggle for the very life of this nation. I feel I may have something of value to say to our warriors, and if I am not perfectly safe among my samurai, I would rather be dead. If I am not interrupting anything, may I speak?'

'It is most irregular,' Munetoki grumbled. 'Unheard of.'

At fifteen, Sametono spoke in a deepening but still youthful voice. 'It is unprecedented that the Sacred Islands should be invaded by foreign barbarians. At such a time all must contribute in whatever way they can. Of course my mother may speak.'

Taniko bowed, the diamonds on her head-dress flashing. 'Thank you, my son.'

The beach was silent as a temple, the only sound the shoreward rush of the waves in the harbour, the whisper of a light breeze and the fluttering of banners. Taniko's voice had, as always, a high, metallic ring, but there was in it a strength Jebu had never heard before. Her words easily reached even the samurai in the rear ranks. It occurred to Jebu that she had never done anything of this kind before. How and when could she possibly have prepared herself? What an amazing woman. His heart filled to bursting with love for her.

'Noble lords and warriors of the Sunrise Land, forgive my temerity in speaking to you, though I am a mere woman. As his lordship the Shogun has said so well, these are unusual times, and they call forth unusual actions from all of us. Though I am a woman, I am also, like you, samurai. So, think that I come before you today as samurai, and excuse my boldness.

'Let me remind you that I was the wife of the great Lord Muratomo no Hideyori, whose wisdom and strength gave us the new system of government best suited to meet this national peril. As you know, I am also the mother of Muratomo no Sametono, the present Shogun, whom all of us worship for his beauty and brilliance. Because of my late husband and my son I claim your loyalty and ask your indulgence.

'Warriors leave their women behind when they go to war, and when they return they expect to be greeted with a simple, modest, "Welcome home". It is not considered becoming in samurai families for husband and wife to display much public affection; this we all know. But we also know that our warriors deeply love their wives, their mothers, their daughters, their sisters. So I come before you representing all those women. Our spirit will be fighting beside you. You fight to defend the Emperor and the nation, you fight for glory, but you also fight for the women who are so dear to you. What will become of us should you fall in battle and we be taken prisoner by the barbarians? Be sure that we will make every effort to kill ourselves rather than fall into their power. And we shall take with us into the Void as many of the enemy as we can. If the invaders come to our cities and our castles and our homes, we women will take their heads. We will be ready for them.' She paused and smiled grimly. 'For, is not Amaterasu Omi Kami, the supreme goddess of our Sacred Islands, a woman too?'

In those words Jebu heard the rage of a woman who knew in her own person what it was to be a captive of the Mongols. Kublai Khan himself had taken her as his property and made use of her. Had she ever had any choice about whether she would lie with the Great Khan?

'Were I not a woman, I would compete with everyone here to take the first head of a Mongol invader,' Taniko went on. 'I envy all of you this opportunity to gain glory. All who take part in winning this war and saving the nation will be heroes never to be forgotten.

'In all this world there is no people like us. Nowhere else is there a nation whose people attack every task, be it fighting a battle, planting a field or writing a poem, with such spirit. We are unique in our love of beauty, which we apply to even the smallest objects we possess. Our language, our poetry, our temples and houses, our paintings, our very thinking and feeling, the life within our families, all of these are special to us.

'Our people have lived in these beautiful islands, protected by the sea, for centuries and centuries, and we have been free to be ourselves alone. Those of us who have travelled to distant places never knew a day's peace or happiness until we could return to this land of the gods.' Taniko paused.

'A priest could tell you of the gods better than I can, and happily there are many priests among you who have come to pray with you for our success in this war. This I know; every rock, every stream, every tree in these islands is the home of a kami, a god. Our Emperor himself is a god in the flesh and a descendant of the sun goddess. This land was created by the gods Izanami and Izanagi. For a foreigner to dare invade this holy soil is sacrilege, and sacrilege must be washed away with blood.'

She had not raised her voice, but this final utterance was greeted with a ferocious cheer by the samurai, who jumped to their feet, waving their arms and shaking their fists. Sametono was looking at his mother with shining eyes, while Munetoki sat sunk in wonderment. Between the two chief men of her family Taniko turned her head up to the sun, radiating light. The samurai quieted down now and fell to their knees, pressing their foreheads into the beach sand.

Taniko rose and gestured. Immediately one of her retainers came forward leading a white stallion. Jebu was reminded of Hideyori's ill-fated horse, but this one was calm and stately. A maid brought Taniko a riding cloak of white silk embroidered with silver dragons flying through silver clouds. A guard knelt and offered his cupped hands to help her climb into the high side-saddle. Another attendant handed her a tall samurai bow and a silver quiver of arrows with pure white feathers. Taniko signalled to Jebu. He stood up in his black-laced armour and strode forward. She handed him the reins with their heavy silver tassels. He was to lead the horse. He smiled up at her and she returned it; theirs were faint smiles that would not reveal too much.

'My honoured son and my esteemed cousin, will you join me in visiting our warriors?' she said to Sametono and Munetoki.

'You mean to show yourself to all the troops, my lady?' Munetoki's face darkened and his thick moustache bristled.

'I'm sure they will be as inspired as we have been,' said Sametono. 'My mother is teaching us an important lesson, my lord Regent. Let us accompany her.'

There was confusion as horses were brought for the Shogun's party, riders jostled one another for position, and runners were sent ahead to warn the troops stationed along the wall of the exalted visitors' approach. With Taniko in the lead, followed by Sametono and Munetoki, they set out. The sun was high in the eastern sky, and Taniko was a radiant vision.

CHAPTER SIXTEEN

This ride of Taniko's, Jebu thought, will do more to put heart into the troops and the people than a visit from the Emperor himself. Around the circle of Hakata Bay the samurai who had come here from the sixty-six provinces were falling out in ranks in front of the high stone defence wall. As the Shogun's party approached the first formations there were hearty cheers. But when the warriors saw Taniko they fell silent, knelt and prostrated themselves.

At Hakozaki, the northernmost town on the harbour, the crews of the kobaya lined up on the piers beside their ships and bowed to the Ama-Shogun. There were hundreds of the little ships at Hakozaki. From this town, nearest the mouth of the harbour, the defenders could strike the Mongol fleet before it even entered Hakata Bay. The old wall that circled the town, built hundreds of years ago against pirates, had been restored and made part of the new defences. Townspeople and samurai lined up on top of the wall and in front of it to watch Taniko pass.

Just outside Hakozaki a shaven-headed man in the saffron robe of a Buddhist monk rushed out of the crowd waving his arms and shouting, 'Homage to Amida Buddha! Homage to Amida Buddha!' Jebu tensed, readying himself to draw his short Zinja sword. Arghun might very well use assassins against them, and assassins could disguise themselves as monks. Indeed, he thought grimly, assassins could *be* monks. But then he

360

realized he had seen this man before. It was the notorious priest Noshin.

In these troubled times, which many called the Latter Days of the Law, with the country ravaged by civil war and now threatened by invasion, many people, especially lower-ranking samurai and common people, sought comfort in new religions. Noshin was one who taught that merely by repeating a certain scriptural verse a person could achieve enlightenment and salvation. He went up and down the country, exhorting large, excited crowds to adopt his simplified version of Buddhism. All the sufferings of the Sunrise Land, he declared, were punishments for its sins, particularly the sins of the nobility, the priesthood and the samurai. He insisted that his was the only true teaching and that all other sects were false and corrupt and should be driven out of the country, by force if necessary. Inevitably, when the land turned its attention to Hakata Bay, Noshin had moved there too, and was now preaching to the troops, leading them in litanies and urging them to defeat the enemy by the purity of their lives and the constant recitation of the prayers he recommended. Some of the samurai found him a noisy bore, but many others became his fervent followers.

Noshin planted himself in front of Taniko and began to harangue her. 'Pray, lady, pray constantly to the Buddha. Ask him to forgive your sins. Renounce the falsehoods of the old Buddhist sects and the new Zen mountebanks. Abjure the superstition of Shinto. There is only one true religion. Pray for enlightenment, lady, and you will be saved, and the country will be saved.'

'Thank you, good priest Noshin, for your prayers and for your counsel,' Taniko said in a firm, commanding tone, as if Noshin had said precisely what she wanted to hear. 'Please ask the Buddha to grant us victory.' With that she gave her white horse a sharp kick, and Jebu, taking the cue, started walking inexorably forward, holding the horse's head.

I'll step on you if you don't get out of the way, he told Noshin silently. Evidently Noshin realized that any more intrusion into Taniko's parade would make him look ridiculous, so he backed away, waving his arms and praying. A group of his followers in the crowd took up his chant, their voices growing fainter as Taniko's party moved on.

'You see, my lady?' said Munetoki in a low, grumbling voice. 'That's the sort of thing that happens when you appear in public. I'd have given anything to be able to draw my sword and cut down that obnoxious wretch.'

'Please, Cousin,' said Taniko softly with a smile. 'You're speaking of a holy man.'

'Holy men don't attack other people's beliefs,' said Munetoki, still angry. 'Nor do they publicly lecture the Shogun's mother. The authorities sent that man into exile once already.'

'And brought him back from exile because there was such a public outcry,' said Taniko. 'We cannot afford to make enemies of his followers.'

It was going to take them all day to make the complete circuit of Hakata Bay, and it became apparent that Taniko had no intention of stopping until they reached the south end of the wall. Jebu feared for her.

'My lady,' he said, hoping Sametono and Munetoki would hear him. 'Perhaps we could stop and rest at Hakata and resume this ride tomorrow.'

Taniko looked at him with an ironic smile. 'Do your feet hurt, Master Jebu? I'll let you ride, and I'll lead the horse for a while if you wish.'

'You can't ride from sunrise to sunset, my lady,' said Munetoki. 'It will kill you.'

Taniko fixed him with a steely look. 'The enemy fleet will probably be here tomorrow. I have only this day. I must complete the ride today, Munetoki-san.' Munetoki opened his mouth, and she cut him off. 'I insist.'

Beyond brief stops, Taniko would permit the party no rest. No one dared complain. If the fragile little Lady Taniko could set herself this ordeal, how could any true samurai say it was too much for him? Every so often Jebu glanced back at her. Her head was high, her back straight. From the way his own legs and feet hurt, he who spent his days in training, he could imagine how her whole body must feel. The only sign of pain he could detect in her was in the tense grip of her hands on the saddle, as if in fear that she might faint and fall off.

The sun travelled slowly across the sky above the bay, the hot sun of the Fifth Month, beating down on them. All along the way the troops cheered and bowed, their faces reflecting the awe and delight they felt at the sight of the famous Ama-Shogun. She's right, it is worth it, thought Jebu, looking at those ecstatic faces. And he longed to take her in his arms and tell her.

The ride continued until after sunset. Taniko refused to stop until they reached the very end of the wall. The Shogun's party had already requisitioned quarters at the small castle of a kenin whose estate was just outside Imazu at the southern end of the wall. The little lord, standing outside his gate, was pop-eyed with pride at being permitted to offer hospitality to the Shogunal party. A group of Taniko's maids had been sent ahead by carriage to prepare her bedchamber. They rushed out of the central tower of the castle, twittering like birds, as Taniko rode through the gate. In the castle courtyard Jebu turned to Taniko, who closed her eyes and slid from the saddle into his arms. Ignoring the shrieking of the maids, he carried her up the steps of the tower. Jebu's heart was bursting with love and pride as he looked down at the small figure nestled in his arms. He went where the maids led him, to an airy chamber in the upper levels of the tower, where he laid Taniko gently on a pile of quilts and cushions. He would not sleep at her side tonight. This place was too public. He would sleep like a guardian, at the entrance to her chamber.

After he set her down he whispered, 'That was the most magnificent thing I have ever seen anyone do. You deserve to be worshipped as a goddess.'

She opened her eyes, the brown pupils turned towards him and she smiled wryly. 'Don't blaspheme.'

'I meant only to honour you, my love.'

'I deserve no more honour than any of those men out there, Jebu-san. Tomorrow they will fight with all their strength for the Sunrise Land, and many of them will die. I wanted to give them a vision, something that would signify everything they will be fighting and dying for.' She sighed. 'How presumptuous of me.' Her voice trailed off and her eyes closed. Jebu sat back, looking down at her, his eyes wet with tears. He looked up to see Munetoki and Sametono, still in armour, staring down at Taniko.

'If she had been a man, what a Shogun we would have had,' said Munetoki. 'I beg your pardon, your lordship.'

Sametono said, 'Don't beg my pardon. You're quite right. It

is unfortunate that she is a woman and therefore subject to women's weaknesses.' He looked at Jebu with troubled eyes. He seemed to want to say more, but shook his head at last and went away with Munetoki, closing the shoji behind them.

Jebu undressed himself and carefully arranged his weapons and armour in a corner of the room. He unrolled a futon across the entrance to the room, set his Zinja sword beside it and lay down. A numbness rushed up from the soles of his feet through his muscles and bones, rendering him unconscious in moments. He had only time to be grateful that the long walk from Hakozaki to Imagu had so exhausted him that he would sleep in spite of the prospect of battle tomorrow.

'Shiké Jebu, wake up. Wake up.' He felt as if he had not slept at all. His entire body ached. What had happened to him? Not in years had anyone been able to approach him while he slept without waking him up. I'm getting old, he thought. Who is this? He opened his eyes and saw Sametono's face. The boy's eyes were bright with excitement. Morning sunlight was pouring in through the openings in the screened windows.

'They're here, shiké. The Mongols. They came up during the night.'

The castle where they had spent the night had been selected because the tower was built on a high hill and was perhaps the best lookout point on this side of the bay. Munetoki was already at the northern window.

'There,' he said. Jebu and Sametono joined him at the window. Past Shiga Island, on the grey, indeterminate line of the horizon, there was a row of light-coloured dots. As they watched in silence, the line of dots extended itself slowly from north to south, across the entire horizon. At first there were spaces between the dots, but more and more appeared until the entire horizon line was covered by innumerable white squares, still tiny – the sails of Kublai Khan's fleet. It was a deceptively peaceful sight, Jebu thought. What they were seeing out there on the sea was only a part of the invasion fleet, the nine hundred ships from Korea. These would eventually be joined by the four thousand ships of the South of the Yang-Tze Fleet, embarking from Linan.

Jebu could imagine the frenzy on those ships as they sighted the shore they were going to attack. The war drums pounding, the horses stamping and neighing in their stalls below-decks, the officers shouting orders. Only the low-ranking soldiers would be silent, staring at the distant shore, wondering what fate awaited them there. Here, too, a terrible dread possessed everyone. Down on the quays of the three towns, all along the wall that curved around the bay, men were readying themselves for the supreme effort of their lives.

'I wish I was out on one of our ships,' growled Munetoki.

'Your work is to stay in castles like this and give orders, Munetoki-san, not to go adventuring,' said Taniko. Jebu, Munetoki and Sametono turned to see her emerge from the stairwell. She looked amazingly fresh and rested and was wearing a pale blue summer costume printed with orange, red and yellow flowers. The three men stepped back to give her the central place at the window.

'There's precious few orders for me to give now, Cousin,' said Munetoki. 'I've given all the orders I intend to, and the defence is in the hands of able generals.'

Considering that it had taken them a whole day to ride from Hakozaki to Imazu, an order now from Munetoki to the fleet back at Hakozaki would be meaningless. Even concentrated in Hakata Bay, the defence line was far too long for easy communication. The defending generals had done as much advance planning as they could and had set up a system of signal banners and lanterns similar to the Mongols', as described by Jebu, that would allow them to send simple orders and messages over a distance. Beyond that, local commanders at each section of the wall were responsible for their own decisions.

'There go our ships,' said Munetoki, excitedly pointing in the direction of Hazozaki. Jebu felt his heart lift as he saw the long, low silhouettes of little galleys racing out to meet the enemy at the mouth of the harbour. It looked as if a hundred kobaya were dashing out. Watching the little ships reminded Jebu that Moko had had a hand in designing them, and with a sudden chill he asked himself, where is Moko? His friend could have been caught out there somewhere. How could any ship escape a fleet so huge?

The ocean was now carpeted with sails almost to the entrance to the harbour, with more of them coming over the horizon all the time. It was now possible to make out some of the ships themselves, craft Jebu recognized from his years in China. The Mongols must have appropriated everything afloat in the ports of Korea and China. There were huge, deep-hulled seven-masted ocean junks that traded with the islands in the southern and western seas, harbour junks with barrel-shaped hulls and high sterns. There were broad-beamed weighty junks and long, light ones, junks with narrow bows and junks with flaring bows, junks with square sterns and with oval sterns, deep-keeled junks and flat-bottomed junks, junks with one mast, with three masts and five masts. There were two-section boats designed by Kublai Khan himself for traffic on China's inland canals. There were innumerable smaller ships, sampans, reed rafts, trawlers, canoes, even rafts made of inflated skins.

'If only I could go out in one of our kobaya,' Sametono said suddenly, fists clenched.

'Don't even think of it,' said Taniko, her eyes frightened. 'Your place is back in Kamakura, not here. And certainly not out at sea.'

'Excuse me, Mother,' said Sametono, staring back at her. 'I'm not going back to Kamakura.'

'Sametono, we've talked about this before,' Taniko said angrily. 'You are not needed here. You would simply be one more source of worry for our samurai, another person to protect.'

'I'm sorry, Mother, but I am the Shogun,' Sametono replied quietly. 'Munetoki has shaved my head and knotted my hair. I am a man. I am ready to take my place with the warriors. I would not go against your advice in many things, Mother, but I will in this, because you are speaking from the heart as any mother would, not from the mind of the Ama-Shogun.'

'That is not true,' said Taniko evenly. 'A samurai woman sends her son off to battle with a smile. You are Shogun, as you say. You are needed in Kamakura to govern the country.'

'I am inexperienced at governing. Cousin Munetoki can do that better than I can. If I stay here, I can continue to do what you did so beautifully yesterday, Mother. The troops will fight all the harder knowing they are fighting under their Shogun's eye.'

'Are you suggesting that I return to Kamakura?' said Munetoki angrily. Jebu suppressed a smile.

'Cousin,' said Sametono, 'I will never forget when you came back after the last attack on our country and told us the story of how the Mongols were defeated. Please let me have the honour of reporting to you, after this war is over.'

Munetoki turned to Taniko with a resigned look. 'The boy has to win the respect of the samurai. It will not do for him to be kept in Kamakura like a child-Emperor. Someone of our family is needed here to inspire our men. You and I will go back to Kamakura. First, though, I mean to make one raid on one of our little ships. I insist on that.'

'Very well, Munetoki,' said Taniko. 'Then you will go back to Kamakura. But if Sametono stays here, then so shall I. And if Sametono does anything foolish, he will answer to me.'

'Mother,' groaned Sametono. 'You shame me.'

'I will not shame you as long as you keep to your proper place. On shore, observing the battle, letting the samurai see their Supreme Commander, but out of danger. If you dare set foot in one of those little ships you had better be prepared for real shame when you come back. Because I will be standing on the beach waiting for you.' Her eyes blazed with a wrath that Jebu found amusing, though he was sure it was terrible to Sametono.

Jebu glanced out the window, saw a sight that transfixed him and called, 'Look!' Flames were rippling along the sides of enemy junks, sails were blackening and heavy, dark grey smoke was coiling into the air. A cheer went up from Jebu and the others as they saw Mongol ships start to sink. It was difficult to see the kobaya at this distance, they were so small. But it was clear that they were among the enemy vessels, boarding them and setting them afire. Blazing lights sailed through the air. There were bright flashes and sounds like distant thunderclaps. *Hua pao* aboard the junks were being brought to bear on the little ships. But more and more of the invading junks were burning.

The battle at the harbour mouth raged for over an hour. Jebu asked himself again and again, where is Moko? Soon the ocean was obscured by smoke, and it was impossible to see the fleet coming over the horizon. At last, though, the smoke began to clear. Jebu could see the low, dark shapes arrowing through the waves back to Hakozaki. He tried to count them. It was difficult at this distance, but it seemed there were no more than thirty. His heart turned to lead. Over a hundred had gone out. The burning junks sank. The Mongol fleet was visible again, filling the ocean as far as the eye could see. Jebu expected the invaders to start sailing into the harbour, but instead the nearer ships were tacking and heading towards Shiga Island.

'They're trying to land on Shiga and get around the wall,' said Munetoki.

'I must go,' said Jebu. He bowed deeply to Sametono and Taniko.

'The fighting for Shiga Island will be over by the time you get there,' Taniko protested.

'It may go on for days, my lady,' said Jebu moving towards the stairway. In a lower voice that the others could not overhear he said, 'Stop trying to protect the men you love.'

'At least trying to protect Sametono gives me an excuse to stay near you,' Taniko whispered. 'Promise me you will not let Sametono go into combat. And promise me you will come back to me.'

'I promise,' Jebu whispered. He squeezed her hand and left.

CHAPTER SEVENTEEN

Red and yellow lights, numerous as the stars, bobbed gently in the darkness ahead. A strong tenor voice floated over the water, singing in Mongolian about a young man who had ridden ninety-nine days and ninety-nine nights to be with his beloved, only to find wild flowers growing over her grave. It was a song Jebu had heard many times around campfires at the edge of the Gobi Desert. It sounded strange to hear it now on Hakata Bay as their thirty-man galley, *Flying Feather*, glided silent as a crane towards the Mongol fleet. There was no wind tonight, so they rowed without a sail. Jebu stood amidships, one hand resting on the mast, the other holding his naginata.

It was near the end of the month, and the thin, waning moon was just rising, well after midnight. As they drew closer, the junks, each with a yellow lantern at the prow and a red lantern at the stern, loomed over their little galley like castles. They had reached the barrier now, a line of fishing nets strung from ship to ship and hung with bells both to block any attacking vessels and to warn of their approach. Hayama Sakagura, Moko's son, stood in the bows of *Flying Feather,* both hands gripping the pole of a naginata fitted with a very long, exquisitely sharpened sword blade of the highest-quality steel. Sakagura swung the naginata three times as the oarsmen, all armed samurai themselves, held the little galley steady. A great square of the net silently fell away, and *Flying Feather* slid through. Munetoki, standing just behind Jebu, expelled a long breath of relief.

There was a distant shout. Blazing arrows shot through the air, a long way off. A kobaya along the net to the north burst into flame. They must have set off the bells trying to get through, Jebu thought. Figures of men, silhouetted by the blaze, toppled from the galley into the water. The distraction would make it easier for all the other raiders to get through.

It was a hot, damp night, and even on the water the air hung thick. Once *Flying Feather* was in among the Mongol ships the smell was nauseating, a mixture of horses, unwashed bodies, garbage, decaying meat and human sewage. The huge fleet was rapidly poisoning the bay. 'Milk drinkers,' Munetoki groaned. Their kobaya pulled alongside a two-masted junk. They drifted till they were just at the midpoint of the vessel, where the sides were lowest. Jebu could hear conversations on the deck of the ship in an unfamiliar language that, he guessed, was Korean. He heard horses stamping on the other side of the hull, and one of them whickered. They would have to act quickly now. The horses were likely to smell them and set up a commotion. Jebu made room for two samurai who went to work with practical speed at the base of *Flying Feather*'s mast. They unwrapped a rope and pulled out an arrangement of pegs and splints. With ropes attached to the top of the mast other crewmen guided its fall. It crashed against the junk's railing, and a cry of alarm pierced the humid night.

It was the third night after the Great Khan's fleet arrived at Hakata Bay. Each night the kobaya had been going out. They filtered in among the big enemy ships and used their collapsible masts, an invention of Moko's, to board the junks. After slaughtering as many of the warriors and crew as they could reach, the raiders set fire to the ships and escaped – or tried to. Each night nearly half the ships that went out did not come back.

'We'll have more ships coming back after the warriors who aren't good at this have got themselves killed off,' Moko's son Sakagura said carelessly when Jebu was arranging for himself and Munetoki to go raiding on *Flying Feather*. Jebu though the remark crude but said nothing. Sakagura was reputed to be the best of the kobaya captains and therefore was the most likely to get Munetoki back safely. That was all that mattered.

Jebu had not seen Moko until earlier that day. It turned out that when the Mongol fleet arrived, war junks had pursued Moko's scout ship, driving it on to the rocks a day's journey north of Hakata Bay. Jebu himself had been occupied, until this morning, in the furious battle that ended in driving the Mongols off Shiga Island. Moko saw *Flying Feather* off from Hakozaki that night, his eyes shining with pride in his son.

Sakagura had promised Jebu and Munetoki the right to be first on the enemy ship. Jebu took a firmer grip on his naginata and set his bare foot on the slanting mast when an unexpected elbow in the ribs knocked him to one side, and Munetoki was clambering up the mast ahead of him. Like the lowliest, youngest samurai, the Regent of the Sunrise Land could not resist the urge to be the first to attack the enemy. Stifling his anger, Jebu scrambled up the mast. It was his responsibility to protect the Regent on this raid.

He glimpsed Munetoki bringing his sword down on the back of a screaming Korean crewman. Swinging his naginata in a huge arc, Jebu dashed for a small lantern beside the door of the stern cabin. He grabbed the lantern, and splashed burning oil on the deck. Mongol soldiers were tumbling up through the hatches now, waving swords, spears and bows and arrows, but the samurai had control of the deck and were cutting them down almost as fast as they appeared. Another fire had started in the bow of the ship. If they're carrying any of the black powder we'll all go up together, Jebu thought.

The Korean crewmen, realizing that their ship was past saving, were diving overboard. The Mongol soldiers were more

370

stubborn – or desperate, since most of them couldn't swim. They had no choice but to stand and fight. About twenty of them managed to form a line across the deck and were steadily shooting arrows into the attackers with well-drilled precision. Jebu jumped to the railing of the ship, took hold of a free line and wrapped it around his left arm. He swung feet first into the bowmen, sending the nearest of them sprawling, killing or scattering the others with his naginata. The samurai rushed the Mongols, their long swords flashing like torches in the firelight. Munetoki was in the lead, and a huge Mongol stood up with his spear pointed at the Regent's chest. Jebu ran at the Mongol, whirling the naginata over his head and bringing it down on the big man's neck. The severed head went sailing off the ship into the blackness. Munetoki took a moment to bow his thanks before decapitating another Mongol with a two-handed swing of his sword.

The Mongols just aren't used to fighting on foot in close quarters, Jebu thought. Sakagura was shouting, 'Sparrow! Sparrow!' the signal to abandon the enemy ship. Samurai were jumping into the water or scrambling down *Flying Feather*'s mast. Soon all the surviving raiders were on board the kobaya. Even the mast was saved, pulled back into place by four crewmen. The rowers pushed off, and *Flying Feather* was racing across the bay to Hakozaki.

Burning ships lit up the vast extent of the invading fleet. In the distance one ship blew up with a roar. There goes another kobaya crew, Jebu thought glumly, as those around him cheered. *Hua pao* mounted on the decks of the junks boomed, and flaming arrows sizzled through the air. The firelight revealed a distant ship that dwarfed the junks around it. It was bedecked with banners and had so many masts it was difficult to count them. On the foremast sail was painted a huge tiger's head, fangs bared. From end to end the ship was Chinese vermilion, vivid as blood. It was Arghun Baghadur's flagship, the *Red Tiger*. I wonder if he knows I survived his arrows in Oshu, Jebu thought. *Red Tiger* was surrounded by a ring of smaller war junks. There was no way to break through.

Jebu asked himself, do I hate him? Do I want vengeance for all he has done to me? Searching his heart, he was relieved to find that he felt no hatred. Arghun was like some dangerous beast of

371

prey – like the tiger painted on his sail – whom one might feel a duty to destroy but could not hate the way it was possible to hate a twisted man like Horigawa. One might even admire Arghun, see beauty in him, as one did in a tiger. Jebu's Zinja insight told him that his enmity with Arghun was part of the necessary pattern of things, the pattern Taitaro had spoken of.

There was an ear-bursting roar and a flash of light from a junk near them. A round, dark object trailing sparks shot through the air. Jebu held his breath, waiting to see if it would fall on *Flying Feather*. It landed in the water far to their left and blew up, sending up a huge waterspout. A man near Jebu cried out and fell, holding his hand over a bleeding ear. The flying chunks of metal were the deadliest part of the Mongol fire balls, Jebu thought. But the *hua pao* were not at all accurate when mounted on ships. They might wreak havoc with masses of troops or break down fortifications, but they were nearly useless on the water.

'The one we raided is going down,' shouted Munetoki, clapping Jebu on the arm and pointing. Jebu watched as the junk, burning from end to end, rolled over on its side. The poor horses, he thought. Munetoki was wild with glee. Now that they had passed beyond shooting distance of the Mongol ships, everyone was chattering and laughing with the dizzy relief that comes to men when they have been in danger of death and have survived.

Sakagura pushed his way back to them. He held up a severed head by its braided black hair. In the other hand he had a rectangular bronze tablet attached to a gold chain.

'I got a general at least,' he laughed. 'That is a general's medallion, isn't it?'

'A hundred-commander,' said Jebu, studying the tablet. To salvage some of Sakagura's pride he added, 'Surely the highest-ranking officer aboard that ship.'

'I'll get a general yet,' said Sakagura excitedly. 'I'll get Arghun Baghadur himself one of these days.' He grinned and stuffed the chain into his belt, then bowed to Munetoki. 'Did your lordship enjoy the raid?'

'I'm only sorry it's over,' said Munetoki. 'I wish I could go out every night as you do. I'm obliged to you, captain.'

Sakagura bowed. 'Forgive my presumption, your lordship,

but I hope you won't forget me. I came when called to arms, and I've fought hard, risked my life many times and killed many enemies. I expect to do a lot more fighting.'

'Your exploits and your reputation for bravery are well known, captain,' said Munetoki with less warmth.

Sakagura did not look in the least abashed. Moko's eldest son had his father's features, but not the crossed eyes and bad teeth, features that without those defects were quite handsome. He had been born the year Yukio and Jebu left for China, taking Moko with them, and was now twenty-three. So he had not met his father until he was about seven years old. Even so, he had Moko's outspokenness and intelligence, it was clear. But he also had some qualities that were, perhaps, peculiar to first-generation samurai — reckless courage, ambition and an air of braggadocio.

'Please forgive me, your lordship,' Sakagura said. 'We fellows who do go out every night, as you wish you could, are hoping the Bakufu will be generous after this is over, with rice land and offices and rank.'

He excused himself as the galley approached the Hakozaki dock. A crowd had gathered along the stone quays and wooden piers. Sakagura stood on the prow of *Flying Feather* holding up the Mongol head. The crowd cheered him. Munetoki watched him with a worried frown as the ship manoeuvred up to the torchlit dock.

'From whom can we take the rice land or the offices or the titles so that we can give them to him and his kind?' he said to Jebu. 'Winning this war means driving off the Mongols, not gaining land. It could be dangerous if there are many who think like him.'

You'd better start thinking about it now, Jebu thought to himself. After the war it will be too late. Aloud he said, 'There won't be that many samurai left to reward after this war, your lordship.' He gestured out over the dark waters of the bay, now lit by the distant fires among the Mongol ships and by the waning moon. 'Twenty kobaya left this town tonight, and I count only twelve returning. In our boat we lost seven men out of thirty.'

'The Mongols are taking terrible losses,' Munetoki agreed. 'But so are we.' The kobaya bumped against the dock, and samurai crewmen jumped out to make fast. The Great Khan has a whole continent full of warriors to send against us, Jebu thought. Most of our fighting men are already gathered here. How long can we hold out?

CHAPTER EIGHTEEN

Returning after the kobaya raid to the camp north of Hakozaki, Jebu stopped suddenly. He had caught sight of two figures crouching at the entrance to his tent. Using a bamboo grove for cover, he moved noiselessly closer. His Zinja-trained senses told him that the two men were relaxed, motionless and breathing regularly as if in meditation. Probably visiting monks, not assassins, he decided. The camp was carefully guarded against enemy infiltrators. He stepped out of the bamboo grove and called a greeting.

'Good evening to you, Master Jebu.' Now Jebu saw that it was the monk Eisen. 'Although it is almost morning. I hear you have been sinking Mongol ships.'

'Sensei,' Jebu said with a bow. 'I didn't know you'd left Kamakura.' He came closer and smiled at Eisen's round, solid face, now visible in the weak moonlight. Behind Eisen was a gaunt, grey-bearded monk with shaved head, who wore black Zen robes.

'I am only here briefly,' said Eisen, 'to assist my colleague here, priest Kagyo.' Jebu and Kagyo bowed to each other. 'I am spending most of my time now supervising the reconstruction of the Todaiji Temple in Nara, since you seem to have abandoned that task.' Eisen's eyes twinkled. Jebu had told him of masquerading as a monk seeking contributions for the Todaiji. 'May we talk in your tent?' Jebu ushered them into his tent and lit a candle. Kagyo looked familiar, but Jebu could not place him. Probably someone he had seen on a visit to Eisen's temple.

'I have news of the Order,' said Eisen without preamble. Jebu was startled. Though Taitaro had told him Eisen was of the Order, they had never spoken openly of it to each other before.

374

'The news is melancholy,' Eisen went on. 'Though it will sadden you, remember that all is happening as it should. The Zinja no longer exist. While the whole attention of the nation was turned towards Hakata Bay, the monks and their women and children simply walked out of the monasteries. Now the temples stand empty. The gates are unguarded. The doors are open. When the people who live near them realize what has happened, they will rush in and doubtless tear the buildings apart looking for the fabled treasures of the Zinja.' He chuckled.

Taitaro had prepared Jebu for this, but when he heard that it had actually happened, grief swept over him. The Zinja monasteries were the only home he had ever known. It was like losing Taitaro all over again.

'Forgive me, sensei,' he said at last. 'When the Order takes this step, why should I weep over it? I'm afraid I'm not a very good Zinja.'

'It is not whether you achieve the ideal that matters,' Kagyo said. He had been watching Jebu with a compassionate smile. 'What matters is the intensity of your effort and the magnitude of your obstacles. By that standard, you are a very great Zinja.' He spoke as if he knew Jebu.

'There is much to be done now,' said Eisen briskly. 'Many of those who were formerly Zinja are coming here to Hakata, Jebu, to help in the fight against the Mongols. We ask you to find places for them according to their abilities. Kagyo here will assist you in any way you wish.'

Jebu looked curiously at Kagyo. 'I know you, priest Kagyo.'

Kagyo nodded. 'We have not seen each other in nearly forty years, Jebu-san. Not since I assisted with your initiation. You knew me as Fudo.' Jebu gasped and leaned closer to study the priest's face in the candlelight.

'Yes. I remember you now. Fudo, the tall, thin one. How you terrified me,' Jebu said. 'A long time ago, when the Teak Blossom Temple was still standing in the hills above Hakata here, and your friend Weicho was the abbot, I asked him what had become of you. He told me you had broken under the strain of initiating Zinja novices and had gone to a Zen temple to study.'

'Our part in the initiations was painful for both Weicho and me,' said Kagyo. 'He was thankful when they made him an abbot, as I was when the Order commanded me to become a Zen monk. I was one of the early ones to cross over. Poor Weicho. The Takashi got him when they destroyed the Teak Blossom Temple.'

'They killed my mother, too,' said Jebu sadly. 'It was Sogamori's revenge because I had killed Kiyosi.'

'Are you still lugging the corpse of Kiyosi about with you?' said Eisen. 'You should have left him at the bottom of the harbour.'

Jebu shook his head. 'Everything I see here in Hakata Bay reminds me of that day and what followed upon it. The destruction of the Teak Blossom Temple, my mother burned alive, Taniko's years of suffering.'

Eisen looked at Jebu sternly. 'You were right before when you said you are not a very good Zinja. Your insight is feeble. Don't you understand that acting without concern for results means not feeling remorse after those results have occurred? You must live as if the consequences of your every action have been perfect.'

Jebu rocked back on his heels, gasping. He felt light as a cloud. Eisen had eased a twenty-year-old pain. He bent forward and pressed his forehead against the woven grass flooring of his tent.

'I am a great fool, sensei,' he said. 'Thank you for taking away the suffering.'

'It will come back,' said Eisen matter-of-factly. 'The cultivation of insight can never cease.'

'I am still very naïve.'

'No, you are not. You are one of the most accomplished members of our Order. You do not realize how important you have become to us. In all the Sunrise Land you have the widest range of experience of the lands beyond the western sea.'

Jebu felt a chill as he guessed what Eisen was leading up to. 'Excuse me, sensei, but you yourself have studied in China.'

Eisen brushed at a fly, taking care not to hurt it. 'I spent five years in a Ch'an monastery. I travelled very little. I'm afraid it's unavoidable, Jebu. Since Abbot Taitaro's death you have become, of all of us, the best qualified.'

'Best qualified for what, sensei?'

'To journey for the Order, as Taitaro did.'

Jebu was appalled. 'But I'm needed here.'

'Yes, your work is here until this war is over. We are telling you about the Order's suggestions for your future to give you time to think about them. As always, the Order wants you to accept the responsibility freely.'

'Why is it necessary to send me, sensei? What am I expected to accomplish?'

'We will talk at length about this another time. To put it briefly, and I am sure unconvincingly, the circulation of ideas and knowledge is the life blood of the Order. If we are a force for life, growth and liberation it is because our view of humanity transcends the limited awareness of the people of any one nation. To make this possible, representatives of our Order must travel to the edges of the world to maintain contact among our branches.'

Jebu glanced out the opening of his tent. He could hear gulls calling, and now he could see the waters of Hakata Bay growing light, the dark shapes of Mongol ships drifting at anchor in the centre of the harbour and extending out to its mouth. They had not even begun to discuss the reason he wanted no part of Eisen's proposal.

'I am the Order's closest link with the Bakufu,' said Jebu. 'Surely that is of more value than my wandering about in faraway lands.'

'What you do now is important,' Eisen agreed. 'But what we want you to do will be even more important.'

Jebu sighed. 'Sensei, I am over fifty years old. Most men do not live to this age. So, I have given a lifetime to the Order already. I have had the good fortune, in the last few years, to be united with the only woman I have ever loved. You know her. I might be killed any day now. But I want to spend the rest of my life with her, however long that may be. I beg of you, do not ask this of me.'

Jebu had expected that Eisen would dismiss with contempt the suggestion that a man might want to set aside his manifest duty for the sake of a woman. Instead the round-faced monk nodded and stared at Jebu with sympathy.

'I know her very well. Even better than I know you. I know what a magnificent woman she is. Each of you has attained deep insight, and the love of man and woman can lead them together to the most profound awareness of the Self. In the embrace of a

377

loving couple, each is drawn out of the illusion of singleness. Yes, Jebu, I know what I am asking you to give up.'

Kagyo said, 'Most of us find our loves within the Order. You have spent an exceptional part of your life in the world outside our monasteries, and it complicates things.'

'Indeed it does,' said Eisen. 'She has a destiny of her own to fulfil. And you are an obstacle to her fulfilment just as she is an obstacle to yours. As with you, the circumstances of her life – the many powerful men she has known, her journey to China, her intimate knowledge of the Great Khan of the Mongols – together with her natural endowment, make her an irreplaceable person. The Bakufu could not function half as well without her. I'm afraid, though, that the liaison between her and you will gradually erode the respect she enjoys now and which she needs to be effective.'

As he listened, Jebu felt he was being torn in two. 'Sensei, again I beg of you – '

Eisen held up a silencing hand. 'Do not commit yourself now. Give your insight time to work on this problem.'

Jebu laughed bitterly. 'Sensei, five years ago the Order helped me to see that I had to yield to her plea that I return to Kamakura. And then our love, which I thought was dead, came back to life. Now the Order tells me that I must give her up again. Does the Order think five years with her is enough for me? A whole lifetime with her would not be enough. I refuse, sensei. Tell them. I do not need time to think.'

Eisen shrugged and patted Jebu's knee. 'Only you can decide. The whole philosophy of the Order is based on that.' He rose. Kagyo following him, and walked to the opening of the tent.

'I will never part with her.'

'It will rain today. The clouds are already covering the moon. Good morning to you, Jebu-san.'

After they were gone, Jebu went out of his tent and sat on a hilltop watching a misty day dawn over the harbour. Samurai paced restlessly along the top of the curving wall that stretched along the beach. Jebu asked himself, where will they attack today? With a grunt of anger he dismissed Eisen's message from the Order. If they think I will give her up after all this time, they are fools, he told himself. But they were not fools, he knew, thinking sadly of the empty temples all over the Sunrise Land.

They were the wisest and the most dedicated people he had ever known. They were his people. Out of habit he reached inside his robe and took out the Jewel of Life and Death. Sadly, he put it away again. It meant no more now to him than a piece of glass. The Zinja gone. The Jewel gone. Yukio gone. Taitaro gone. Now they wanted to take Taniko. They were systematically stripping away anyone or anything that he cared deeply about. But a Zinja was not supposed to have attachments. He had started out in life knowing that. How had he acquired so many?

CHAPTER NINETEEN

In the middle of the Seventh Month, the South of the Yang-Tze Fleet, long delayed in its rendezvous with the fleet from Korea, arrived at Hakata Bay – four thousand ships carrying a hundred thousand Chinese troops. The day after the huge new invasion fleet appeared, the defending generals held council before sunrise in the pavilion north of Hakozaki. There were ten of them, and among them they represented every region of the Sunrise Land. Each wore a slightly different style of armour and spoke with a different accent, but they were alike in their air of calm gravity which masked deep anxiety. In the position of honour on the raised platform under the pavilion sat the young Shogun Sametono, his eyes burning with excitement, eagerness, concern. Jebu was sitting with a group of lesser officers and kenin who had been called to give counsel and receive the generals' orders. He noted with a twinge of worry that Sametono was wearing battle armour and had the sword Higekiri at his belt.

Sametono had little to say until the generals were finished outlining their plans for meeting the new threat. Then he raised his young voice. His hands, as he gestured, were trembling.

'Honoured generals and brave officers, today and the next few days will decide the fate of the Sunrise Land. Until now I have stayed out of battle, persuaded that the life of the Shogun should not be risked. But if we lose now, it does not matter whether the Shogun lives or dies. Today, I go into battle. I ask you generals to assign me a place in the defences.'

There were cheers from many of the officers. Jebu himself was stirred. He did not want to frustrate the boy, but he had promised Taniko he would do everything in his power to keep Sametono out of combat, and there was good reason for doing so besides Taniko's maternal fears. The death of Sametono would be a disaster from which the forces of the Sunrise Land might never recover. Jebu asked for permission to speak.

'I have fought in many battles, honoured generals,' he said. 'I ask you to imagine what it would do to our warriors, brave as they are, to hear in this moment of crisis that the Shogun himself has been killed in battle. Precisely because it will be so difficult to hold back the enemy now that they have three times as many troops as before, it is all the more important that nothing happen to our Shogun. I beg his lordship to spare us any fear for his safety, and I beg you honoured generals to intercede with him not to expose his exalted person to danger.'

There was a muttering of agreement as Jebu sat down. Dawn was starting to break over Hakata Bay. Looking down the beach, Jebu could see mass pyres where stacked enemy corpses were being burned by slaves. The dead samurai had been taken inland for more ceremonious cremation. Wrecked Mongol siege machines were being chopped apart by labourers so the wood could be re-used. Here and there beached ships were being salvaged. The hulks of enemy junks sunk in the offing were left there as a barrier to other landings. Out on the bay many of the invaders' sails were up and their ships were beginning to move towards shore. Shrill voices could be heard shouting war cries across the water, and the drums on the ships were taking up their inexorable beat. Jebu turned his attention back to the generals. Sametono was glaring at him as if he wanted to kill him.

Miura Zumiyoshi, the senior officer among the generals, addressed Sametono. 'Your Lordship, we think the Zinja monk has spoken well. To lose you might be the very blow that would weaken our men's morale enough to let the Mongols break through our lines. We humbly suggest that you refrain from going into combat.'

Sametono's face turned a deep red. He was the Supreme Commander of these generals, of all samurai in the Sunrise

Land. But leadership in the Sacred Islands was traditionally never a matter of one man's will. Leaders who disregarded the opinions of their supporters soon lost that support. Sametono knew that Jebu had turned the consensus against him. He nodded abruptly and uttered his acceptance of the generals' 'suggestion' in a low voice.

Shortly afterwards the meeting ended. Jebu felt a tug at his sleeve and turned to see Moko's son Sakagura smiling and bowing to him. The young man looked thin and wolfish after two months of leading forays against the Mongols nearly every night.

'Master Jebu,' he said, 'I wish to ask a favour. I have never had an opportunity to meet his lordship. Would you introduce me now, while he is here?'

'I don't think the honoured Shogun wishes to speak with me just now,' said Jebu.

'Shiké, I may die today. I may never have another chance.' As he called Jebu by the title Moko always used, Sakagura looked so much like his father that Jebu decided to help him. Motioning Sakagura to follow him, he approached Sametono, who was striding angrily and silently through rows of bowing officers.

'Excuse me, your lordship,' Jebu said. 'May I introduce Captain Hayama Sakagura? It is Captain Sakagura who plans and leads the kobaya night attacks which have been so effective.'

Sametono stared angrily at Jebu, as if about to reprimand him for daring to speak to him. But his expression changed when he turned to Sakagura. The young men were ten years apart in age and both of the same height. Jebu towered over them. Sakagura bowed deeply to the Shogun.

'Your father is an old friend of my family, captain,' said Sametono with a smile. 'Your exploits are marvellous. How many heads of Mongol generals have you brought back?'

'Seventeen, your lordship,' said Sakagura, baring his teeth with pleasure.

When Sakagura retold his adventures, any Mongol officer whose head he took was posthumously promoted to the rank of general, Jebu thought.

'I am proud to meet you,' Sametono said solemnly. 'Just to man an oar in one of your kobaya would be a privilege.'

Sakagura bowed, then beckoned to a servant whom Jebu had

not noticed before, who handed him a bag made of shiny crimson silk. With a low bow Sakagura offered it to Sametono. 'May I present your lordship with a small token of my esteem?'

Sametono opened the bag with curiosity and drew out a wooden statue of a shaven-headed seated figure holding a disc-shaped gumbai, a kind of war faa carried by generals, in one hand and a Buddhist rosary in the other. The delicate carving clearly delineated a stern, unyielding face. The pose was traditional, but the vigour in the small teakwood statue could only have come from the hand of a talented artist. The fan identified the figure as Hachiman, god of war, patron of the Muratomo. The statue had been left unpainted, the sculptor having the good taste to realize that the warm tones of the natural wood were sufficient adornment.

'There is much life force in this,' said Sametono. 'I am most grateful to you. By whom was it carved?'

Sakagura bowed. 'My unworthy self, your lordship.'

'Not only are you a great captain of ships, you are a remarkable sculptor as well.'

'I inherit my small skill from my father, who was a carpenter, you'll remember, before your lordship graciously elevated him to the samurai.'

'Your father builds the ships and you shed glory on your samurai family name by the way you captain them,' said Sametono. 'Now, I thank you for your gift, and I would like to have a few words with this Zinja monk in private.' Jebu sensed suppressed anger in Sametono's voice. Sakagura bowed himself out of the Shogun's presence. Sametono gently put the statue of Hachiman back in its bag and handed it to one of his men standing nearby. Then, as if possessed by the war god, he turned a face dark with fury towards Jebu.

'I can never forgive you for what you did today, Master Jebu. Meeting Sakagura only reminds me what heroic feats other young men accomplish, while I remain no more able to do anything than that wooden statue.'

Jebu knelt before Sametono. He felt he could not conduct an argument with the Shogun while looking down at him.

'May I suggest that there is a lesson in that seated statue, your lordship. Our highest symbols of religion and the nation are not expected to plunge into the thick of battle.'

Sametono was obviously close to tears. 'I am not a statue. I am a human being who wants to fight to save my country's life. The generals will not let me plan strategy and they will not let me go into battle. There is nothing I can do.'

'You may not fight where and how you want,' said Jebu gently, sitting back on his heels and looking up at Sametono. 'No one can. A nation whose fighting men did not obey orders would lose in any war. Do you suppose that there is one warrior, the Shogun, who is exempt? You must do the duty appropriate to your station, as everyone else must. Eisen and your mother tell me you were unusually enlightened as a child. But one does not light a lamp once and have it stay lit for all time. You must keep fuelling it. Do you understand what I am saying?'

'I understand that you can preach at me like any other monk,' said Sametono staring at Jebu with hostile eyes. 'But you are not like any other monk. You worship neither gods nor Buddhas. What are you but an adventurer in monk's robes? You're my mother's lover, and you carry messages from her to the generals. Yes, I see very well that you want to keep me helpless, like a wooden statue that you can place wherever you wish. You killed my grandfather, and you were involved in the killings of my father and my foster father. And yet my mother lies with you. What kind of power is it that you have over my mother? It is becoming a national scandal that the Shogun's mother goes to bed with a warrior monk in whose veins flows the blood of our enemies. You and I are both fortunate that I am under obligation to you for saving my life. It is said that a man may not live under the same heaven with the slayer of his father.'

Jebu held out a hand pleadingly. 'Sametono. I understand what you are going through.'

'Address me properly.'

'Your lordship. I have felt hatred. I have wanted revenge. I have been torn by the urge to fight and kill when it was my duty to refrain. I beg of you, do not lose what you have always possessed. Do not let your mind be clouded by the passions this war has stirred up.'

'It is you who have clouded my mother's mind. Stay far from me. I do not wish to see you. You are dismissed.'

Jebu knew that if he spoke another word Sametono would draw the sword Higekiri that hung at his belt. He stood up reluctantly, bowed deeply and backed away. Sametono turned on his heel and walked stiffly to his horse, followed by the retainer carrying Sakagura's statue. As he watched Sametono go, Jebu discovered that he was crying. Until now there had been a love, almost like father and son, between himself and Sametono. He wept for the loss of that love. And even more for the boy's loss of enlightenment.

CHAPTER TWENTY

Jebu kicked his horse into a gallop. It raced up the stone ramp to the top of the wall. The thousands of Mongol ships that dotted the bay were moving steadily shorewards under an iron-grey sky. Behind Jebu the rest of his fifty cavalrymen topped the wall. They were all carrying short Zinja bows and wearing armour with black laces. To themselves they were known as the Former Zinja. Together they charged down a removable wooden ramp on the seaward side of the wall.

A three-masted junk with staring eyes painted on the bow had pulled in so close to shore, its flat bottom was nearly scraping on the beach. Chinese infantrymen by the hundreds, armed with murderous pikes, were leaping from the deck of the junk and splashing up the beach. They wore light armour constructed of metal scales adorned with red and green capes and helmet scarves. Their iron shields were painted with fierce beasts – dragons, tigers, eagles. They were larger than the men of the Sunrise Land, expert at fighting on foot with spears and swords, and they moved in tight, well-drilled formations, walled in with shields and bristling with spears.

The former Zinja stood up in their saddles Mongol-fashion, firing arrows into the Chinese squares. The pikemen in the front ranks were falling, slowing the advance of the invaders. The Former Zinja rode into the midst of the pikemen, forcing openings with the weight of their horses and the bite of their swords. A huge man with long black moustaches thrust at Jebu with a pike. Jebu fired an arrow into the man's face. It crashed into his head just at the bridge of the nose. The pointed steel head of the man's pike grazed Jebu's leg, stabbing into his saddle. Another spear hit Jebu's arm and was deflected by his armoured sleeve. Jebu turned and jerked the pike out of the infantryman's hands and hit him in the chest with the butt end. The man fell, and Jebu rode his horse over him.

Something struck him on the back of the head like a club and knocked him stunned from his horse. For a moment he lay deafened and blinded. He forced himself to stand, and the reek of the Chinese fire powder filled his nostrils, and the screams of his horse tore at his ears. The animal was lying on its side, legs flailing, the left front leg a stump. Jebu killed the horse with a quick thrust of his short Zinja sword through the eye into the brain. Crouching behind the horse Jebu looked around. Near him were dead men, Former Zinja and Chinese, and dead horses. Beyond the range of the *hua pao* blast, Zinja riders were circling and Chinese infantrymen were falling into attack formation.

Jebu started running for the wall, a few of his comrades on foot following him. The men on horseback moved in behind them to cover their retreat and shoot at the Chinese. The wall looked much further away now that Jebu was on foot, and his legs ached as he ran as hard as he could through the sand. He reached gratefully for the rope ladder the samurai on the wall threw down to him, and pulled himself up as a dart from a ship-based Mongol crossbow smashed stone fragments from the wall beside him. On top of the wall he crouched behind the battlements. More platoons of Chinese were wading ashore. Those of his contingent who were still mounted were riding back and forth below the wall, raining arrows on the invaders.

It was typical of the Mongols to fire their *hua pao* into their own Chinese troops, just to kill a few of their enemy. They were using the Chinese soldiers much as they had the civilians at Kweilin, as a kind of expendable advance screen. The Chinese were courageous and skilled fighters, but they could not have any heart for this war. Only a few years ago they themselves had been fighting against the Mongols. Now even the highest-ranking Chinese were treated like slaves. From invaders captured the day before, the samurai learned that as soon as the South of the Yang-Tze Fleet had arrived, Arghun had sent for the Chinese admiral and had him beheaded on the deck of *Red Tiger* as punishment for having taken so long to get there.

Arghun had put his old second-in-command, Torluk, now also a *tarkhan*, in command of the Chinese ships and army. Though the Chinese might not want to fight, their arrival could be enough to defeat the samurai. They brought not only a hundred thousand men, but tens of thousands of horses and shiploads of siege equipment – catapults, mangonels, giant crossbows and many more of the terrible *hua pao*.

When the Great Khan's invasion fleet arrived at Hakata Bay, two months ago, there were seventy-five thousand warriors waiting for them, the largest samurai force ever assembled, and there was a constant trickle of reinforcements as men arrived from distant parts of the country and young men newly come of age were sent by their families. But when the fighting was fiercest thousands were killed on both sides. There were battles in which four men out of every five were killed. The samurai could not hold the defences much longer, losing men at this rate. Men were getting scarce, and horses even scarcer.

But their inability to establish a permanent beachhead was hurting the Mongols. From captives the samurai learned that dysentery had swept through the insanitary, overcrowded ships and over three thousand Mongols had died. Hundreds more succumbed to simple heat prostration, for which the sons of the northern deserts were quite unprepared. Several hundred had been killed in shipboard brawls; the confinement was driving them mad. The Korean captains and crews were constantly on the edge of mutiny and had to be kept under control by ferocious punishments. Late in the Sixth Month, Arghun moved the fleet out to sea under cover of darkness and tried to land on the island of Hirado, south of Hakata Bay. Samurai raced overland on horseback by the thousands and drove the Mongols off before they could entrench themselves. The samurai, as Taitaro had said years ago, were the finest fighting men in the world. Now they had adapted to Mongol tactics and their skills had been sharpened by the spread of Zinja arts and attitudes, and they were even more formidable.

A fire ball sailed overhead and burst behind the wall. Soon exploding black balls were falling by the hundreds. Jebu crouched down behind the battlements to protect himself from the whizzing bits of iron. Looking out through the smoke he could see movement among the ships in the harbour. A long line of junks was coming in, sails spread like the wings of bats. It looked as if the Mongols now had enough flat-bottomed junks to land all along the shoreline, from the northern arm of the harbour to the southern. Many of the junks had mangonels, catapults and giant crossbows set up on their decks, and a murderous rain of stones, huge spears and iron darts as well as the deafening, stunning fire bombs fell on the wall and its defenders. The Chinese infantrymen swarmed all along the beach. Now came galleys and rafts bringing mounted Mongol warriors to shore.

'Stay back and shoot the Mongols off their horses,' Jebu called to his small contingent. Those of the Former Zinja who still had horses drew up in front of the wall firing arrows, making no attempt to charge the attackers.

'Make every arrow count,' Jebu ordered, remembering the words from his long-ago initiation.

Now the ranks of Chinese infantrymen parted as the first boatloads of Mongol riders hit the beach. With wild screams the Mongols raced forward to storm the wall. As they came on, they unleashed flights of arrows from their powerful compound bows. Jebu fired as rapidly as he could and did not bother to count the numbers of Mongols he shot out of their saddles. He kept repeating the Prayer to a Fallen Enemy over and over again to himself, the repetition helping him to free his mind from anxiety and allow his body to function instinctively.

The heat on the beach became more intense. It was an overcast day, and the sun was a white disc in the midst of swirling clouds. By noon the beach was covered with enemy troops, living and dead. The flat-bottomed junks shuttled back and forth between the beach and the fleet, bringing boatload after boatload of warriors to shore. Siege machines were now set up on shore, and the engineers were assembling prefabricated towers to attack the wall. Here and there an enemy junk, hit by flaming arrows, burned down to the waterline.

A samurai rider came flying along the back of the wall shouting, 'They're breaking through at Hakata. Every man is needed there at once.' Riders galloped, men on foot ran. The enemy troops on the beach, Jebu noticed, were rushing towards Hakata as well.

Jebu managed to get a horse. He raced southwards along the

top of the wall with some of the Former Zinja. He could see the hand-to-hand fighting along the stone quays as the town came into view. The buildings near the shore were all in flames.

The huge junk *Red Tiger* rode at anchor just off shore, as if to signal all invading forces on the beach that their place was here. An enormous bronze *hua pao* mounted on its top deck near the bow boomed again and again, sending a steady stream of exploding missiles into the blazing port. If Arghun were to appear on deck, I might hit him with an arrow from here, Jebu thought.

Now Jebu could see the Mongol siege towers in the centre of Hakata. They had broken down the town's seaward wall. The heat from the flames stunned him as he rode closer. The roadway along the top of the wall led directly into the town, whose streets were empty. The people of Hakata had long since fled to the countryside. As Jebu rode forward, followed by a band of Former Zinja, a crowd of Mongols on steppe ponies came around a bend in the street ahead of them. The Mongols charged with shrill battle cries. The street was too narrow for the Mongols to bring their numbers to bear. Jebu drew his Zinja sword and galloped forward, bent low along his horse's neck. A red-bearded Mongol rose up in his saddle and tried to bring his sabre down on Jebu's head. The steel of the Zinja sword was better than that in the Mongol sabre, and when Jebu parried the sabre stroke the Mongol blade broke in two. The Mongol was still cursing his sabre when Jebu's thrust to his throat silenced him.

Jebu and his men fought their way through this band of Mongols and then others that they met as they rushed through the streets. The Mongol siege towers were burning. At last Jebu and the Former Zinja reached the rear wall of Hakata and took a stand in front of it.

It was man against man, body against body, for the rest of that day and long into the night. The Chinese and the Mongols kept coming in waves. By nightfall Jebu was exhausted, and wounds all over his body hurt him. Most of his comrades were dead. The samurai were forced at last to move behind the wall they had been defending. Now they were the besiegers of the city, with the Mongols on the inside. The beachhead the samurai had been trying for two months to prevent had been established.

Aside from the stone wall around it there was little left of the town. Most of the buildings had burned during the battle, and the low-hanging clouds above Hakata were painted red by firelight. The Mongols would spend all night pushing into that burnt-out space within Hakata's walls as many warriors as they would hold. Korean and Chinese boats would be plying back and forth all night, ferrying troops into Hakata. Tomorrow morning the Mongols would try to burst out of their beachhead. Tonight the kobaya would be out, all of them that were left, trying to sink the enemy ships and drown as many of the troops as possible. For now, fighting was gradually dying down like a fire that had used up everything that would burn. The samurai were too exhausted to make any more sorties into the captured town, and the Mongols and Chinese were entrenching themselves now, not advancing.

The samurai moved out into the hills behind the town and set up camp. A light rain had begun to fall, and many of the men sought shelter under trees. Rain-soaked armour was a nuisance. It took days for the lacings to dry. Jebu make a one-man tent out of his riding cloak and a stick and sat cross-legged under it, cleaning and polishing the blades of his sword and his naginata and tending his wounds. He covered a bad gash on his hand with medicated paper and bound it up with a strip of cotton cloth. Then, using his cloak to keep the rain from his head and his armour, he lay down to try to sleep. There was a strange tension in the atmosphere that made his scalp prickle. The drizzle became a steady downpour. That was a setback. It would be harder for the kobaya raiders to set fire to Mongol ships. But tonight it was all up to the kobaya. Designed by Moko, so fast and manoeuvrable, so easy to build and replace. Easier to replace the ships than the warriors who manned them. Thinking about the little ships, he drifted off to sleep.

CHAPTER TWENTY-ONE

Footsteps near his tent woke Jebu. Moko was standing close by, his eyes red with weeping. Jebu's first thought was, Sakagura. Then he sat up and saw Sakagura standing behind Moko. The two men were barely visible. Jebu sensed that it should be dawn, but it was still dark. It was utterly silent. Not an insect buzzed, not a bird sang. Pulling his head all the way out from under his cloak, he saw that there were no moon and stars. Sakagura was wearing only a fundoshi. His lean body was dripping water, and he was shivering despite the oppressive heat. Sakagura's ship might have been sunk, but if he was alive why was Moko so upset, and why did Sakagura himself look as if he had suffered a mortal wound and was holding himself erect only by sheer will?

There was still that strange feeling of tension in the air that Jebu had noticed the night before, but the rain had stopped. He heard the voices of many samurai gathering in darkness for combat near the base of the town wall. He could not see them; they carried no lights that would attract enemy archers. He stood up, tightening the laces of his armour and checking over his weapons.

'I was thinking about you before I went to sleep last night,' he said. 'About you and Sakagura. What is wrong?'

'Sakagura,' said Moko. 'If only he had been killed yesterday. If only he had never been born.' He turned and struck his son in the face, full force. It was amazing. Jebu had never seen Moko strike anyone. What was even more amazing was that Sakagura stood there and took it. A chill crept into Jebu's bones. He knew what was wrong.

'Something has happened to Sametono,' he said flatly. His entire body was cold now. 'Tell me exactly what happened,' he snapped at Sakagura.

'Give me permission to kill myself, shiké,' said Sakagura in a low voice.

'Don't be a fool,' Jebu snarled. 'What good would that do?' It was all he could do to keep his hands from the woebegone figure before him. These samurai – death was their solution to everything, their way of running from the problems they had created. Succeeding his anger, a feeling of shocked desolation began to grow. How would he tell Taniko, how would he face her?

'Is Sametono dead?'

'If I knew that for certain I would already have killed myself,' said Sakagura with a groan.

'I assume he went to you yesterday and asked to be taken along when you raided the Mongol ships last night. And you agreed.' Jebu could not keep the fury and contempt out of his voice.

'He is the Shogun, shiké. How could I disobey him? Did I not take Lord Munetoki on one of our raids? Did anyone find fault with that? Then why not the Shogun himself?'

'Don't pretend to be more stupid than you are, Sakagura. Just tell me everything.'

Sakagura began to cry, and he blurted the story out between sobs. 'As soon as it was dark enough we went out. Their ships were all clustered around Hakata. I had it in mind to try to set fire to some of the junks further out in the harbour that hadn't yet unloaded their troops. His lordship insisted on going for *Red Tiger*.'

'Oh, compassionate Buddha!' cried Moko. It seemed Moko himself didn't know everything that had happened.

'His lordship said that killing Arghun Baghadur would be better than sinking a thousand junks, because it would break the Mongols' spirit. We sailed in among the Mongol ships. They were so busy trying to land troops at Hakata that they didn't even have the nets up. We made for *Red Tiger*. Think if we had succeeded, shiké.'

'Thirty of you against the four hundred or more warriors on that huge ship? Madness. What happened then?'

'They must have seen us. Just before we got alongside *Red Tiger* a fire ball struck us amidships and exploded. Most of our men were killed. His lordship and I, standing in the prow, were thrown into the water. The Mongols began fishing around in the water for us with hooks and rakes from the portholes and deck of *Red Tiger* and other nearby ships. When last I saw his lordship, he was being hauled aboard *Red Tiger*. As long as our

Shogun might be alive, it seemed to me it was my duty to get word back to our side. I spent most of the night swimming back to Hakozaki. I didn't know who to tell, realizing that the news of our lord's capture might panic our troops. So I went first to my father. And ever since we've been looking for you.'

'Swimming back with the news was the only intelligent thing you did,' said Jebu. 'Of course, by now they might have tortured him to death. Or killed him outright. Could they find out who he is? He certainly would try to keep them from knowing.'

'He was wearing an ordinary low-ranking samurai's armour. He did have his family sword with him, though. Higekiri.'

'Arghun would know that sword. We must prepare for the worst, that they know who they've got and will try to use him against us.' Even in his anguish he realized what agonies poor Moko must be going through now. He turned to the little man and put a comforting hand on his shoulder.

'What are we going to do, shiké? Sakagura and I must commit seppuku at once, don't you agree?'

'There will be no more talk about anyone's killing himself,' Jebu said. 'We will do what we can to help Sametono. That should be enough to satisfy anyone's lust for self-destruction.' He realized that the Self was speaking through him, and with that realization came the glimmerings of a plan.

Moko and Sakagura stood silently, awaiting orders. 'You must be very careful that word of this does not get out,' Jebu said. 'I will tell those who must be told. Moko, you will have to ride at once to Lady Taniko at the governor's castle at Dazaifu. Tell her what has happened. I should bring her the news myself, but I have much to do here and there is no time. Tell her that I have a plan, if she is willing to trust his life to me. Of course, if she had any orders of her own, I will follow them.'

'Shiké, don't ask me to break this news to her,' Moko wailed. 'I couldn't bear it.'

'A moment ago you were telling me that you were ready to cut your belly open with a knife. Tell Lady Taniko that if she wants to let me try my plan, she should gather all the finery for men she can find in the chests at the governor's palace. Court dress, robes, hats, jewellery, that sort of thing. She should have it sent by carriage to Hakozaki as quickly as possible. Sakagura, I want you to get me a ship, preferably not a warship, but a large, handsomely decorated one, a gozabune, a governor's galley, something of that sort. I presume you are enough of a famous sea captain to be able to requisition a ship.'

'One thing, shiké,' said Moko as father and son turned to go.

'Yes.'

'I owe you so much already that I cannot find any way to thank you. I could praise you for a thousand lifetimes and it would not be enough. I have one last favour to ask. Whatever you do in this rescue attempt you're planning, you must let me go with you.'

'Moko, you are not in any way to blame for what happened to Sametono. A raid of this sort is hardly the place for you, and you do not need to risk your life to expiate something which is no fault of yours.'

'Fathers are always accountable for the deeds of their sons. Everyone says so. As for my being out of place, I respectfully ask you to remember what I accomplished in Oshu. Furthermore, I know ships, I know this harbour, I know quite a bit about Mongols. If you do not take me, shiké, you will find me dead when you return.'

Jebu put his hand on Moko's shoulder. 'Still ready to go anywhere with me, are you, old friend? Well then, I won't leave you behind this time, either.'

CHAPTER TWENTY-TWO

Taniko insisted on coming to Hakozaki from Dazaifu along with the wagonloads of Court dress Jebu had sent for. While the costumes were loaded aboard Jebu's ship, he sat with her in her carriage. She was dry-eyed. She had been through these crises of terror and grief so many times, it seemed there were no more tears to shed.

'I don't think he's still alive,' she said faintly to Jebu. 'In a way I hope he isn't. I can't stand to think of what they might do to him. I don't want you to risk your life trying to save him. You are all I have left. A storm is coming. If you go out there you will never come back.'

'Yes, he may be dead and I may not come back,' Jebu said. 'But it is not true that you will have no one left. I said that same foolish thing to my father, Taitaro, when he was preparing to die. I had everybody then. As you have everybody. You are the mother of this nation, the Ama-Shogun. Do not fear, my love. You can never be separated from me, because we are both the Self.' He held her in his arms and kissed her, and his tears wet her tearless cheeks. Then he pushed himself away and climbed out of her carriage.

General Miura Zumiyoshi was standing near the carriage, staring gloomily at Jebu's ship. Jebu had secretly notified him of Sametono's capture, and he had passed the disastrous news on to the other generals.

'I don't know what I can wish you,' he said. 'What you are attempting to do is impossible, but it is a noble attempt. May you be reborn in Amida's Western Paradise.'

Jebu bowed and thanked him, then ran across the dock to the great beribboned state galley.

The ship rose high and fell far, hawsers screaming in protest, as tall waves rolled into the Hakozaki docks. The moaning wind whipped the red and white ribbons and the embroidered banners that adorned the sides of the vessel. The hull itself was richly carved and decorated with red and gold dragons. The ship's name was *Shimmering Light*, and it was, as Jebu had ordered, a gozabune, a state galley with a high bridge and a deck covering the sixty rowers, used in normal times to transport provincial governors and the like.

Timing his jump to catch the ship on the rise, Jebu made the perilous leap from pier to deck. Kagyo, Moko and Sakagura were waiting for him.

'Were you able to get the items we need on such short notice?' Jebu asked Kagyo.

'All the men had to do was search their own tents,' Kagyo laughed. 'Each one has his little souvenirs from the monastery armoury. But moving around in these prisons of drapery will not be easy.'

Kagyo and the other Former Zinja had already donned the costumes sent by Taniko. Kagyo wore what the courtiers called a hunting costume, an outfit that had nothing to do with actual hunting, a tall, shiny black cap advertising high rank, an embroidered dove-grey jacket with trailing sleeves and billowing apricot trousers with legs as round and full as a pair of paper lanterns. He carried a folding fan and an oiled-paper parasol. The forty Former Zinja gathered on the deck of *Shimmering Light* were similarly dressed, like a delegation of ineffectual courtiers from Heian Kyo. They wore tall black caps, jackets of pink, green and lavender, and full trousers printed with diamonds, leaves, blossoms or birds. All carried parasols and fans.

Jebu turned to Sakagura. 'You did well, this ship is perfect.'

'Shiké, what if Sametono isn't alive?' said Sakagura, his eyes filled with suffering.

'Then we will avenge him by doing what he set out to do with you last night,' said Jebu quietly. 'Assassinating Arghun Baghadur. Now let us push off, Sakagura-san. These seas will crack our hull against the dock if we stay here any longer.' It had begun to rain again.

Sakagura called orders. Crewmen slipped the hawsers and jumped aboard. They used long poles to push the brightly painted ship away from the pier. Another order, and a drum began to beat below the deck, where the rowers sat.

It was already midday, and Sametono was probably dead. The Mongols, like the samurai, took prisoners only to get information about what the other side was doing. Captives were questioned, sometimes tortured, finally killed. Jebu looked out at the harbour. The fighting was still fiercest where the shoreline curved in to Hakata. The town was a smouldering ruin, only its walls still standing, within which the Mongol beachhead held firm. Samurai battered the entrenched Mongols as the waves in the harbour smashed on the beach. There was fire everywhere. Junks burned on the water. On the land, trees, houses and war machines stood in flames. The smoke billowed horizontally over land and water from south-west to north-east, pushed along by the howling wind. The low clouds overhead were shiny white, like a fish's belly. They darkened to the south and were almost black along the southern horizon.

Jebu climbed down a hatchway ladder into the bottom of the ship, where the rowers sat. The sixty men wore only fundoshi. They were all samurai, unarmed, like everyone else aboard the gozabune. Jebu walked to the bow of the ship so he could face them.

'We've kept this a secret until now because we did not want to spread panic among the troops on shore,' he said, raising his voice so he could be heard over the beat of the drum that kept the men rowing in time. 'The Mongols have captured his lordship, our Shogun, Muratomo no Sametono.' There were gasps and cries of shock. The rowers lost the beat, and the rowing masster had to stop them and start them again. Quickly Jebu outlined his plan of action for them.

'If Mongols come aboard to inspect us before we get close to *Red Tiger*, try to look like slaves,' he concluded. 'You were chosen for your skill in empty-handed combat, but I'm sure that when you get aboard *Red Tiger* you won't remain empty-handed very long.'

The rowers laughed. 'I thank you for inviting us to share this exploit with you, shiké,' said the first oarsman. The others called out their agreement.

Above deck, Jebu assembled the gozabune's beautifully dressed passengers and told them the news of Sametono's capture. They were as shocked as the rowers had been. Kagyo was the only one of the Former Zinja in whom Jebu had confided. Now he explained his plan to them, as he had to the samurai below decks.

'Remember to act as though you are terrified by everything,' Jebu told them. 'And try not to let the wind blow your parasols apart. They're a very important part of the effect.'

He lined the Former Zinja along the railing of the gozabune so that they could be clearly seen from the Mongol ships they were approaching. The Former Zinja stood with their backs and parasols turned towards the wind and rain. Jebu stationed himself in the bow, holding the rail. Rain and spray lashed his face. They were out past the breakwater now, and the waves in the harbour were like the mountains of Kaga. At once moment Jebu was plunging down into a valley of black water. The next moment he was shooting up into the cloudy sky. The sensation was sickening, and he had to keep his eyes shut part of the time. Moko came and stood beside him.

'I am the most unfortunate of men,' said Moko, 'to have such a son.'

Moko's pain made Jebu think of his years of regret over the killing of Kiyosi. 'Your son did what he thought he should do. He couldn't refuse the Shogun.'

Moko's eyes widened. 'But, shiké, the consequences could be –'

'The consequences are regrettable, but should not be cause for shame. Forget the past. Forget the future. What matters is now.'

After a silence Moko said, 'Thank you, shiké. I feel better.'

In the valleys of water it seemed as if their ship were alone in an empty ocean, but when the prow of the ship topped a crest he could see the entire harbour and the Mongol fleet, most of its junks anchored in orderly lines. Some distance out from shore, *Red Tiger* rode at anchor, four times longer and far higher than any other junk in the fleet. The tossing of the waves made it impossible for Jebu to count how many masts the Mongol flagship carried, but there were surely more than twelve, perhaps as many as sixteen, those in the rear slanting towards the stern, those near the front slanting towards the bow. It looked more like a monstrous sea dragon than a tiger, and like a dragon it could spit fire. The huge *hua pao*, a bronze tube as long as three men, mounted on its foredeck roared repeatedly, sending missiles arcing an incredible distance to the beach, where they landed among the samurai attacking the Hakata beachhead, blowing craters in the sand. But above the boom of the *hua pao* Jebu heard another rumbling sound at once more terrible and more hopeful – thunder. Of course, many thunderstorms had swept over the bay since summer began, none of them doing much damage to the enemy. But this was the time of year for the big storms.

Shimmering Light had to pass a whole line of violently rocking junks at anchor, sails all reefed, to reach *Red Tiger*. An arrow whistled down and thunked into the planking, directly in front of Jebu. Good shooting, Jebu thought, if he meant to miss. He signalled to Sakagura to halt the rowers. From the nearest junk a voice challenged them in the language of the Sunrise Land, broken and heavily accented.

Jebu called out his answer in Mongolian. 'This ship carries ambassadors of the Emperor of the Sunrise Land. We seek to parley with your great commander, *Tarkhan* Arghun Baghadur.'

397

Despite the wind and rain the forty Former Zinja managed to put on a great display of bobbing parasols, trailing silks and waving fans. Mongols lined the rails of the nearest junk, and Jebu could hear hoots of laughter. There was a long wait. The wind rose and the sky grew darker as the junk captains relayed Jebu's mssage along the line of ships to *Red Tiger*. At last Jebu heard a cry ordering him to move ahead.

Red Tiger was due south. Sakagura ordered *Shimmering Light*'s steersmen and rowers to point the ship's bow obliquely into the great waves rolling from south-west to north-east across the bay to keep the galley from being swamped. Jebu's robe was already soaked and plastered to his skin by rain and spray. Pitching violently, *Shimmering Light* made painful progress across the bows of the long line of enemy junks, subjected to derisive laughter, insults and curses in Mongol, Chinese and Korean. There was no garbage throwing, probably because after two months there was little left on the junks to throw. Jebu counted on the Mongol rule of the sacredness of an ambassador to protect them from violence.

Red Tiger's scarlet-painted hull spread before and above them like a wall. Mongol warriors jumped into a longboat moored in the flagship's lee and rowed to *Shimmering Light*. Jebu felt a hollow of fear in his stomach. He was in the heart of the invasion fleet, and now the enemy was boarding his ship. Whatever had made him think such a mad plan would work? Crewmen dropped nets to the longboat and helped two Mongol officers over the rails. Their polished steel helmets were ornamented with silver and their exquisitely-wrought chain-mail armour was covered by surcoats of light crimson silk. Their fur-clad grandfathers, thought Jebu, would hardly have recognized them. They asked Jebu who he was, who the nobles were, and what they wanted.

Jebu gave his name, thinking it would pique Arghun's interest, and explained that he was simply an interpreter. He listed titles and offices for the pretended ambassadors.

'As for why we have come,' he said, 'we have reason to think a certain distinguished prisoner is aboard *Red Tiger*. If so, the ambassadors are most anxious to discuss the possibility of his release. They are also willing to open talks with the *tarkhan* on the subject of the war in general, if he is interested.' The two

Mongol officers looked astonished and pleased. Silently they searched Jebu for weapons, running their hands over his wet robe, which he had emptied of its usual deadly contents before coming on this mission. They went among the Former Zinja, fingers probing their silks and brocade. They hefted parasols to make sure there were no sword blades concealed in the handles. The men in Court costume shrank away from the Mongols with little cries of alarm. The contempt on the faces of the Mongol officers deepened with every passing moment. They searched the bridge and the cabin below it. They went below deck and carefully examined the rowers, who sat slumped wearily over their oars. Finally they returned to their longboat.

The enormous prow of *Red Tiger* rose high into the air with each wave as if it were about to fall upon the smaller gozabune and crush it. High above him, at the rail of *Red Tiger*, Jebu saw the familiar bearded face of Arghun looking down at him. The flesh between his shoulder blades crawled at the sight of his oldest enemy.

Possibly, Jebu thought, Arghun and his officers were not at all deceived by this spectacle and intended to massacre the lot of them. Even if they did get safely aboard *Red Tiger*, he had best prepare his mind for the prospect of seeing Sametono's mutilated body or severed head.

At last there was a hail from *Red Tiger* and an order to come alongside. The Mongol flagship's crewmen lowered a scaffold, and at a gesture from Jebu a group of the costumed Former Zinja crowded aboard and were hauled up to *Red Tiger*'s top deck. Listening to their wails of feigned terror, Jebu smiled grimly, thinking how easily these Former Zinja could have scaled the side of the ship. He waited until the last few of his men were on the scaffold before stepping on himself. He looked around for Moko and realized that the little man was already up above. Jebu had not meant him to go aboard *Red Tiger* yet, if at all.

He turned to Sakagura. 'You stay here. You can lead the oarsmen up when I give the signal.' Sakagura was obviously disappointed, but pressed his lips together and said nothing.

The scaffold lifted Jebu to the deck amidships. The ship's many masts rose from the deck like a row of temple columns. The after-cabin was like a small Chinese palace. A Mongol officer, his armour glittering with silver ornaments, motioned Jebu to go forward. Jebu looked to the south. The sky was black as night, and the southern arm of the harbour had vanished into the blackness. In front of the foremast a wooden shed occupied most of the bow end of the deck. It was decorated with wind-whipped pennants, their bright colours darkened by rain. In the shed, relaxed in a big cane chair draped with scarlet silk, sat Arghun Baghadur. A group of officers – Mongol *tuman-bashis*, Chinese generals and Korean admirals – hovered around him. The rear portion of *Red Tiger*'s huge *hua pao* was protected from the rain by the shed. The stink of the black powder assailed the nostrils and the smoke burned the eyes, bur Arghun did not seem to mind. He stood so that two of his guards could turn his chair to face the delegation from the Sunrise Land, and he signalled the Chinese *hua pao* crew to suspend the barrage.

Unlike the other Mongols, Arghun still wore the plain, battered leather and steel armour that had served him on the edge of the Gobi Desert long ago. His once-red beard had turned iron-grey, just as Jebu's had turned white. I'm fifty-four, thought Jebu, so he must be over seventy. Yet Arghun seemed ageless, his body vigorous and powerful even sitting at ease, his face hard, his blue eyes as always empty of feeling.

'You are far more difficult to kill than your father was,' were Arghun's first words. 'Perhaps your Order does have magical powers. I was sure I killed you in Oshu. Then came word that you were still alive and teaching your Zinja tricks to a new generation of samurai. You have inherited Mongol endurance, son of Jamuga.'

Jebu bowed courteously but did not answer. His eyes searched the shed piled with ropes, racks of spears, bows and arrows and casks of the black powder for the *hua pao*.

'Have you come looking for the boy?' Arghun asked. 'There he is.' He pointed out of the shed in the direction of the foremast. Sametono was hanging from a rope attached to the yard of the forward-raked mast, swinging in the wind, lashed by the rain. Jebu's men gasped in horror, as much at the insult to a near-sacred personage as to the injury done him. Jebu stepped out of the shed for a closer look. Sametono's eyes were open and they looked down at Jebu with suffering and shame. He had been stripped of his armour and was wearing a torn crimson under robe. On his head his captors had left a white hashimaki, a headband with a red solar disc, the emblem of the Bakufu. The rope holding him had been passed under his shoulders and around his chest. It was run over the yard and securely tied to the bottom of the foremast. Jebu was torn between relief that Sametono was alive and apparently unhurt and anguish at the pain and indignity he was forced to endure.

'Please observe that I have archers stationed all around the deck,' said Arghun. 'At a signal from me, that boy's body will be filled with arrows.' A semi-circle of warriors stood around the base of the mast, their arrows nocked and trained on Sametono. 'Now then,' Arghun went on, 'have you come to surrender?'

'We have come to ask what you want in return for the release of the boy.' Jebu wanted to have done with the masquerade and strike as soon as possible, but he needed something to distract Arghun's men. If only the storm would get more violent.

Arghun laughed, a harsh, brassy sound. 'Is he really your Shogun, then? I wasn't sure, and he denied it, of course, but I know this sword.' He patted the silver-dragon hilt of Higekiri, which lay across his lap. 'I kept him alive in the hope that he would be of value to us. Son of Jamuga, do you speak for these officials, or am I to negotiate with them directly?' He gestured contemptuously at the men in drenched silken finery, who backed away from him and spread out over the deck, moving in a planned pattern, as he glared at him. The officers around Arghun laughed at them.

'Your samurai deserve better leaders than these women-men,' said Arghun. 'When I am deputy king of the Sunrise Land they will have a ruler they can respect.'

The blackness from the south was almost upon them. A huge wave, a storm swell, struck *Red Tiger*'s starboard side and sent it rolling to port. Arghun stood up and braced himself as his chair crashed over on its side. Both Former Zinja and Mongol guards slid across the rain-slick deck to the port rail. The *hua pao*, set in a bronze base plate which was bolted to the deck, creaked in its mountings, and the Chinese who served it chattered among themselves. Jebu looked up and saw that Sametono had swung out over the water. The Mongol archers kept their arrows trained on the boy's body as best they could, but they had to scramble. These steppe-bred horsemen had no sea legs.

401

'Tell these ambassadors what concessions you ask for the return of Sametono,' Jebu said. 'I will interpret for you.'

'I can speak the language of your country as well as you can speak mine,' said Arghun. 'But you may speak for me. Tell them that there is only one agreement the Great Khan will permit me to accept from you. That is unconditional surrender.'

Jebu translated this into the language of the Sunrise Land. The emissaries made a great show of horror, giving them a pretext to back away a few steps more. They were now quite close to the ring of archers menacing Sametono.

'*Tarkhan*, these men are not empowered to surrender our whole nation,' Jebu said. 'Nor would they, in return for just one life, even one so precious to us as Sametono's. I advise you to demand some tactical advantage, something our defence forces could reasonably give up without feeling we were losing everything.'

Arghun looked out through the open side of the shed at the slanting rain and the darkness covering the harbour. Thick black clouds rolled before the wind like lines of Mongol cavalry. It was so dark now that crewmen on the bridge were lighting lanterns.

'Then let us all come ashore. Give us the rest of this day to disembark all our troops on that beach, so that our ships can weather this storm in the open sea.' Jebu saw the uneasiness in Arghun's blue eyes. The man knows, he thought, that the wind and the rain and the waves can wash away everything he has been living and working for. Again Jebu translated, drawing out his speech and adding details and comments, taking his time.

What he was waiting for happened. A wall of water pushed by the storm smashed into *Red Tiger*, throwing everyone on the top deck off-balance and swinging Sametono's body far out over the sea again.

'The *tarkhan* is no more capable of negotiating fairly than a shark is,' Jebu said quickly.

The word 'shark' was the signal. Twenty of Jebu's men unsnapped wooden caps from the tips of their parasols and put the long handles to their lips. Twenty men took deep breaths and expelled them powerfully. Two poisoned darts struck the neck of each Mongol bowman. The archers had their arrows nocked and aimed, but only a few had time to draw their bows and shoot before they died. All the arrows went wild. All forty Former Zinja fell upon Arghun's officers and guards. Folded, the beautifully-painted fans they carried became rigid sticks which they used to parry sabre thrusts, to stun their victims and to smash their temples or windpipes. In moments the Former Zinja were armed with bows and arrows, and of all the invaders at this end of the deck only Arghun was left alive. He roared for help.

'Cover him,' Jebu snapped, and the *tarkhan* fell silent as two Former Zinja pressed the points of captured sabres to his throat. Jebu leaned over the rail and called to the samurai on *Shimmering Light*. He and the other Former Zinja threw ropes and nets down, and Sakagura and the loincloth-clad samurai came swarming up. They joined the Former Zinja, seizing weapons from the fallen invaders and readying themselves to meet the remaining enemy warriors on this deck.

Jebu judged that there must be three or four hundred Mongol warriors and Korean crewmen aboard the ship. A line of invaders swinging sabres and battle-axes was charging down the deck from the stern cabin. More were climbing up through the hatchways. The Former Zinja used captured bows and arrows to bring down the first few warriors to come out of the hatches. Their bodies blocked the way out for their comrades. Now Jebu's men stripped off their silk robes and trousers, revealing the plain grey tunics of warrior monks. They tore the ribs and paper tops away from their parasols, turning the handles into fighting staffs. Armed with these or with captured weapons, the Former Zinja and the samurai attacked Arghun's warriors. Mongols sabres, of inferior steel, broke when struck precisely with the strong wooden sticks. Mongol skulls broke, as well. In confined shipboard quarters Zinja fighting arts easily overcame men used to making war from horseback on broad plains. Within moments Jebu and his party had control of the top deck of *Red Tiger*.

Jebu ran to the *hua pao* shed, where the Chinese crewmen lay sprawled around the base of the monstrous device. He took the torch used to ignite the *hua pao* from its iron brazier. He set fire to a discarded silk robe and stuffed in into the nearest hatchway. Other Zinja followed suit. Some set fire to arrows and shot them belowdecks. When flames burst up through one of the hatchways, Moko ran to it with a cask of the black powder in his hands. He threw the little barrel down the hatch, and he and Jebu both jumped back. After a moment there was a muffled boom from below deck and a great puff of black smoke shot up out of the hatchway. There were screams from below and more fire and smoke. Moko and Jebu and the other men threw powder casks down the hatches as fast as they could. Explosions shook *Red Tiger* from prow to stern, like a dog shaking a rat. Jebu turned to look at Arghun. The Mongol warlord was staring at the death and destruction all around him, and for the first time there was an emotion in his eyes. Fury.

Red Tiger was rocking wildly from side to side, and the rain was almost horizontal. It was pitch dark. The only light came from the fires below deck. They had used the black powder just in time, Jebu thought. This rain would probably put all fires out. Still a lurid glow came from the innards of the ship. Would nearby ships see that there was trouble aboard the *Red Tiger* and try to send help? He slipped his sandals off. Bare feet gave better traction on the wet deck. He ran to the rail.

Red Tiger had been deserted. He could see no ships near at hand. A junk with all sails up vanished into the blackness of the storm even as he watched. It seemed to be sailing towards the harbour mouth, but he could no longer be sure of his directions.

The colonnade of masts that ran the length of *Red Tiger*'s deck was creaking fearfully as the huge, crippled ship rolled first to one side, then the other. It sounded as if the masts might begin breaking loose and crashing down on them at any moment. The explosions belowdecks had probably destroyed the bases of many of the masts, blowing them loose from their beds. Hearing screams and cries from below, Jebu ran to the rail and saw arms and heads bobbing in the water. The Mongols and Koreans left alive belowdecks were abandoning the ship. Jebu's heart sank as he saw some of them swarm aboard *Shimmering Light*, manning the oars and cutting the gozabune loose from *Red Tiger*. If the Mongol flagship went down, Jebu's party now had no way of escape. Jebu watched the undermanned galley sluggishly pull away. It spun out of control on a foaming white crest, then slipped sideways into a trough. A wave as tall as a pagoda fell upon it, caught it broadside, swamped it and turned it over. The screams of drowning men were tiny doll cries in the roar of wind and waves. The flat brown bottom of *Shimmering Light* floated for a time awash in the swelling seas. In the brief illuminations of lightning, Jebu could see the other ships tipping over under the force of the storm and the huge waves that came from all directions at once.

Red Tiger could hardly last much longer. The mast to which Sametono was tied might break off at any time. With each roll of the ship the boy's body swung out over the waves. If the rope holding him broke, he would be thrown into the sea. With his arms bound he would have no chance at all. The rope was tied to the mast. Jebu realized he had nothing to cut it with. He had not picked up a weapon for himself and there was none near him. He had only a fan, one the Former Zinja had brought aboard *Shimmering Light*. Still he hurried to the base of the foremast. Doubtless he could untie the rope. Then he froze in horror. Arghun was standing there with a Mongol battle-axe in his hand, poised to cut the rope. One blow and Sametono would fly off into the sea. Jebu started walking towards Arghun.

'Come no closer,' the Mongol commander shouted above the storm. 'I was a fool. I let you trick me. You are the only people in the world who make weapons out of parasols and fans.'

'What do you want?' Jebu called.

'Still bargaining? I want nothing. I've lost my fleet. All I can do is kill your Shogun. That's the only way I can hurt you.'

Jebu tried to appeal to the Mongol's sentiment. 'What use to kill a brave boy?' Arghun's only reply was a wild, derisive laugh.

'We'll let you live,' Jebu shouted. 'We'll send you back to Kublai Khan. I swear it on the honour of my Order.'

'I would rather die than face Kublai Khan. I had your country in my grasp, and I lost it, because of you.' A malevolent light dawned in his face. 'There is one bargain I will make.'

'Anything,' Jebu cried, frantic.

'You, more than anyone, stopped me from conquering this land. I will end my life victorious in this one thing. I will kill the last of Jamuga's seed, even as Genghis Khan commanded me.' The blue eyes glowed with rage. 'Stretch out your neck to my axe, and I will let the boy live.'

Jebu did not hesitate. 'I will.' He strode towards Arghun.

'No!' screamed Moko. Jebu had not noticed the little man

come up beside him. Moko rushed past Jebu, his fingers clawing for the Mongol giant's axe.

And now it was Jebu who screamed, 'No!' as the axe blade bit into Moko between neck and shoulder.

Surprised by Moko's unexpected attack, Arghun's instant reaction had been to defend himself, rather than cut the rope holding Sametono. Moko's sacrifice must not be wasted. Empty-handed except for his fan, Jebu threw himself at Arghun. The axe came down again, and Jebu side-stepped it, jabbing the end of the folded fan hard into Arghun's wrist. The Mongol grimaced in pain but did not let go of the axe. Jebu whirled and ran for the bow of the ship, exposing his back to Arghun to draw him away from the mast. The ship tilted and Jebu slid across the wet deck towards the rail. The axe smashed into the planking just behind him. Jebu looked back at the foremast. Sakagura and other samurai were cutting the rope that held Sametono. Sakagura was tying the end of the rope around his own waist. Kagyo was kneeling beside Moko, holding him, keeping him from being washed overboard. Blood had soaked the front of Kagyo's grey tunic.

The ship rolled to starboard, and Arghun backed into the shed at the bow, waiting for Jebu to slide within reach, battle-axe in one hand, in the other a long dagger he had drawn from his belt. He had braced himself against the base of the huge bronze *hua pao*, whose bolts were creaking in the deck. Jebu grabbed the portside railing and clung to it, keeping himself away from Arghun.

Sametono was dangling over the water. Sakagura, with the rope holding Sametono attached to his waist, was climbing the raked foremast. If he slips, thought Jebu, they'll both go into the sea. The higher Sakagura climbed, the more the rope holding Sametono lengthened. At last Sakagura stopped climbing, wrapped his arms and legs around the mast and waited. The ship started its next roll, tilting back to port. Just at that moment one of the men at the foremast turned and saw Arghun advancing on Jebu. Aiming carefully, he launched a spear at Arghun. But the wind defeated his aim. The spear planted itself in the deck just in front of Arghun. The ship reached the midpoint of its roll, and Arghun seized the haft of the spear for support, stepping away from the *hua pao*.

406

Sametono came over the deck as the ship rolled. The rope holding him was now so long that he swung right into the arms of four samurai waiting to catch him. They cut him loose with a sword stroke. Jebu saw with relief that Sakagura was shinning down the mast. Then Arghun was upon him.

Now the big Mongol was coming at him with spear and battle axe. 'Slay Jamugu and all his seed!' he screamed.

Both of them were tumbling towards the roaring black water. Each time the ship rolled, it seemed it would roll on until the railing went under the water, until the whole huge vessel turned over completely, just as *Shimmering Light* had. Even a ship this big could not survive in a storm like this unless it was manoeuvred. Anchored, with no captain or crew to move it to evade the force of wind and wave, it was doomed. It was only a matter of time before the *tai-phun* sank Red Tiger and all aboard her. Indeed, if *Red Tiger* was doomed, then so was the rest of the Mongol fleet. Even though it was mid-afternoon, the sky was dark as night, and Jebu could not see beyond the confines of this ship. Most of the batten-reinforced sails on *Red Tiger*'s many masts had been blown loose and were flapping wildly. The masts were bending like trees in the wind. The two mizzen masts at the rear had been broken off and had fallen to the deck. Some of the samurai were back there cutting the masts away. The timbers of the ship screamed under the pressure of the storm, louder than the wind and thunder and booming of the waves and hammering of the rain. In a sudden flash of lightning Jebu was able to see the wreckage of a few junks tossing on the black waves. Pieces of spar hurtled through the air overhead.

Arghun advanced on him, clinging to the rail with one arm as the starboard side of the ship tilted towards the water and this side rose into the air. The battle-axe swung at Jebu, and without thinking, Jebu leaped, barefoot, to the railing of the ship. The axe crashed into the oak at his feet. He looked down into Arghun's enraged, frustrated face below him and laughed. Arghun thrust at him with the spear, and Jebu parried the spearhead with his folded fan.

In the lightning flash he saw Yukio. He was holding a fan just like Jebu's, and he was standing beside Jebu, balanced on the railing of the *Red Tiger* on the balls of his feet, just as he had stood so many years ago on the railing of the Gojo Bridge. He was laughing. He was only fifteen years old, as he had been the night Jebu first met him.

'I knew you were fighting beside me,' Jebu said. He looked to see if Arghun had seen Yukio, but the Mongol's blazing blue eyes seemed only to see Jebu. Arghun threw the spear, and Jebu jumped into the air over the tilting railing, just as Yukio might have in his boyhood. The spear passed under him. He dared not watch it. He had gauged his leap so that he landed gripping the moving, slippery railing with the soles of his feet.

'Eternal Heaven fights on my side,' Arghun roared. He swung the battle axe and Jebu jumped again. This time he teetered and barely caught his balance before falling overboard. The ship had come to the top of its roll and the railing was dropping beneath his feet. He hooked his toes over the inner edge, bracing himself to jump again as Arghun lifted the battle axe with both hands for another blow.

There was a monstrous crack. The huge bronze tube of the *hua pao* broke loose from the deck, smashed through the side of the shed and was sliding towards them. Jebu danced backwards along the railing. Like a falling elephant the enormous mass of metal struck Arghun and crashed with him through the railing. There was not even a cry. Jebu saw arms and legs flail briefly, then Arghun was gone. With both arms wrapped around the broken railing, his legs dangling into the rolling sea, Jebu watched the shadowy bulk of the fire-spitting weapon disappear into the depths. He whispered the Prayer to a Fallen Enemy.

CHAPTER TWENTY-THREE

Someone grabbed him and pulled him back to the deck. Kagyo. Jebu felt the sea slide under the giant ship as the deck began to tilt to starboard again. He was still numbed by Arghun's sudden vanishing. He pulled himself up against the railing. His surviving men were huddled around nearby masts, clinging to the huge wooden pillars and each other to keep from being washed overboard.

'Where is Moko?' Jebu shouted.

'We took him to the captain's cabin,' Kagyo called back. He led Jebu along the deck, running in a crouch, clinging to ropes or masts whenever a gust of wind threatened to blow them overboard or a huge wave turned the deck into a raging torrent. By the time they reached the captain's cabin at the rear of the junk a mountainous wave had broken over the starboard side, dumping rivers into the open hatches and holes in the deck. One or two more waves like that and the junk would surely go under.

Moko was lying on cushions in the shelter of the captain's cabin. The Former Zinja had done their best with bandages and the Chinese needles to staunch the flow of blood, but Arghun's axe had gone too deep. Moko's blood was pouring out on the floor, and there was no way to stop it. The little carpenter's arm and shoulder were almost severed from his body. Sametono knelt beside him, crying silently, and Sakagura sobbed above him.

'Don't die, Uncle Moko,' Sametono said softly. 'I need you.'

Moko's voice came faintly. Jebu had to strain to hear him above the shriek of the storm. 'Indeed you do, your lordship. If we don't get this ship moving it's going to sink with all of us on board. And then what was the point of coming out here to rescue you?'

'Can you tell us what to do, Moko?' said Jebu.

'Yes, shiké. Sakagura, get as many men as the tiller will hold to keep the rudder steady. Set the rest to bending every scrap of sail you can find to the masts. The ship is sideways to the wind now. It's a wonder we haven't turned over already. Put sail on and get the wind behind us. Let it blow us right into shore. With a *tai-phun* pushing it, this ship will end up inland as a fine castle for all of us.' He tried to laugh, and gasped in pain.

'Run her aground?' Sakagura stared at his father, momentarily startled out of his grief.

'Of course. We don't want to save this ship. We only want to save ourselves. And in your haste don't forget to raise the anchors. There are two of them, one at the stern and one at the bow, and each is raised by a windlass. Now do it.' Jebu thought, Moko won't live to see *Red Tiger* make the shore. Sakagura ran outside to shout orders to his men as another enormous wave

409

swamped the ship and threw everyone against the port side of the cabin.

'I'm so glad you're still alive, shiké,' Moko said. 'What of the Mongol?'

'Dead.' Jebu told Moko how the *hua pao* had fallen on Arghun and carried him beneath the waves.

'"The mighty are destroyed at the last, they are but as the dust before the wind,"' said Moko, quoting a popular poem. 'So are we all,' he added, 'but it pleases me to know I have outlived Arghun Baghadur. And that you will outlive him, shiké, is wondrous joy.'

Jebu fell to his knees, weeping. He took Moko's almost-lifeless hand and pressed it against his face, letting his tears run over the broad, hard fingers.

'I owe you so much, I can find no words. Moko, Moko, my friend. I wish I might die and you live. Only you can help me now. Tell me what I can do for you.'

'You have already done everything for me, shiké. You appeared on the Tokaido and gave me a marvellous life. You gave me China, ships, the War of the Dragons, a family name. Because of you my sons are samurai. Because of you I know the beautiful Lady Taniko. Salute her for me now, shiké. Tell her I apologize for not being able to bid her farewell in person. And if you wish to do me any other last favour, look after my foolish son.'

'What I owe you cannot even be calculated,' said Jebu. 'If I spent my whole life caring for your family it would not be enough.'

Moko smiled. 'If you feel such an obligation to me, remember who I am. Remember what your father taught us before he went into oblivion. Remember who I really am. Do you want to return to me what good I have done for you? Then be true to the Self.'

The terrible rolling motion of the ship had stopped. It felt, there in the cabin, as if the ship had righted itself and was plunging forward, like a whale, through the waves. Jebu looked out the open cabin door. There was nothing but blackness ahead and rain was spraying in through the door in sheets. Jebu started to shut the door when Sakagura appeared in the doorway. He came into the cabin and Jebu slid the door shut behind him.

'Oh, Father,' Sakagura cried. 'Are you alive?'

'Sakagura-chan,' Moko whispered. 'Come to me.'

Weeping and groaning, Sakagura knelt at Moko's head. 'I have disgraced our family, Father,' he wept. 'Dishonoured the family name you founded.'

'Listen to me, Sakagura.' Moko's voice was stronger, firmer now. 'You will not commit hara-kiri.'

'But, Father – '

'This is your father's dying command. You must live.' Amazed, Jebu remembered how, so many years ago, his mother, Nyosan, had said almost the same thing to him. *Live, Jebu.* 'You will live in order to carry on the family name,' Moko went on. 'See that the proper observances are performed for your father. Bring glory to our family.'

'I have brothers,' said Sakagura brokenly.

'Your brothers were too young to fight in this war. Only your deeds can bring glory to our family name. You must stay alive to see that they are remembered.'

Sametono said, 'Uncle Moko, your son bears no shame. I ordered him to take me out in the kobaya with him.' Sametono turned anguished eyes to Jebu. 'This is all my fault. If Sakagura commits hara-kiri, I must, too.'

'Then it is settled,' said Moko with a peaceful smile. 'Neither of you will kill himself. Shiké Jebu, I have gone through life fearing death, and now at last I know how foolish I was. I feel no pain and no fear. I wish I had always had the wisdom to contemplate death with a smile, as your father, the holy abbot, did. Surely, today's exploit is the greatest of my life. What better day to end my life?'

He closed his eyes and let his head fall back. Sakagura held one hand and Jebu held the other. They watched Moko's breathing slow, grow fainter. Then it stopped altogether. He was lying on the cushions with his eyes closed and a look of bliss on his face, not breathing at all. And Jebu knew that he would never look into those crossed eyes again.

As if impaled by a spear, Jebu groaned and fell, face forward, beside Moko. He lay howling with grief. After a moment he felt strong hands helping him to his feet. He opened his eyes and blurrily saw Sametono, who draped one of Jebu's arms over his shoulders. Yes, thought Jebu, I want to get out of this cabin.

Together Sametono and Kagyo dragged Jebu out into the rain and wind and darkness, leaving Sakagura lying beside his father's body. The three men huddled against the carved and painted wall of the captain's cabin. The air and spray stinging Jebu's face helped clear his head. He looked forward, trying to see the shore. The curtains of rain were almost opaque. A lightning flash revealed a stretch of beach, stripped of buildings and life, some distance away. They were travelling towards it with incredible speed. The masts and sails screamed protest against the force of the wind pushing them along. The speed of such wind was inconceivable.

'He was my oldest friend,' Jebu wept.

'I know,' Sametono said into his ear.

'He had so much to live for. So much yet to do. He was learning. He had his work. His family.' The pain of losing Yukio had been terrible, Jebu remembered. But he himself had expected to die shortly. And Yukio knew he was finished, that he had no future in the Sacred Islands, that even his wife and children would not be allowed to live. Yukio's life had ended in hopelessness and helplessness, and Jebu had been glad that his suffering was over. Moko had had many good years ahead of him.

Kagyo put his head close to Jebu's and said, 'Do not sorrow for a man whose life is cut off in fullness. Such a man has made the most of life.'

Of course, Jebu thought. That is why we Zinja never mourn for one another. The image of the cherry blossom came to him. The samurai are right.

The black waves rushed past. Those waves were Arghun's tomb. Arghun had haunted him all his life. He could not remember when Taitaro first told him of the man who killed his father. And Arghun's last act had been to kill Moko. Jebu felt no satisfaction in the *tarkhan*'s death. He had not killed him, it was Arghun's own weapon that killed him, in the end. Moko learned and built. Arghun brought only death and destruction wherever he went. Moko's death was a calamity, but Arghun's whole life was a calamity. Moko sacrificed his life for mine, Jebu thought. To repay him for that sacrifice, for the extra years he has given me, I must try to fulfil more truly the purpose of the Zinja.

Be true to the Self. Jebu knew what his future must be as surely as he knew that this ship was about to wreck itself on the shore of Hakata Bay. It was clear what the Self, acting through him, intended for him. Only the Order offered hope. In a flash of lightning, the *tai-phun*-driven waves before *Red Tiger* seemed to turn crimson as he saw all the blood that had been and would be spilled in all humanity's murders and robberies, oppressions and wars. An ocean of blood, the blood of millions of men, women and children. It was unbearable. He screamed aloud.

Then in another lightning flash he saw a great tree rising before the ship, its roots sunk deep in the blood, but living things appearing in its branches. A tree that shone with the brilliance of an eternal lightning bolt and shed, in the midst of the cold ocean, the warmth of the sun. It glowed with a pure, white light above the red sea. The Tree of Life. I'm seeing it without the help of the Jewel, he thought. Taitaro was right. The magic is in my mind. And just as all living things were part of that great tree, so all consciousness was part of the one Self, and no one was ever lost. Not Moko, not Taitaro, not even Arghun. There were many branches and leaves, but the Tree was one.

A wave avalanched on the ship's stern. Jebu heard screams and shouts from the bridge. He scrambled up the ladder, followed by Sametono and Kagyo. Of the four men who had been holding the great bar that controlled the rudder, two had been swept overboard, one lay unconscious and one clung frantically to the tiller, which swung back and forth unaffected by his weight, scraping his legs bloody on the deck. Jebu and Kagyo threw themselves against the tiller. Sametono carried the unconscious man below. The ship had already started to swing athwart the waves, and the creakings of the masts were louder than the screaming of all damned souls. The tiller fought the three men like some giant animal.

Sametono was back moments later with Sakagura and two other men and a length of rope. Lightning flashed, and Jebu was able to make out the rocky shore between Hakata and Hakozaki dead ahead. The *Red Tiger* was making its final run. It would crash them into the rocks or it would sink here in the deep water and take them all with it. The six men tied themselves to the tiller. The junk was riding lower in the water than it had been. There were holes belowdecks blown by the exploding black powder. Actually, the water down there had acted as ballast, steadying the ship against the gusts of wind and the waves that battered it from every side, giving it extra mass to hold it on course.

There were moments when the junk was balanced on the crest of a wave, both stern and bow out of the water, the rudder cutting uselessly through empty air. Jebu tried to imagine the size of a wave that could lift an enormous vessel like this out of the water. He had never heard of waves of such size or winds of such force as these. For good reason, he thought. No one has ever experienced them and lived to tell about it. Water tumbled over the high stern, knocking their feet out from under them. The ropes held them to the tiller, but the tiller threatened to break their ribs. Jebu's hands froze to the long board like claws. Each flash of lightning revealed the rocky shore a little closer. Once as the waves were going out the lightning showed Jebu the floor of the sea and the roots of the great black rocks near shore. A jumble of wood that might once have been a ship clung high on the side of one of the rocks. The wind whipped black beards of seaweed on the rocks. Another flash and all was sea as far inland as the wall, the rocks completely covered, the beach under swirling, foaming water. At times the wall itself appeared to be under water, only the stone watchtowers standing above the waves. Jebu remembered that there had been a tall forest behind this section of the wall. Now there were no trees. The forest was gone, the trees blown flat. What of the towns, he wondered? What of the samurai? Had this tremendous storm killed everyone on shore?

There was a crack as loud as the boom of a *hua pao* and the rear mast, directly in front of them, broke loose. To Jebu's amazement it did not fall. The wind got under the sail, which was still attached to the mast, and lifted it like a kite to splash into a wave some distance away. And then another deafening snap, and the next mast broke loose and flew away. The next, and the next. The masts blew away in succession, snapping like straws, swooping through the air. With each booming break, with each flight of a pillar of wood and its flapping batwing sail, the ship lost ground in its race for shore. There were only three masts left now. Those three sails remained their only hope of reaching shore before the ship sank or broke up on the rocks.

Sakagura shouted, 'Everybody to the bow. We'll have to jump for it when the ship hits.' Jebu, Sametono and the others untied themselves from the tiller. Together with Sakagura they rounded up the survivors huddled along the deck and rushed them to the bow. There was another skull-numbing snap, and one of the remaining masts crashed down on the fleeing men like a felled tree. Jebu looked back. The mast had fallen across the bodies of three men. They were crushed. But the fourth man was pinned by the leg only. Jebu went cold. It was Sametono. Their eyes met, and Sametono shook his head and waved Jebu on. Unable to make himself heard over the volcano roar of the storm, Jebu grabbed Sakagura and Kagyo and jerked them to a stop, pulling them back to help him with Sametono. Other men saw and joined them. All got their hands under the mast and tried to lift. It wouldn't move.

'Save yourselves! I order you!' Sametono shouted.

'No!' Jebu roared back. Sametono looked amazed, as if he had made a sudden, overwhelming discovery.

The ship struck ground. They were all thrown flat to the deck. The mast that had been pinning Sametono tipped up and fell away from the junk. There was no blood and no broken skin. Probably the bone was broken, but Sametono would have to hobble on it as best he could. With his arms around Jebu and Sakagura, Sametono started towards the bow of the ship. They had only moments to jump off before the ship was swept out again by the next big wave. The last two masts, the foremast and the one behind it, had broken off and lay toppled forward. *Red Tiger* had fallen on the beach itself. It had been lifted over the rocks and grounded on the sand. The men ran to the broken masts and climbed down them, using them as bridges from *Red Tiger*'s bow to the ground. Just like the collapsible masts Moko had designed. Moko!

'Your father!' Jebu shouted to Sakagura. 'We can't leave him to be swept out to sea.'

Leaving Sametono in the care of Kagyo and another Former Zinja, Jebu and Sakagura raced back to the cabin where Moko lay. The little body was crumpled in a heap in one corner, where it had been thrown by the wild careening of the ship. Jebu picked up Moko by the arms, thankful that the wound that had killed him was bound up. Moko's head lolled back, pale as white

415

paper, and his mouth fell open. He was so light that Jebu could almost have carried him alone. Jebu taking the head and Sakagura the feet, they ran out of the cabin and trotted down the deck. Jebu looked over his shoulder. A wave as tall as Mount Fuji was falling upon them out of the black sky. The stern cabin of *Red Tiger* vanished under water, and then the ship rose up under them. Hanging on desperately to Moko's body, Jebu was almost washed overboard. As he and Sakagura stood up and started running for the bow, they saw with horror the shore recede and the black tips of the rocks rush past the sides of the ship as it was carried out to sea. Then another wave caught *Red Tiger* and threw it like a javelin back at the shore again. As it struck the beach with a stunning crash, Sakagura and Jebu reached the bow with Moko's body. There was nothing they could do but lift the body over the rail and let it drop. Then they jumped – a distance five times the height of a man – to the sand. The soft wet sand and martial training saved them from broken limbs as they hit and rolled. Another colossal wave was coming at them. It caught the ship and began to pull it out to sea. It dragged them off their feet and nearly carried them back into the water. Struggling frantically, each hanging on to one of Moko's arms, they clawed, crawled and floundered up the beach towards the safety of the wall which now seemed impossibly distant. At last, reluctantly, the water released them, flowing back into the bay. Jebu saw the scarlet bow of *Red Tiger* disappear behind a wall of green-black water. He collapsed on the sand with a sigh.

The *Red Tiger* was upon them again. Riding the crest of yet another wave, the ship's bow loomed gigantically over them, threatening to fall upon them and crush them. Somehow Jebu managed to get his numb limbs moving and help Sakagura with Moko's body. Just behind them *Red Tiger* hit the beach with a thunderous crash and a cracking of timbers. The storm was using the huge junk as a plaything, Jebu thought as they staggered towards the wall, tearing it slowly to pieces as a cat destroys a mouse.

They dared not stop to rest again. One wave after another pursued them up the beach, seizing them and pulling them back. Some waves, larger than others, rushed past them to crash into the base of the wall. These knocked Jebu and Sakagura down again and again, so that by the time they reached the wall they were bleeding and nearly dead from fatigue. Men in loincloths lowered a wooden ramp from the top of the wall and helped them up. They identified themselves at swordpoint to samurai who still had no idea what might have happened to the Mongols, and then they were allowed to seek shelter on the leeward side of the wall. Tenderly laying down Moko's body, Jebu and Sakagura collapsed, exhausted.

A voice beside him said, 'I feared I might never see you again, Shiké Jebu.' It was Sametono. His leg was tied to a broken board with a white piece of silk that was wrapped around it many times. He had crawled painfully over to Jebu on hands and knees, dragging the broken leg behind him.

Jebu closed his eyes and let his head fall back on the rough stone of the wall against which he was sitting. 'I'm happy to see you, too, your lordship. Please forgive me for letting your leg be broken.'

'Don't be absurd, Jebu.' Jebu opened his eyes and saw that Sametono's eyes were glowing at him, catlike. He certainly did look like Taniko. 'Have you ever heard of Joshu's No?'

'No. That is, I never heard of it.'

'It's a Zen *kung-an* set me by Eisen.' Sametono told him the story of No. 'I've been trying to work it out ever since. All the time I was dangling from Arghun's masthead I was thinking about Joshu's No. Over and over to myself I said, No, No, No. That was the only thing that kept me from going mad. Today I learned that No can affirm as well as deny. Thank you for improving my understanding.'

'I am your lordship's servant,' said Jebu wearily, wanting to sleep, not discuss philosophy.

'If I hadn't had that small satori it would be awfully hard for me to bear the burden of my obligation to you, Master Jebu. I have been a fool. I defied your advice. And now many brave men are dead because of me. Uncle Moko is dead because of me.' Sametono's voice broke. 'Everything that happened was my fault.'

Resignedly, Jebu opened his eyes. The rescuing was not over. The boy's spirit needed rescuing, too.

'When you set sail with Sakagura last night, you thought you were doing right. Remorse because your actions did not have the results you wished is a waste of your time. All you can truly say is that you might do things differently on the next occasion. There is no right or wrong.'

'No right and wrong?' Sametono looked excited. 'Then there is no Yes or No. Yes and No are both Yes. I see, I see!' Laughing wildly, he crawled away. Jebu stared after him, watching him climb painfully to the top of the wall, where he pushed himself to his feet with his broken leg propped under him. He waved his arms and shouted something into the teeth of the storm.

One word or sound, over and over again. Jebu could not hear it, but knowing Sametono he was sure it could be only one cry: 'Kwatz! Kwatz! Kwatz!'

CHAPTER TWENTY-FOUR

Though Jebu sensed that it must be mid-morning, it was dark as midnight in Taniko's bedchamber. She was awake beside him, and he could feel her quietly sobbing. The old mansion house at Dazaifu creaked under the force of the wind, and the steady drumming of rain on the roof was so loud and had kept up so long that he forgot he was hearing it. Here and there in the corners of the room a drop of water from one of the many leaks in the roof would plop into a puddle, a sound strangely audible above the roar of the *tai-phun*.

'Are you crying for Moko?' he asked her.

'Oh, Jebu, why did he have to die? He didn't even have to go with you. He wasn't a warrior.'

'He said he would kill himself if we didn't take him, and I believe he meant it. Though he wasn't a warrior, he attacked Arghun with his bare hands. Sametono and I would probably be dead now if he had not.'

'I have lost so many loved ones,' Taniko said. 'Why do men kill and kill and kill?' As she spoke, Jebu saw in his mind the ocean of blood.

'My Order exists in part to find the answer,' he said. 'If I could do a little bit towards finding it, I would think my life well spent.'

The fury of the *tai-phun* had blown most of the buildings at

Hakozaki flat. Taniko's retainers had insisted that she return inland to the governor's palace at Dazaifu, which was better protected. As soon as Jebu had gathered his strength, he brought Sametono to Dazaifu in a carriage. They arrived in the middle of the night, Sametono sound asleep and unwakeable. Taniko put her foster son in the care of priests and took Jebu to her bedchamber, where he collapsed, exhausted, and went to sleep immediately, while Taniko lay awake most of the night, weeping over the news that Moko had been killed.

Now her arms went around him in the darkness and she pressed her wet face against his. 'You brought Sametono back out of the very heart of hell. You have given me back my life. I did not think I could love you more than I did already, but I find that love grows deeper, like enlightenment.'

'And I love you more every day and every night,' Jebu said, holding her tightly.

A maidservant knocked at the bedchamber door. 'My lady, there is a messenger from Hakata for Shiké Jebu.'

'They do not even pretend not to know you are here any more,' said Taniko. 'I'm afraid our love is no longer a secret anywhere.'

The messenger was from Miura Zumiyoshi. Even though the storm was still battering Hakata Bay, the defence command had decided to launch an attack on the Mongol beachhead at Hakata. Yesterday they had seen countless Mongols and Chinese swimming or riding out to their junks, fearing they would be left behind by the fleet retreating from the *tai-phun*. Overloaded junks had turned belly-up in the water, others had been the scene of battles as those on board tried to prevent any more from crowding on. The men who had decided to stay on shore were shooting arrows and even missiles from siege machines at their retreating comrades. The messenger's account reminded Jebu of the Takashi rout at Ichinotani. Now the Mongol beachhead was undermanned and would be vulnerable. No one knew what had happened to the Mongol fleet. After the storm passed on, they might be back. The time to destroy their forces on land was now. Perhaps the Mongols at Hakata could be persuaded to surrender, and Jebu was needed as one of the few warriors who could speak Mongolian.

His armour, he thought, was probably lost in the wreckage of

419

the camp at Hakozaki. Taniko helped him find an old corselet and shoulder guards in the Dazaifu governor's armoury, as well as a naginata in good condition. Jebu covered himself with a straw hat and a straw raincoat. He said goodbye to Taniko and rode off westwards with the messenger.

It was early afternoon, the Hour of the Horse, when the first samurai leaned their scaling ladders against the shiny-wet black stones of the wall around Hakata and started to climb. The invaders put up a feeble defence, dumping rocks and throwing spears down at the climbing warriors. But it was too late for that. Jebu glimpsed some fighting on top of the wall, and soon after a gate swung open and the several thousand samurai Zumiyoshi had gathered for this assault trotted heavily through the mud and into the ruined town.

Within, all was grey black, the grey of ashes. The town had been levelled by fire. Remains of walls and blackened stone statues rose above the expanse of charred wreckage. The first group of invaders they encountered had thrown down their weapons and were kneeling in the downpour when they approached. The samurai brandished their swords and awaited the order to start taking heads. Jebu questioned a middle-aged man whose rain-soaked robes looked as if they might once have been a splendid officer's uniform. They were Chinese, he told Jebu. They had been forced to come here under threat of death to themselves and their families. They had no quarrel with the noble warriors of the Sunrise Land. They begged for mercy.

'We always kill prisoners,' Zumiyoshi said, when Jebu pleaded for the Chinese.

'They did not willingly take up arms against us,' Jebu said. 'The true samurai is compassionate to the unfortunate, and these are here only through misfortune. These Chinese are highly-skilled, hard-working and civilized people. It would be a terrible waste to kill them.'

'In short,' said Zumiyoshi, 'they'll make good slaves. The Bakufu will have little land to give away to reward our victorious warriors. In place of land we can give away free labour. Round them up and march them off to Hakozaki.' That wasn't what I meant, Jebu thought, but life on those terms might be better for these men than death out of hand.

Bodies were everywhere. Lying in the muddy ashes they were hardly recognizable as human. Few were civilians because most of the people of the harbour towns had been evacuated when the Mongol fleet arrived. Many of the samurai dead were found with their armour stripped off, hands tied behind their backs and Mongol arrow wounds in their bodies, the arrows themselves having been retrieved. That their helpless comrades had been slaughtered angered the samurai, even though they would have done the same to any Mongols they captured.

Several hundred Koreans also surrendered. They were even more vociferous in denoucning their Mongol overlords. The surviving Mongols, they informed the samurai, were planning to make a last stand on the west side of the ruined town, close to the water in case their fleet should come back.

'These Koreans would have loved nothing better than to conquer us,' said Zumiyoshi sourly. 'They provided the ships and seamen for two invasion fleets. They've always hated us.' Once again, though, Jebu's arguments prevailed. The prisoners would be more useful alive.

The Mongols, when they came upon them, were crouched in the rain in wet brown rows, spears and swords ready, taking advantage of what little cover was provided by the broken walls of a temple. There were over a thousand of them, those who had stayed behind or been left behind when the invasion fleet fled the storm.

'We'll lose many men finishing them off,' said Jebu.

'Our men want to draw blood today,' Zumiyoshi growled. 'They're angry, they've come out here in this storm to fight, and it's Mongols they want to kill.'

'I came out in this storm because I can speak to the Mongols and might persuade them to surrender,' Jebu said. 'General, it's one of the oldest military principles never to attack a cornered enemy. It's too costly.'

'Go ahead, then.' Zumiyoshi turned away in disgust.

Jebu selected a spot half-way between the samurai and the Mongols. He planted his naginata in the ground and tried to think of arguments that might move the invaders.

'We know how to honour a brave foe,' he said. 'It is a waste of your lives for you to fight on. The storm has destroyed your fleet. You are the last of your army left on our shores. We are willing to accept your honourable surrender. It is no disgrace. It is foolish to shed blood for no purpose.'

Someone called out, 'You will make slaves of us. We would rather be dead.' A spear, well aimed and thrown hard, came whistling through the rain. Jebu deflected it with his naginata. More spears flew. Now, behind him, he heard the battle shout of the samurai. They ran past him, slogging through the wet grey ashes, rank after rank, swords and naginatas at the ready.

In man-to-man, hand-to-hand combat the fighting style of the samurai was far superior. Without their horses, with their bows and arrows made useless by wind and rain, the Mongols were outmatched. And they were outnumbered. Samurai swords rose and fell like farmers' sickles in a field ripe for harvest. Jebu had no stomach for fighting today, and he certainly wasn't needed. Sickened though he was by the killing, he stood where he was and watched.

In the centre of the Mongol square, standing on a little hill of rubble, stood a familiar grey-bearded figure shouting orders and encouragement – Torluk. Jebu remembered hearing that Torluk had been put in charge of the Chinese troops and the South of the Yang-Tze Fleet. He must have taken personal command of this all-important beachhead and now intended to die defending it. Using the pole end of his naginata as a flail, Jebu plunged into the fight. He pushed men aside right and left until at last he was in the front rank of samurai.

'Torluk,' he called. 'Torluk, come to me.'

Torluk's eyes met his in shocked recognition. With a roar, the old Mongol was off his mound and charging at Jebu, swinging his sabre. Jebu threw his naginata to a startled samurai nearby and awaited Torluk's rush with his open hands held out before him.

Suspecting a trick, Torluk checked his rush and began circling Jebu slowly. Age, Jebu saw, had affected Torluk more than it had Arghun. His movements were slower, less certain than they had been. A flicker of superstitious fear crossed his face.

'So, you still live,' said Torluk. 'I had heard you were alive, but I could not believe it.'

'Yes, I am alive, and your master, Arghun, is dead,' said Jebu. Something – fear, grief? – crossed Torluk's bearded face, then was pushed back by the determined, concentrated stare of the professional fighting man.

'And now you mean to kill me and complete your revenge?'

Jebu laughed. 'You wish to die in combat, of course, but I have a crueller fate than that in mind for you.'

At that, Torluk charged, raising his blade and bringing it down at Jebu's neck. Jebu swung his body to Torluk's right, so that the Mongol commander brushed past him, the sabre grazing Jebu's chest. Jebu seized Torluk's extended sword arm in a grip that twisted the wrist, leading the grey-bearded man around him, slowly applying more and more pressure to force him to drop the sword. Torluk pivoted in Jebu's grip, swinging behind him. Over his shoulder Jebu caught a glimpse of a dagger in Torluk's left hand just before the point of the blade struck Jebu's corselet, failing to penetrate. Jebu got his shoulder under Torluk and threw him through the air, to land on his back with a thud. While Torluk lay stunned, Jebu tore the weapons from his hands and bound him quickly with his own rawhide lariat.

Samurai and Mongols were fighting all around him. Jebu turned away in despair. It was as he had warned Zumiyoshi; killing off the last Mongols would be costly. Even though the samurai outnumbered the Mongols and were their superiors in combat skills, every Mongol who died was managing to take at least one samurai with him. They were fighting with the strength of those who already count themselves dead. The circle of fighting warriors grew smaller and smaller. It was surrounded by a much larger circle of the dead. Samurai and Mongol lay side by side in death as they never could have done in life. Oceans of blood, thought Jebu. Oceans of blood.

When Jebu dragged the captive Torluk to him, Zumiyoshi said, 'Now I see why these barbarous warriors coming out of a desert place have conquered half the world. They have true fighting spirit. You can't tell that about a man until his back is to the wall. Who have we here?'

'The commander of this beachhead, *tarkhan* Torluk,' said Jebu. 'Now that we have their leader, perhaps the rest of them will surrender.'

Torluk understood the language of the Sunrise Land and spoke it, though with an accent. 'It has been my misfortune to be captured, though I hoped to die in combat. These, my fighting men, will never surrender. And our desert lands will breed tens of thousands more warriors. Do not think that you samurai have won a final victory today. When news of our deaths reaches the ears of Kublai Khan his rage will be as terrible as this *tai-phun*. We will come again. We will come again and again until we are victorious.'

'We never give up either, friend,' said Miura Zumiyoshi, drawing his long blade.

'Wait, general,' said Jebu quickly.

Zumiyoshi turned a face of outraged wonder towards Jebu. 'Surely you don't expect me to let this man live? He was one of those responsible for this war against us.' Zumiyoshi sputtered, 'Why, he doesn't even want to live.'

'I know,' said Jebu. 'But, general, I urge you to send him back to his Great Khan with perhaps a few other captured Mongols. I want the Great Khan to have a first-hand account of what happened here to his fleet and his army. He should be told that we will never surrender, and that we will wipe out every expedition he sends here just as we did this one. How do you think *tarkhan* Torluk will feel, being one of the only Mongol generals left alive, bringing Kublai Khan news of defeat? That will be punishment enough for his complicity in this war. Of course he wants to die. That would be much less painful for him.'

'I dislike it,' said Miura Zumiyoshi, 'but what you say makes sense.' He turned to Torluk. 'I order you to go back to your Great Khan and tell him how great this defeat was, and that the samurai will never surrender to him.'

'You do not have to order him,' said Jebu. 'He will report all this to the Great Khan because it is his duty as a Mongol.'

The battle was still going on. Under sheets of rain a mob of samurai surrounded a determined little circle of Mongols. Jebu looked questioningly at Zumiyoshi, who nodded. Jebu strode off towards the struggling warriors. He worked his way to the front rank of samurai, roaring for the fighting to stop. The ground beneath his feet was soaked with so much blood that even the downpour could not wash it away.

At last he was looking into the few remaining Mongol faces, angry, frightened, determined, ready to die. With a gesture he pushed back the ring of samurai, bristling with swords and naginatas.

'All right,' he called in Mongolian, raising his voice to be heard above the wind and the rain. 'There has been enough fighting. Your *tarkhan* Torluk has been captured. He is going home, and those of you who are alive now are going with him.' First one Mongol dropped his spear, then another threw his sabre down on top of it. With a clatter, all their weapons went down in a pile. The samurai opened a path for them, and Jebu led them away.

CHAPTER TWENTY-FIVE

Although the Mongols had never landed there, Hakozaki was almost as completely levelled as Hakata. It was water, not fire, that had destroyed this town. At the height of the *tai-phun*, waves higher than the walls had reduced the walls to rubble and carried away most of the houses. The buildings that were not swept away were nothing but piles of broken timbers mixed with dislocated rocks and pieces of ships. As Jebu trudged up the beach past the ruins of the town he saw bodies of drowned men and horses that had been thrown upon the beach by the waves. The storm had also scooped up sea creatures, fish and crabs, and black-green heaps of seaweed and tossed them on the beach to drown in the air. Flies were starting to swarm.

There were blue breaks in the clouds that suggested the sun might even emerge today. The tempest had raged for two days and two nights, and that morning the rain had stopped at last and the wind had died down, and the dazed people around Hakata Bay were beginning to take stock. It was once again becoming oppressively hot. Beyond Hakozaki people were gathering around a pile of wood that had been the wreckage of *Red Tiger*. The ship was so huge and had been thrown so far up on the beach that it had survived the pounding of the storm. Sakagura and his men had chopped the great timbers and ribs into smaller pieces which they built into a rectangular pile.

Shortly after Jebu took his place in the front rank of

mourners, Taniko's carriage rolled up, and she stepped down, leaning on Sametono's arm. Her eyes were red with crying and her face was haggard. Jebu moved silently to her side. Now there came a procession of priests, followed by samurai carrying a small fifteen-man kobaya. Seated amidships, dressed in a white kimono, was Moko. Drums and bells and gongs shattered the silence, and the priests began chanting the sutras. The music and chanting went on for a long time. Once Jebu caught himself wishing he could hear what Moko would say about how tedious all this ceremony could be. At last the priests came to the end of their rites. Sakagura went up to Jebu.

'Does your Order have a chant or a prayer that might be said for the soul of my father?'

'I will say something,' said Jebu. He stood beside the pyre, his white robe blowing in the faint breeze, and faced the people who had assembled to do Moko honour.

'Over three cycles ago in the Year of the Dragon, I met this man on the Tokaido Road, and he was my friend from that day to this. When I first met him he was a simple man from a small village, but he had been trained as a carpenter, and he was skilled at his work. His work was his way of penetrating the mysteries of life. He travelled to the far places of the earth and brought back discoveries to the great benefit of his people. He designed and built the ships that helped us defend outselves against the Mongols. His sense of duty drove him to volunteer for a raid into the very centre of the Mongol fleet, and he died on that raid. He died saving my life.' Jebu stopped, realizing that if he spoke another word he would sob aloud. The sun was out now and it dazzled him. He looked at Taniko. Tears were again running down her face, as copious as yesterday's rain. At last Jebu felt able to continue.

'And yet, when I have said all that about Hayama Moko, I have not said enough. What was the meaning of his life? When Moko died of his wound, a wise brother of my Order said to me that those who die at the height of their powers, of whom we say, death cut them off too soon, are least to be mourned. Moko lived in such a way that if he had lived a thousand years we would still have to say his life was too short. He died without a weapon in his hand, sacrificing himself to save others, without striking a blow. He took no priestly vows, yet at no time in his life did he injure another being. His life was dedicated to the creative principle. Why did he die at the hands of another human being? We must never tire of asking that question. Moko has by his death sent us on a quest, a search for the answer to the question, why do men kill other men? That quest itself is the meaning of Moko's life and death.'

There was a long silence after Jebu spoke. Then Sakagura stepped towards the pyre, holding in one hand a blazing torch.

After the funeral, Sakagura and Jebu took one of the few kobaya that had survived the storm to see if there were any sign of the enemy fleet. It was a fifteen-man ship, like the one they had burned with Moko. The sun was now hot and high, the waves in the bay sparkling and tame. Jebu and Sakagura had little to say to each other on the way out to the harbour mouth. Each remained sunk in his own grief for Moko.

Their ship rode so low in the water that they did not see the wreckage until they had nearly sailed into it. As they came opposite Shiga Island they began running into huge broken timbers and fragments of decks and hulls drifting across their course that had to be pushed out of the way. Then, at last, they could go no further. A barrier of splintered, water-soaked wood, rocking in the waves but solid as far ahead as they could see, blocked their way. There were bodies, too, many bodies of men in soldiers' and seamen's garb. They floated in the water or lay tangled in the wreckage of the Great Khan's fleet. And there were sharks, black fins cutting the water all around the piles of wood, scavenging.

'It's solid all the way from here to Shiga Spit,' said Sakagura, standing on the prow of the kobaya.

Slowly they rowed south along the wooden barrier, looking for an opening out to sea. But no matter how far they went it was the same, a wall formed by the wreckage of ships, a wall too solid for their little ship to penetrate.

'Nothing like this has ever been seen before,' said Jebu, 'and perhaps nothing like it will ever be seen again.' This is for you, Yukio, he thought to himself. If you still exist in any form, if that was truly who stood beside me on the rail of Arghun's ship, then behold this. Your people, inspired by your spirit, have triumphed over those same Mongols who destroyed you.

'They must have jammed together in the harbour entrance trying to get away,' said Sakagura. 'They got stuck, and the storm wrecked them.'

'They may have lost half of their fleet here,' said Jebu. 'They probably lost many more out on the open sea. We will have to send scout ships out after them, of course, but I don't think they will be coming back. This expedition of Kublai Khan's, at least, is finished.' Tens of thousands of men drowned, whole armies. It was difficult to picture, terrifying and pitiable. It was as Taitaro had prophesied to Yukio and Jebu years ago in China: 'The jewels created by Izanami and Izanagi shall be protected by the Hurricane of the Kami.' With a sigh, Jebu sat down cross-legged in the bow of the kobaya, his long-haired, bearded head sunk on his chest.

'Compassionate Buddha!' Sakagura said, looking at the remains of the Mongol fleet. He ordered his rowers back to Hakozaki, then dropped down beside Jebu.

'Shiké, I thank you for speaking so beautifully at my father's funeral this morning, but your words were strange for a warrior monk. What did you mean about finding out why men kill one another?'

'The Zinja were founded for the purpose of protecting people from war and killing, so my words were in keeping with the spirit of my Order. After many generations we have been forced to admit failure. That is why the Order has been dissolved.'

'No group as dedicated as the Zinja simply disappears, shiké,' said Sakagura with a knowing smile. 'There is more to it than that. My father hinted to me that your Order has simply decided to make itself invisible.'

'And why should that interest you?' said Jebu. The resemblance to Moko in the young face was strong.

'Shiké, I am at a crossroads in my life.' Tears appeared in Sakagura's large brown eyes. 'I thought of myself as a great hero. I enjoyed the praise of other samurai. Then I made the great blunder that cost so many lives, including my father's, all through my foolish pride and hunger for glory. I've dreamed all my life of preferment, land, power, rank. I wanted those things as much for my father's sake as for my own, shiké. I respected and loved him. I knew him for the wise and compassionate man he was. And brave. He was brave, even though he kept saying he

428

wasn't.' Sakagura paused a moment, unable to go on.

'He was brave but never foolish,' said Jebu.

'There were those in Kamakura who laughed at him, shiké. I wanted our family to rise so high no one would ever dare laugh at my father again. But instead I caused his death. One of the other kobaya captains is going to hire an artist to paint a scroll depicting his heroic deeds. He will present it to the Bakufu along with his petition for rewards. A few days ago I thought I would do the same thing. Now it seems ridiculous to me. When you said this morning that my father's death sent you on a quest to find out why men kill one another, I thought, if a warrior monk can ask that question, so can a samurai. Shiké, I think I want to follow you on that quest, wherever it takes you.'

The good teacher begins by discouraging the would-be student, Jebu thought. 'I am not seeking followers,' he said abruptly. 'I have no idea what I myself am going to do now. In any case, this feeling that the life of a samurai is not right for you is doubtless only a passing phase. Your grief for your father will naturally come to pain you less in time, and the samurai way of life will seem good to you again.'

'You don't understand, shiké—' Sakagura began. Jebu turned a thundercloud face towards him.

'Leave me alone. I am meditating.' Jebu folded his hands in his lap and half closed his eyes. Sakagura sighed and said no more. To the rhythmic beat of the oars the kobaya glided across the dancing waters of the harbour. Time passed, while Jebu reflected that what he told Sakagura was partly true. He was indeed uncertain about his future, and there was much pain in that.

Sakagura did not speak to him again until the kobaya was tied up at a makeshift pier at Hakozaki. Then, after they had both climbed out, he turned and faced Jebu.

'Excuse me, shiké, but what you don't understand is that I am very much like my father. He told me how he once promised to follow you anywhere, even to China, and how he kept that promise. Since my father has commanded me to live, I want to take the place he left vacant. I too will follow you. Anywhere.' Giving Jebu no chance to reply, he turned on his heel and marched off into the town. Jebu stood there smiling after him, hoping his beard would hide the smile.

CHAPTER TWENTY-SIX

Taniko and Eisen walked together at twilight between a broad, still carp pond and the stone outer wall of the Todaiji Temple in the old city of Nara. Everything around Taniko whispered of age and tragedy. The Todaiji had been built by Emperors five hundred years earlier, when Nara was the capital of the nation. Thousands of people who lived here had died by fire and the sword in the War of the Dragons, when the Takashi in their wrath descended on the temple. Now new buildings were rising on the Todaiji grounds. Under the direction of Eisen, whose authority among the Buddhist priesthood had grown greatly because of the favour of Kamakura, the monks and people of Nara were rebuilding the temple. Taniko, making a state progress with Sametono from Hakata Bay to Kamakura, had stopped for a time at the Rokuhara in Heian Kyo. At her first opportunity she made the two-day journey from Heian Kyo to Nara to see Eisen and inspect the rebuilding. Ceremonies over, they walked in the garden to talk confidentially.

'I am sorry to tell you that your father has entered the Void, my lady,' said Eisen. 'I just received a message for you from the head priest of the Rikyu-in Temple.' The Rikyu-in was a small temple established by disciples of Eisen near Edo, a remote fishing village north of Kamakura. There Shima Bokuden, his head shaved, had idled away his life and dreamed of his days of power under the careful eyes of Zen monks who had formerly been Zinja.

'What did he die of?' The news surprised her, but she felt no grief. She was momentarily ashamed of her cool reaction. In fact, she realized to her greater embarrassment, she felt rather relieved that one problem at least was over with for good. Her father would never trouble her again.

'Pheumonia,' said Eisen. 'He had the best possible care. He died shortly after the news reached the temple that the Mongol fleet had been destroyed. I'm told he was pleased about that.'

'He might have had some word of praise for his family,'

Taniko said wistfully. 'No matter. Please say prayers for his soul.' Was the face I had before I was born my father's face? she wondered. But she felt no more enlightened.

'As soon as I get back to Kamakura,' she said, 'I'll have this temple's income increased. All our wealth has had to go to the war. I want you to complete the casting of the giant statue of the Buddha which will replace the one that was destroyed here by the Takashi. And later on I want to have a Buddha just as big built at Kamakura in memory of my husband, the late Shogun. I promised that to him when he was dying. Without him we would not have had the armies we needed to hold off the Mongols.'

Eisen held up an admonishing finger. 'These are worthy projects, my lady, but please remember that when the Buddha was alive, he asked only for what people could spare him after taking care of their own needs. There are many families bereft, many people homeless, many children fatherless. I beg of you, use the wealth of the Bakufu to relieve the suffering of those in want, before we cast any statues. There is an old story about a monk who took shelter in a temple on a winter night and used a statue of the Buddha for firewood. That is the true attitude of Zen.'

Taniko laughed bitterly. 'You seem to be the only priest who thinks so. There isn't a temple in the country, large or small, whose priests are not claiming personal credit for defeating the Mongols. It was their prayers, they say, that brought the *tai-phun*. They are all calling it the Kamikaze, the Hurricane of the Gods. Noshin is the worst of all. He claims that the day of the storm all the flags on his temple pointed straight at Hakata Bay. He demands – he does not request, he demands – that the Bakufu endow his temple with more rice land than any of the older temples now possess.'

'Kamikaze,' said Eisen musingly. 'That *tai-phun* did not save our Sacred Islands by itself. It was our samurai who held that enormous Mongol army to the beach for two months. If the Mongols had entrenched themselves on our land, the storm would not have defeated them. The true Hurricane of the Gods is the spirit of our people.'

'They're not inspired any more,' said Taniko sadly. 'It's only a month since the Mongols were driven away, and already that

431

wonderful spirit that filled the country is gone. Everybody is clamouring for riches, hounding the Bakufu for lands, titles, offices. And we have practically nothing to give. In fact, we have to ask the samurai and the people to sacrifice even more. Kublai Khan will want to try again. We will not be safe until he dies, if then. We have to keep our defences in repair, build new walls and more ships, keep armies permanently stationed along the threatened coasts. We'll be straining our resources for years to come.'

'And you want to build gigantic statues of the Buddha?' Eisen said gently.

'I thought it might remind people not to be so selfish.'

'There is only one way for leaders to inspire the people, my lady,' said Eisen. 'By example. You enjoy the privileges of a ruler. Stop feeling sorry for yourself that your subjects make demands on you. Remember, there is no guarantee from the gods that your family will hold power perpetually. These are dangerous times for governors, my lady. In addition to bands of impoverished, disgruntled samurai roving the countryside, you have preachers like Noshin stirring people up, claiming that their sufferings are caused by the sins of their rulers. At such a moment as this, it would take very little to provoke rebellion. If you want your regime to remain in power, the lives of the country's leaders must be beyond reproach.' He stopped walking, stood with his back to the carp pond and stared meaningfully at her.

'What are you suggesting, sensei?'

He hesitated, then a look of resolve came over his face. In that flicker of expressions she saw to her surprise that even the great master Eisen could be reluctant to say something unpleasant.

'My lady, I suggest that it would be wise for the monk Jebu to leave the country for a while.'

Taniko was speechless for a moment. This sudden turn of the conversation shocked and angered her. How dare this man speak to her of Jebu? How dare anyone? Jebu leave the country? Along with the joy of victory over the Mongols, her happiest thought in the last month had been that at last she and Jebu would be united and that nothing could separate them again for the rest of their lives. She could not believe her ears.

'Please forgive me for disturbing your harmony, my lady,'

Eisen said. 'It is simply that a journey has been proposed to the monk Jebu.'

'Proposed by whom?' Her anger grew stronger. Someone wanted Jebu out of the country. When she found out who, she would set the samurai on them.

'Those formerly known as the Zinja, my lady.'

'Are you one of them?'

'I and others of the Order have been doing our best to look after your welfare and that of your family for many years.'

'Why do you want to separate me and Jebu?' She was on the verge of tears.

'Of all of us in the Sacred Islands, Jebu is the one who can carry out this mission, a journey to the West. He will speak for us to our brothers in distant places, he will represent us in the Councils of the Order, he will learn what is happening in the rest of the world, and he will come back here with precious knowledge. You cannot imagine, my lady, how uniquely important such a journey can be. A single man travelling across the world from east to west or from west to east in these times can change the course of history.' He went on to tell her a little about the Order and its purposes, its far-flung branches, its constant need to keep its parts in communication with one another. She was amazed and rather frightened to realize that all this had existed without her knowledge. Jebu had kept his Order's secrets even in bed.

'All lands everywhere are going through a time of great and painful change,' said Eisen. 'From all this change can come great benefit as well as suffering on a scale never before known. We who call ourselves the Order must be in a position to spread constructive ideas, to influence. Jebu's foster father, Taitaro, undertook the same sort of responsibilities for the Order before him. Indeed, he left Jebu's mother for years of meditation and travel.'

'You are asking me to let my happiness be destroyed by a secret society I scarcely knew of before, for the benefit of people I have never seen.'

'For the benefit of your people, my lady. If you knew that Jebu's journey could help insure that the Mongols would never again threaten the Sacred Islands, could you accept his going?'

433

She thought long. 'You play upon my love of country to persuade me to sacrifice the man who is my life.'

'The first branches of the Order Jebu visits will be those in China and Mongolia. He will meet with people who are trying to influence the course of events in those countries.'

'You can't promise me that Jebu's leaving me would accomplish any such wonders, can you?'

'Indeed, I can guarantee nothing,' said Eisen. 'But it is knowing you should act in a certain way, and acting in that way regardless of the effect of the action, that leads to enlightenment.'

'Do not try to divert me with promises of enlightenment.' Her voice was hard, angry. 'I want Jebu.'

'As I told you when we first met, the strength of your love shows that you are already greatly enlightened. But one of the Bakufu's most important sources of strength is the esteem, almost like worship, in which most samurai hold the Ama-Shogun. Unfortunately, the rumour is spreading that the real power behind the Bakufu is your lover, a monk of the disreputable Zinja Order who, even worse, is half Mongol.'

Taniko was outraged. 'I have a right to my privacy. From the Emperor on down, there isn't a nobleman on these islands who doesn't sleep with several wives and assorted courtesans. And what's more, Jebu is a hero. His deeds are legendary. How could anyone say anything against him?'

Eisen shook his head. 'Our lords may disport themselves as they wish, but our ladies must be chaste. I disapprove of such a state of affairs as much as you do, but we cannot change it. As for Jebu's heroism, there are many who envy and hate him. Yukio was a hero, and still the people turned away from him.'

Now Taniko was in tears. 'I won't do it. I won't give him up. It's not fair. I have loved him all my life, and I've never been able to spend more than a few months at a time with him. Even in the last six years we've only been together for brief visits. Now, for the first time in our lives, we can live together as we have always wanted to. We have so little time left, sensei.' She was pleading now for understanding. 'We can't expect to live much longer. Surely we have a right to the few years of happiness left to us.'

Eisen shook his head. 'The only thing you are promised in this life is suffering.'

Anger boiled up within her. She took a breath and opened her mouth to shout a protest, to say no to the belief that life was nothing but pain, no to his demand for sacrifice, no to all suffering and loss of her life, no to more years of separation from Jebu. But as she drew in her breath, it seemed some tremendous force took hold of her and drew her breath in for her, as the water near shore is drawn into a great oncoming wave, till her lungs were full to bursting. Then the wave broke.

She let her breath out in one terrible scream, a long-drawn-out wordless shout of rage and agony, a cry from the very centre of her being. The muscles of her abdomen knotted and her throat burned and the cords in her neck ached from the force she put into the scream. She went on screaming until every bit of air in her chest was gone.

She opened her eyes and saw to her amazement that Eisen was sitting in the shallow carp pond, staring at her with a surprise as great as her own. After a moment, he began to laugh.

There was a clatter of weapons all around them. Taniko's samurai guards had heard her scream and had come rushing to her aid. The warrior monks of the Todaiji saw Eisen fall into the pond and came running to their sensei's aid. The two groups of armed men stood in a circle around Eisen and Taniko glaring at each other, tense and ready to fight. Taniko and Eisen dismissed them with assurances that they were both all right and that neither had in any way hurt the other. Before anyone could help him up. Eisen sprang dripping from the pond, as if to demonstrate by his very agility that all was well.

'Sensei, what happened?' said Taniko in a low voice when they were alone again.

'It is a phenomenon that was developed by the *Ch'an* masters of China and which we students of Zen are introducing in the martial arts here,' said Eisen. 'It is called kiai, the shout. After many years of practice a student of this art can produce a shout that will stun a man or kill him. In your case, under the pressure of the situation, you produced such a kiai shout naturally.'

'Yes, but what happened to *me*, sensei?'

Eisen looked into her face. It was long past sunset now, and the garden of the Todaiji was illuminated by many bronze and stone lanterns, their reflected lights twinkling in the pond. A nearly full yellow-orange moon was peeping over the temple wall.

'Ah,' said Eisen, after carefully examining Taniko's face. His little sigh of satisfaction and his look confirmed what she suspected. Even as the moon was rising, she felt a light dawning within her. The suffering of a moment ago was replaced by pure, limitless joy. She had broken through. The scream was the cry of life itself, the life that had been in her parents and which they had passed on to her, that had been passed to them through countless generations of ancestors, that was the same as the life in Eisen, in the carp in the pond, in the trees around them. To be alive is to suffer. The scream of pain and of protest against pain is the original cry of life. The first utterance of each of the children she bore had been such a cry. It was the cry of *yang*, the creative principle, goaded by its very suffering to overcome its afflictions and grow stronger and wiser. She felt the connectedness of all things. It was an ecstasy she had previously known only during her most exalted moments with Jebu.

'That scream, sensei,' she said, 'is the face I had before I was born.'

Eisen knelt and pressed his palms and face to the ground before her in humble acknowledgment of her enlightenment. She was so preoccupied with her new thoughts and feelings that she scarcely noticed what he was doing.

'I do not feel as if I have made a discovery,' she said as he stood up again. 'I feel as if I am remembering something I have always known.'

'It is one thing to know that fire burns flesh,' said Eisen. 'It is another to learn that truth by putting your hand into the flame of a torch. Now I will have to find a new *kung-an* for you to work on.'

'Must I go on solving *kung-an* for the rest of my life?'

Eisen laughed. 'Does one who trains in the martial arts ever say, 'Now my training is complete, I need no more practice'?' Then the round face grew grave and compassionate. 'Sometimes lift gives us a *kung-an* to solve. Now that you have found the face you had before you were born, perhaps you will have the wisdom to decide what you and Jebu should do.'

Taniko thought a moment, searching within herself to see if she felt any different about Jebu. Nothing was changed. She still wanted him at her side for the rest of her life, and she still resented the Order for trying to part them.

'Your Order has no right to send Jebu away from me,' she said firmly. 'I will make him stay with me. We deserve to be united after all these years, and I defy you to try to separate us.'

Eisen nodded. 'You must do what you think you should do. That is the very essence of enlightenment. As for Jebu, he has been given time to think about this journey. I do not know what he will decide. Perhaps he will tell you. When do you see him again?'

'I will see him the day after tomorrow at Heian Kyo for the first time in a month. He stayed behind at Hakata Bay, helping to rebuild and to aid the victims.'

'Please greet him for me when you see him. And also tell his lordship Shogun Sametono that I hope to see him at his convenience. I am anxious to learn what progress he has made with Joshu's No.'

CHAPTER TWENTY-SEVEN

Taniko's heart fluttered nervously, partly in happy excitement, partly in fear, as she rode ahead of Jebu along the path up the side of Mount Higashi. She had managed to slip away from all her ladies, maids, retainers and samurai guards. Those at the Rokuhara thought she was at the Imperial Palace paying a visit to the young Emperor and the Imperial family. Those in the newly rebuilt Imperial Palace thought she was at the Rokuhara. She and Jebu could be alone together, celebrating the full moon of the Eighth Month in each other's arms in the place where their love had begun for them so many years ago.

They tethered their horses by the old statue of Jimmu Tenno. The first Emperor of the Sunrise Land looked as fierce as ever but a little more weathered. She stood a moment before the statue, silently reporting to the founder of the nation that the barbarians had been driven from his shores. Then they turned and walked hand in hand along the path until they came to the spot where they had lain together years before and exchanged vows of love. These twisted pine trees on the hillside now might have been seedlings when we first came here, she thought. Will Jebu remember our vows, and is he still willing to keep them? As for her, she had never forgotten his words, 'I am yours for the rest of my life and the rest of your life.'

In the sunset Heian Kyo seemed to rise out of a violet autumnal haze mixing mist from the rivers on either side of the city with the smoke of cooking fires. The capital looked much the same as it had that other night. There was hardly a part of it that had not been levelled by fire or earthquake over the past thirty-seven years, but its people were indefatigable rebuilders. Taniko took off the rice-straw hat and veil she had worn to conceal her features and sat down on the grass mat Jebu unrolled for her. They talked about the war.

'We had a message from one of our people in Korea,' Jebu said. 'The Great Khan lost three thousand ships and eighty thousand men. It is the worst defeat the Mongols have suffered since the rise of Genghis Khan. Kublai flew into a rage when he got the news and ran about his palace shouting, "Arghun! Arghun! What have you done with my fleet?" He collapsed and had to be punctured with the Chinese needles and put to bed. Now he is saying he intends to attempt another invasion.'

'Oh, no.' Taniko's heart sank. 'We can't go through an ordeal like that again.'

'Neither can the Mongols. This defeat has weakened Kublai's authority over his vassal kings and nobles. I don't think he can raise another army and fleet. Of course, we can never be sure. We will have to remain prepared for war for many years to come.'

Taniko visualized Kublai's barbarian wrath with satisfaction. What do you think of us now, Elephant? she thought. You who were always so contemptuous of our little country. Would you still like to have me back in your harem?

'He's sixty-five years old now,' Jebu went on. 'That's on in years, as members of his family go. I think after his death his successors won't be so interested in conquering our islands, and the Mongol empire will fall apart. It's already starting to.'

'That storm convinced the priests and the people that no invader can ever conquer us,' said Taniko. 'They say the gods were helping us. Some of the samurai think it was the angry

438

ghost of Yukio that brought the storm. They say Yukio was fighting beside them, seeking vengeance against Arghun and his Mongols.'

'I actually saw Yukio,' Jebu said, his voice filled with wonder at the memory.

'You saw Yukio?'

'He was standing with me on the railing of *Red Tiger*, laughing, when I was fighting Arghun.'

'Do you think it was truly a vision, or was it only in your mind?' Taniko asked him. 'You must have been terribly wrought up in that moment.'

'Just before he died, my father, Taitaro, taught me that a mind that creates such visions is miraculous enough. One can attain insight in combat. Sometimes in a moment of insight you see visions.'

Taniko let her small white fingers rest on his long, brown hand. 'I had a satori, a flash of enlightenment, talking to Eisen last night. It was one of the most profoundly happy moments of my life.'

He smiled, strong white teeth flashing in his beard. 'Then you understand a little better what I've been looking for all my life.'

'Jebu,' she said, 'my satori happened when Eisen told me your Order wants you to travel to the West.'

Jebu was silent for a while. At last he looked at her with eyes full of pain and sadness. 'I am going to go, my love. I have to.'

She shuddered, as if struck a physical blow that she had been anticipating. She rocked back and forth, her face in her hands, weeping. He took her hand, and she pulled it away. How dare he try to comfort her with such a banal gesture. She looked up at him and he was crying, too. For a moment she felt pity for him.

'Don't say you have to go. Eisen told me the decision was left to you.'

'If the Order had commanded me to go, I would have felt more free to refuse. I did refuse at first. In the last month, since you left Hakata Bay, I have suffered a lifetime of agonies over this decision. Taniko, I love you. I don't want to leave you. And yet, there is so much I can do by making this journey. Eisen must have explained to you why it is so important to the Order. And I will be the first person from the Sunrise Land to travel all the way to the other end of the world, to that unknown land of the white barbarians. Taniko, travelling and learning are my whole life. Were it not that I love you and can't bear to be parted from you, I would be overjoyed at the thought of making this journey. I couldn't wait to leave.'

'I'm sorry our love is such a burden to you, Jebu. But it seems you have the strength, somehow, to part from me.' He seemed to be trying to make it sound as if his sufferings were equal to hers, which could not possibly be true.

'For me to refuse this responsibility would leave me with my insight beclouded and my contact with the Self broken.'

'And I – and our love – must be sacrificed to your spiritual attainment? That's what I dislike about all this pursuing of insight or enlightenment, whatever you wish to call it. It's nothing but a selfishness of the spirit.'

Surprisingly, Jebu nodded. 'A long time ago Taitaro abandoned my mother, Nyosan, to follow his inner voice. She died in the holocaust of the Teak Blossom Temple. When he told me how she had died, there was a moment when I hated him for having left her. As you must hate me now. But you have known satori. So you must know that we realize in enlightenment that the individual self is an illusion. We are all part of one Self.'

She was crying again. It was so frustrating to be unable to touch him with her anger. She had experienced enough of what he was talking about to understand him. Still, she could not, would not, give him up.

'How do you know that denying our love won't damage your precious insight?' she demanded. 'How can you be so sure that what you have decided is right?'

'I can't,' he said. 'Being sure that you are doing right is one of the easiest ways to go astray. We Zinja have ways of reminding ourselves that what we are doing is not necessarily right. But I know I must do this just as I knew, six years ago, that I must answer your call and come to you in Kamakura. The deeper my insight, the more the Self chooses for me.'

She sneered. 'When you ask monks hard questions, they always retreat behind words that are impossible to grasp, like clouds of smoke.'

Surprisingly, he was crying again, and he took her sleeve and wiped his eyes with it. 'That reminds me so much of what my

440

mother said to me once when I was preaching at her. "Sayings that boom like a hollow log in the temple," she called my words. I know how you feel. Even so, you know that at the bottom of my words, hollow as they are, there is a reality.'

'The reality is that you are going to leave me,' she whispered in a choked voice.

'I am not going to leave today or tomorrow, my love,' said Jebu. 'In the spring I will go. Sakagura and I will outfit a small ship and sail to China. Sakagura doesn't know yet that I have decided to take him with me. But he wants to be my student, and I need someone to help me cross the ocean and to be my companion after that. I will be back, Taniko. Be sure of it. Much of the reason for my making this journey is so that I can return to the Order with new treasures of knowledge. I will be back, and then we will be together forever after. That I promise you.'

Her rage and grief burst out, not in a scream as on the night before, but in a flood of speech, broken by sobs. 'And I promise you that when I am asleep my angry ghost will leave my body and go wherever you are in the world and torment and plague you until you go mad. As I will go mad here, if you leave me. I believe you are mad already. After we have been forced to be apart so much of our lives, can you turn your back on me of your own free will? Even if you do return you will surely be gone ten years or more. I may be dead by then. I will be dead. Have you forgotten that when we were a boy and girl here in this spot so long ago, you swore you would be mine forever? You don't really love me. You never have. I've just been someone for you to come back to after your legendary exploits. If you leave me now, Jebu, I will always hate you. Always.'

Jebu put his arms around her. She tried to push him away at first, but he held her tightly, and in spite of her anger at him it was comforting to be held. The pain tore at her from within, like some monstrous crab that had been conceived inside her and was trying to tear its way out. With his forefinger he wiped the tears from her cheek. Crickets chirped in the forest. Was it Taniko's imagination, or was there a sadness in the sound because winter was coming and the little insects would soon all be dead? He and I will soon be dead, too, she thought, and our love lost forever.

441

'There is another reason why it would be good for me to leave now,' he said softly. 'Did Sametono tell you about our quarrel before he went out in Sakagura's kobaya?'

'He told me that he was angry because you persuaded the generals not to let him go into combat.'

'He said that our love is becoming a national scandal. The temples, the warrior families, the people are losing respect for you. He would never have said those things to me if he weren't angry, but they are true.'

'Ridiculous.'

'Taniko, you said yourself that our being lovers is no longer a secret. Munetoki and Sametono need you. They'll need you until Sametono is grown up. Most of the time, the path that leads to enlightenment is simply doing your duty as well as you can, according to your place in the world. For you, the path is to accept my going and to work to make the Bakufu strong. Your duty is to keep the figure of the Ama-Shogun bright and shining.'

He was still holding her. Part of her wanted to lift her head and kiss the lips that looked so inviting surrounded by his white beard. Part of her wanted to push him away, leave this mountaintop whose meaning for them he had betrayed, and never see him again. She hated all this talk about enlightenment. It had nothing to do with life and love. But she knew it was true. She was trapped in her position. But – she could give up her position. Or offer to. If he realized that she was willing to give up everything for him, then surely he would be willing to turn his back on his Order for her.

'Very well, then,' she said. 'If you won't stay with me, I will go with you.'

His grey eyes widened. 'You will give up your position, leave your family and home, and travel all the way across the world with me?'

'Will you take me?'

After a long silence he said, 'It would make the trip more difficult, of course. You are very strong, but still the Order will object. They'll say that my having you along will slow me down. And they would be right, but that doesn't matter. I have decided to make this journey despite the suffering it inflicts on you and me. They'll have to accept my making it on my terms. For the sake of our love, if this is what you think you must do, I cannot refuse you.'

She felt like a charging warrior who falls on his face when his opponent unexpectedly backs away. She had not thought he would agree to take her. She had thought that what he really wanted was to be separated from her.

'You really would take me with you?'

'Taniko, I must make this journey. I thought that to do it I had no choice but to part with you. It never occurred to me that you would be willing to go, too.'

Too late she saw the trap she had fallen into. It was not a trap of Jebu's making. It was karma, or life itself, that had built this trap for her. Sometimes, as Eisen said, life becomes the sensei and sets a *kung-an* for us to solve.

'I can't go,' she said. 'I didn't think you would say yes.'

His sad smile was beautiful. She reached up to stroke his white beard.

'You gave me hope for a moment,' he said. 'That was cruel. I used to be so angry with you, Taniko-san. Always you wanted to be at the centre of things, at the Court, in the midst of public affairs. I always hated your ambition. But now I know that you are no longer driven by ambition. It has been transmuted into something else. You are staying because it is what enlightenment chooses for you. You can't give up being the Ama-Shogun, even for the sake of our love, because the Self tells you this is what you must do.'

Taniko searched her heart. He was right. Even though her love for Jebu was the most powerful force in her life, she could not leave her post. But it was no longer ambition that kept her there. Hers was a vast, unfinished task. She felt the same powerful bond that keeps a captain aboard his endangered ship, that keeps a samurai fighting to hold a threatened position. Kamakura needed her, and she could not abandon it.

'I helped to build it,' she whispered. 'And it's not finished. I can't desert it now.'

He took her hands tightly. 'Be the chaste goddess, and the samurai will never rebel against the Bakufu. But now you know why, even though it tears me to pieces, I have to go. And when we are very old, we will live the last years of our lives together and pass from this world together. And if you believe in rebirth, believe that we will be reborn as a couple of peasants who will have twenty children and live together in peace for ninety years. Surely we have accumulated enough good karma in this life to deserve that. Believe whatever you can believe, my darling, but above all believe that we can never be parted.'

'Nothing can destroy our love,' she said. 'I believe that.'

'Taniko,' he said, 'most people are blind to the fact that we are all one. Men gather behind their boundaries, their walls, rivers and seas, and make war on one another. The Order trained me to be a warrior, and I have spent most of my life at war. I have done my duty in the place where I found myself. But now I hope I may live out the rest of my life without ever again killing another human being. Taniko, when I was in that chaos in the harbour I saw other visions besides Yukio. I saw an ocean of blood, all the blood that has been spilled and will be spilled because men kill. I saw the Tree of Life, a vision that tells me all beings are one. I want the Tree of Life to grow. I want men to stop spilling blood into that ocean. How can men make war if they realize they are all part of one being? We must lose the illusion of separateness. People can break down boundaries by freely crossing them to share what they have with other people. The day will come when all boundaries fall and when we will have the knowledge we need to end the killing of man by man. That is what the Order works for and what I work for. That is why I am going.'

'I understand.'

'And also,' he said, 'I am going for Moko. Moko was a man who broke down boundaries and learned. Why are there men like Arghun and Kublai Khan, like Sogamori and Hideyori, who bring death to their fellow human beings and never question what they are doing? I'm going to find out why Moko was killed.'

'Such a huge question. Do you really think you will find the answer?'

'I may bring the Order and the people of the world closer to the answer. The lands of the far west are strange, from what little I know of them. Perhaps they go to war for different reasons than we do here. And by finding out what is different and what is the same, I may know more about what war is.'

'I can tell you some things about the West. While I lived with Kublai Khan one of my friends was a princess from a country called Persia.' She reached for him and put her arm around his neck. He sank down beside her, holding her. It had grown dark while they talked and he was shadowy beside her.

He stroked her cheek. 'We will pass the winter with you telling me tales of Kublai Khan's harem.'

She laughed. 'Some of them are not for the ears of a monk.'

'Even a monk like me? Sametono said I was nothing but an adventurer in monk's clothing.'

'That is all you are. See how easily you decided to abandon me.' It seemed she had come to a point of reconciliation, for now she could even joke about it.

But Jebu did not join in the joke. 'Do you still love me?' he asked, his grey eyes fixed on hers. 'Can I take that with me through the world? Can I have the hope of coming back to you to help me keep going?'

The tears spilled over, but she laid her head on his chest and whispered, 'Yes.' Oh, but how lonely I will be, she thought. How I wish you would not go.

He slid his hand into the breast of his robe and brought out something that sparkled in the light of the rising full moon. He put it into her hand. The surface felt rough to her fingertips, but when she held it up she saw that it was intricately carved. A tracery of fine lines too complex for the mind to encompass flowed across its surface, compelling her to try to follow its weavings until her eyes ached. In its depths there glowed a tiny fire, bright as satori.

'Jebu, what a beautiful thing.'

'It is a gift to you from the land of the Mongols.' He told her the story of the Jewel. 'Taitaro used it as a talisman in my spiritual training, but in the end he told me it has no magic. Yet carved on its surface is the Tree of Life, a very beautiful design. You may find it helps you to concentrate when you are meditating. Look at it every day and think of me, and perhaps you will discover that we are one, as I said, and are not really separated.'

'It has a very great magic,' she whispered. She put it in a pocket in her sleeve and then pressed herself against him. She slipped her hands into his robe and caressed the pattern of scars on his chest, just as she had tried to trace the pattern on the

445

Jewel. His fingers crept under the layers of silk she wore and brushed her skin lightly, following its smooth surfaces. The bright rays of the full moon of the Eighth Month, the most beautiful moon of the year, dappled the ground around them and their robes and their bodies. Strings of lanterns dotted the streets of the city below. It was all as it had been long ago, but they had changed immeasurably.

'Oh, Jebu,' she whispered. 'That we have known and loved each other though everything was against our love is the greatest of all blessings.'

That night under the full moon and the pines of Mount Higashi, their bodies and their spirits melted together. What they had suffered before, what loneliness they might know in time to come, no longer mattered. On every plane they became one in an eternal now.

From the pillow book of Shima Taniko:

I have decided that I will not let him read my pillow book now. Not till he comes back to me. In that small way I will punish him for leaving.

We have this one winter together, and then I will truly be both nun and Shogun. After Jebu is gone I will sleep alone and devote myself to the Bakufu. I will be a mind and a voice, neither woman nor man.

Why this lifelong urge to involve myself in affairs of state? Even though Eisen dismissed the idea, this passion does arise from the face I had before I was born. When I was in my mother's womb nobody knew whether I was male or female. And if I strip away being a woman and all that is expected of me because I am a woman, then I am simply a living being who does not want to be a helpless piece of property, who wants to matter, to accomplish things. These are the needs of my deeper self. It is not that I wish to stop being a woman. I am glad I have tender feelings and can show them openly, as no man dares to, because I am a woman. It delights me that men desire me, and I love the pleasure I receive from men. Even though I lost both my children, the times another human being grew inside my body were among the most marvellous experiences of my life. But I do not want to be a woman at the cost of leaving my deeper needs unfulfilled.

And so, because I am driven to achieve, and because of karma or luck, I have become the Ama-Shogun. I seem to be quite alone among women in rising so high. When I was a girl and the Court in Heian Kyo ruled the Sunrise Land, women often had great influence. But now this land is governed by the samurai. Women cannot compete with men in battle, and as long as warriors rule the nation, women will be more and more reduced to servitude. Perhaps I can use my position to help women. But the forces working against us are powerful.

Our best hope lies in an end to wars, because that will end the dominance of the samurai. Peace, the thing Jebu dreams of. Women can help themselves by nurturing peace. If I could communicate my thoughts to other women, I would tell them that.

Perhaps Jebu will bring back the secret of peace to the Sacred Islands. I have learned to live with the fact of his going, but just as I screamed at Eisen, I scream inside whenever I think of his leaving me alone. I remember the story Eisen told me long ago about the enlightened monk who screamed as he was murdered. I understand that story much, much better now.

If I did not have Sametono to love and look after, I do not think I could hold back the scream. After Jebu is gone I will help Sametono to mature and become wise in statecraft. And, in a few years' time, surely there will be great-grandchildren to occupy my time. Little Taniko, a great-grandmother! Perhaps I have reached that happy stage in life where one grows by simply loving, acting and giving, and does not need to receive.

But that man – so different from all the other people of the Sacred Islands, so wonderful a lover – who came into my life when I was a girl – he is my life. When he sails away in the spring, he takes my life with me.

But he will be back. It may be five years or ten years, but he will be back. And then I will withdraw altogether from public life, and we will find some little cottage on a mountain-side with a pleasant view, and I will make *ch'ai* and raise flowers. He will sit with brush and ink and write down what he has done and learned. And we will never be apart again.

447

While I am alone I will remain myself. And as myself, I will always love him. As he says, our selves are one Self. So I have him within me, and we will be together always in this life, and sit side by side on the same lotus blossom in the next.

—Eighth Month, seventeenth day
YEAR OF THE SERPENT